THE ONE

by

William J. Millman

SB

Sunset Beach Press

SB

Sunset Beach Press

This book is a work of fiction. Names, characters, places, and incidents either are products of the author's imagination or are used fictitiously. Any resemblance to actual events or locales or persons, living or dead, is entirely coincidental.

Copyright © 2014 by William J. Millman

Manufactured in the United States of America

Cover photo: NASA

ISBN: 978-0-9857918-6-5

To all the kids
And grandkids…

PROLOGUE

As the school transport moved through the crowded airspace above Mining Colony Phoebos, Vers Leitstell looked out at the drab, industrial cityscape that whizzed by. The principal star's light was slightly exaggerated by the transparent dome that separated the city from the emptiness of space, but the UV filters and CO_2 scrubbers kept the environment safe for all the Terrans living inside. If you could call it living. He still retained memories from Terra 3, where he'd been born and where his mother and father lived until his Dad had been assigned to the job in the mines. T3 had been green, lush, with running water. No dome.

Not for the first time, Vers found himself wishing they'd never moved to Phoebos. But he understood: you went where the government told you to go, or you didn't work at all.

He saw a small gathering of Watchers flash past out of the corner of his eye. It looked like they had some poor young woman surrounded; probably making her life miserable.

'Lousy black buzzards,' he mused with a grimace. The God's Watchers were the Seven's eyes and ears throughout the Terran system. Draped in black from head to toe with just a tiny band of visible-light and IR sensors where their eyes should be, the Watchers were recruited as children and raised as True Believers at the Institute of Light on T1. At eighteen they were assigned to one of the Terran planets, where they would spend the rest of their lives – watching, harassing, enforcing the dictates of the Seven.

Vers took a deep breath and let it out slowly. No need to let them get to him so early in the din.

"Man, what's your problem?" the slight red-haired kid sitting next to him said as he saw his friend's distorted face and heard the long sigh.

"Eh, just the usual." Vers and his friends never talked about the Watchers, or the Seven, in public. That's how you got disappeared. But Jafar knew Vers well enough to know what he was thinking about. He knew his friend blamed the Seven for the death of his father, and that he couldn't wait to graduate next cycle and get the heck off the mining moon. If they let him. As Worker Caste kids they didn't have all the privileges reserved for the Ruling Caste brats, but enough to give them some hope. After all, they went to the same school as the RCs, didn't they? Maybe he'd get lucky. Maybe they both would.

"Yeh. It sucks. But hey, what did you think of the Raiders' game last night – pretty awesome, eh?" he continued with the high energy enthusiasm he was so well-known for.

Vers smiled. With friends like Jafar, maybe he'd make it through the din after all.

CHAPTER 1

Terra5

Rogen Antavar wasn't happy. And when he wasn't happy, the whole Seven quaked, or so the saying went.

"I have felt his power growing: the cycle is about to begin anew," he said, pacing back and forth in front of the massive floor to ceiling windows in the Chancellery. "Yet we still do not know where this *child* they call The One is hiding. This is inexcusable!"

Even in his impressive robes of office he appeared a small man, his head shaved with just a short steel-gray braid plaited tightly beneath the jeweled crown of Arod – the ultimate symbol of power in the Terra system. His prominent jaw seemed to stick out just a little further as he spoke, his thin cheeks a bright, unhappy red.

As he paced, twelve eyes followed his every move. Although each of the Seven was a power in his own right (they were all men), none of them approached Antavar for influence in their society. His was the face that appeared on SightScreens all across the seven planets as well as on all moons. His was the signature that transformed a whim into law. Most importantly, his was the name that struck fear into any Terran who thought, or lived, or believed differently than The Seven.

Sitting at the long metal table that served as the meeting place for their regular meetings, Ofran Belinger was the only other member to have any public identity whatsoever. His actual title was Defender of the Faith, but everyone knew him as The Fist, the number two man in the Church/State hierarchy. The longest-serving of the Seven, his straggly gray hair and craggy, creased face belied a sharp mind and a ruthless disposition. The other five ranged in age from 44 to 91, and were nondescript in every possible way. As opposed to Antavar, whose bejeweled crown, long magenta robes and gleaming ring of power made him an instantly recognized figure, or even Belinger, who wore the woven latinum glove that both symbolized and made all too real his appellation as Fist, the others were all dressed in the traditional deep gray of humility, their heads hooded, their faces rarely seen. Even if someone had managed to peek beneath a hood, it is unlikely they would have remembered the face they saw long enough to describe it to anyone. A combination of truly unremarkable features, modesty reinforced by solar cycles of theological training, and the use of the Kin-zah mind control that was the foundation of their sect made it nearly impossible for them to be identified. No, they were the steel backbone of the Seven, with Antavar as their public face and Belinger their gloved fist. It was an efficient, powerful, deadly melding of talents and influence.

Of course, those Terrans who were courageous enough to discuss the Seven, even in the relative privacy of their own living spaces, all knew that the true power behind the throne was Octana, Antavar's first wife and the mother of three of his 22 children. She was almost never seen in public, but rumor had it that hers was the only opinion the High Priest considered, though how often and to what extent was truly just speculation. The manner by which the Seven made their determinations, and specifically what role the High Priest played, were utterly opaque to the Terran public.

What they did know was that the Seven had been created personally by Arod Tolanfar, the Redeemer of the Faith, the Light in the Darkness, the Savior and Founder of the Terran system. Eight hundred solar cycles earlier, after a series of horrible, bloody wars on all six of the other Terran colonies, Arod led the Flaming Sword brigades that brought peace to a system that had seen 300 solar cycles of war and inhumanity. His was a Ruling Council of Belief, demanded by a grateful populace. For over five hundred solar cycles the Seven had ruled wisely, allowing each of the seven Terras to elect their own representative to the Council. But then, in 3831.4 the High Priest at the time – Rogen Antavar's great-great-grandfather, Oden – disagreed with a decision of the Seven: even though they had all voted to allow proportional representation regardless of home planet, with one member of the Council to represent every 4.2 billion citizens, Oden insisted they maintain the old ways, that they keep the Council at seven. Not surprisingly, his method of selecting representatives maintained the relative strength of Terra5 – his home planet, and greatly diminished the possibility that anyone from any other planet could be elected High Priest. A proud, haughty individual, he thought his opinion should carry more weight than that of the other six. They disagreed.

And so began the Sixty Cycles of Cleansing.

From colony, to colony, to colony, the Armies of Arod swept across the galaxy to cleanse all seven Terra colonies of any thoughts that contradicted Oden's, even long after he died. Despite the fact that Terra5's army was not as large or as well-armed as some of the others, they managed to crush all opposition and impose their will on the 30 billion Terrans. Part of their success can be attributed to Oden's strategic brilliance. But the greater part must be ascribed to the fact that he could trace his lineage directly back to Arod himself. The force of that linkage, and the uncommon traits inherited from his illustrious ancestor, gave him and his forces an aura of invincibility that eventually proved itself true.

But it was from that same lineage that Rogen's current problem evolved. For although he was a direct ancestor of Arod, he was not the only one. The first High Priest of the Seven had two sons, as well as several daughters. The eldest son, Rathma, inherited his father's dynasty upon the great man's death. The younger son, Volis, barely escaped with his life when Rathma's followers attempted to assassinate him the din of his father's funeral. The tales that come down from that time suggest Volis was the smarter, the stronger, and the more worthy of the sons. But he was not the eldest. In all the solar cycles that followed, the sons of Volis lived lives of quiet solitude, hiding from their pursuers and even from each other. Some were found, and died before their existence could be confirmed. But legend has it that in generation after generation, true believers in the Word of Arod ensured that one son survived, and that one din one of those sons would step forward to claim his rightful position as The One, upon whom a growing legion of Terrans pinned their hopes for a life free of the Seven's tyranny.

In good times, few spoke of The One. But in times such as these, the whispers for change began to grow into shouts. As the centuries passed, all traces of the early solar cycles were meticulously erased from the data banks, and many assumed He was but a myth, created by opposition forces as a rallying point for their faithful. But Rogen knew all too well that The One was not a fiction. The High Priest alone had access to the archives that catalogued his predecessors' efforts to find and eliminate His challenge. As of yet, no descendant of Volis had ever laid claim to the office of High Priest, and despite the growing dissatisfaction among the Working Caste, Rogen intended to be sure his reign would continue that success.

Ofran Belinger was the only one of the Seven who would dare speak when the High Priest was in such a state of agitation.

"We will find him, Holy One," he said calmly, with no trace of the doubt he felt.

"Oh, really? And how will you do that?" the High Priest asked, his words sharp with sarcasm.

"We have every CompuData terminal in the system sifting through every news report, every blog, every police report, every security vidcam, every local report from the Watchers – all are being cross-referenced, checked against facial recognition software, evaluated to the nth degree. Sooner or later he will reveal himself. And then we will have him!" The Fist's eyes glowed with the fervor for which he'd been named to his post in the first place. It did not sway Antavar.

"Sooner or later?" he repeated, his voice threatening. "What exactly does that mean?! If our calculations are correct, the boy nears his sixteenth cycle din. Upon that anniversary, his *talents* will come to full force! That *cannot* happen!"

Some of the Seven chanced quick glances at their Councilmates. All had seen the High Priest in an excited state from time to time, but few if any had seen him as agitated as he seemed now. As frightening as he could seem in the steely calmness of their regular meetings, this fervor frightened them even more. For if the High Priest were afraid, their world was teetering.

"I don't care what it costs, how many people it takes, you *will* find him. And I mean sooner, not later – *without* it becoming common knowledge!" The last was directed squarely at Belinger, but the other five knew they were as vulnerable as the Fist. "Do you understand?"

The last was phrased as a question, but the remaining six members of the Council knew it was actually an order. They nodded in unison.

"Good. Then go. I don't want to see you again until He is found."

Antavar turned his back to them as if to illustrate his pledge, and his fellow Council members fell all over themselves trying to get out of the room. All except Belinger. He had always had a special relationship with the High Priest, dating back to when they were children together in Asia2 Prime. He waited patiently for the others to depart, feigning difficulty packing up his datapoints. When the last of the others was gone and the door had closed behind them, he turned to Antavar, who still stared out the massive windows.

"Holy One, do not despair. We will find him," he said softly, with all the conviction he could muster. "We have several very strong leads."

For several moments the High Priest did not answer. At first Belinger thought he hadn't heard his pledge. But then he began to speak, his voice soft as silk yet pointed as the finest Valluvian blade.

"The only reason we are not at war even as I speak is that the Old Man has not moved against us," he whispered. "But we know he has put the pieces in place for a rebellion that endangers everything that all of us, all the High Priests throughout the ages, have worked so hard to create. The ancient legends speak of The One that will come…"

"They are but legends, Holy One. Surely you do not believe…"

"I believe that a new millennium dawns with the first rays of the Morning Star in less than one revolution of this planet! Beyond that, I do not want to *believe* anything. I want to *know* that our empire is secure. I want to sleep easily at night. I want my family to be safe. I want to know that The One is dead."

"It shall be so."

The High Priest turned to face his Fist and Belinger relaxed ever so slightly, expecting words of encouragement, or at least hopefulness. What he didn't anticipate were the two smoldering coals of fervor that burned into his psyche, turning his legs to rubber.

"It had better be! Or you will wish you had never been born."

In that one instant, a wave of inestimable pain shot through every cell of Belinger's body, tossing him to the ground like a rag doll. His teeth clenched so hard his jaw felt that it would break. He looked up at his old friend – to beg for mercy? – but saw nothing but a shadow enveloped by waves of blood red emanations. He thought he would die. He hoped he would.

Just as he thought he could not possibly stand the torment a second longer, it stopped. He felt his body rise off the floor, and drift toward the now open door.

"Do not fail me," a voice rumbled. It was the voice of Rogen, yet not. It was a voice he would never forget.

CHAPTER 2

Phoebos

I have heard the stories so many times, sometimes I almost think I was there when all this began.

But I wasn't, of course. My mother was young then, not much older than I am now. My father just two solar cycles her senior. They had moved off Terra3, their home planet, like so many others during those difficult times, looking for a better life. The orders came down from the powers-that-be on T5: he was '*assigned*' to Phoebos – the mining colony where I was born.

They'd met back on Terra3 when Mom was just 14 and Dad 15. She told me that it was anything but love at first sight.

"He was loud, and cocky. First time I saw him, at a Council of Light dance, I thought he was too big for his britches. He came up to me as I was standing with two of my girlfriends and without saying a word took my hand and pulled me out onto the dance floor. The nerve! Worst of all, I was so startled that I went with him! I *still* remember my friends laughing."

The contortions in her face eased into a gentle smile. "But he was a good dancer. I can't say he wasn't. He twirled me around that floor as if we'd been dancing together for solar cycles. And then, when the dance was over, he bowed to me – bowed! I didn't know what to think. I mean, here I was, a little country girl from the West District. I'd never seen anyone like Davis before. Was he crazy? Didn't know. But, crazy or not, he was mighty good looking. With those bright blue eyes and long hair – for a second there I thought he might be from the Ruling Caste. Of course, he wasn't, was just one of us Workers, but you sure couldn't tell just by looking at him. Truth be told, I think I fell in love with him during that very first dance. I didn't tell *him* that, of course; I'm not sure if I even admitted it to myself. But looking back, yeh, he was the one for me from the very first."

She must have told me that story twenty times. It was usually in the dins just before his birth din celebration, often after a glass of synthahol. It would be early evening, with the shadows growing longer, or even after star set. I'd be tucked into my bed, or we'd both be sitting in front of a roaring fire in the big room, and she'd get that far-off look that told me she was thinking about him again. As much as I loved to hear that story, and all the others, I must admit it made me a little sad. I mean, I never really knew him, you know. I was only three when the accident at the mine happened... But I've heard the stories, from Mom and the others. I think I remember Mom crying on his birth din anniversary when I was little, and some neighbors coming by with food. But maybe I'm just making it up. Maybe I just want to remember.

I know it was during a bad time, not just here, but back on Terra5. The food riots had only just been put down. The Seven were worried that further insurrection was likely, and so had passed the Blasphemy Laws.

"You don't know what it was like, before," Mom told me again and again. "It was so different. Men and women attended functions together, and worked together. People would discuss the government, and the Ruling elite, openly, even at parties! It was another world... But then, after the riots, they decreed that any criticism of the High Priest or the Council was blasphemous and could be punished by death. Death! And then they gradually limited what we women could do, not just in the workplace, but even in our homes. Do you remember Evna Kinesh?" she'd ask, forgetting that she'd asked the same question so many times before. "No, of course you don't. You were so young when they took her. She taught at the university, and when the Laws were first announced she was one of the leaders of a movement to have them withdrawn. She was a wonderful woman. Nothing scared her. She'd march in public, give speeches, even appear on the SightScreen.

"At first, I think the Council didn't see her as a threat. They thought they could intimidate her, and the others. But they were wrong. The more they attacked the protests, the more they limited public expressions of outrage over the new Laws, the more committed she became. And people began to see the truth in what she said! The protests grew, a few of the more radical elements became violent – that's true. But it was only a few. And I'm certain Evna wasn't a part of that. She always spoke of peaceful resistance and told her followers to shun violence. But that didn't stop us.

"One night, I think it was literally one or two in the morning, the Security Force kicked down her door and arrested her. I remember how frightened we all were when we heard. Even those of us who weren't active participants in the protests. I mean, if you'd said anything that could possibly be interpreted as critical of the Seven, even among friends, you could be at risk. The SF informers were everywhere. It was a terrible time...

"Her trial was a huge event, both because the government wanted to make an example of her, and because those who supported her wanted to try to protect her, or maybe make her a martyr if we were unable to embarrass the Council enough to force them to let her go. It was on all the SightScreen channels. It was all everyone talked about. But it wasn't enough to stop us. After a two sept show trial, she was declared guilty of transgressions against the State and sentenced to death.

"Hers was the first broadcast execution of our time. It was *mandatory* viewing. A citizen could be fined, even arrested, if they were found ignoring the decree to watch. And so we watched. They didn't de-atomize her, as they would any common criminal. No, they reverted to the barbaric practice of hanging. Said that her crime was so heinous that it deserved a special execution."

It was immediately after Evna Kinesh's death that we moved to Phoebos. There had been a severe shortage of dilithium crystals on T5 and so the government had sent an entire unit of would-be miners to Phoebos, where dilithium had only recently been discovered. Of course, the miners didn't really have a choice, but to make it look good in public the Council offered anyone who worked in the mines for 10 consecutive solar cycles a bonus and annuity that would provide them with the basics – meager though they might have been – of life back on their home planet. Of course, between the long-term toxic effects of exposure to dilithium, and the myriad dangers in the mining itself, the number of people who laid claim to the bonus was limited. But that didn't stop thousands – tens of thousands – of would-be miners from hoping.

My father was one of them. I still keep a digi-still of him on his first din at the mines, wearing the protective dig-suit that was supposed to keep him safe. His big smile and happy eyes spoke of his hope. It was hope misplaced.

We'd been living on Phoebos just over three solar cycles when they brought the news of the cave-in. There was an investigation, of course, and it was *determined* that the company had followed all regulations and had all safety procedures in place. No one was at fault. But he was dead.

Mom got a small death benefit, just enough to allow her to move from their company-provided enclosure to a small unit on the periphery of the company town. She told me that she considered moving somewhere else, but all her friends lived on Phoebos by that time. Her parents were dead. There was really nothing much to draw her back to her home planet. Her friends helped her start the laundry service that she ran for so many solar cycles, and so we stayed.

"I was thrilled and frightened at the same time," she used to tell me. "Thrilled to start something that was really mine. But what if the laundry didn't succeed? What if I got sick? Somehow, I like to think it was a gift from your father. I was able to overcome my fears, the laundry took hold from the very first, and the lunar cycles passed."

But that wasn't the part of her story that made me uneasy. No, it was a story from three solar cycles earlier. No matter how many times she told me, I always got a nervous feeling that I couldn't quite shake.

"It had been the full 10 lunar cycles since I learned I was pregnant," my mother would recount, usually after a long sept in the laundry, "and I was ready to get you out and on your own two feet. Very ready! It was a Kirak night – I remember it as if it were yesterdin. I had closed the laundry early – I wasn't feeling too well. Tired, my feet hurt. And then, once I was home, I began to have cramps. If you can believe it, even though I knew full well it was time, somehow I didn't link the cramps with my pregnancy. I had eaten a cold sandwich for lunch that afternoon, and I thought that it might have been bad. Stomach problems weren't unusual in the mining town during those early dins. Anyway, for over a stunde I put up with the pain. Drank some tea. But then it finally dawned on me that this was more than just indigestion, and I called my friend, Andar, to come help me get to the clinic. Andar was young, like me, and Davis and her husband had worked in the mines together. They lived in another sector of the Bubble (which is what we called the protective dome that enclosed the community and provided both a breathable atmosphere and protection from space junk), but she said she'd be right over.

"As I was waiting for her to get there, the pain and exhaustion overwhelmed me, and I had to lie down. T5 had almost set, and the light was dim, gray. I thought of increasing the interior illumination (we didn't even have auto-control in those dins), but didn't have the strength. I must have been drifting, almost asleep, when I thought I heard something. I thought it might be Andar, and despite the pain I opened my eyes, just a crack.

"'Andar?' I whispered.

"But the voice that answered was not Andar's.

"'Be at peace,' a low, soothing male voice directed. My initial reaction was to cry out, to scream for help. But somehow, I don't know how even now, somehow his words calmed me. I did not call out.

"'Who are you?' I asked instead.

"'I am a Son of Arod. Your son will be The One who shall set us free.'

"I thought I was dreaming, or perhaps hallucinating. I tried to force my eyes to open further, but the pain – or something else – kept them nearly shut. All I could make out was a dark figure, a shadow really, standing by my bed. I should have been terrified, but I wasn't.

"'Have no concern. You and your son will come through this in good health. You will name the boy Vers, and you will raise him here on Phoebos. Should anyone ask you about this night, you will remember my visit as nothing but a dream. But as his sixteenth birth din nears, I will return to show him the path that lies before him. Now I must go. Close your eyes and rest. The bad times cannot last. The future brings hope through The One.'

"The next time I opened my eyes, it was Andar, not the shadow figure, who stood by my bed. She and her husband rushed me to the clinic, where you were born three stundes later.

"At first I thought of telling Andar about the strange vision. But I didn't. And as the solar cycles passed, the whole incident seemed more and more like a dream to me. I began to doubt that it had ever happened, choosing – or maybe persuaded, to believe that it was a nightmare brought on by the stress of childbirth.

"'And yet I never completely forgot it. Never rid my dreams of the shadow figure. Never forgot his words: 'As his sixteenth birth din nears, I will return to show him the path.'

"The time has passed so quickly. You have grown strong, my son. But what will happen now?"

CHAPTER 3

I was so sick of school, I could barely force myself to get up each morning to catch the transport to class. It's not that I didn't enjoy learning – quite the opposite. I wanted to know more about us Terrans, and our history, about who we were in this vast universe. But school? That was a different story. Especially after my Dad died.

There weren't enough kids to divide us up by castes like they do on the home planets, so classes on Phoebos were mixed – Ruling, Managerial and Workers all together. More or less. We all knew that there were special classes for the Ruling Caste kids, but since they rarely if ever interacted with us, we didn't know if their curriculum was any better than ours. Looking back, I doubt it. The Ruling Council has no interest in seeing its citizens get a good education so we can analyze its decisions and actions. Heck, they'd prefer a nice, dumb, docile population, I'm sure. But I'm getting ahead of myself.

When I was younger I never thought about the RC, or about justice and injustice. I guess I was pretty much a typical kid: I hung out with my friends, got into a little trouble every now and then, but not much, really. I was pretty happy, I guess. Ignorance is bliss, or so they say. If they're right, I was as blissful as they come.

As I approached my 16th birth din, I was happily ignorant of the changes that were headed my way. Although my mother had told me the story of the mysterious visitor many times, she'd never revealed his promise to return. Afterwards, she said it was to protect me, to keep me from worrying about something that might never happen. I think she still thought it was a dream, or perhaps just hoped it was. Whatever the reason, I went about my normal life with neither cares nor premonitions.

Getting back to my school: Vaden Upper Level was the name of the place. Linth Vaden was some RC type who supposedly had helped draft the New Constitution after the Religious Wars. They had a plaque in the entry hall that talked about the guy, but I never read it. Don't think many other kids did either. When you go to school, you usually don't read the educational stuff that's splattered all over the building. That's for the parents. Or maybe it's just for the administrators, so they can say they've toed the party line. I don't know. I only know that I never saw a kid read that plaque in the two solar cycles I attended.

My first solar cycle at Vaden, I was too young and too shy to enjoy much of anything, even if it happened to actually be enjoyable, which was doubtful. I don't remember much of it, really. What I do remember is the friends I made that solar cycle, friends that have stayed by me ever since, even with all that's happened.

I think I met Jafar Quimby on my very first din. In any case, it was definitely on the transport. He was a little guy, no more than one and a half meters tall, while by 13 I was already nearly a half-meter taller and 40 pounds heavier. If I remember correctly, I was keeping to myself, as I usually did, when this little guy with the bright red hair and grass-green eyes that marked him as Worker Caste for sure, plunked himself down next to me.

"First din?" he asked with the excitement and confidence that I later learned were his trademarks.

"Yeh," I probably mumbled. "You?"

"Yeh. You WC?" he asked, using the popular shorthand for Worker Caste. He probably asked because I didn't really look the part. My hair is jet black and my eyes as blue as the oceans on T3, as Mom always says. As I think about it now, he was taking a pretty big chance asking, because if I wasn't WC he could get himself in a lot of trouble just for talking to me. He was too young to realize that everyone on that transport was WC – the other castes had their own transportation.

"Yeh. You?"

He smiled. "Look at me – what else could I be?" Of course, he was right. But the warmth of his smile and the easy way he joked about his appearance made an immediate impression. They say opposites attract, and I suppose by that they mean men and women. But I can tell you, it works for friends as well. At least it did for us.

"Jafar. Jafar Quimby," he said holding his hand up for me to slap.

"Vers Leitstell," I replied.

"That's a different name," he said, his face scrunched up as if he'd smelled a slag pile.

"I don't know. I suppose."

"It is, take my word for it. Do you play jimur?" That's something I really like about Jaf. He doesn't dwell on things. He speaks his mind and moves on. We've been friends ever since.

Adjusting to the Upper Level was not so easy, however. In my Mid-level school all the kids were from the same sector of the Bubble, but in Upper Level the kids came from all over the colony, from the three other Bubbles in addition to our own. I hadn't had much interaction with kids from other Bubbles. I wasn't prepared, to put it mildly.

That first din we arrived at school to find that transports form the other Bubbles had already arrived. Large groups of students milled around in front of the structure, more people than I had ever seen! More than the shift change at the mines, more than at the shopping malls at holidin time. Jafar and I were making our way toward the entrance to the school, since we had arrived only a few clics before the scheduled start of classes, when a huge WC'er stepped in front of me and poked a finger painfully into my chest.

"Where do you think you're going, RC? This isn't your sector." Of course I knew that I looked different than most of my friends, but no one had ever accused me of being part of the Ruling Caste before. I was shocked, to put it mildly.

"I'm not RC," I said, trying to keep my voice as modulated as possible.

"And I'm Rogen Antavar," the kid said with a sarcastic sneer, mentioning the name of the High Priest of The Seven. Some kids standing nearby snickered. I could tell they were friends, or at least part of his clique.

"Leave him alone," Jafar said, even though he barely came up to the middle of the kid's chest. "He's WC, just like the rest of us."

"Did I ask you?" the bigger kid asked with a tone that suggested he expected no talkback.

He didn't know Jafar. "You didn't, but I'm telling you anyway." I had to control myself to keep from grabbing him by the shoulders and getting the heck out of there.

The other kid had no such compunction. He grabbed Jafar by the front of his shirt and lifted him up off his feet. Some of his 'friends' jeered and urged him on.

I was hoping that that would be the end of it. But I didn't know Jafar either.

"Put me down, you big oaf!" my new buddy ordered indignantly.

The big guy stared at him as if he'd been slapped. "What did you say?"

"I said, 'Put me down!'"

I heard the big guy start to say something and then I saw him pull back his hand for what I was certain would be a punch that would knock poor Jafar into the next sector. I don't know what came over me, but I reached out and gave the kid a light shove with my hand. What happened next was a shock even to me. Especially to me.

The kid flew three or four meters across the lot and slammed into a knot of his friends, knocking them to the ground like a game of 10 pins. Jafar fell to the ground where the kid had dropped him, landing in a heap at my feet.

Heads turned, from every part of the lot. For just an instant everything went quiet. A whistle sounded immediately, and First Level Monitors – their bright red armbands cutting like hot knives through the crowd – hurried to where the kid was slowly picking himself up, his face even redder than his hair. I was stunned. I think I must have been in some kind of daze or something, because the next thing I knew Jafar was standing next to me looking up into my eyes with what could only be described as awe.

"What the fates was that?" he asked.

I was about to tell him that I had no idea, when one of the Monitors stepped into the confusion and grabbed the big kid by his arm. The Monitor was tall, very athletic looking, and obviously an upper classman. You could tell he was used to giving orders and having them followed.

"What's going on here?" he asked, his face set and hard.

"Nothing," the kid answered. "I tripped."

The Monitor turned to me.

"Is that right?"

"That's what he said." I was so nervous that I had to struggle to get the words out.

I could tell the Monitor didn't really believe us, but he didn't have any proof that we were lying so he pretty much had to take our word for it.

"Watch your step," he said to both of us, giving us a hard look that was surely meant to frighten. "I don't want to have to talk to either of you again." I don't know how it affected the other kid, but I was shaking inside.

Worse yet, the look the big kid gave me when he turned to go back with his friends was pure death.

"You just made yourself an enemy," a voice suddenly announced, echoing my thoughts so exactly I thought for a moment I was thinking aloud.

I turned and saw the most striking violet-colored eyes I'd ever see, before or since. It took me a few moments to tear myself away from those eyes and realize they were part of a face so lovely, so breathtakingly beautiful, that I was absolutely stunned. I'm not sure I even took a breath.

The girl – tall, thin, with deep reddish hair that seemed to shine like the late afternoon glow as the principal star set each din – looked at me with an expression that seemed half pity and half fascination.

"Nobus is not one to forget having been made to look a fool," she continued, undeterred by my mute paralysis.

"Is that his name, Nobus?" I finally managed to ask.

"You didn't know? You're not from D Sector, are you?"

"No, I'm not. You are?"

"I was, until two solar cycles ago. We moved to F."

"We're from B Sector," a familiar voice spoke up, and only then did I realize that Jafar had been standing next to me the whole time. "I'm Jafar."

"You should look after your friend a little better, Jafar," she said with such seriousness that I swallowed hard. "You're not in B anymore."

I was trying to think of something to say that wouldn't sound utterly stupid, when suddenly the buzzer sounded announcing the beginning of classes.

"Guess I'll see you around, Jafar, and …?" She looked right at me. I'm sure I blushed twelve shades of purple.

"Vers," I finally muttered. Vers Leitstell."

"Vers." She said the word as if tasting it. And then she smiled. "Good name."

Without waiting for me to say another word, she turned and headed off into the throng of kids moving toward the entrance. Several girls her age immediately surrounded her and an animated conversation began.

"Hey!" I shouted above the roar of the crowd. "What's your name?"

She stopped and turned slowly, her smile a quizzical cross between smirk and satisfied grin.

"Amanda," she called back over her shoulder. "Amanda Velding."

Her coterie of friends wouldn't wait for further conversation, but pulled her ahead toward the entrance.

"Velding?" Jafar asked. "Like Somar Velding?"

I shrugged. Somar Velding was someone that everyone in the mining colony knew, or at least had heard of. In fact, he was something of a legend. He was one of the very few off-worlders who had worked their way up from WC to a managerial position at the mines. Everyone said he was exceptionally smart, exceptionally competent, and had married a well-to-do RC to cement the deal. I realized that if this Amanda was his daughter, the chances of any kind of relationship were pretty darn dim. Once someone had clawed their way out of the Worker Caste, they rarely allowed anything – or anyone – to endanger that move. 'Oh well,' I remember thinking, 'it was exciting while it lasted.'

That first morning passed in something of a blur, as my thoughts were focused on those amazing violet eyes and the taunting smirk. I couldn't get her out of my mind, even though I knew full well that I wasn't the kind of kid her parents would want her associating with. Those first classes dragged interminably, until finally it was time for lunch. With so many kids in the school, they divided us up into three different seatings in the cafeteria. I only hoped Amanda was in mine.

I guess I was making small talk with Jafar as we walked to the huge dining area, but truth be told I wasn't concentrating on whatever he was saying. My eyes were scanning the dozens of tables packed into the huge room, when suddenly I saw the deep red hair that could only belong to one person. It sounds fey, I admit, but I think my heart literally stopped beating for just a second before it roared back at twice its normal speed.

Jafar followed my eyes. "You've got to be kidding," he muttered. "She's way out of your caste."

"Her father married above him."

"You're not Somar Velding."

"Not yet."

When they got their food, Jafar started off toward a small group of kids we knew from B Sector. I, on the other hand, headed straight for Amanda.

"What's the matter with you?" Jafar asked, grabbing me by the elbow. "Are you trying to look like an idiot on your first din here?"

"Eat with those guys if you don't want to come."

I didn't see his reaction, but I'm betting it was part shock and part exasperation. But he came with me.

As we were making our way toward her table, two girls got up directly across from Amanda. I didn't hesitate. Even as I debated what to say, I saw her sneak a peek at us.

"Are these seats taken?" I asked, my heart pounding.

She looked up, feigned disinterest, and said, "No, I don't think they are."

I sat down and Jafar sat next to me, smiling broadly at the girls on either side of Amanda. At least two of them giggled nervously.

"Vers, wasn't it?" she asked as soon as I sat down.

"It is. And you're Amanda?"

She smirked. "I am. So how's your first morning been at Vaden? Since you threw Nobus half-way across the pavement, that is."

"I didn't, throw him I mean." I didn't really know what I meant, but I knew I had to say something. I could tell from the way her friends looked at me when I came into the cafeteria that word of our little scuffle had spread widely.

"Could've fooled me."

"He must've tripped."

"Ah. Yeh, that must be it. So, other than Nobus tripping, has your first din been uneventful?"

I don't know what came over me, but I stared into those hypnotic violet eyes and said, "I wouldn't say *that*." I'm sure I must have been blushing. She, on the other hand, smiled calmly.

"What *would* you say?" I think she liked torturing me.

"I'd say, well, I guess I'd say I've met some interesting characters."

"Interesting characters... I suppose that's one way to look at it."

She stared at me as if daring me to contradict her, or at least reconsider. I felt as though the air had been sucked out of my lungs.

Just as I was about to say something undeniably witty, one of her friends – I later learned her name was Devy – touched her arm. "We should be going," she said with the raised eyebrows of secretive girl-to-girl communication.

"Yes, I suppose we should," she said. "Enjoy your lunch, Vers."

"I'll enjoy mine too," Jafar spoke up, never one to be left out of a conversation.

Amanda laughed, not a mean, snobby laugh, but an open, caught-by-surprise guffaw. "I'm sure you will," she said. "See you around."

As she and her small herd of girlfriends walked away from the table, the chatter that enveloped us generated more giggles and furtive looks back at where I was sitting.

"You seem to have made an impression," Jafar said matter-of-factly. "Not exactly sure what kind, but an impression."

As I sat there watching them leave, all I could think of were those eyes...

*****

The rest of that first din passed in a blur of new teachers, new classes, new everything. Nothing particularly good, or bad for that matter. Just school. I think my brain was elsewhere during much of that time. I know it was. That's the only excuse I can give for what happened at the end of the din when we were leaving school to board the transport home.

Jafar and I were talking as we went out the front exit, about nothing in particular. At least nothing I remember now. We both agreed that Vaden seemed like a decent-enough place to spend a few solar cycles of our young lives, when suddenly a veritable wall of humanity appeared directly in front of us: Nobus and his buddies.

"Going somewhere? You didn't think it was over between us, did you?" the human mountain asked coldly.

"Hey, I'm not looking for trouble," I said, hoping against hope that a meek demeanor would satisfy him in front of his friends.

"He's not looking for trouble," Nobus echoed snidely to his gang. "What is he looking for – his mommy?"

The small circle of drooling idiots laughed on cue. Despite the bravado, they looked a bit nervous to me.

"Don't be a dick," Jafar chimed in. "He took it easy on you last time. Don't push your luck."

I felt like pushing *his* luck, but I kept my face blank. I saw his challenge ripple through the hangers-on, but not much reaction from Nobus.

"Last time he caught me by surprise with his martial arts, or whatever it was. This time I'm ready for him."

"We're going to miss the damn transport," Jafar mused aloud.

"Ooo, poor little boy gonna miss his transport," Nobus said, moving threateningly toward my friend.

"Leave him alone," I said, maybe a bit tougher than I had planned.

"Or what? You gonna pull that same zee-rhat crap as last time? Go ahead, take your best shot." His face was already red. I could see a vein bulge in his forehead. To be honest, I was about ready to piss in my pants.

Just as it seemed that I was going to have to take him on, a welcomed voice rose above the hubbub of the departing crowd.

"Hey, get a move on! We're not going to hold the transports for you two!" It was one of the Monitors. The same one as in the morning. I couldn't tell for sure, but I had a feeling that he knew what was going on and decided to stop it. Whatever the reason, I sighed with relief.

"Looks like you'll have to wait a bit to get your ass kicked again," Jafar spoke up before I could get us out of there. Right then it wasn't Nobus's ass I wanted to kick.

"You have a pretty big mouth for a little piece of pluda."

"I said, GET MOVING!" the Monitor interrupted, closer now.

I didn't wait for a third invitation. I grabbed Jafar's elbow and hustled him past the nonplussed Nobus and onto the transport. As soon as we got onboard, the Monitor motioned for the driver to close the airlock and take off. I saw him point to the next transport in line for Nobus and crew.

"Are you out of your warping mind?!" I yelled at Jafar as soon as we sat down.

"You can't let those big glooks push you around," he said, seemingly unconcerned. "Take my word for it. I've been dealing with them my whole life."

"He could've ripped our heads off!"

"Maybe. Maybe not. You'll have the chance to find out if you're going to let him set the agenda. He's an idiot. The only way you're going to end this is either by kicking his butt or buying him off."

"With what?" I don't know if we were the poorest kids at Vaden, but we sure as heck weren't the richest.

"I have no idea. You're always telling me you're the smart one. You figure it out."

Amazing. He'd almost gotten us killed, and there he was pouting. I was tempted to give him some more grief, to make it clear to him that I had no desire to pick fights – especially with the biggest, meanest kid in the whole school. But somehow I didn't have the heart for it. Somehow I understood that he'd had to put up with a lot more harassment growing up than I had, being such a shrimp. Whatever the reason, I let it go. But his words stayed with me.

*****

I had expected another confrontation with Nobus the next din, but it never came. Or the next. Looking back, I think maybe the Monitor who'd intervened, whose name I later learned to be Marcus Onwell, told him that he either backed off or he'd pay the consequences. No matter what the reason, it was a great relief to be able to go to school without the possibility of a beating hanging over me. Or perhaps even worse, the possibility that whatever happened that first din, when the massive Nobus was launched across the lot, might happen again. I didn't know what had sent him flying, but I knew that it scared me. Like most people, I want to believe that I can control my own world – at least for the most part. Whatever force, or energy, or whatever is was that lifted Nobus off the ground and tossed him three meters or more, wasn't under my control. At least not then.

Without his giant shadow to blot out the reflected light of Terra5 I was free to study, play some sports, and – above all – continue to pursue Amanda. I wasn't much of a student; I thought my future entailed nothing more complicated than the kinds of jobs our Caste members always got. Truth was, I was bored. Except for Math, all the subjects we were forced to study were either related to the Light, or something equally dull. Almost all WC kids on Phoebos, at least almost all the boys, went straight from Upper Level to manual labor anyway, no matter how well they did at school. The Upper Caste kids had a choice; RC had a *lot* of choices. We, or most of us anyway, had *one*.

Our situation was quite simple: my Mom earned enough to feed and clothe us, and the subsidy that we received from the mining company because of my father's death kept a roof over our heads. Beyond that, we had very little. We had no private transport. No SightScreen. Our air recirculator was so old that the CO_2 alarm was constantly sounding whenever there were more than two people in our apartment.

In short, I was headed for some kind of dead-end job and school was just a short detour I'd made because of a promise that I'd made to my Mom. You wouldn't have called me a good student. I didn't skip classes, usually, but I didn't spend any more time than was absolutely necessary studying either. I never failed a course – that would have earned me a tongue-lashing from Mom. I did just enough to get by. Even Jafar got better grades than me.

"You know, if you actually studied you might do a little better," he used to goad me. "You're really not as stupid as everyone thinks."

He was just needling me. I don't think anyone actually believed that I couldn't do the work. At least not the people I cared about. My Mom, Jafar, maybe a couple of other friends – and Amanda, of course.

In fact, she was pretty much the main reason I never complained about school. From the very first time we met I knew she was the girl for me. Jafar and my other friends all told me I was reaching beyond my grasp. I told them you can't ever know how far you can reach until you try. And so I reached.

For the first few lunar cycles our friendship consisted of little more than passing comments in the halls and lunches whenever our schedules overlapped. She, of course, was in the Advanced Studies grouping, while we called my section Retards and Dips. We were actually labeled Slow Learners, but kids have a way of cutting to the essence of reality.

One thing I liked about her from the very beginning: she never bragged about how smart she was, or put me down for my R&D banishment. She always acted as though I were in A.S. as well, and truth be told, I guess I could have been if I'd wanted to work at it. But back then getting out into the real world was all I dreamed about. A chance to earn a real salary. A way off that moon.

I'm not sure I would've stayed in school until graduation if it wasn't for her. Even when we hardly knew each other she was always smiling, and talking about a future that seemed to include the two of us, and listening to my gripes without complaining. Even when we were just friends she was special.

But in May of that first solar cycle she became very special.

At the end of each school solar cycle in Upper Level, each class holds a dance to celebrate their survival – or advancement, if you prefer the school's version. I'm not much for dancing. I understand it's meant to be fun and exciting, but I'd prefer a din of virtual hunting on the 3D deck, or even a good e-book. It seems to me that dances are really just occasions for the girls to dress up and compete with one another for attention (as well as a few of the boys.) Of course, that was before Amanda.

I knew that the end-of-class dance was coming – no one could miss all the posters and banners pasted all over the school. In my case, I also had Jafar constantly nagging me, ("Have you asked her yet?") and Amanda patiently waiting for me to do just that. It's not that I was scared, exactly. I mean, I guess I always knew she'd say yes. But when I learned that a Third Form boy had asked her, it gave me pause. If a kid with 18 cycles wanted to take her to *his* dance, was I being selfish by inviting her to our little affair? What if she felt she had to say yes to me, after all the time we'd spent together over the solar cycle, and so missed out on the graduating class event? I suppose I felt guilty.

As was so often the case, Jafar set me straight.

"I thought you said she's smart," he said one afternoon as we walked home from the transport.

"She is."

"Then why don't you let her make up her own mind? She doesn't need you to tell her what she wants. But you'd better do it soon. If she starts thinking you're not going to invite her, she might say yes to that other kid just to avoid being embarrassed with no invitation at all."

I really couldn't argue that logic. So the next din at lunch, I asked her. Or to be more accurate, I asked her to walk with me so I could ask her. I didn't want to chance having her say no with all her friends, and mine, sitting around listening.

"So what's so important we couldn't discuss it in the cafeteria?" she said after we'd walked all the way to the outdoor recreation area. We were two of the very few students who had left the temperature-controlled comfort of the main building to make the trip to the decidedly cool-ish tree and flower-lined walkway. It was the closest thing to Terra we could find on Phoebos – just the flora, a few birds, and the force field-enhanced dome above us. Beyond that, just the blackness of space and the twinkling of stars, at least until T5- rise, when the planet occupied a full third of the sky.

"Well, you know the end-of-cycle dance is coming up in a couple of septs..." I began, trying to let her know that I really wanted her to come with me, while at the same time not wanting to sound like I expected it.

"So, you noticed," she said.

"Yeh, I noticed. And anyway, I was wondering..." At that point I got nervous and hesitated. She was having none of it.

"Yes, what were you wondering?" she prodded, her face now filled with expectation.

"Well, I mean, I heard that some guy in Third Form asked you to go with him to the big Graduation Dance..."

"Darien? I've known him my whole life. I don't think he knows any girls in his class well enough to ask them."

"Are you going?"

"I don't have any other option."

"Of course you do!"

She picked up on my tone at once.

"Oh really? And what would that be?" Torturing me was becoming something of a specialty for her.

"Well, I mean, there's always *our* dance…" I managed to stammer. Just then the buzzer for the beginning of the next period sounded. She glanced over at the entrance back into the school with ill-disguised irritation.

"Vers Leitstell – are you asking me to the dance?"

"Well, yeh, I guess I am…"

I was standing there, looking, I'm sure, like some overwhelmed farm kid from Ag Sector, when she leaned forward and planted a more-than-friendly kiss on my shocked and unprepared lips.

"Then yes, of course I'll go. Gotta run!" With just the briefest glance back at me, her smile shining nearly as brilliantly as her eyes, she was gone. And there I was, face and ears burning, heart pounding, with no one to tell. So I yelled at the top of my lungs.

The echoes were still bouncing around the dome when Marcus Onwell, the Monitor, stuck his head into the rec area.

"Is somebody dying out here?" he asked, only partly in jest.

"Sorry. Just… had to let it out."

"Yeh, well next time try to keep it in. And unless you intend to be very late to your next class, I suggest you get a move on." His face was stern but his words were friendly. I suppose even then I had an inkling that he wasn't out to get me, but it would be several more septs before I learned just how good a friend he would be.

I mumbled some lame thanks and rushed past him back into the main building. I'm not sure my feet even touched the floor as I ran.

CHAPTER 4

The next two septs passed so quickly that I had little time to think about the dance or worry about the fact that I'd never been to one in my life. Thankfully, my mother wasn't so distracted. One night a few dins before the big affair, just after we'd finished dinner, she came to my room – where I was hard at work studying for finals – and literally dragged me away from my books. Quite unlike her. But, as I was about to learn, she had her reasons.

"I think we should go over a few details before the dance," she began.

"Mom, I was studying for finals!" I argued, not so much because I was incredibly dedicated to my studies; as I've already mentioned, I wasn't. More that I was embarrassed how little I knew about dances, or even dates. It wasn't my thing and I felt like the proverbial saltran out of kimizzit.

"Your studies are important, but so is this. Come on, it won't take long." She led me by the hand out to the big room. Or bigger room. It wasn't so big in absolute terms, but it was a lot bigger than the other rooms.

"Let's start at the very beginning," she began. "When you get to Amanda's house, be sure you say something pleasant to her parents."

Her parents! I'd have to talk to her parents? I mean, I don't mind talking to Jafar's folks, or some of my other friends, but this would be different. Even I could see that much.

"What should I say?"

"Don't worry, nothing too complicated," Mom said with a smile. "Just 'good evening', 'how are you tonight?' – that kind of thing."

"Okay, sure." Sounded simple enough.

"Now, when you escort Amanda from her house out to the transport, how will you do it?" she asked.

For a moment I didn't know what to say. I must admit I hadn't given even a second of thought to escorting Amanda, just to being with her. Finally, I admitted as much.

"I'll…just walk with her, I guess."

"No," she said with a tone that broached no discussion. "You will take her arm like this…" she hooked her arm into mine, "and walk beside her at *her* pace – not yours." I was well-known for walking at a speed that left most of my friends, Jafar in particular, begging for relief. "And you will tell her she looks beautiful." At my unspoken objection she added, "Or whatever word you want to use that means the same thing. It's not the word that counts, but that you notice and let her know it."

I didn't think I'd have any trouble with that part of the evening; Amanda is the most beautiful girl I've ever seen. But my mother wasn't through.

"And if you really want to gild the lily," she continued after a short pause, "you'll tell her while her parents are near enough to hear."

I had no idea what gilding a lily meant, but I could see that any parent would like to hear nice things about their kid. It would be embarrassing, but I could do it. Heck, I *would* do it.

"Okay. Can I get back to studying now?"

"Not yet. That just gets you out of the house. Do you know how to dance?"

Ah, the crux of the matter. I'd watched a few dances on the SightScreen and it didn't look too hard. Just move to the beat of the music. But no, I had never actually done it in real life.

"Not exactly," I said, as inexactly as I thought I could get away with.

"Hmm," she said, shaking her head with that look all parents seem to use to convey 'I knew it!' without saying so. "Let me bring up a few songs on the Digitact and we'll see if we can remedy that situation."

I stood in the middle of the room as she programmed the music, thinking 'Does every kid have to go through this?' Yet if I were pressed, I'd have to say that part of me was pretty happy she was doing it. There's probably nothing more embarrassing than appearing like a dork in front of all your classmates. If her tutoring made me appear only part-dork, I'd be thrilled.

"Okay. We'll start simple and get a bit more complicated," she said as a familiar popular tune began to play. "Watch me."

At that she began to move to the music. There's nothing more amazing, at least to me, than discovering that a parent is more, or at least different, than I'd supposed. In this instance, her graceful, even artistic moves absolutely blew me away. I mean, I knew that she'd been young once, and had seen photos of her and my Dad all dressed up for some dance or another. But to actually see her, at her age, moving to that music – I was dumbfounded!

She danced with eyes closed, as if in some kind of trance. She whirled and twirled, and moved her hands as though carving sculpture from thin air. The room was transformed in that moment into some sort of portal between two different realities: the mother I knew and the woman she actually was.

Perhaps she felt my awe, for suddenly she opened her eyes and motioned to me with a smile so sweet I almost sighed. "Come on. You do it."

To say I felt self-conscious would have been a gross understatement, but she seemed to be having so much fun I was moving to the music before I even realized what had happened.

"Great, great!" she said, "but let yourself go! Let the music carry you away!" She closed her eyes again and followed her own advice. With no one watching me, I felt my insecurity fall away as I stopped thinking about what I was doing and just reacted to the music.

It was incredible! I actually felt as if I were flying, carried along by the emotion and power of the melody. I realized that until that moment I had only experienced music with my ears; now I felt it in every part of my body! I closed my eyes and flew.

When the song finally stopped, I opened my eyes to find my mother standing just a few feet away, smiling broadly as she watched me.

"You're a natural," she said.

"How could I not be?" I said, and her smile grew even wider.

"Your father would have been very happy. He loved music."

That, I knew. Even though I hadn't been born when he died, I'd seen digi-vids of him humming, and whistling, and listening to music of every variety imaginable. At least, that was how it seemed to me.

"Before your head gets too big for the room," my mom interrupted my reverie, "let's try some slower music. Once you get this down, you're home free." She turned toward the Digitact and ordered, "Selection 3, please."

At once a large orchestra began to play music I didn't recognize, the kind of music I'd always referred to as fuddy-dud. "Now, put your right hand here," she continued, placing my hand on her left hip, "and your left one here." She lifted my hand to hold hers. "It's just a simple pattern, repeated with a bit of ad-libbed expression." She showed me a box-step that seemed anything but exciting. "One, two, three," she counted as my step followed hers. "One, two, three…"

I thought I was catching on pretty well, when suddenly she turned and said "Pause!' in the general direction of the Digitact. The music stopped.

"Vers, this isn't a forced march," she said gently. "I know it feels a lot more structured than the other dance, but you can still relax and let the music move you. You just need to stick more or less to the basic steps."

"All right," I said with a sigh. "Let's try again."

The second time I was merely terrible, and each successive time I got a little better, until after about a stunde of repetition I was able to move my feet without thinking of each step ahead of time.

"Not bad," my mother said appraisingly when she finally surrendered. "Not bad at all."

I didn't know if she was just making me feel good or whether I'd actually improved to any great extent, but at least I wasn't dreading the experience. And as I understand my Dad used to say, confidence is eighty percent of success. I wouldn't say I was exactly confident, but at least I wasn't pathetic. That was improvement.

I practiced my dance moves a couple of more times in the dins before the dance, and by the time the big din rolled around I was almost passable. At least *I* thought so. Of course the big test would be how Amanda reacted to my newfound ability on the dance floor. I'd be lying if I said I wasn't worrying a little, but not so much that I wasn't looking forward to the whole experience.

The night of the dance I was more than a little excited. I tried to maintain a cool exterior, but my Mom saw right through it.

"Relax," she told me as she took over tying the ridiculous little piece of colored cloth that is mandatory with formal wear. I'd been fussing with it for ten clics and it still looked like something that fell off a bird's nest. "It'll be fine."

"I know, I know. It's just…"

"You want to impress her."

I probably wouldn't have put it so directly, but yeh, I *did* want to impress Amanda. I was so powered-up that I was all decked-out and ready to go by quarter to eight. In my mind I ran through the handful of dances that I'd almost mastered, trying to imagine Amanda and me swirling through the crowd like something out of one of those old Earth movies. I could see my classmates all pull back in stunned amazement as we moved effortlessly to the rhythm of the music. She'd be looking at me, I'd be looking at her, and everyone else would be looking at us.

I was just about to drop her into one of those massively cool dips that Mom had demonstrated to me, when suddenly the front door buzzer sounded with its crow-like squawk. It was like getting awakened by a face full of cold water.

"Yeh?" I said as I opened the door with perhaps a bit more attitude than I intended.

"Glad to see you too," Jafar responded, stepping by me with little regard for either my attitude or its cause.

"Sorry about that. I was off in another zone."

"Yeh, well you'd better get yourself back down into this one. We've got to get going."

I took one look at him and had to restrain a smile. The image that leaped to mind was a bunch of carrots wrapped in black crepe paper.

"Looking good," I said. "You'll wow 'em."

"Undoubtedly. But only if we get there. You about ready?"

I was. But I had to go find my Mom for the last reassurance before stepping out into deep space. She wasn't hard to find.

"I thought I heard the front buzzer," she said, hurrying into the big room carrying a Digistill. "Let me get a few memories of this night."

Both Jafar and I did our mandatory complaining, but I think both of us were kind of happy that someone would capture the moment for all posterity. Little did I know that it would be my last such event, ever.

We laughed, and posed, and laughed some more, until even my Mom was ready to see us go.

"Just have fun," she whispered as she kissed me on the cheek. "Keep an eye on him," she told Jafar with mock sincerity.

"And who's going to keep an eye on me?" he answered with the sly smile that was his trademark.

As I stepped out their front door I couldn't resist one surprised "Wow!' as I set eyes on our luxury transport. All gleaming metal and tinted oversized windows, the thing must have been half a block long.

"Couldn't get anything bigger?" I asked Jafar.

"Not and have it qualify for standardized routing."

"Then it'll have to do."

"I guess it will."

The driver actually got out of the vehicle and opened the doors manually for the two of us.

"That's the first time anyone's ever done that for me," I said, mouth ajar.

"Stick with me, kid. We're going places."

That we were. First stop: Amanda's parents' place. As the transport neared her sector, I must admit that Jafar's incessant chatter dissolved into simple background noise. I don't remember a word he was saying. All I kept thinking was, *Don't screw up, don't screw up...'*

As we drove the last few kilometers to her house, we passed dozens of electronic billboards with the High Priest's scowling face staring down at us, reminding us that he – and the Great Creator – are *always* keeping an eye on us. As if we needed reminding, with the black buzzard Watchers on most every corner. By the time we got to Amanda's I was sweating, and not just from the fancy clothes.

The car stopped in front of her house, the driver opened my door, and I froze.

"What are you waiting for, dude?" my friend asked. "Do you expect her to come out here to meet us?"

"Just getting my head together," I said, which was a bit of a stretch since my head was anything but together.

"Well try to do it sometime this sept. We're paying this driver by the stunde."

Finally, I focused on the task at hand and forced myself to leave the relative safety of our huge transport. As we walked up the path to her door, I felt like a condemned man on his way to execution. I must have looked like it, too.

"Hey, get a smile on," Jafar said, just as I was about to ring the door buzzer. "You look like your dog just died."

I took a deep breath, forced my rigid lips into some semblance of a smile, and pushed the button. In an instant the door swung open, and there stood Somar Velding, the Manager of the entire Phoebos Mines system, his expression more questioning than welcoming.

"Hi, Mr. Velding, I'm Vers Leitstell," I said, my voice on the verge of cracking. "Is Amanda ready?"

"Vers," he said with nothing that could be interpreted as a welcoming smile, "I'm told that she'll be out in a clic. Come on in."

I'd been hoping that Amanda would already have her coat on and be ready to flee, but no such luck.

"And who's this?" he asked as Jafar came in on my coattails.

"Jafar Quimby," the crepe-wrapped carrot said without hesitation. He shook Mr. Velding's hand with forceful confidence. "I'm a friend of Vers."

"Pleased to meet you," her father said, but he didn't sound very convincing. "Have a seat."

He gestured for us to come into their big room, which made ours look like a closet. I think my mouth might have actually dropped open as I looked at the expensive furniture and rugs, the walls covered with paintings and sculpture.

"You have a beautiful home," I managed to say, and I could see I'd finally scored a point. His rigid jaw relaxed into something resembling a smile.

"Thank you. Amanda's mother has more to do with that than I do."

Even as he mentioned her, Mrs. Velding emerged from a room in the back of the residential space. I could see at once where

Amanda got her good looks. Even at her age (she must have been pushing 40), she was still very attractive.

"Mr. Leitstell here was just commenting about how beautiful our home is," Velding said lightly. "I told him it was principally your doing."

Mrs. Velding feigned modesty. "Oh, don't you listen to him, boys. He has a very sharp eye for beauty."

"I can see that," I said unthinkingly as I put out my hand to touch hers; from her pleased smile I realized she interpreted my words to include her as well as her home. I turned three shades of crimson.

"I'm Vers Leitstell," was all I could manage to get out.

"And I'm Jafar Quimby," Jafar thankfully spoke up, stepping forward to touch hands as well.

"It's a pleasure to meet you both. Can I get you anything? Something to drink?"

"Oh, no thank you. The transport is waiting."

"Oh, yes, of course. Let me see what's keeping Amanda." She disappeared back the way she'd come.

"So, Leitstell, is it?" Mr. Velding asked to break the awkward silence that ensued. "Haven't I heard that name before? Does your father work at the Mines?"

"He used to. He died in the big explosion in 3317.8," I said.

"Ah, right. I'm so sorry," he said, and I could tell he was embarrassed. He fidgeted and looked around for some way to change the subject. I felt sorry for him. I'd talked about my Dad so many times that I was kind of used to it, or as used to something like that as you can get. But I knew how it affected other people to hear about how he died. Especially the Mines Manager.

"No problem. It was a long time ago," I said, hoping to lessen his embarrassment.

Just then, as if summoned, Mrs. Velding reappeared from the back room. In her wake, still fiddling with some button or pin, came Amanda. She was almost to where we were standing before she looked up from what she was doing to greet us.

"Oh! Sorry I'm late," she said. "I can't seem to get this silly snap to catch."

She looked so great that even Jafar was struck speechless. "It was worth the wait," I finally mumbled. The pride in her parents' faces made me happy to have said something. Her smile made it even more worthwhile.

"You two are looking pretty good yourselves," she said as her mother helped her with the snap. "You clean up well."

"Here, this is for you," I said, pulling a wrist corsage out of my jacket pocket. It was a little the worse for wear, but she pretended not to notice.

"Oh, it's lovely!" she said with more enthusiasm than it deserved. "Will you put it on me?"

I hadn't practiced that maneuver, but thankfully it turned out to be nothing more than a wristband with flowers. I only hoped she didn't feel my hands shaking as I did it.

"Let's get a few DigiStills before you go!" her mother suddenly decided. "Som?"

Her husband went over to a desk and pulled out the recorder. I was feeling a bit self-conscious, but it only took a few moments to save our smiling faces for posterity.

"Now all of you have a wonderful time!" her mother said as we finally made our way to the door.

"And you take good care of my little girl," Mr. Velding said in a voice so low that only I could hear him.

I nodded to him with a look that probably fell somewhere between terror and confirmation. It seemed to do the trick.

"Try to be home before 1," he said as he touched my hand and Jafar's at the door.

"Oh Daddy," Amanda interrupted, "we're not babies! We'll be back when it's over."

She kissed her mother on the cheek and took my arm just as my mother and I had practiced. Feeling more relieved than anything, we headed out into the Phoebean night. As we slid into the transport I chanced one look back at the house. Her mother stood watching us with an expression of sheer pleasure, while her father held up one finger: "One o'clock," I saw him mouth. I made believe I didn't see him.

"Wow, this is pretty nice," Amanda said as she looked at all the accessories in the transport.

"I hope so," Jafar said. "Cost an arm and two legs."

"Not *so* much," I corrected, even though he was pretty much right. I'd be working at least a lunar cycle to pay off my half of the rental. But it was worth it.

Next stop was at Jafar's date's house. Her name was Elinine, and although she was even shorter than Jafar, she was pretty cute. Looked good in her dress too. The routine at her house was pretty much the same as at Amanda's, except her parents insisted on even more DigiStill moments and were even more in awe of our ride than we were. By the time we finally piled back into the transport we were running very late. I thought we'd miss the first dance and the formal DigiStills, so I asked the driver to try to step on it. Boy, did he ever!

By the time we pulled up at our school, Jafar, Amanda and I were laughing hysterically from being bounced all over the inside of the transport like a Digitact SightSee game. Elinine, on the other hand, looked like she was ready to burst into tears. Her wrist corsage had gotten smushed from one particularly sharp turn, and her dreams of a perfect evening were bruised, if not entirely ruined.

I have to hand it to Amanda, she stepped in and gave Elinine a pep-talk that would have made Coach Wezen proud. Good thing too – Jafar was having too much fun to even notice the tears starting to pool in his date's wide eyes. But by the time we stepped out of the transport, we were all smiles again. That's the DigiStill we caught. The one I still keep in my reader. The one I take a look at whenever it seems that my life has moved so far from those simple, fun dins that it'll never be the same.

Enough of that.

As it turned out, we weren't the only ones running late. About ten per cent of the kids showed up at or after the 8 o'clock start time. Luckily, the Admins were used to that kind of irresponsibility, and the real shindig didn't kick-off until 8:30. We got our DigiStills, had a chance to meet with our friends, and even had a glass of punch before the speeches and the introductions of all the chaperones began. You'd think we were bang-bangers in a Rehab Facility the way they brought in so many adults to keep an eye on us. Then again, as I looked around, I suppose more than a few of the kids there either had been, or soon would spend some time in confinement.

It makes me laugh to think back to that night. I tried so hard to seem cool and collected, when all the while I was hyperventilating as I waited for the first dance to begin. I mean, I was pretty confident that I could do the basic moves and all, but doing them with my mother was a far cry from doing them with Amanda. And in front of 400 kids! Yeh, I was nervous.

Amanda, on the other hand, seemed like she was born for just such an evening. I'd never realized how popular she was until that night. It seemed like some kid or another was coming over to talk to her five times a clic. And guys I'd never said two words to before came up to me, most all of them with the same basic question:

"How did a big dufus like you ever land Amanda for the dance?"

They were trying to be funny, I know. I mean, I was pretty popular too. Nothing like Amanda, but pretty good in my own way. But I understood what they meant. If a SightScreen star had been there with Amanda, they'd probably ask the same question. Any guy would look kind of feeble in comparison to her.

So when the Director finally announced that the music was about to begin, I was already pretty jumpy. Some kids, mostly girls, rushed out onto the dance floor as soon as the lights dimmed. I hesitated, trying to clear my head. Amanda would have none of it.

"This is what we came here for," she announced. "Come on."

Before I could say a word, she'd taken my hand and led me out to the dance floor just as the first strains of music began to blare from the omni-sound diffusers. I didn't have time to think or object. Before I knew it, I was dancing!

I'd thought that I'd be completely self-conscious, thinking everyone would be looking at me since I was with Amanda. But the way it worked out, I was so drawn to her eyes I don't even remember thinking about anyone else. It was almost like it was just the two of us out there.

Well, almost. At one point we were having so much fun that somehow we moved closer than the 25 centimeters allowed by the Council. In clics a chaperone was standing next to us with one of those pludy morality sticks, demonstrating to everyone in the room that we had transgressed against the wishes of the Great Creator – as if they had any idea what His wishes might be.

I was about to say something that probably would've gotten us a stunde or two of 'reflection time', when Amanda spoke up.

"Sorry about that. We'll keep the allowed distance from now on." I wondered if anyone else could see the sarcastic glint in her eyes. But it worked.

We danced for over a stunde before taking a break, by which time I was sweating so much I needed a napkin to dry my face and hair.

"I could use a breath of air," Amanda said as she watched me mop up the flowing rivers on my face. "How about you?"

"Are you kidding? Let's go!"

We went out the front exit, where we found at least a dozen other couples had come to the same conclusion. Some wanted to cool off, some wanted to smoke, others to sneak sips of whatever concoction they had managed to smuggle into the dance. We stood off to one side, eying our classmates with mild amusement.

"Looks like a scene from a bad SightScreen," I joked.

"Really bad," she said, and smiled. There was something about that smile...

I don't know what came over me, but I leaned over and kissed her – full on the lips! To my great relief, she didn't pull back in disbelief or cry out for help. In fact, she put her hand behind my neck and held me there, in full pucker, for what seemed like a stunde.

"You're full of surprises," she said when she finally took a breath.

"I...I don't know what came over me," I stumbled. I'm sure I was blushing, but in the dim light she probably couldn't tell. Or at least I hoped not.

"Whatever it was, I hope it's not the last we see of it." Her eyes sparkled.

I was just about to come back with some snappy reply, or at least I was trying desperately to find one, when suddenly a voice I hadn't heard for several lunar cycles brought my moment of ecstasy to a crashing halt.

"Hey Leitstell, what'd you do, pay some skank to go to the dance with you?" It was Nobus Wentwell, with three of his leering buddies. From the way they were dressed, I was pretty sure they weren't there for the dance.

"Don't answer him," Amanda whispered. "Ignore the big glook."

But Nobus had no intention of being ignored. He led his pack of braying jackasses so close to us that I could smell the heady mixture of intoxo, scrum and body odor. We were only a few feet away when Nobus realized his earlier error.

"Cremny Shalt!" he said loud enough to be heard a few districts away. "Is that the prissy Miss Velding I see there with you?"

"Lay off," I said before I even had time to think. "Go smoke some more scrum."

"Oh ho! Look who's grown a pair! Or maybe Amanda lent them to you?"

I took a step in their direction, but Amanda put her hand on my chest to restrain me. I was so mad at that moment I didn't even realize what a favor she was doing me.

"Don't," she said softly. "They're not worth it."

"You should listen to her, Leitstell. You caught me by surprise last time, but tonight will be a different story."

"You are such a glook, I can't even believe it," I said, pulling my best verbal punch. Nobus just smiled.

"Grab him," he ordered his flunkies, and before I knew what was happening, each of my arms was held tight behind my back. I struggled to get free, but there were two of them and they held on for dear life.

"Leave him alone!" Amanda suddenly yelled loud enough so that heads turned all over the entrance plaza.

"Mind your own business!" Nobus answered, grabbing her by the arm.

I don't know what came over me, but it was as if something exploded in my head. I threw my arms straight out to the side and Nobus' two buddies went flying across the pavement. I don't know what I had planned to do next; I'm not sure I was even thinking clearly. But before I could do anything else, Nobus' huge right fist came flying through the air and caught me flush in the stomach.

I doubled over in pain, the wind rushing out of me like a burst balloon. I fell to my knees, tears welling up in my eyes despite my best efforts.

From somewhere in a red haze I heard Amanda cry out, "You leave him alone, you big glook!" I would have smiled at her choice language if I could have managed it. But it was all I could do to suck in small gulps of air, let alone smile.

The next thing I knew, there was a loud scream and I heard a scuffle break out. I thought for an instant that Amanda had gone after Nobus, but as my head cleared I realized that the voices belonged to Nobus and... Jafar! I tried to struggle to my feet. He was going to get killed! I was just barely able to lift my eyes enough to see Jafar clinging to the big guy's back, riding him like a wild stallion, his arms tight around Nobus' throat.

"I'm gonna kill you, you little dwerb!" Nobus yelled, his face so red I feared it might explode.

Jafar didn't answer him, but from the look on his face I could tell he took the warning seriously. He hung on for dear life. If I could only get enough strength back to help him…

I was just starting to get my wind again when suddenly shrill whistles screamed from seemingly every direction.

"Stop that − now!" a welcomed voice called out. It was Marcus Onwell and two of his Monitor buddies, coming at a full run.

At first the words had no effect, but after an interminable delay, Nobus stood − with Jafar still glued to his back − and watched numbly as the three upper classmen roared to his side.

"I said, STOP THAT!" Marcus screamed with all his strength as he slid to a halt.

"I'm…not…doing…anything," Nobus croaked through a bruised larynx.

Marcus turned his furious gaze on Jafar, who slowly loosened his grip on Nobus' throat and slid to the ground.

"What is going on here?" Marcus demanded.

"We were just coming out for some air, when this glook punched Vers in the stomach," Amanda offered at once, ignoring the seething hatred in Nobus' eyes.

"Nobus! What are you doing here?" one of the other Monitors asked. It was clear he didn't expect to find the big glook at a dance.

"I was just walking past. Thought I'd say hi to my old buddy Leitstell." The sarcasm was unmistakable. Nobus obviously wasn't intimidated.

"Do you realize we almost called the sector Watchers?" Marcus said, his voice low and threatening. They were the Keepers of the Faith, the neighborhood muscle for the Seven.

"Go ahead. Call them. I've got a few friends here who'll testify that these two losers jumped me out of the blue," he said, nodding in the direction of his two buddies, who were just then dusting themselves off. "It'll be our word against theirs."

"Well here's *my* word," Marcus said, leaning in so close to Nobus that their faces almost touched. "Out! Get out of here before I take you up on your offer to call the Watchers. I don't think you'd enjoy their…questioning."

In fact the Watchers were known to use the worst of both old and new interrogation techniques. It was said they didn't really care what you confessed, as long as you squirmed long enough before doing so.

"Hmmph," Nobus grunted with a sneer. "Why would we want to stay around this dump?" he said. "It sure isn't the company." He turned to his friends. "Come on – let's go someplace where they know how to have a good time."

As he turned to leave, Amanda stepped forward with a flushed face.

"Is that it? He attacked Vers for no reason, and he gets to talk away?!"

"We're even," I said, trying to diffuse the whole issue. I saw Nobus glance back over his shoulder. From the look in his eyes, I'd say he didn't exactly agree.

"Yeh, what is this?" Jafar suddenly added. "The guy should be locked up!"

The look in Nobus' eyes turned utterly unforgiving.

"I said, we're even!" I nearly shouted, trying to get Jafar to back off. He looked at me with a bit of surprise, but got the message.

"Okay, all right. You're even. Good for you."

Amanda wasn't mollified. "You can't let him get away with this!" she insisted, grabbing me by my arms. "People like him thrive on intimidation. They have to be taught a lesson!"

"We'll see who's taught a lesson!" Nobus called back to us. This time it was my eyes that burned with fury.

"I said get out of here!" Marcus interjected, "unless you want to meet the Watchers tonight!"

Nobus looked like he wanted to answer back, but he simply mumbled something unintelligible and strutted off with his friends. The whole bunch of them started laughing a few clics later.

"Idiots," Marcus said with a shake of his head. Then he turned to me. "What's going on between you two?"

"I have no idea," I said truthfully. "For some reason he doesn't like me."

"That's obvious. Why?"

"Because he's a glook!" Amanda said. "He likes to scare people. It's how he shows he's a big shot."

"You need to stay away from him," Marcus told me solemnly. "He's bad news."

"I'm not trying to spend time with him. Sometimes we just run into each other."

"Well don't. When you see him coming, go in the opposite direction."

"I don't believe this!" Jafar said indignantly. "You're blaming this on Vers?!"

"I'm not blaming it on anyone," Marcus said. "I'm just saying that someone has to break the cycle, and I think Vers in the only one mature enough to handle it. Am I wrong?"

He looked right at me with a stare that actually sent a chill down my spine. He wasn't asking me; he was daring me.

I wasn't one to pass on a dare, especially not when it involved a big glook who wanted to take my head off.

"I'll keep my distance," I said.

"Good. Sometimes being right isn't enough. Sometimes we have to be smarter as well."

Something in the way he said that made me flinch, but not in a bad way.

"Well I think you were wonderful," Amanda said, taking my arm and leaning against me protectively. "No matter what anyone else says." She looked right at Marcus, and then turned to me and threw her arms around my neck. Without any warning she kissed me on the lips, (and I don't mean a little peck!) I heard a few catcalls from the other kids standing around watching, but I can't say I cared. I was lost again in Amanda's eyes, which gleamed with anger and...something else?

Before I could get my mouth working to say something, she took my hand. "Let's go back inside," she said, leading me in that direction. "It's too cold out here."

I saw Marcus following me with his eyes as I walked past him. He seemed to be watching me closely, more closely than I liked. What was up with him? He knew it wasn't my fault! Why was he giving me the eye? And this wasn't the first time!

I wanted to ask him, wanted to find out why he was paying so much attention to me, but Amanda's hand was warm and inviting and I had no intention of dropping it to chat with an upper classman I barely knew. So I followed Amanda back into the dance with Jafar and Elinine trailing just behind.

There isn't too much to tell about the dance itself, except for one short moment that really gave me the jeebies. Amanda had dragged me back out on the dance floor for about the fourth time, and we were dancing a waltz, when I decided to get fancy and do a big dip with her at the very end of the song. So there we were, swirling around the floor, and doing a pretty good job of it, if I may say, when it comes time for the dip. Well I put one arm under her back and the other behind her neck, as my mother had demonstrated, but maybe I'd gotten a little cocky, or maybe my hands were wet from sweating so darn much, but just at the bottom of the dip I felt her sliding out of my hands!

There wasn't anything I could do but wait for her to splat on the floor, and then apologize profusely as I scraped her up. Only…she never hit the floor! I sort of put my hands out in panic and the next thing I knew she 'flew' right back up into my arms and we finished the dance looking like pros! A few kids actually clapped and whistled! Amanda looked at me with obvious confusion, but I just smiled and bowed.

"How about that?" I said, at a loss to say anything else.

"Yes, how about that?" she answered cautiously.

I wasn't about to get into it then and there, so I changed the subject. "I'm dying of thirst. Want something to drink?"

"Yeh, okay. Thanks."

I dragged her back to our table and then took off without saying another word. I was hoping that the conversation there would divert her attention from our little magic dip. For a little while it seemed to do the trick. We took a nice long break chatting with Jafar and Elinine, where the choice of topic was mostly Nobus and his buddies. None of us could explain why he seemed to hate me so much, but we all agreed that we'd stay as far away from him as possible.

When the dance finally ended, right at midnight, we all said goodbye to a bunch of kids we knew and piled into the transport. I must admit I snuck a peek out of the corner of my eyes as we left the building trying to see if Nobus had come back, but there was no sign of him anywhere. We dropped off Elinine first, and like a good escort Jafar walked her back to her front door. Although we weren't trying to be nosey, Amanda and I couldn't help but notice when she stretched up and kissed him on the cheek.

"She likes him," Amanda said with that dreamy girl tone that all the girls in our school seem to use whenever they're talking about love, or kittens, or stuff like that. I just grunted, figuring it could be taken almost any way.

When it came time for us to drop off Amanda, however, I was more focused.

"I really had a great time," she said as we walked the pathway to her door.

"Yeh, me too," I said. At this point all I could think of was whether or not she would give me a kiss as well. "You're a great dancer."

"You're not so bad yourself," she said. "Especially that dip move where you drop me but I don't fall." She stopped and looked at me with her brows all knitted up in question marks. "How did you do that, anyway?"

"I…" For just an instant I thought about lying, making up a real big one to try to change the subject. But then I changed my mind.

"I really don't know," I said. "I mean, I really don't know what happened. One clic you were falling, the next you were back." Then a thought hit me. "Are you sure *you* didn't do it?"

She laughed, right out loud. "Oh sure. You knock big old Nobus half-way across the parking lot with just a shove, and then send his two buddies flying with a flick of your wrist, but *I'm* the one who did it. Right."

She had me there. "Yeh, well whatever it was, how about we don't talk about it – with anyone."

"A secret?" she whispered, and I heard that kitten tone again. Yes!

"Just between the two of us. Okay?" I put out my hand to touch. She looked at it and made a face as though I'd handed her a plate of kibwaw and brittons.

"Just the two of us," she repeated, and then she leaned forward as if she were in slow motion and kissed me. A real kiss. This time I was ready. I wasn't exactly sure about all the details, but I'd seen enough SightScreen kisses to fake it pretty well, if I do say so myself. When we finally pulled apart, I could hardly catch my breath.

"Deal," she said with a sly smile.

Just then her front door swung open and there stood Mr. Velding. I wasn't sure what he'd seen, so I just stood there looking as innocent as possible. Turns out, his timing was perfect. He didn't see a thing. Or at least he didn't let on, if he did.

"There you are!"

"Daddy!" Amanda nearly screamed, grabbing my arm so tightly I thought she'd break the skin. She turned to me with a panicky expression that demanded my attention.

"Got her back on time," I managed weakly.

I noticed Mr. Velding glance up at the time and date information displayed in his eyeglasses. "So you did!" he said a bit too jovially. "Even a few clics early. I'm impressed. Did you have a good time?"

"Wonderful!" Amanda said with real emotion. "The music was great, we saw a lot of friends – a perfect night." This time she looked at me with dreamy eyes and a big smile. I smiled back.

"Well you can't ask for more than that," her father agreed. "But now it's time to get some sleep. Don't want to be waking the neighbors!" His attempt at humor was transparent, but it worked.

"I guess I've got to go in," Amanda said with just the least bit of a pout.

"Thanks for a terrific night," I said.

"There'll be others."

"There will?"

"Of course, silly!" She kissed me lightly on the cheek. "Sweet dreams."

Mr. Velding gave me a nod of his head as he shepherded his daughter inside. I guess it was a sign of approval. I couldn't help looking past him, though, for one last glimpse of Amanda. She turned and waved, just as the door closed. And there I was, standing in the dark, by myself, smiling like an idiot.

As I walked back to the transport I kept sighing, like I was short of breath or something. Of course, I knew what the something was.

"It's about time," Jafar grumbled as I slid back into my seat. "I thought for a second there you were trying to suck her tongue right out of her mouth!"

I punched him in the arm, a pretty good shot.

"Hey! I'm just saying it like it is!" he complained, massaging his bicep.

"Well say it some other way," I said.

"Uh oh, is Vers in love?" my friend said, rolling his eyes and puckering his lips. I just barely held off popping him another one. He threw up his hands in defense. "Just asking. No harm, no foul."

The look on my face must have said everything, because the conversation did not venture back into those waters for the rest of the ride home. We did discuss Nobus a little, but even that dumb glook couldn't spoil my night. By the time we dropped off Jafar and got back to my house, it was after 1. I should have been exhausted, but I was flying high. Maybe that's why I didn't even notice the strange transport parked in our space until I was halfway to the front door.

"What the heck is that?" I wondered when I finally noticed the expensive looking 55-D sports model. Every once in a while someone parked there when visiting one of our neighbors. Since we couldn't afford a transport ourselves, I guess it didn't really matter. But a 55-D? Wow, never saw one of those in our sector before.

So I was only half-surprised when I opened the front door and there was my mother, looking a whole lot dressier than when I'd left, sitting next to a strange man showing him something on the porta-SightScreen. She looked more surprised than me.

"Oh, Vers! Is it so late already?" she asked, jumping up with what looked to me like a pretty good blush.

"Yeh, guess it is," I said, trying to act cool and all.

Mom glanced to me, and then to the man, and then back to me. "But I'm being rude," she finally managed. "This is Mr. Mallett," she went on, presenting the guy with her hand. "He works at the Mines."

"Oh? Are you a miner?" I asked, thinking maybe this guy knew my Dad.

"Not exactly," he said, standing to touch my hand. He was tall, a few inches taller than me, even. Short dark hair. I guess women would say he was pretty good-looking. Light eyes.

"Mr. Mallett works with Mr. Velding, in Administration," my mother explained quickly.

"Eden," he corrected. "Call me Eden." My mother's smile was genuine.

"We were just looking at some old DigiStills."

"You're quite the athlete," 'Eden' said. There was something about the way he said it that struck me as phony, but maybe he was just being polite. The two seem pretty much the same sometimes.

"Not so much anymore. I played a bit a few solar cycles back."

"Looks like you're still in good shape." He slapped me on the shoulder like we were old pals. But we weren't.

"Guess so."

At that the conversation looked like it was about to stall out when Mom came to the rescue.

"So, how was the dance? Did you have fun?"

I didn't really feel much like telling all about my night with some stranger in the room, so I kept it simple. "Yeh, it was good. Real good." Then we all just stood there for a few moments, none of us really having too much to say — at least not all together like that.

I guess I was signaling my discomfort a bit more than I'd realized, because 'Eden' got the hint right away.

"Well, I think it's about time for me to head home," he said, stretching dramatically (for my benefit, I suppose.) He looked to my mother, maybe hoping she'd disagree with him. But she didn't.

"I had a wonderful time," she said.

"I did too. Maybe we can do it again? Or, perhaps dinner?" They were talking like I'd already left the room, which is what I felt like doing but was hanging around just to be polite.

"I'd like that," Mom said, and there was something in her voice that I hadn't heard for a long time, maybe ever. I can't say what I was thinking just then, but I know I was wondering what was up.

Mr. Mallet shook my hand and told me how happy he was to meet me, but all the time he kept looking over at Mom as though I was just a box he had to check before leaving. I can tell you, I wasn't impressed.

When he finally left, Mom came over to me with a big smile. I expected her to ask again about the dance, and Amanda. So I was pretty surprised when she asked about her 'date'.

"What did you think about Eden? Did you like him?"

What could I say? I'd only met the guy for five clics and he was grandstanding for my Mom the whole time. "Seemed okay," was the best I could do.

"I know it was a little awkward. I didn't expect him to stay so long."

"What was he doing here, anyhow?" I couldn't stop myself. In all the solar cycles since Dad died, that was the first time a guy had ever hung around so late.

Mom seemed so flustered that I almost felt sorry for having asked, but I wanted to know. "Well, you know, there was a change in Dad's annuity payments, and Mr. Mallet wanted to explain all the details."

Sure he did. I may have only been 15, but I knew that my mother was still a good-looking woman. I'd seen lots of guys eying her when we went out somewhere, and more than a few had come over for dinner or whatever over the solar cycles. But 'to explain annuity details'? Sounded sketchy to me.

"Seems like you two hit it off," I said, trying to sound nonchalant.

"Oh, well, I don't know if I'd put it quite like that," she stumbled, falling all over herself to try to sound noncommittal. "He *is* a nice man, though."

"Yeh, good. He seems nice enough."

That was all the space she needed. "Speaking of nice – things went well with Amanda?"

I went through the whole evening step by step, in more detail that I'd planned because of all her questions. Of course I edited out a few things, like Nobus for instance. I really didn't want her getting worried about nothing. But there was something I needed to know about what happened out there, and I was hoping she might be able to tell me.

"Hey Mom," I said after all the grilling about the dance was pretty much over and we were just about to head off to bed, "did Dad ever have any... *unusual* abilities?"

She looked at me with narrowed eyes. "Like what?"

"Oh, I don't know," I hemmed, "like anything out of the ordinary."

She stopped to ponder for a moment. "Well, he could touch the tip of his nose with the tip of his tongue," she said with a laugh.

"Nothing more... *unusual?*"

Now her look had become positively concerned. "How do you mean?"

"I don't know," I began, starting to wish I hadn't started the whole line of questioning, "something that other people just can't do."

She shook her head and smiled. "Is this because of Mr. Mallet's visit?" she asked. "Because if it is, you don't have to worry. No one will ever take the place of your father in this family."

"No! It's not that at all. It's just, well, I don't know. I was just wondering."

"Well, whatever it is, I'm sure it can wait until morning. Time for us to get some sleep!"

And so it ended. I think it took quite a while for me to fall asleep that night, but once I did I remember having incredible dreams of Amanda. Some of which I can't really talk about. But all of them good. Real good.

Still, my *power*, whatever it was, had now shown itself twice. The first time I could justify it with all kinds of logical excuses. But the second time? I had more to think about than just Nobus.

CHAPTER 5

Time passes quickly, especially when you're fifteen and there's a special girl involved. Jafar kept joking it was love. Or, something like love. Whatever it was, it made my life a whole lot more interesting and a whole lot more pleasant being around Amanda. Oh sure, there were some downsides: I didn't really get along with all her girlfriends. Some of them were just too catty and nasty for my taste. Of course, they didn't show that side to Amanda too often. They wouldn't have been part of her 'group' if they did, I imagine. But when she wasn't around, I saw more of it than I would've liked. I was tempted to tell her how her friends weren't as smiley and nice when they weren't with her, but I'm not a snitch. I figured she'd work it out on her own, eventually.

There were a few guys who came with the girls. Most of them were okay, to me anyway, but I heard how some of them treated Jafar when I wasn't around, and it wasn't the best. He's a tough little guy, and although he never really dwelled on it I could tell he wasn't too thrilled with some of them. So, I just didn't spend much time with the glooks. No problem.

What really concerned me more was the increasing presence of old Mr. Mallett – 'Eden'. I had hoped that he would fade from the scene like a bad memory, but instead he started showing up at our house for dinners, to take my Mom to eat-houses and public DigiScreens, and even at my Upper Level solar cycle-end ceremony. It wasn't a big deal really. Just an assembly where the Director tells all the first solar cycle kids how great we're all doing and what high hopes he has for all of us. A bunch of pluda, I'd call it, though not when he was around. The only thing was, they also gave out a few awards, and I was going to get one. Nothing spectacular. 'Best First Solar cycle Math Student.' I was always pretty good at math. I think my brain is just wired that way. I see solutions to math problems almost before I start to try to solve them. It's really the only subject I liked a lot. Some Tech classes were okay, but most of the rest were kind of boring. For me, anyway.

So when 'Eden' showed up, I was kind of wondering what was going on. It made me worry what would come next. And, as it turned out, I had every reason to be worried.

I remember that din pretty clearly. After all that's happened, more clearly than part of me would've liked. I got my award, we took a few DigiStills, Amanda got an award as 'Best First Solar cycle Creative Writer', and 'Eden' touched our hands and told us how proud he was of our 'accomplishment', as if I really cared whether he was proud or not. I thought that we'd go home then. Maybe Mom would have a cake or something for Amanda and me and Jafar.

But 'Eden' wanted to take us all out to eat.

"Someplace nice," he suggested with the cheesy smile that adults use when we think they're really being nice to you.

"Oh, wouldn't that be wonderful!" my mother said, and I could tell she was all excited about the prospect so I said, "sure."

'Eden' tried to hint that maybe it would be more 'family oriented' if just he and Mom and I went. But I really wanted Amanda to come, and so I asked, figuring it wasn't a big deal. But I hadn't even gotten the words out of my mouth before I saw 'Eden' and my Mom exchange a look that said 'Oh, this isn't going the way we want. Let's make up some pluda to get him to change his mind.' Or at least that's how I read it.

I was about to argue that it would seem more like 'family' if Amanda, and maybe even Jafar came along (a lot more than it would with him...) when Amanda's Dad came up to her and told her that they had plans and was she ready to leave. I could tell she wasn't thrilled with the idea, but there are times when every kid has to go along with their parents' idea of a good time, just to keep things peaceful at home. So she sighed, gave me a kiss on the cheek, and off they went.

That would have been that, except as they were walking away – Mr. & Mrs. Velding and Amanda – Mr. Velding turned back over his shoulder and I could swear he winked at 'Eden'! Well, I knew they both worked at the Mines, but this wasn't a workplace wink. This was a 'Glad to have helped, go get 'em!' kind of wink. Or that's how it seems to me now, after the fact. I'm not really sure, but think I had my suspicions right then and there. I know I should have.

We went to a restaurant, a pretty nice one I have to admit, just the three of us – one big happy family. Things were going along just fine (or as fine as could be expected), when 'Eden' asked to have a bottle of syn-cham brought to our table. Now, I don't know what kind of childhood you had, but I'd never seen my mom sipping syn-cham, *ever*. It's something the Seven tolerate, but just barely. In fact, I think I'd only seen it in SightScreen programs. So I must admit I was kind of impressed that ol' 'Eden' was ordering some, just to celebrate my award ceremony.

He wasn't.

After seeing that the server poured us each a glass – ("Even Vers?" my mother had asked, aghast. "Sure, why not. It's a special din," 'Eden' answered. I should've known right then and there something was up) – he held his up and offered a toast.

"To my beautiful Morgan, and her math-whiz son, Vers – may we have many more dins as happy as this one!"

He seemed so thrilled by the whole idea that I turned to my mother with a questioning look, as if to say, 'what's going on?'

"I know this will come as a bit of a surprise," my Mom began.

"Not too much of a surprise, I hope," 'Eden' interrupted.

"No, but a bit, I imagine. Vers, Eden and I are going to be married!" She smiled as if it was the greatest news I'd ever heard in all my life. The two of them stared at me with expectant looks. I tried really hard not to groan.

"Wow, that *is* a surprise," I finally said.

"Are you happy for us?" my Mom asked. I was glad that she'd asked the question that way so I didn't have to lie. I'm usually not a good liar.

"Oh, yeh, sure, I'm real happy for you," I answered. And I was. Happy for them. Not so much for me.

"Oh, honey, I knew you'd be!" Mom half-shouted as she hugged me so hard I thought she was going to break a rib. 'Eden' slapped me on the shoulder again.

"Good man!' he said as he grabbed the bottle to refill our glasses. "You see, Morgan, I told you he'd be fine with it."

Well, the rest of the evening was pretty much just listening to the two of them tell me all their plans for the joining, and the Acclimation Holidin, and even how I was going to fit into the new scheme of things. I wasn't really asked what I thought about everything that was going on, but I suppose between the syn-cham and their excitement, they probably were flying too high to even think about my opinion. Actually, I guess I was kind of glad for my Mom. I mean, I know she'd had me with her all those solar cycles after my Dad died, but I'm old enough to know that a kid doesn't take the place of a wedman. So she'd finally have another man in her life. I just would've been happier for her – and me – if it hadn't been 'Eden.'

*****

Everything moved so quickly with my mother and 'Eden' that I barely remember the details of their engagement. It seems to me that one din everything was going along like normal, and the next our world was turned upside down. Or at least my world.

From a regular, if not overly welcomed visitor, 'Eden' became a daily fixture. At first it was just a nightly visit 'to see how you are.' Then he joined us several times a sept for dinner, and by the time the joining approached it was every night. I rarely had any time alone with Mom. Maybe a few clics in the mornings before I left for school and she for work, but we were both running around so much that we hardly had time to say two words to each other.

I must admit, they kept me in the loop about all their plans, but it was hard to fake interest when all I hoped was that something would happen to scuttle the whole affair. It didn't. As the din of their joining grew closer, I must have lost my smiley face persona a bit because one morning Mom cornered me with the 'I'm worried about you' look that I'd seen repeatedly during my childhood.

"Is there something wrong?" she asked as she struggled to slip her foot into a dressy brown shoe while gulping the last dregs of morning javo.

"No! What could be wrong?" I'd learned early-on that answering a question with a question was often the best way to avoid really answering. Unfortunately, my mother had learned it long before me.

"I don't know, but you seem a bit…down in the mouth lately."

Wow. 'Down in the mouth.' I think that was one of my Dad's, and I hadn't heard it for solar cycles. But I didn't let that throw me. Even though I wasn't wild about 'Eden', I knew she was and I refused to let my own feelings ruin her big din.

"Nah, probably just a bit nervous about the joining," I said, turning away slightly so she couldn't detect my lying eyes. She always said she could tell when I was lying by my eyes.

"It *is* coming awfully fast, isn't it?" she asked, but I could see from the look in her eyes that she was excited, not sick to her stomach.

"How are you holding up?" If one question is good, two must be better.

"Oh, it's a lot to handle, but I'm doing okay. What can I do to make your smile a little brighter?'

That was one thing I'll never forget about my Mom. Even when she was swamped by her own life, she always tried to make mine a little better.

I took the hint and smiled. "Just be happy," I said.

She smiled too. "I am."

I guess I remember that moment so clearly because of what happened. But whatever the reason, whenever I think back to Mom, it's that smile I remember first.

Anyway, as the big din approached I somehow managed to keep the corners of my mouth pulled domeward as well, if for no other reason than to keep Mom happy. The din before the joining I took Amanda to the rehearsal and the big dinner that followed. She was all starry-eyed, which worried me a bit – but not much. I had no thoughts of being bound at such an early age, and despite all her glowing words I knew Amanda well enough to know that she wasn't serious either. At least not yet.

The ceremony took place at the Mines' Devotion Center, a large richly-decorated space brimming with paintings, computerized windows that showed mosaic images of the life of Arod that changed every clic or so, and the largest indoor SightScreen I'd ever seen. (I knew there were bigger ones on the home planet, but on our little mining moon, that was it.) Since 'Eden' was a bigshot at the Mines, and Mom was the widow of a Hero of the Seven (basically one of the hundreds who had died mining the crystals that powered and financed the Council's activities), we were given access to a room that most miners never saw. I couldn't help but wonder what Dad would have said, and if he ever saw the Center. Probably not.

On the Big Din, I was bundled off with 'Eden' and several of his friends, or at least people with whom he worked. Mom was assisted in her preparations by her old friend, Natha, and by 'Eden's' mother, a pleasant-enough older lady who showed none of the stodgy falseness that made him so difficult for me to accept. We went to a very expensive Men's Club at the Mines Headquarters, where we all were steamed, cleaned and massaged within an inch of our lives. I suppose he meant it as a bonding exercise. I found it excessive, unpleasant, and just plain boring. 'Eden' made the occasional attempt to include me in the conversation, but statistics about crystal production, inside jokes about Mine MC staffers, and unending praise for the Council and its Seven did not entice me to pay close attention. After a while I think they all just forgot I was there. After three or four rounds of synthahol, I'm not certain they even knew where *they* were.

The stundes passed, slowly, and finally it was time to head off to the Center. Mom had picked out for me a tunic of brilliant white highlighted by dark purple that I thought was a little flashy, but she said it was perfect and 'Eden' said it 'would do,' so white and purple it was. 'Eden' was dressed in the most traditional joining garb ever: black, sack-like, with no fancy stitching or cuffs; he could certainly not be accused of betraying the guidelines of The Seven. I know he pressured my mother into wearing something similar, probably in hopes of gaining favor with his superiors at the Mines. But Mom would have none of it. She insisted on a reproduction of an antique Terra1 outfit, all in white as well, with a long train that trailed out behind her and a translucent veil that suggested more than it revealed.

'Eden' and I left for the Center nearly a stunde before the scheduled start of the ceremony; Mom went over with some friends. 'Eden' was worried that the transport would have problems, or the computers that controlled the traffic flow would suddenly go berserk and strand us on some out of the way thoroughfare until dinbreak. After all his chattiness at the Club, he was determined and reserved as we made our way the short distance to the Center.

"Vers, I hope you understand that there will need to be some changes made, after the ceremony," he said a few clics into the trip.

"No, I didn't know that," I answered truthfully, for although Mom and I had talked in general about the joining, we hadn't gone into any particulars. I'm not sure if it was because she didn't know what 'Eden' was planning, or whether she just chose to let him break the news.

"Yes, well there will probably be a number of changes, but I thought we should discuss two in particular while we have this time alone."

I didn't know what to say, so I said nothing.

"First of all," he continued, seemingly unconcerned by my silence, "although your mother's living facility is a cute little place, it really won't suit us once we are joined. I'm sure you understand that an MC must look the part as well as act it, so we'll be moving to my place. It's considerably more... suitable."

"All of us?" I asked before I could stop myself.

"Well, yes, of course. It wouldn't do to have a young man of your age living alone, now would it?" He actually seemed shocked that I would even suggest such a thing, although, in reality I hadn't even considered it until that very clic. "Of course, that brings me to my second point," he plowed on, and I had the sensation that he had rehearsed his whole speech. "As I mentioned, it's important for a member of the Manager Caste to *act* like an MC. You wouldn't learn *that* at your current school, I can assure you." He chuckled humorlessly. "So we have arranged for you to attend a *very* elite private school back on Terra5. I can tell you, it was no easy matter to get you accepted."

"But, I *like* Vaden," I said without thinking.

"Oh, I'm sure you do," he said dismissively, waving his hand as if to shoo away my absurd protest. "But that's not the point. The point is, you will now be moving in different circles, young man, and it's critical that you are fully prepared to do so."

Looking back, I suppose he thought he was being really nice to me, or at least he might have thought so. But that's not how I saw it then.

"I won't go!" I said.

He looked as if I'd slapped him.

"Of course you will. It's already been discussed."

"Not with me!"

He stared at me with a look of utter confusion. "Well," he huffed after a bit, "we'll discuss this later."

"Nothing to discuss," I muttered, half under my breath.

He shook his head and looked out the side window in silence for the remainder of the trip.

Once we were at the Center, everything moved so quickly that the discussion about going to school on the home planet faded into the background. I had been designated Second to 'Eden', though I'm certain it wasn't his idea. My Mom probably thought it would bring us closer together. Really. Anyway, the first part of my job was to see that everyone got seated in their designated seats. For some reason I don't really understand, the woman's friends and family are supposed to sit in one section, and the man's in another. Since the whole idea of a joining is to bring together not just two people, but their respective tribes, I'd think they'd want everyone to mix without artificial boundaries. Nope. Mom's folks on one side; 'Eden's' on the other.

It was pretty easy, really. Most people knew someone who was already there, so they just took off and went straight towards them without my having to say or do much of anything. A couple of times some of the older folks got a bit confused (or maybe saw the ridiculousness of the whole set-up) and I had to gently steer them to their 'correct' seats, but it didn't happen often. The high point of my ushering was when the Veldings appeared. I knew from Amanda that they'd been invited (apparently Mr. V knew 'Eden' from the Mines, vaguely), but I still felt my heart race a little faster when I saw the two senior Veldings appear in the doorway. But that was nothing compared to the way it took off when Amanda followed them in, her long pale blue gown the most elegant piece of outerwear I'd ever seen. I was awestruck.

"Looking good, Mr. Leitstell," Mr. V said as he touched my hand, breaking me out of my daze.

"*Very* good," Amanda whispered as she gave me a peck on the cheek.

Both her mother and father seemed so relaxed and comfortable that I thought they must have been drinking before they arrived. It was only later that I realized the real reason: I was about to be lifted up into the lofty ranks of the MC, and so was seen as a more *suitable* friend of their daughter. Whatever. As long as Amanda was there, I was happy.

Their arrival did create one little controversy, however. After I seated her parents – on 'Eden's' side, of course – I went to guide Amanda over to 'our' side, since I'd assumed she'd sit with me.

"Aren't you joining us?" her mother asked loud enough for me, and everyone else within five meters, to hear.

I started to tell her that she could sit wherever she wanted, I'd understand, when she cut me off.

"No Mother, I'll sit with Vers," she said, with such finality that there really wasn't anything her parents could say about it. To their credit, they gave in without a fight.

The ceremony was very nice. I can't really say more than that, since I paid more attention to Amanda than to the service, and…well, because of what followed. I do remember loud music, lots of flowering flora, and of course Mom – looking absolutely unbelievable in that old style white dress. The presiding Priest made a long speech about how Arod had always wanted to see upward mobility in this sphere as well as the next, and so would've been just tickled green by an MC reaching down into the depths of the WC to choose a mate. (He didn't actually say that. But that's what I heard.) I wondered then, and now, why it was so hard to move between castes if that's what Arod wanted for all of us.

When it was finally over, Mom and 'Dad' led the way down the aisle, followed by me and Amanda. I remember how happy I felt just then, even with my new 'Dad' threatening to send me into educational exile on Terra. (I figured I could handle that; maybe get a stay of execution through my Mom.) Amanda was radiant by my side, Mom looked as happy as I'd seen her.... Maybe ever. It was one of those brief moments when every biowave comes into synchronization, when time seems to stand still, when the Principal Star shines a little brighter and our very senses seem more acute. I was content.

But if life has taught me anything in my few solar cycles, it's that happiness and sorrow are balanced in equal measure. And so it was on that awful din.

After we had all posed for a thousand more DigiStills, 'Dad' virtually dragged Mom from the Center so that we could stay on schedule and get to the reception on time. The stretch transport was parked just outside the Center, and all the invited guests waited patiently to shout their best wishes and throw flora bits at the departing couple. 'Eden' bustled Mom and her Second into the transport and then stood at the door, looking expectantly at me.

"Well? Are you coming?" he asked.

"I'm going with Amanda," I said, not having been informed that I was expected to travel with the newly-joined, not as their son but as his Second.

"But it's tradition!" 'Eden' wailed, seemingly truly upset that I was flaunting some unwritten code of joinings.

"Let the kids have some time together," Mom said, and I got the feeling she meant let us spend some time together before I was shipped off to school.

I realized then and there that I'd have to fight to stay on Phoebos if I hoped to forestall their plans for me. I'd start as soon as we got back from their post-joining holidin...

It was not to be. Those next few clics still replay in my dreams at least once every rotational cycle.

Mom waved to me.

"See you at the reception!" she called out.

Eden climbed into the transport. The door closed behind him.

We all threw our flora bits.

I put my arm around Amanda's waist and we joined the crowd in waving and shouting best wishes.

If I close my eyes, I can see it still: The transport pulls away slowly. I turn to Amanda, and she to me. She smiles.

But just as she does, I see the flash of light reflected in her eyes. Then, the explosion.

We were knocked to the ground, all of us, by the force of the blast. Pieces of metal rained down all around. I got to my knees and found Amanda, blown two meters away from me. She was bleeding from a small cut on her forehead.

"Are you okay?!" I shouted, not just because there was a great deal of shouting and moaning from all the people around us, but because I had a buzzing in my ears that made everything sound as if I were underwater.

She nodded, dazed and befuddled.

"What happened?" she asked. She scrunched her eyes trying to focus on my face.

"I don't know. I think it was the transport..." Just then, the full meaning of what I'd just said hit me. "Stay here – I'll be right back!" I said, and scrabbling to my feet, I began to stumble in the direction the transport had taken.

It wasn't until I stood that I realized how much my head hurt, but I didn't care. I had to know. I had to see.

I picked my way through friends and family as quickly as I could until, finally, I made my way to where the explosion had taken place. I stared in disbelief at the gaping hole in the pavement, smoke still rising in wisps from the cavernous abyss. I instinctively looked skyward to see if the protective sphere had been pierced. I could see no breaks in the physical barrier, and was certain the energy enclosure was still in place.

But there was nothing left of the transport. Nothing bigger than the palm of my hand. I scanned the area, probably more in shock than consciously, and saw a small scrap of white sticking out from a pile of rock and permaphalt. It wasn't until I'd picked it up that I realized it was a piece of cloth, possibly from the antique white dress.

Suddenly it all was too much. My head began to swim and I bent over, retching violently. Tears streamed from my eyes. If I had died right then and there, I wouldn't have complained.

Then, seemingly from nowhere, I felt a hand on my shoulder. I immediately assumed that Amanda had come after me, and tried to clear my head and catch my breath so that she wouldn't see me like that.

"They're gone," I said, the best I could do in that state.

"And you must go as well," a voice answered. It wasn't Amanda.

I turned my head just in time to see Marcus Onwell quickly scan the chaos that surrounded us. I could barely hear faint sirens approaching.

"What? Why…?" I couldn't even process his presence, let alone what he had told me.

"I'm sorry!" he half-yelled, grabbing me lightly under one arm. "We *must* go – now!"

We must go? Where? Why? My mind was inundated by questions and impulses.

"No time to explain – come!" He pulled me up, harder, more urgently now. Part of me wanted to argue, to protest that I had to get back to Amanda, to help the injured. But he allowed no objections and my will was not my own. He dragged me from the spot where I'd collapsed, across the roadway to where a nondescript carrier transport awaited us. He pushed me inside and hopped in after me.

"Go!" he shouted to the driver, an older man I'd never seen before. The rapid acceleration that threw me back into my seat was unlike anything I'd ever experienced in a carrier class transport before. I barely had time to turn and look out the side window, where for just an instant I saw Amanda, leaning over her prostrate mother. But before I could yell to her, or even gesture, we were

gone and the entire blast site was disappearing in the backview
screens into flickering flames and the pulsing colored lights of more
emergency vehicles than I'd ever seen in my life.

CHAPTER 6

I must have passed out, since when I finally opened my eyes we were no longer in the transport but in a small but extremely well-equipped physician's office.

"Take it easy. You had a nasty blow to the head," an unfamiliar voice directed as a hand gently pushed me back to the bed.

"Where...? What...?" The blast still echoed in my ears, but everything else was fuzzy and my head still ached.

"It's okay," Marcus interceded, stepping into my field of vision. "You're safe now." '*That's right,*' I remembered, '*Marcus! He pulled me out of there. But why?*'

Then I remembered everything – the wedding, the transport...

"Amanda!" I half-shouted. The same gentle but strong hand restrained me.

"She's okay," Marcus reassured, pushing me back to the bed. "A cut on her forehead – that's all."

I didn't want to ask the next question, but I had to. "My mother?"

Marcus took a deep breath and then shook his head sadly. "I'm sorry."

I suppose I already knew. I'd seen the huge hole where the transport exploded. No one could've survived that. But somehow it seemed more real when I heard it from Marcus. I felt tears well up in my eyes and I choked on the realization.

"We let you down," Marcus said. "We never thought they'd go after you like that."

What? "*Me*? Who'd go after me? Why would *anyone* go after me?" I asked, too shocked for anger.

"You can get into that later," the first voice said to Marcus in a commanding tone. "For now, he needs to rest."

A middle-aged man wearing a white lab coat stepped out from behind the bed carrying a hand scanner. He adjusted his glasses as he looked at the readout more closely.

"It's definitely a concussion. He needs rest – now."

I saw Marcus hesitate for just a moment, as if he might argue the point, but just as quickly he apparently decided to follow the med-tech's advice.

"Tech Wiltorr will watch after you for the next little bit," he said instead. "Until you're recovered enough to move."

"And that won't be for a couple of stundes yet," the Tech added. "So you may as well settle in and get some sleep."

Sleep? I didn't want to sleep! I wanted to find out why someone would be trying to go after me, and I wanted to talk to Amanda, and…

I saw the Tech depress a syringe into the medline they'd hooked into the back of my hand. Within an instant I felt as if I were floating, and then – nothing.

*****

When I awoke again, I was in a different room, just as small but with scarcely any medical equipment and pale yellow walls instead of the medicinal white of the first one. My mouth was as dry as the lunar landscape outside the dome. I tried to sit up, but a bolt of pain shot through the top of my skull and I felt like I might throw-up again. I had barely fallen back on my pillow when the door opened and an attractive young nurse came hurrying in.

"So, we're awake," she said cheerfully as she went straight to the digital readout at the head of my bed. "Feeling any better?"

"A wibble bit," I mumbled, my dehydrated tongue unable to form the words.

"Sounds like you could use a sip of water."

"Pliz."

She poured a glass and brought it to me.

"Your vital signs are looking good. We'll get a med-tech in here to take a look in a little while. Can I get you anything else?"

"Maybe something to eat?" I said, my mouth once again fully functional.

"I think that can be arranged."

"And some information," I added, and just like that her cheery smile disappeared.

"About?"

"About what I'm doing here. About why someone would 'come after' me. About…"

She held up her hand to cut me off. "Sorry. I'm just a nurse here. I think you'll have to talk with someone in the PolMil section about that."

"The what?"

She seemed to catch herself just as she was about to explain further. "They'll explain, when it's time. For now, you just take it easy."

"How can I take it easy when someone just killed my mother, nearly killed my girlfriend, and might still be trying to kill me?!" I said, louder than I had intended. But I was mad. And worried.

"You're safe here. Don't worry about that," she said, and suddenly her smile was back. "I'll see what I can find to eat."

I wanted to stop her. To scream at her. To do whatever it took to get some answers. But I knew she wasn't going to be the one who gave them to me. So I leaned back into the pillows and watched her leave. As the door swung open I saw a man dressed in a mottled tan camoform – holding some sort of weapon – standing guard at my door. Was I a prisoner?

The nurse returned in a half-stunde or so with warm cereal and a mug of javo. Other than that, I saw no one and spoke with no one for the entire morning. I began to think that I was being held incommunicado when finally the door swung open and Marcus strolled in, accompanying an older man who looked somehow familiar to me.

"Vers!" the older man said with soft-spoken vigor and more friendliness than I'd expected. "How're you doing?"

"I...I'm feeling a little better, thanks," I said, not quite sure what to make of his presence.

"You're looking a whole lot better than when we got you here," Marcus said.

"It's a good thing you have the Leitstell hard head," the older man said with a smile. "It takes more than that to bring us down."

He must've noticed my confused look, for he continued immediately.

"I know, I know. This is all alien to you. I'm sorry about that. But it was necessary – to protect you. Now that they've shown themselves, you need to know what's going on."

I didn't say a word. Just waited for him to continue. But he gave a look to Marcus, who went on with the explanation.

"Vers, first of all, we want to tell you again how sorry we are about what happened to your mother and her husband."

"The only thing I can say at this point – and I know it's not much – is that they did not die in vain," the older man interrupted. "They *will* be avenged."

I could not hold my tongue a moment longer. "Who *are* you?" I asked.

"Well, Vers," Marcus began, but the old man stopped him.

"My name is Andres," he said softly. "Andres Leitstell."

I thought I had misheard and just stared at him, waiting for a correction.

"He's your grandfather, Vers," Marcus said.

My grandfather? My mother's father had died when I was little, and my Dad's grandfather solar cycles earlier. Or so I had been told.

"What grandfather?" I asked, my head swimming with the implications.

"Your father was my son," Andres said. When he saw my reaction, he quickly added, "It wasn't your parents' fault that you didn't know about me. They thought I'd died solar cycles earlier."

"This is nuts! Why would anyone make their own son think that they were dead?"

"To protect him," Malcolm explained.

My head began to ache again and my temper flared. "I'm starting to get pretty sick of that answer!"

"I know, I know," Andres soothed as he gently pushed me back to my pillow. "It's a long story."

"I'm not going anywhere soon."

Andres and Marcus exchanged a look, and then the older man nodded. "All right. I suppose this is as good a time as any." Marcus pulled over two chairs, and they sat.

For the next stunde or so my grandfather, supported from time to time by Marcus, told me a story that I could barely believe, let alone embrace. He started by reviewing the history of our people's exodus from the original Terra, called Earth, to a succession of similar Class M planets that could support our life-forms without the necessity of external equipment. I knew much of what he told me, of course, from the history classes all Terrans received from the time of our first classroom lessons. I knew, for example, that lax stewardship of Earth's air and water resources, compounded by the radiation and biological elements released during the 40 star-cycle War of Beliefs, poisoned the planet to such a degree that a number of starships were sent out as 'arks', containing flora and fauna, including thousands of Terrans, to all parts of neighboring space.

By the time the inhabitants of these 'survival pods' reached their ultimate destinations, and were reanimated from the space-sleep that allowed them to survive the many cycles that were required to reach even the nearest systems, Earth was already a barren rock spinning slowly in the vastness of space, every vestige of intelligent life wiped from its surface.

I knew that the War was brought on by conflicting *beliefs*, as speculation about the Great Creator was called then. I knew that different groups on Earth held differing beliefs, and that those differences led to a long series of smaller battles that lasted many solar cycles before the War of Beliefs ended it all. What I had never heard, however, was my grandfather's version of what happened next.

The Class M planet nearest to Earth was Terra1, or so the small band of refugees from Earth named it when they settled there. The leader of that small group, Irod Antavar, the First High Priest, outlawed any beliefs other than those of the Kingdom of the Light, as the sect that launched the ark called itself. Irod knew, as all Terrans now know, that differences in belief lead inevitably to conflict. Irod and his followers vowed that this would never happen again under the KoL.

For over one hundred cycles the people of Terra1 lived in something approaching functional harmony. It was not always an easy life. They had limited machinery, limited manpower, limited sources of energy. They had to work together, to work as one, to survive and eventually prosper. For despite their limitations, they did have fertile land, clean air, and unspoiled water. They created self-replicating machines to rapidly increase the mechanization of their society. They modified their impulse engines to provide clean abundant power. And, most controversially, they used lab-birthing, first on a limited scale and eventually as a standard procedure, to grow their population geometrically from the first few tens of settlers to many millions in just a handful of generations.

It was a true rebirth, Irod had said, blessed by the Great Creator. But it did not end there, not with Irod or with Terra1.

When Irod finally died, as even High Priests inevitably do, he was succeeded by his eldest son, Iron. And he by *his* eldest son, Aron. And when Aron died in 327.4 AW (After the War), the greatest High Priest of all, Arod, came to power. He was to change the history of our people.

Just a few cycles before Aron died, Terra1 made first contact with another of the ark planets, as the societies created by survivors of the Earth disaster were then known. Terrans from both colonies were ecstatic, since until that time neither knew that any of the other expeditions had survived. Curiosity of each people with the other soared. An exchange of visits took place, despite the lengthy voyages required and the extreme cost involved. SightScreen programs, DigiScreen epics, advertising boards, even personal body art that celebrated the long-lost neighbors exploded (though the last was frowned upon by the Council.) But after the initial euphoria, the hard reality of philosophical differences set-in all too quickly.

The Council of Light, led by the ultra-orthodox High Priest Arod, sent an interstellar expedition to bring his version of The Light to the *heretics* of Terra2 (as the Council had designated the newly-found planet.) The expedition never returned. Terra2 responded to inquiries curtly, if at all.

Arod was outraged, not only because the expedition had been lost, but because Terra2 had not immediately and gratefully acknowledged the error in their *beliefs*. Some on the Council advised patience; others suggested a second expedition. The planet was in an uproar. Then, in what is still celebrated as The Revelation, Arod revealed that the Great Creator had spoken to him in a vision and had told him to bring the Light to Terra2, personally. But he did not mean to go alone.

"For five cycles the people of Terra1 prepared for the *Crusade of Truth,* as Arod termed it. What he meant, was *war,*" Andres explained to me, the pain on his face a clear sign of how he viewed the decision. "For five solar cycles Arod diverted his people from the hardships of their lives, from the tyranny of his rule, by using every media at his disposal to paint the colonists of Terra2, their brothers and sisters, as violent heretics who threatened their very way of life. And when he had assembled a massive fleet of battle cruisers and an army of nearly 100,000, he attacked."

I could barely believe what I was hearing. For my whole life I had been told a completely different version of the story. About how Arod had protected the Light from outsiders that would have destroyed it. About how he had tried the path of peace but had been forced to fight back against far more powerful hegemonic forces. Could it all have been a lie?

"It was slaughter, pure and simple," my grandfather continued. "Terra2 was an agricultural society. They had not tried to recreate Earth, but instead had opted for a simpler world, a more peaceful world. In the blink of an eye that was all destroyed." His voice caught in his throat.

"After Terra2, Arod knew no limits. The Council was his to command. Naysayers were branded heretics and *removed*. The people of Terra1 rejoiced in the victory of their forces, but more than anything in the victory of their *beliefs*. For the slaughter of Terra2 was interpreted by the Council and their toadies as the work of the Great Creator. 'This is His victory!' Arod told his people at the famous Tarkan Square sermon. 'The first of many!'

"The people cheered. They vowed to honor the Great Creator by bringing his Word to all the universe, beginning, of course, with the other three Terran colonies that had been located by that time. And the spirit of our planets changed," Andres whispered sorrowfully.

"We forgot our history," Marcus said. "We forgot the War of Beliefs."

"Not all of us!" my grandfather corrected with no little agitation. "There were some – many actually – who saw Arod as the madman he was."

I gasped in spite of myself. *No one* I knew had ever spoken like that about the Great Arod, the Prophet of the Light. There was no one who was so honored, so revered on Terra5. On all seven Terran colonies, or so we'd been told. Now, I didn't know what to believe.

"They were many, and yet a small minority in a society gone mad," Andres continued. "They vowed to struggle against Arod's insanity, but to do so without violence, without hatred. Their leader was a man nearly as revered as Arod himself – his brother, Volis."

What brother? I hadn't heard of any brother.

"He was your seven-times removed great-grandfather," Marcus said softly as Andres watched me closely.

At that they paused, waiting for my reaction.

I think my heart stopped.

"What did you say?" I finally asked when it became clear he didn't intend to say anything further until I responded.

"Ever since that time, for seven generations now, we have kept that hope alive, by ensuring that at least one descendant of Anton's line survived throughout the long darkness of The Seven. Our hope, our plan, was that one din, when we had organized our forces on all seven colonies, we would free our people from the oppression of The Light and return the peoples of the Terran system to the self-determination that is their right. Vers, we believe that that time has come."

I stared in disbelief. "You mean you intend to revolt against the Council? You'll be slaughtered!"

"Not if we are led by The One, a direct male descendant of Volis Antavar," Andres said with the passion of a true believer.

"I'm not a descendant of Antavar – my father was Davis Leitstell, a miner!" I half-screamed. I sounded shaken even to myself.

Andres took a deep breath before putting his hand on my shoulder. "Vers, Davis wasn't your father – he was your stepfather. Your father died before you were born."

What?! It was hard enough to believe that I was a descendant of Anton Antavar, but now this? I began to think maybe this Andre person was a little crazy.

The old man saw my reaction and plunged on without waiting for me to respond. "I know, I know – and I'm sorry that we never told you. Your mother was waiting for your 16th birth din before she explained. But it's true. Morgan and your father met when she volunteered to help our cause back on T3. Morgan was just a few cycles pregnant with you when the Council found Atlan and killed him – with a bomb." Andre cleared his throat of emotion but his determined stare never wavered. "He died without knowing that he had a son. By the time Morgan found out herself, the High Priest and his goons had already moved on, not knowing that she carried Atlan's child."

"But how...? I began. He raised a hand. When he spoke again his voice was softer, apologetic.

"Your parents never actually married, Vers. So there was no public link between them. No way for the Council to know of your existence. They loved each other very much, but it wasn't the time or place for official commitments... Anyway, what matters is that we smuggled her to Sensay – the second largest city on T3 – and there she remained, until we introduced her to Davis – her *bodyguard*, if you will. You were born eight cycles later – we 'manufactured' some papers to suggest Davis was your father. Once we were confident the Council was no longer interested in your mother, we arranged for them to come here to Phoebos."

"Why should I believe you? I don't even know you!" I said, probably a bit too harshly. But I didn't care. I wasn't buying any of his story by then. It was too weird!

"I don't blame you," he said softly. "I don't know if I would've believed it myself. But it's true. We have the DNA analysis to prove it. You *are* Volis' successor and you will become The One – if you choose to do so."

My head was swimming.

"How can one person make a difference against the Armies of the Light?   They control *everything*." I knew I sounded disheartened. I didn't care. What they were saying was insanity!

"Throughout our history, one person – determined, dedicated, and true to themselves and their cause – has often made a difference," Andres said. "From the Christ, to Ghandi, to Bera Wingeft, all of them changed their world for the better – without resorting to the kinds of totalitarian repression that the Council of Light has made their trademark."

"All three of those men ended up dead," I said before I even had time to think what I was saying.

My grandfather nodded sadly. "And many more who followed them. But change came, and their children and grandchildren all benefited from their sacrifice."

Sacrifice? Is that what he was asking of me? That I sacrifice myself for the dream of a better life for future generations? I didn't like the sound of that.

"But I'm just a kid!" I argued. "No one will take me seriously."

"Once they know that you have accepted your birthright, they will follow you," he said with complete confidence. "Even now thousands of your followers await only your blessing to act."

My mind was racing. "Did you ask my father to lead your movement? Did he turn you down?"

Part of me was hoping it was true, while the other half feared to learn that my father had been a traitor to their cause.

"We did not," he answered without flinching. "We decided that the Council had been too successful infiltrating our forces and was coming too close to uncovering our leadership organization. I was still fit, so we decided to try to throw them off the scent by skipping a generation, if you will. I saw my son born, and then, as best I could, I watched from a distance. We thought we'd hidden him from their prying eyes. We were wrong." He sounded old, tired, and his eyes moistened. I could feel the pain he still carried from his decision.

"But now you are approaching your 16th birth din," Marcus intervened, putting one hand softly on the old man's shoulder. "Already you are demonstrating some of the powers that male descendants of Volis Leitstell have always possessed. I suppose it was only a matter of time before the Seven learned of your location."

"And that's the reason for the explosion," I said, the words catching in my throat.

Andres nodded. "They know that we have little chance without The One. They wanted to end it all – now."

"But *you* are still alive," I answered. "Aren't you this *One*?"

"I am just *a* descendent of Volis; you are *the* successor, the only one who has inherited all his gifts and powers," he answered with a hint of sadness. "My time is nearly up. With the powers that our ancestor has passed onto us come certain…limitations as well. I am nearly at the end of my allotted solar cycles. Soon, only The One To Be will be able to lead our people to their promised future."

"Me?" I still couldn't believe it. It was like some kind of weird dream, or nightmare.

"You," the old man said firmly. "You are the hope and the promise. Yours is the power and the right. If we are to succeed, The One must lead us. It is your choice," he added, and I could see a look of consternation – or was it fear – pass from Marcus to Andres. "You must decide. No one can force you to take this responsibility."

My head was swimming. I couldn't have answered them then even if I knew what I would decide. I needed time! I needed some space where I could be alone and think this through!

But I also knew that my 16th birth din celebration was only a few lunar cycles away.

CHAPTER 7

Terra5

"What do you *mean*, you aren't certain whether the boy was in the transport?"

The High Priest's menacing tone left no doubt as to his frame of mind. The security operative standing before him tried to stop his body from shaking, but was none too successful.

"We are still analyzing all the DNA that's been collected. It was…distributed over a very wide area," the operative managed to croak.

Rogen stared out the huge window in his Council office. "How much longer?"

The operative glanced over at Ofran Belinger, his direct superior, his eyes begging for help. He would receive none.

"I…the tests should be completed in another 48 stundes."

"You are sure of that?" The High Priest's voice sounded composed, but something told the operative to be careful – very careful.

"Our people are working diligently," he began.

"I asked if you were sure."

The operative took a deep breath. "Yes, yes I'm sure."

A crease that might have been a smile appeared next to Rogen Antavar's mouth.

"Do you understand the penalty for failure?" he asked.

"I…yes." The man bowed his head as if accepting his fate.

"Good. Because if that boy lives still, many of 'our people' will not. Understood?"

"Yes, Your Grace." His voice was barely audible.

"Get out of my sight!"

The man nearly jumped across the room. His hand was on the door release when Rogen stopped him.

"I will expect your report – in full – within 48 stundes."

The operative just nodded. No words would come.

As soon as the door closed the High Priest slammed his hand down on his imposing black oxyl desk.

"The Light take us all!" he shouted to no one in particular.

"Perhaps the boy died after all," his Fist ventured calmingly.

"He did *not!*" the High Priest spit through clenched teeth. "I would have known, I would've sensed it if he had. He lives still."

"But you just told that security overseer…"

"I told him I wanted success! I didn't say I thought we had it. You will need to redouble your efforts."

Belinger's eyebrows arched unconsciously.

"We already have nearly every one of our security people looking for the boy. Surely he will not escape our grasp."

The High Priest turned toward his Fist very slowly. The look in his eyes sent a chill through the underling's body.

"We have been trying to eliminate the infestation of his line for centuries, and yet they survive still. Are you so sure your people will succeed where thousands have failed before?"

The Fist wanted to fervidly reassure the High Priest. But he found he could not.

"I will redouble our efforts," he said instead.

Antavar nodded. "You do that, Ofran. You do that."

The Fist understood full-well the fragility of his position. "We will find him. I give you my oath."

The crease at the corners of the High Priest's mouth broadened ever so slightly. "My patience is not unlimited you know. I would hate to see our…association come to an end."

'As would I,' Belinger thought. 'As would I.'

CHAPTER 8

Phoebos

I had lain in bed as long as I could bear. I needed to get out of that place, to walk and think.

I didn't know if I were a guest or prisoner, but my head was feeling a little bit better so I decided to find out for myself. I pushed the call button by my bedside and one of the young nurses, Reta, came in nearly at once.

"What can we get you? You hungry?" she asked as she turned off the call and glanced at my vitals readout.

"Actually, I think I'd like to go for a walk," I said.

Her conflicted look told me she wasn't expecting anything of the sort.

"I'll have to check with a medtech. You haven't been cleared…"

"I feel fine. I won't go far. Just a little ways to clear my head and get the blood pumping."

"Let me check. I'll be right back."

Even as she slipped out the door, I was already disconnecting all my tubes and wires and searching out my clothes. I wasn't going to wait for some tech to decide if I was able to take a short walk. Thankfully, my clothes had been cleaned and smoothed and I was able to get up and dressed with no problem at all. I was slightly surprised how well I felt, considering how banged-up I'd been just two dins earlier.

When I pushed open the door to the hallway, the armed guard at my door snapped to attention with his hand on his weapon.

"Sir – no one told me you were leaving," he said nervously.

"Just taking a short stroll," I said easily. "Need to get my legs back under me."

"Understood."

As I took a step past him, however, he turned as if to follow.

"That won't be necessary," I said. "I'm not going far."

"My orders are not to let you out of my sight."

Since I'd been in the room for the past 48 stundes, out of his sight, I had my doubts as to the specificity of his orders, but I decided not to argue. Better to walk with a shadow than not walk at all.

"Ok. Let's go."

It didn't take me long to realize that I was still a bit weak. My legs kept me upright, but I didn't feel the usual spring to my step. Weak or not, it felt wonderful to be up and moving. The nightmare of the transport bombing and my mother's death still weighed heavily on me. But what Andres and Marcus had told me required serious thought. I needed to clear the cobwebs from my brain and think it through from beginning to end. After about five clics wandering through what appeared to be a refurbished warehouse structure, I passed by chance through a set of double doors that led to a small circular chamber, with a water fountain at its center and star-panels overhead. It was like finding an oasis in a Terra desert.

"What is this place?" I asked my silent shadow.

He shrugged. "Never been here."

I glanced around. In addition to the fountain, there were small Terran flora in grow-pots scattered throughout the room. The subdued lighting and soft gurgle of the water made for a serene, soothing environment. I found myself suddenly content to sit by the fountain and just *be*. The place seemed inordinately peaceful, almost intoxicating. I closed my eyes and drifted.

I don't know how long I sat there; maybe five clics, maybe a stunde. But I remember having the strangest sense of calm and security in that place, as if all my cares and sorrows had suddenly been washed away.

I was startled back to the moment by someone clearing their throat close-by.

"So you found our little Shangri-la," Andres said as I opened my eyes to find him looking down at me with a grandfatherly smile. I glanced around but the guard was nowhere to be seen.

"Shangri what?" I asked.

"It's from an old Earth legend," he explained. "May I join you?"

I motioned to a spot on the fountain next to me and he sat stiffly.

"The old bones don't move as they once did," he said with a sigh.

"You don't seem so old to me."

He chuckled. "If you spent a stunde in this body you wouldn't say so. But I'm an old man. What can I expect? How are *you* feeling?"

"Much better, thanks. In fact, better than I would've thought possible."

Andres nodded. "Yes, so I would suspect. Part of the Gift. And as you get nearer your 16th birth din, you will see even greater changes."

"So you said before." I wanted more than just predictions. I wanted to know exactly what was supposed to happen to me and why. My grandfather seemed to understand.

"You deserve an explanation," he began, leaning toward me to tell his tale. "Back when Irod first led his group of exiles to Terra1, he somehow acquired a number of *qualities* that had not existed back on Earth. We don't know how he came to have those qualities – whether they were a fluke of genetics unlocked by Terra's environment, or whether his scientists developed them purposely to help ensure the line of succession. We don't even know if he was the only person to develop such qualities. All of that has been lost – or concealed – in the mists of history.

"What we do know, is that he made very effective use of his talents during the War of Beliefs. Most historians – even those not completely controlled by the Council – think that his powers made the difference in the outcome. You must remember, Irod defeated each of the other six colonies with an army less than half as large as some of his opponents', and did it all on their home planets. In theory, he should have lost, more than once. But he never did. In each case, a key leader, or a key commander, or someone of influence, made a bad decision or took a wrong step that allowed the outnumbered and thinly-provisioned invaders to beat the odds. It was an incredible series of victories."

I knew all this from my Terran History classes. Of course, we had been taught that Irod's victories had come from the Great Creator himself, as a reward to Irod and his forces for their devotion and belief. This was something else. Something...dangerous. The Council would call it heresy.

"Yes," Andres said as though he'd read my thoughts, "this is quite different than what you've been taught. Their version of the Wars conveniently bestows all blessings of the Light on them, and them alone. There is no mention of the powers that Irod possessed. Powers which this din's Council would condemn as blasphemous and enchantment, may I add.

"For all the cycles since that time, the eldest son of the eldest son has continued to rule as High Priest. But there have been other sons. From the very beginning. When Irod died, his eldest, Iron took his place on the Council. But he had a second son, Inod, who had a son, and so it went down the ages. At first the lineage of Inod was treated as an honored offshoot of the ruling family. Inod himself was a principal advisor to his brother – the first Fist. For generations his descendants were treated with great reverence and held important government posts.

"But with Arod, all that changed.

"Whether all the bloodshed he'd seen in his many solar cycles of warfare had made him doubt the loyalty of his extended family, or whether it was always a part of his character, Arod decided upon the birth of his second son that the eldest male offspring of Inod's line was not only unneeded but dangerous. The eldest son – Oron – was seized, imprisoned, and then sacrificed in an elaborate ceremony witnessed by only the very highest echelons of Council supporters. 'A gift to the Light,' is what it was called. Murder is what it was.

"The rest of Oron's family were supposed to be eliminated. The more distant relatives dispersed and forgotten. But they were not. A sympathizer tipped them to the High Priest's plans before they could be carried out, and Oron's wife and three children fled just before the Forces of Light could capture them. In all the long cycles since that time, the Inodian Line – *our* line – has persevered. It has not been easy. We have had to hide our identity and rely on the help of our supporters to stay one step ahead of the Council's spies.

"But we have not been idle. Terran by Terran, town by town, cycle by cycle, we have built a secret Opposition to the horror that Arod's descendants have created. At first we were but a handful. Then dozens, hundreds, and more. This din the followers of the Inodian Line number in the tens of thousands, on all seven Terran colonies and their moons. We have kept hidden in order to gather our strength, kept in the shadows until the great prophesy is fulfilled. Our time has finally come! We, the descendants of Inod, have built an army that will end the despotic rule of Arod's line forever! All that we need is a leader: The One.

"You."

The transformation that had come over Andres frightened me. His eyes shone with the same Messianic gleam that I'd seen in the eyes of Rogen Antavar when he'd given his cyclical SightScreen address to the colonies, exhorting all of us Terrans to follow The Light. His words carried the same unshakeable certainty as the High Priest's. He wasn't asking me to lead his forces, *our* forces, so much as demanding it. For him, I was The One whether I liked it or not. And at that moment, I wasn't at all sure that I did. Or that I even could.

"This is…a lot to take in," I said. I think my voice quavered a bit. I know my pulse did.

My grandfather's eyes widened and he took a deep breath. I think he realized he'd been pushing too hard.

"Of course, of course," he said, his voice calmer and more controlled. "I'm sorry if I've brought this upon you too quickly. But with the attempt on your life it's clear that Antavar's forces are closing in on you and time is short. I'm afraid that your only choice now is between a life on the run or the life for which you have been destined. You must run, or you must fight. Either way, if the Council finds you, you *will* die."

I could see that he believed what he said utterly. But should I? How did I know that the Council had been behind my mother's death? How did I know they were even looking for me?

"It's up to you," Andres went on after a short pause. "I can't make that decision. No one else can. Whatever you decide, your life is about to change forever. I am sorry for that. There was nothing I could do. We tried to keep you hidden, but the Council and its Forces of Light are strong. We still don't know whether the explosion that killed your stepfather was the accident it appeared, or something else. Perhaps they hadn't found him tucked away on this mining moon until then. Perhaps they know more about the prophesy than we do. Whatever the reason, it's clear they fear you. Even now, they are out there – their spies, their machines, their sympathizers – scouring this little chunk of rock looking for you. It's only a matter of time before they hear or see something, or find someone who thinks as they do, or can be bought, or frightened into giving you up. We must act, and soon."

At that moment I wanted to tell him to just go away, to leave me alone! Prophesies, bombings, *war*? I wanted to stand up and tell him I was going home. I wanted it all to be a bad dream.

But I knew it wasn't.

"Let me think on it," I said, hoping that time might bring me alternatives, if not clarity.

"Yes, you do that. But don't think too long. We must move from this place, with you, or without you. I hope you will see fit to join us. To lead us."

"I will give you your answer by nightfall," I said.

"Good. I pray the Great Creator gives you His guidance."

"Yeh. Me too."

As Andres stood, I thought he was about to leave when he reached into his cloak and pulled out a small hand screen. "This may help you decide as well." He handed it to me.

"What is it?"

"You will see."

He patted me on the shoulder and left me sitting by the fountain, my mind completely confounded.

*****

I activated the small hand screen and found myself staring at a series of digi-stills and vids. For the most part they were youthful stills of my Mom and a man I didn't know, but who I recognized at once as Andre's son. My father? I didn't want to believe, but I couldn't look away until I'd seen every one.

After that, I sat and stared up through the dome into the blackness of the night sky for quite some time. All I could think of was my parents – all of them. My Dad had been dead for so long, you'd think I would've gotten over it, but I hadn't. Still haven't. And my mother's savage death burned within me unlike any pain I'd ever felt before. Then there was a father I'd never know. If the Council was to blame…

Eventually my mind worked its way back to the present and the dilemma I faced. I needed to make a decision, but I wasn't at all sure I had enough information to do it. I didn't know my grandfather at all. I didn't even know for sure if Andres *was* my grandfather, although every instinct told me he was. With everything so ill-defined, should I accept his explanation at face value and go running off with him to who-knew-where for who-knew-how-long?

Of course, there was Marcus to consider as well. As I thought back about the past solar cycle at Vaden Upper Level, I remembered quite clearly all the times that he had appeared, seemingly out of nowhere, to help me out. I didn't doubt for a moment that Nobus would've tried to pound me into pudding if it weren't for his intervention. So was this the reason he'd always been close by? Was he my *guardian angel*, sent by Andres and his people to keep me safe?

At that moment I felt more alone than I'd ever felt in my life. I thought again of my mother, and how she'd always been there for me whenever I needed someone to talk to. If only I could see her just one more time! But it was not to be. I would never see her smile again. Never hear her reassuring words.

To keep my sanity I allowed my thoughts to wander to Amanda and Jafar: what were they doing just then? I needed to talk to someone, someone I could trust. Even though there were a great many other people in that building, it was painfully obvious to me that I was the one who had to make the decision. The only one who *could* make that decision. I don't mind admitting that tears welled up in my eyes. I guess I cried a little.

But then, something very strange happened. A light suddenly illuminated the fountain and I heard a voice, the most soothing, reassuring voice I've ever heard, telling me to stay strong, that I was indeed The One, the true Defender of the Light. My path would be a difficult one, it said, but if I remained true, not just me but all Terrans would benefit.

"Who are you?" I asked aloud, looking skyward to where the light seemed to come from.

"You know me," the voice answered. "And you know what you must do."

And in that moment, I did.

CHAPTER 9

I made my way back to the room where I'd been convalescing to await Andres. Although my determination never wavered, I couldn't stop wondering if the entity I'd encountered was some illusion created by Andres to influence my decision. Or perhaps some kind of hallucination brought on by all that had occurred. Or, perhaps something else?

I felt exhausted when I got to the room, and I must've fallen asleep. When I awoke, Andres was sitting next to my bed, waiting patiently.

"It's good you got some sleep," he said as soon as I opened my eyes. "Even with your natural gifts, you are neither immortal nor immune to illness or injury."

I had planned to tell him about my decision, about the light and the voice from above. But now that he had spoken of my gifts, I couldn't resist learning more.

"You keep talking about all these qualities that I supposedly have as a descendant of Inod. But I don't see anything all that special about me. I think I'm pretty normal."

"That is as it should be. The gifts do not begin to show themselves until the 16th cycle. I don't know why that is," he added, holding up one hand to stop the question that I was about to ask, "but I suspect it has something to do with keeping the heir to Inod's line safe and concealed until he is old enough to make important decisions on his own."

"So I'll get these powers on my next birth din?"

He smiled. "You've already been given some of them." When he saw my puzzled expression, he continued. "Think back.

Hasn't there been a time, or maybe more than one, when you did something, or knew something, that you didn't know how you could've possibly done it, or known it? Maybe it was something relatively small. But I'm sure it was there."

It didn't take long for me to think of Nobus, and then my dazzlingly unexpected dance moves. Were *those* my gifts? If so, I wasn't as thrilled as I'd hoped.

"One time I managed to push a big guy who wanted to beat on me halfway across the Upper Level lot," I said. "And then there was the time I was dancing with my girlfriend and I should've dropped her, but she didn't drop." I felt foolish even mentioning the second.

My grandfather cocked his head. "That was the beginning. In both cases, they were unconscious reactions to strong emotions – fear being most prominent. You didn't *will* those reactions, at least not consciously. The protective mechanism that is given to all of us in Inod's line asserted itself in response to your need. Beginning with your sixteenth birth din, both the number and intensity of your gifts will grow quickly. And you will learn to summon their power when you want it."

"Cool," I said, and immediately wished I hadn't. I sounded juvenile even to myself. When someone tells you that you're about to inherit capabilities beyond those of anyone you've ever known, 'cool' hardly seems enough.

But Andres seemed pleased.

"Yes, it is…cool. Your rapid recovery from your head injury is another gift that is revealing itself. There will be many more."

"Is hearing voices and seeing things that aren't really there part of this gift as well?" I asked timidly, afraid that he'd simply tell me that I was absolutely nuts.

The stunned look I received in reply increased my anxiety.

"What is this? You've heard voices? And what did you see?"

I felt foolish, but there was no going back. "It was when I was in that fountain room. I was trying to decide what to do, about my destiny and all that, when I saw – or felt, I don't know – a light that seemed to come from outside the dome, and a soothing voice spoke to me."

"The Argia," he whispered reverently. "Tell me – everything."

The urgency in his words spurred my own, and in a flood of confession I told him everything that had happened. He sat listening intently, saying nothing to interrupt me. When I'd finished he remained silent at first, seemingly weighing all he'd heard and all he would say. Finally he nodded and sighed deeply.

"So, you said you were trying to decide about your destiny. Did you? Decide?"

"I did. But that light…"

"What did you decide?"

I remember feeling a tingling, or perhaps it was just a tremble, as I found myself answering: "I will go with you."

"You will accept your role?"

"Look, I'm only fifteen. I'm not the commander of some revolution…"

"You are The One."

"I don't know anything about leading an army!"

"You will learn. I will teach you."

"I'm not a great student."

"You will learn."

I looked deep into his eyes, hoping to see what, I don't really know. My heart was pounding when I spoke.

"What if I can't do it?!" I cried out, the words as much an accusation as a question.

There, I'd said it. My greatest fear. I was willing to risk my own life, but thousands of others? How could I take that responsibility unless I was sure?

Andres smiled and put a hand to my shoulder. "It is a lot to ask, but you *can* do it. The time has come, and you are The One. Have faith."

I must have been crazy, or maybe the words I heard in the fountain room finally made their way to my heart. In any case, I found myself nodding.

"Okay, I'll try," I said, expecting some kind of excitement, or gratitude in reply. Something. But for seven long heartbeats the old man said nothing. The quiet in the room finally overwhelmed me. "What now?"

"Now," he said, "we prepare for a long journey."

*****

I knew we'd have to leave that place, wherever it was. If the Council knew I had escaped the bombing, they wouldn't rest until they found me. But I had no idea how far we would travel.

The next stundes passed in a whirlwind of preparation, though nearly all the activity took place around me. I was left pretty much to myself, told only by Andres: "Get yourself ready. We leave soon. Don't take anything you don't need."

It didn't require much thought on my part, since all I had were the clothes on my back, ill-fitting Worker Caste gear that had been given to me to replace the bloody, torn shreds I wore when they brought me to that place. I spent the vast majority of the time thinking about the Light, and Andres, and above all the revolt that I suddenly found myself about to lead, if only in name at that point. And thinking back – to my parents, my friends, my life before the explosion. It seemed to me then that my entire existence had been destroyed in that bombing, to be replaced by a future as ill-defined as the distant mountains to the west during one of our frequent sandstorms.

I guess I was pretty depressed, although if you'd asked me then I'd probably have said I was just sad. I didn't realize that the listless, teary-eyed private moments that were to recur over the next dins and septs were a sign of serious emotional problems. I suppose I had no time for problems beyond those we were to encounter during our flight. Even if I had realized, what could I – or anyone else – have done about it?

As soon as the night sky darkened to the inky black that only a moon without atmosphere could provide, our band of four travelers slipped out of the unremarkable building that had served as my hospital those past two dins and into an equally unremarkable transport. My grandfather led the way, followed by me, my young nurse (in case I suddenly collapsed, I supposed), with Marcus securing our backs. The same driver who had brought me to that place sat behind the controls, with another of Andres' supporters – carrying an ion beam weapon that looked capable of bringing down a building, if need be – stationed in the rear seat. Neither man said a word.

"Let's go," Andres said, and just like that my old life, my old world, disappeared behind me.

For the first few clics we traveled in silence. I don't know about the others, but I was half-expecting to see a Council security transport move to intercept us, or perhaps obliterate us on the spot. But as the distance between us and the main Mining colony rapidly increased, the tension in the vehicle palpably diminished.

"How are you feeling?" the nurse, Reta, finally asked, breaking the long stretch of mute anticipation.

I had to stop for a moment to think. I was so absorbed in my thoughts that my personal feelings were as far removed from me as my former life.

"Okay," I said, not wanting to say much about the unwanted tears. "Pretty good, actually. Now."

Marcus chuckled, and I remember that sound seeming like the sweetest music I'd ever heard. "It's been a tough few dins for you, hasn't it? But it'll get better soon. You'll see."

I didn't know whether I believed him, or just wanted to, but either way it took a huge weight off my shoulders. I can't say I relaxed, but I got a lot closer to relaxing than I had for dins.

For a while we exchanged small talk, saying nothing of tremendous importance. Looking back, I suppose they had been directed to studiously avoid any discussion that might upset me. I, on the other hand, was just happy to be engaging in real, simple, human conversation that didn't include talk of death, or destruction, or revolution. The bleak lunar scenery swept past in a blur, and after a short time we sat silently, each lost in his (or her) own thoughts.

It didn't take me long to realize that we were headed for the Quinby Mountains north and east of the Mining base. I wasn't surprised, since any clandestine operation would need cover, and on Phoebos, at least, the mountains were just about the only place where Council satellites, security drones and spies might not be able to find a sizeable rebel base. But even I was surprised to find how large the opposition force actually was.

After traveling for nearly one-half din, we found ourselves deep in rugged mountain terrain, moving ever higher and deeper into the towering range. The transport switched to hover mode not more than a clic into our ascent, as the transport passage all but disappeared beneath us. I was a little surprised, since I knew that hover was both louder and left a more discernible heat signature than surface mode, but I decided that speed was more important than invisibility at that point. I only hoped that some Council computer somewhere wouldn't recognize the anomaly in a routine sweep analysis.

Some time later, as Terra5 began to dip below our moon's horizon, we came to a sudden stop in a deep ravine carved into the solid black rock of the mountains surrounding us.

I must've been more nervous than I thought, for as we braked to a stop I asked, "What's the matter? Is there a problem?"

Marcus smiled and patted my knee. "No problem, Vers. But here the limo ride ends. From here on out, we walk."

I was about to protest that I hadn't brought a pressure suit that would allow me to survive even an instant in the near-vacuum outside the transport, but before I could say a word the unnamed escort behind us was pulling out four suits from the rear storage bay.

"You've used one of these before?" Andres asked me.

"Of course. You don't think we stayed in the bubbles all the time, do you?"

"Don't know. Some colonists never leave the domes."

"Well my friends and I got out whenever we could."

"Good. Our climb is not an easy one, and it will be much easier if you know how to adjust the suit and the breathing mixture. These are older, manual models. You'll have to adjust the oxygen mix yourself – more on steep inclines, less on the flat. Understand?"

I nodded, although to be honest, my friends and I had never explored anywhere even remotely as rugged as what I saw through the transport windows. I just hoped I wouldn't embarrass myself and slow them down.

When we'd all finished a final round-robin check of each other's suits (a critical safety measure that even my friends and I always followed), Andres thanked our driver and guard and bid them a safe journey back to the Mining Center.

"Same to you," the driver said, and then turning to me, added, "And may the Light lead you and empower you." He bowed his head and made a strange movement with his right hand.

"Thank you," I said, not knowing what else to say.

I felt that the driver expected something more from me, but Andres ended the brief awkward moment by tapping me on the shoulder. "Let's go. We have a long hike ahead of us."

As the four of us stepped out into the colorless depths of the ravine, I saw the faintest hint of star-rise in the distance. I wasn't the only one to notice.

"Come on. It grows light. We must get further into the mountains where their *eyes* can't see us," Marcus said.

"Are you feeling up to this?" Reta asked in passing.

I didn't know if she were just being polite or if she really wanted to know my condition, but since I doubted we had any alternative to the climb, I answered, "Absolutely," even though my legs still didn't have the spring I would've liked. She didn't investigate further.

And so we set out, Marcus leading the way along a narrow, worn path, followed by me, then Reta, and Andres at the rear. It didn't take me long to see why we had abandoned the transport. The terrain was so rugged that we could only move single-file, and slowly at that. The path wormed its way between sheer rock walls, towering boulders and sudden drop-offs, nearly always moving upwards. I could hear my breathing amplified in the helmet unit of my pressure suit, a loud rasp that sounded more like a Terran hawk's cry than a human being. I began to wish I had kept up with my exercises once athletics season had ended, but it was too late by then.

Every once in a while one of the others would check with me to be sure I wasn't having a heart attack or something, and every time I'd tell them I was fine even though sweat was dripping down my back in rivulets and I felt my heart pounding as if it were going to burst from my chest. I was amazed that the old man, and even Reta, could navigate the steep, treacherous slope with seeming ease while I labored. But then, I guessed that they had been doing this rebel thing a lot longer than I had.

We rarely stopped to rest, and when we did it was only for a brief moment. The Prime Star made its way to a point nearly directly above us, and still we climbed. I was getting light-headed and found myself stumbling over small bumps in the stone beneath our feet, but I refused to be the first to ask for a stop. If they could continue, so could I.

Thankfully, whether because he saw me struggling or because he was getting tired himself I don't know, Andres called for a short break. I sipped some lukewarm water from the mouth-spout of the suit's recycler, and took a few bites of some energy pellets dispensed through the same tube. It wasn't much, but at that moment it was heavenly.

"You ready to go?" Andres asked after a brief time.

"How much further?" I asked, trying not to sound anxious.

"Depends how fast we go," Marcus cut in. "And how many breaks we take."

I got the message. "Well I'm feeling a lot better. All ready when you are!"

As we got to our feet and started back up the mountainside, I heard Reta's voice in my headset. "If you need to stop, just say so," she said. I couldn't tell if she were talking to me on a direct link or whether our two companions also heard her advice, but no one said a word in opposition. I silently thanked her.

The Prime Star continued its arc through the blackness above, and soon enough had descended to no more than 15 degrees above the horizon. Unless I was very much mistaken, in a short while we would be walking in pitch darkness. Given the infinite possibilities for disaster on that route, the prospect did not appeal to me. But I was the newcomer, the junior partner in our little unit, so I held my tongue.

We pushed on as the shadows lengthened, turning our narrow path into little more than a vague slash in the deepening gloom. I was tripping and stumbling every few steps, and our pace had slowed to barely a crawl. Then, suddenly, it seemed as though the trail just disappeared, coming to an abrupt end at the base of a cliff that vanished into impenetrable blackness above! I was about to tell anyone who was listening that I was getting worried, when a small red light blinked once, then twice from a ledge just 100 meters above us.

"Did you see that?" I asked nervously, not entirely sure that I'd actually seen it myself.

"Welcome to Base Camp Bravo," Andres announced. "Let's see if we can get up there without breaking our necks." It wasn't until I saw his slight figure begin to disappear into the darkness that I realized we were meant to scale the cliff that separated us from the camp. I took a deep breath.

Tired but mentally energized by finally having our goal within reach, we did our best to maintain a solid pace while keeping our concentration focused on the near-vertical stairway that had been carved into the cold black rock. About halfway up the sheer cliff-face we were met by two representatives from the rebel camp on a landing just barely large enough for the six of us. In the dim light I couldn't make out any features through their faceplates, but from their actions and gestures I could tell that they were discussing something with my grandfather. I had a funny feeling they were talking about me.

"Is there a problem?" I cut into their com-link after the discussion dragged on a little longer than I thought justified. Besides, I don't like heights all that much and we were probably 30 meters above the boulder-strewn ground.

"No, no problem at all," Andres answered without hesitating. "They just wanted to confirm that the rumors of your arrival were true."

"Okay. So what was all the discussion about?"

"They wanted to find out if I would approve a rather large welcoming ceremony. I told them we appreciated the offer but were a little bit tired right about now. I suggested tomorrow morning, early, before we take off."

"Were they ok with that?"

"A little disappointed, but they'll get over it." He looked up as the two envoys from the camp scrambled up the stone stairway. "I think they're hurrying to shut the ceremony down before you get there."

"What? No synthahol or virtual beef? I'm heartbroken," Marcus said good-naturedly.

"Watch your step to be sure that's all that gets broken," Andres said with an edge I hadn't heard before. Marcus must have heard the same inflection, since he didn't pursue that line of humor any further. Instead, with a tiny shrug in my direction he led the way up into the darkness.

We climbed for what seemed like a full stunde. The last 50 meters or so seemed to stretch on forever, as my calf muscles began to cramp and my fingertips grew sore from grabbing so tightly to the stone wall. But finally, just as I was beginning to wonder if the whole affair was just one long bad dream, a hand reached down and half-guided, half-pulled me up the last step or two. I stumbled on the last step, and fell to my knees at the very top of the stairway.

"Plenty of time to give thanks later," a pleasant high-pitched voice teased as I knelt there trying to catch my breath, my gasps roaring in my headset. "Here. Up you go!"

This time the tug was a good deal more forceful and I lurched to my feet as if shot from a proton cannon.

"Not much to you, is there?" the same voice said, and as I looked up to give thanks for the help, I choked to realize that my helping hand had come from an absolutely bangin' blonde, my own age or maybe even a bit younger. Her smile shone even in the darkness.

"You're a girl!" I couldn't help remarking, wishing I hadn't almost immediately.

"Wow, I can see now why everyone's so excited about your arrival. Very perceptive."

I fumbled for a clever comeback but instead received a brief tongue lashing from my grandfather.

"Hey – do you think you could clear the way up there? Two of us are still hanging onto this cliff face," his aggravated voice came up to us from down below.

"Sorry!" was all I could manage as I stepped aside to let first Reta, and then Andres, wearily climb up onto the ledge at the top of the stairway.

"Andres!" the girl who had helped me called out when she saw him appear at last. "We were getting worried."

"About me? You should know better than that, Vera."

Vera. So that was her name. Now my only question was what was she doing up there. But apparently my questions would have to wait.

"Come," the old man said as he took my arm and led me toward the entrance to a medium-sized cave. "It will soon be light and we don't want to be outside where their eyes can see us."

Marcus was already talking to a young man in the shadows of the cave entrance, while Reta and Vera followed close behind us.

"We had begun to wonder," the young man said after clasping Andres' arm and pulling him close for a welcoming bear hug.

"Better than worry," Andres said pointedly, sneaking a glance back at Vera.

"But here you are, and I take it this is…"

My grandfather stepped aside to introduce me. "Vers. Vers Leitstell," I cut in, putting my hand up for a touch.

To my surprise, and embarrassment, the young man knelt at my feet. "We are yours to command," he said eagerly.

I didn't know what to do, and when I looked to my grandfather for guidance I saw him watching me closely. Was this some kind of test? Whatever it was, I wasn't comfortable with some guy ten solar cycles older than me acting as if I were the Great Creator.

"Get up, get up," I told him, grabbing him by the elbow to help get him to his feet. "Whatever we do, we will do together."

Out of the corner of my eye I saw Andres smile.

"People are waiting for us," he said. "Let's not keep them waiting any longer."

With that, he led the way into the shadowed entrance, the four of us following close behind. Just a short distance inside, however, we came to what appeared to be the back wall of the shallow cave. *What the heck?'* I remember thinking. He bent down as if to examine something on the rock, then said "May the Light shine forever" aloud. To my amazement, a massive reinforced door swung open as if from the rock itself. As I got closer I could see that it was actually an ingenious use of camouflage, melding the entranceway into the cave walls so perfectly that even from a single step away an unknowing eye would've been hard-pressed to detect it. I did see a tiny impression in the rock just to the left of the doorway, and decided that it was probably a retina-scanner. Impressive. It was clear to me that this wasn't the rag-tag band of rebels I had been picturing in my mind.

We stepped into a narrow tunnel carved into solid rock. It was tall enough for even the tallest of Terrans, but wide enough for two at most. I assumed it was designed as a choke point, to limit the number of unwelcomed guests who could rush into the base camp at any one time. Made me wonder if there was an exit that would allow our people a fast departure should it become necessary. It briefly crossed my mind that there I was considering strategy after less than five clics at camp, but I didn't have time to dwell on it.

About twenty paces from the entrance, we turned at a sharp angle to the right and found ourselves in a huge cavern, perhaps thirty meters tall and twice that from side to side and front to back. Artificial light was augmented by natural star shine brought down through optical light tubes. Dozens of rolled sleeping mats dotted the sides of the room, and a line of rebels holding mess kits snaked toward a sizeable food preparation area off to one side. A loud buzz of activity from the eighty or more men and women in the chamber suddenly died away to a whisper. All eyes turned toward us – toward me.

Andres stopped and began to pull off his pressure suit. A young woman ran to help him. I began to remove mine as well, when a tap on my shoulder stopped me.

"Let me," Vera said, appearing out of nowhere to take my helmet.

"Thanks, but I think I can handle this myself," I answered, painfully aware of all the eyes watching us.

"Let her do it," Andres said softly as Vera stowed the helmet in a locker with many others. "It is an honor she cannot be denied."

I didn't understand, but I wasn't about to argue. Besides, it didn't seem like she had been asking my permission.

"You must be tired," Vera said as she came back to help me get out of the awkward suit. "We will welcome you more appropriately tomorrow before you go."

"I am a little beat," I said, understating my exhaustion by ten-fold.

"Let's get you introduced, at least, and get some food into that skin and bones."

If the light hadn't been so dim in there, I'm sure the entire band would've seen my cheeks blush a bright red. What was it about the young rebel that made her seem so much older than me? I felt like a little kid whenever we spoke. But my grumbling stomach spoke louder than my ego, so I allowed her to lead me to where Andres, Marcus, and the young man who'd greeted us at the entrance stood talking to a man nearly as old as my grandfather.

"Vers," Andres said as soon as I came up to us, "here are a couple of people I want you to meet." He indicated the older man first. "This is Winder Ebram, the Commander of the Light Rebellion here on Phoebos, and his son, Tiber."

The Commander put out his hand but looked into my eyes as if he were trying to see through me. Tiber bowed his head in acknowledgment.

"Vers. We've been awaiting your arrival for a long, long time," Winder said. "It's good to finally have you here with us."

I couldn't tell if his words bore a hint of criticism, or if I were just being overly sensitive. Before I could say anything, however, Andres intervened.

"What's important is that he's here now," he said. "We old lions can't continue the hunt forever."

"We are old, not dead," Winder answered, and this time I was certain I heard an edge to his voice. There was something going on between those two, and I had a feeling I'd better find out what before too much time passed. For the moment, however, my empty stomach took priority.

"I'm sure there's plenty of fight left in both of you," I ventured, figuring that a compliment could help smooth things over, "and we all want to end the Council's rule. But to do that," I added, trying to lighten the mood, "we'll need to keep up our strength. I, for one, could use some food!"

Thankfully, Tiber jumped in with support. "That makes two of us! Come, let's get in line before there's nothing left!"

"First things first," the Commander intervened. "The traditional welcome ceremony may have been postponed, but we still need to make an introduction. Come." He took me by the arm and led me and my grandfather to a podium on a raised platform.

"You all know Andres," he began, "but there is someone else he has brought with him that you should meet as well." He stepped back to usher my grandfather to the podium.

"People of the Light!" Andres called out, and his voice boomed so loudly that every eye turned toward him immediately. For a moment I wondered if this was another of the family *gifts*, but then I realized that a vocal amplifier in the podium had been activated. "It is my great honor, and pleasure, to introduce all of you to my grandson, The One to Be, Vers Leitstell."

As if they had rehearsed, the dozens of rebels dropped to one knee and murmured in unison, "Praise the Light!"

I looked out at the mass of people below me and for the first time the impact of what it meant to be The One really hit me. Until that moment I hadn't fully grasped that I wasn't just being groomed to be a rebel leader, but as their go-between with the Great Creator as well. My knees felt weak.

"Say something to them," my grandfather whispered, turning from the podium so no one but I could hear him.

Say something?! Couldn't he have warned me? I stepped to the podium, my mind whirling in a jumble of impulses. I was so tired, and so hungry, my thoughts were a muddled mess. I decided to speak from my heart.

"Two dins ago a bomb killed my mother and her new husband, as well as a half-dozen innocent bystanders," I began, and then the words just poured out of me. "If what I've heard is true, they were trying to kill me. I must live with the knowledge of that fact for the rest of my life. But what I refuse to live with, what I refuse to accept, is a brutal, totalitarian government that corrupts the teachings of the Great Creator, that distorts the vision of the Light, that exists only to serve itself. They may kill me, or you, or any of us. But they will never kill our cause. We will triumph, and the true Light will once again shine upon the Terran colonies!"

I have no idea where all that came from. It was as if the words already existed somewhere inside of me and were just waiting for that place, that time. My head suddenly felt light, and I stumbled a bit as I stepped back from the roaring cheers that greeted my speech.

"I think we'd better get him some food before he collapses," Andres announced with a smile. "Very nice," he said softly to me. "Didn't know you had it in you, did you?"

As we turned to go down toward the food preparation area, I saw a blur of smiling, cheering faces, some with tears in their eyes. And off in a corner, nearly hidden in deep shadow, I caught a glimpse of Winder, his arms crossed over his chest, watching my every step.

He was *not* cheering.

*****

I fully expected to wait in line with everyone else. But whether it was due to my stature among them, or my obvious weakness, Vera pulled me from where Andres and I stood and took us to a waiting table.

"Come," she ordered. "I've prepared your place already."

I wanted to tell her I preferred to wait, but her look told me I was better off following her lead. My grandfather did the same, so I guessed it was probably the Base routine with honored guests. I was having trouble keeping my legs under me anyway, so it was probably for the best.

I was very much aware as we sat that nearly everyone in the cavern was either staring in our direction or sneaking a quick peak every now and then. It wasn't something I was used to, and I can't honestly say it was particularly pleasant. I kind of felt like I did when I had to stand up in front of class to give a report, but this was even worse. I knew that all those people expected big things from me. Only problem was, I didn't know if I could come through for them.

It didn't affect my appetite, though. By that point, I could've eaten a whole real chicken, if we'd had one. But given the situation, I was very happy to see some steaming synth-chick with what could've passed for real mashed potatoes and a textured protein spinach-y concoction that tasted better than it looked. I'm afraid I gulped it down as though I hadn't eaten in dins. Truth was, I hadn't eaten much since the explosion, so I suppose I had a good excuse.

Without really thinking about it, my eyes wandered to the corner where I'd seen Winder standing seemingly unimpressed by my talk. He was gone. Why hadn't he joined us? Just how bad were relations between my grandfather and the rebel Base commander? I decided to find out.

"I thought Winder and his son might join us," I said matter-of-factly between forkfuls of food.

"Those two do pretty much whatever they choose," Andres said with what I took for a touch of irritation. "Especially the old man."

"Why's that? Is there some bad blood between you two?"

Andres looked up at me with a bemused smile. "Your intuition is pretty developed for one so young. Has it always been that way?"

I hadn't really thought about it, but now that I did, I'd have to say it hadn't. "Not really. Maybe more the last few lunar cycles."

He nodded. "As I suspected." He went back to eating, but I wasn't letting him off the hook that easily.

"And relations between you and Winder?"

This time the look was pure frustration. "I suppose now is as good a time as any," he began, putting down his fork and leaning in closer to me. "Winder began fighting with the rebels while my father was still leader of our people. So I think he thinks of himself as the senior member of the rebellion, at least here on Phoebos, and he rarely misses an opportunity to make that point clear to me."

"So that's why he didn't kneel with the rest?"

"You caught that, did you?"

"Hard to miss."

"Yes, well don't take it personally. He's a good man, and a good commander. He just has his…idiosyncrasies."

"And Tiber?"

"A good boy. Man, I should say. But his ties are closest to his father, as you'd expect. I've never had a problem with him."

"Will I?"

Andres arched his eyebrows. "I hope not. His father influences him, but he's got a good head on his shoulders."

I was about to ask more questions, when Vera suddenly popped up at my side.

"You weren't hungry, were you?" she said sarcastically, staring down at my spotless plate.

"A bit," I answered. I could feel the warmth creeping into my cheeks once again.

"Want more?"

I was about to shout 'yes' when I saw that fully half the rebels hadn't made their way through the line yet.

"I think I'll let my stomach go down a bit," I hedged. I didn't want to create hard feelings on my first din in camp. Better to be a little hungry than make everyone think I didn't care about their welfare.

"You sure?" Vera asked, looking askance.

I glanced over at my grandfather, who nodded ever so slightly.

"Yeh, I'm sure. But thanks for the offer."

"No problem. If there's anything you want, just let me know."

I was glad she turned and left before she could see my pink cheeks turn bright red. For some reason I thought of Amanda at that moment, and my embarrassment heightened.

"Pretty girl," Andres said simply.

"Yes, she is."

"You do her a great honor by allowing her to serve you."

What? I thought she'd been assigned the task as some kind of punishment. "You mean she *wants* to wait on me?"

"As does nearly every young person in this cavern."

"Because I'll somedin be The One?"

"And because you will lead the combined rebel forces. Being close to you means she will be close to all the major decisions of this struggle."

"Are you saying I should let her stay on in that duty, or something else?"

"That is up to you. I've already seen enough of your intuition to trust your judgment on that score. But you could do much worse."

I nodded. It was becoming increasingly clear that this wasn't going to be easy, with all the personalities, all the moving parts, all the intrigue. But I had a job to do, just like all of them. And I had a score to settle.

*****

After dinner I could barely keep my eyes open. Vera and my grandfather showed me to a sleeping place in the far back corner of the cavern – as far from any enemies entering through the front entrance as possible, I decided. I wasn't about to argue.

There were three other bedrolls laid out in the same section.

"We have company?" I asked Andres.

"You, me, a bodyguard, and Vera," he said, ticking off the rolls one by one.

"Vera?" I said before I could stop myself.

"We all share the same quarters here," he answered. "Every soldier of the Light is equal under His eyes."

"Except The One."

He opened his hands in wordless response. "We do not demand it. They insist."

"And you cannot object?" I was feeling as though my life had suddenly slipped out of my control, and I didn't like it.

"You're not going to make this easy, are you?"

"I just want to understand. Why is it so important that people serve us?"

"Because we – you – are the one thing they can believe in, the focal point of all their hopes and dreams. They want you up on a pedestal. They *need* you there. If they see you as one of them, then it's as though they are hoping that *they* can overthrow this terrible government. And although we eventually *will*, until it happens they need more."

He seemed so sincere, so certain, that I was almost convinced on the spot. Almost.

"It's just…"

"That it seems so self-serving?" Andres interrupted. "So much like the very people we are trying to replace? Yes, I know. But sometimes motivation matters. Sometimes we must do things that seem distasteful in order to achieve a positive outcome. The one thing we must not do, however," he said, his voice suddenly more pointed, "is allow these momentary lapses to become commonplace. We must not become that which we despise. We *cannot.*"

I'm not sure if I was too tired to argue, or if his argument was just too good to be denied. In either case, I nodded, accepting.

"Then we will do what we must," I said. "And right now, that's sleep."

The old man smiled. "You do that. Morning will come all too soon. I'll go find Winder and see what he's in a snit about this time."

I wanted to ask more details, to better understand the dynamic between the two of them, but my eyes were closing of their own accord. "Say hi," was all I could manage.

I didn't even bother to slip out of my clothes. I think I was asleep before my head touched the bedding. But my sleep was not peaceful. Images of the bomb blast and the pieces of metal raining down on me kept coming back in different guises. And all the while I knew, or felt, the eyes of the Council, the eyes of Rogen Antavar, watching me. I had to get away, I had to find a place where he couldn't find me...

I awoke to find Vera shaking me by the shoulder, none too gently.

"Rise and shine," she said cheerfully. "You've got a lot to do before you leave here."

I sat up, my head thick and confused in the dim light of the cavern. "What? What do I have to do?" I asked, just barely conscious.

She pulled back in mock alarm. "First thing is brush those teeth," she said. Then sniffing the air added, "and a bath wouldn't hurt. Shall I bathe you?"

Bathe me!? This whole thing was getting out of hand! "I, ah, I don't think that will be necessary," I mumbled, pulling the covers to my chest nervously.

"What, you won't *let* Vera bathe you?!" a voice called out sarcastically. "I know people who'd *kill* to get her to do that to them." I turned to see Tiber striding toward us with a huge smile on his face, carrying a bundle of clothing.

"Don't get your hopes up," Vera shot back.

"I'm a patient man," he answered easily.

"If you'd just point me in the right direction for the baths," I cut in.

"Back there," Tiber said, pointing to a narrow tunnel off the rear of the cavern. "But I should warn you, they're not private. We don't have the space for everyone to have their own bathing tub."

"That's okay. As long as it has water – preferably warm."

"That it has. And when you're done, put these on," he added, handing me the bundle. "Andres wants you to look the part."

His skepticism, though clad in humor, still stung. I tried not to show it. "Thanks," I said. "I'll do my best."

"Of course you will," Vera said, and for the first time there was no trace of sarcasm or levity. I glanced in her direction and caught her glowering at Tiber.

"Ooo, the she-wolf has fangs," he taunted. "Look out, Vers. This one's bite is worse than her bark." He turned and walked off without a second look.

"At least I have a bite!" Vera called after him, and I couldn't tell if she were angry or…?

I didn't have time to think about it. Pulling myself out of the bedroll, I threw the bundle of clothes over my shoulder and headed toward the bathing area.

"We're expecting you back here in a stunde. You don't want to keep us waiting," Vera informed me in no uncertain terms.

"Heaven forbid," I muttered. "Hey, by the way, are the baths co-ed?"

She laughed. "No, we are not *so* egalitarian. We have our own tubs."

"Just wondered."

I felt her eyes on me as I walked off. What *was* it about that girl?

The bathing facilities were basic but welcome. The warm water was both soothing and invigorating and for the first time in dins I felt almost human again. But when I went to put on the clothes that Tiber had given me, I wondered if he'd made a mistake. Instead of the travel clothes I'd expected, I found instead a richly colored and elegant outfit befitting a king! 'Or The One', I realized. Would there be no end to the changes required of me because of the accident of my birth?!

Part of me wanted to protest, to yell to the high heavens that I was no royalty, just a kid trying to make it to his 16th birth din. But part of me, a surprisingly insistent part, reminded me of my grandfather's words: "They demand it." I took a deep breath and dressed. When I'd finished I collected my dirty clothes and started back toward the main cavern. I happened to glance in the steamy mirror that hung by the entrance to the bath, and was stopped dead in my tracks. The person who looked back at me bore little resemblance to the kid who'd just finished his first solar cycle at Vaden Upper Level. I looked more like...The One.

My head spinning, I continued out the short hallway to the main hall. To my amazement, the sleepy room I'd left just a short while earlier had been transformed in my absence into a hubbub of activity. A small stage had been erected where the podium had been, decorated with two flags I'd never seen before. A group of five or six people stood off to one side of the flags, while virtually the entire population of the base stood in front of the riser. When I came out, all eyes turned toward me and recorded brass instruments played some kind of flourish to announce my arrival. I knew then what a Terran deer must feel like in the road lights of a transport.

I stood motionless, utterly stunned by the reception. Thankfully, Vera appeared at my side and took my elbow as if I were ancient and decrepit.

"Don't worry. It won't hurt," she whispered to me. "Much."

I let her lead me past the mass of people and up two steps on the side of the stage. Andres stepped forward to give me a warm hug. Winder followed, with just a nod of his head. Two other oldsters touched hands with me, and a dark-haired woman of around 40 or so kissed me on both cheeks. I had no idea what I was supposed to do, so I just waited for someone to tell me. My grandfather must've sensed my confusion, for he took my arm and placed me between the two flags, to his right. Winder stood off to my left, and the others behind us.

"Time is short, so we will be brief," my grandfather began, his amplified voice filling the large cave. "This din we welcome into our community my grandson, The One-to-be, Vers Leitstell." I half-expected a big cheer. The quiet was eerie. "He has come to us at a sad time, for him, and at a critical time for us. In just two lunar cycles he will come of age and will take his rightful place in the insurgency. I ask you to support him as you have me. Together, the Terran system will soon be free of the Council, and all Terrans will be able to live the life promised us by the Great Creator. May the Light shine on him, and on all of us!"

Now the cheering was loud and genuine. But after just a short moment, Andres raised his hands for quiet.

"Now, Winder Ebram will give the benediction," he said, stepping back to allow the Base Commander to come forward.

"It is premature to bless an investiture before its time," he said, sounding none too thrilled to be there. "But it is what it is. And so, let all of us pray that this *boy*," (his emphasis) "will find the strength and the courage and the fortitude to confront the darkness of the Council, and that through him the Light will shine once more on every corner of Terra."

Once again the crowd exploded as my grandfather took my hand in his and held it high over our heads. I glanced out of the corner of my eye at Mr. Ebram, who had stepped back and stood next to us with head down, neither cheering nor clapping nor doing much of anything. I tried not to look shaken, nodding to the crowd as if I knew what was going on. After several long moments of cheering, Andres turned to me. "Your turn," he said.

My turn? Again? Now I was certain that I was being tested. For what, and why, I had no idea. But I've never been one to turn down a challenge.

"Thank you, all," I began, stalling for time until I could think of something more inspiring. Nothing much was coming, so I decided to wing it. "*You* are my strength, my courage, and it is through you that the Light shall once again illuminate the hearts of all Terrans, everywhere." I waited for the cheering to die down, feeling the moment at last. "I am young, and inexperienced, I know that better than anyone. But I promise you this: I will not rest, I will not stop, until the Council and all its spies and secret police and hangers-on are brought to justice, and we are free of them forever!"

The cheers were deafening. I was all warmed up by this time, and was about to go on, when my grandfather put his hand on my arm. "I think that's enough for now," he said through clenched teeth.

"Oh, yeh, right," I replied, a surge of adrenaline just beginning to subside. Turning to the crowd I added one last, "Thank you!' and waved as my grandfather virtually pulled me off the stage.

"You seem to have lost your reticence," he said as we stepped down into a mass of waiting people.

"Funny thing is, I never liked speaking in front of people."

"It's in your blood," he said as a phalanx of bodyguards appeared from nowhere to move us through dozens of rebels eager to reach out and touch us. Or me, really. It was weird.

Andres made it clear to me that we were on a very tight schedule in order to match our departure with the rotation of Phoebos. The plan was for us to launch while our sector of the moon was facing away from Terra5, and then slot into a high orbit like one of the interplanetary freighters using the gravity of Phoebos to give a boost to their propulsion systems. It saved us fuel and gave us perfect cover to leave Phoebos without prying eyes being aware.

I was led to a small chamber where a pressure suit and undergarments had already been laid out for me. I was only slightly surprised to find Vera waiting for me as well.

"May I help you suit up?" she asked, a good deal more demure than the last couple of times.

I was about to tell her I could handle it myself, but thought better of it. "Thank you. I'd appreciate that," I said instead, and the thoughtful smile I received in return convinced me that I'd made the right decision.

It was a little embarrassing at first, undressing down to my din shorts, but she seemed utterly unconcerned and so, eventually, was I. I had to admit that she knew her way around a pressure suit – better than me, actually. She had me all strapped in, adjusted and tested in no time.

"Let's get you over to the launch platform," she said after she'd walked all the way around me twice to be sure that nothing had been left undone, or poorly done.

We didn't go through the main cavern, but instead left the dressing chamber though a simple gray door that I'd assumed led to a closet. We walked a surprisingly long way, maybe a kilometer or more, through a narrow channel cut out of the solid stone. We crossed several intersecting tunnels, but Vera led the way without hesitation. I wanted to ask her about herself, about how she fit into the rebel organizational structure, but she kept silent and so I did as well. Time passed all too quickly, and I had just built-up the courage to start a conversation when we came to a huge cave housing a launch platform that looked out over the sheer cliffs of the Quinby Mountains. Just as the fueled and prepped space transport came into view, a host of rebels and dignitaries saw us and came hurrying over to bid us farewell.

Probably a dozen people, young and old, walked with us to the boarding ramp. I say *us*, though in reality I noticed about halfway across the platform that Vera had somehow disappeared. I wondered if the invitations to those who would see us off were extended according to rank, or connections, or some other criteria I couldn't even imagine. Apparently Vera didn't possess the right status. I felt suddenly alone, and kicked myself for not having thanked her more explicitly for everything she'd done for me. Despite all the thanks and expressions of good fortune their departure committee provided, I couldn't help wondering when I'd see her again, if ever.

The high-pitched whine of the electro-generators told me that we were getting close to departure. I looked around for my grandfather, or anyone I might recognize, but the only familiar face I saw was Winder's, standing behind the techs in a small control room, looking none too interested in me or my journey. But then a burst of excited talk and movement made me turn in that direction. I saw my grandfather leading three other suited rebels toward where I waited.

"All set?" he called out when he'd come closer.

"I think so."

"You are."

I looked to the other three, but they already wore their helmets with the reflective facemasks pulled down into protective position. I couldn't make out any features through the mirror-like finish.

The five of us posed for some DigiStills and the next thing I knew the ramp door was swinging shut and Andres was directing me toward my launch recliner. I was just about to ask him for more information about the flight and our companions, when our three unknown crew members began removing their helmets. I recognized the first as the bodyguard who had shared our sleeping cell the previous night. When the second helmet popped off, I was more than a little surprised to see Tiber's smiling face.

"Didn't think we'd let you have all the fun, did you?" he asked as he settled into his heavily padded gyro-seat.

Before I could answer him, the final member of their quintet removed the heavy helmet that had hidden her from view: Vera!

"What are *you* doing here?!" I asked in total shock.

"Who's going to wash and dress you if I'm not around?" she said with her usual caustic wit.

"Actually," Andres cut in, "Vera is one of our more talented tele-guides. She can get a ship through space junk that even the navigational computers can't handle."

A telepath. Why didn't that surprise me?

"And Tiber here is one of the finest battle strategists and weapons techs we have in our force."

"At your service," he said with a nod of his head. I knew full well, of course, that he was also Winder's eyes and ears on our journey to Terra5. What I didn't know was if that was a good thing.

"Jans, you already know from last night. If anyone can keep us safe and sound, it's him." The big man didn't even blink.

"What Andres didn't say is that if I say 'jump', you'd better already be in the air or you may well not be around to hear my next sentence," he said, his voice low and utterly calm. "I don't say much, but when I do, you'd best listen. Even someone with your powers can't avoid a direct hit from a proton beam, or worse."

"Listen to what he says, Vers," my grandfather affirmed. "He's already saved my life so many times I've lost count."

A direct hit from a proton beam?! I didn't like the sound of that at all. But I knew who my new best friend was.

We strapped ourselves in and waited while the flight crew went through the final stages of its pre-launch systems check. Tiber and Vera chatted about nothing in particular, while Jans, my grandfather and I pretty much just lay there, our thoughts our own.

As launch became eminent, Andres spoke to me over the helmet communication channel. I assume he must've made the link person to person, since none of the others reacted to his words.

"I know this is a big leap for you," he said reassuringly, "but I just want you to know that I'm very proud of how you handled yourself back there. I don't think you could've done any better."

Whether he knew my doubts or just wanted to make me feel better, I didn't know. I only knew that as the roar of the engines and the vibration of lift-off cut short his message, I was smiling.

CHAPTER 10

From the relative brightness of the launch bay we moved into the absolute blackness of the back side of Phoebos in just a few clics. My viewport looked forward and to the right as we left, so I couldn't see the moon fade away behind us. But as I left the only home I'd really ever known, I couldn't help but wonder if I'd ever return again.

Once we reached escape velocity the main engines cut off and we switched to the impulse engines. The quiet and calm was disorienting. An unsecured wire casing drifted off to my left, telling me that the artificial gravity system was not yet activated. Moments later, the casing dropped out of the air as if shot, just as the transport Commander's voice came over the intercom.

"This is Gemri Ota, your Commander on this din's flight to Terra5. Just wanted to welcome you all onboard the Leitcom Windsong, and wish you a safe and comfortable flight. We'll need to work our way into the transport shipping lanes to avoid detection, so it may take us a bit longer than normal. If there's anything I or the rest of our flight crew can do to make your trip more comfortable, feel free to let us know."

"Just get us there in one piece," I heard Tiber mutter. He didn't sound like he was joking.

"So, I bet it's been a while since you've been up in one of these," Andres said to me.

"Last time was before I was born when the family moved to Phoebos," I told him. "I haven't been off the moon since then."

The old man pursed his lips. "Oh? I hadn't realized that. No…anxiety?"

I hadn't even thought about it. I know some people talk of interplanetary flight as if it were torture, but for me it was as natural as breathing.

"Nah. I'm fine," I said. "Can't get over the views."

"The Great Creator has given us all of this. It is up to us to make the best use of his gifts."

There was something in his words that struck a discordant note, but I was enjoying myself too much to pay much attention. Andres only gave me a short while to sightsee, however, before he pulled Tiber, Vera and I off to the officers' mess and began to brief us on the details of our trip – and beyond. It was a definite relief to get out of the pressure suits, but his words carried such gravity that I found my mood greatly sobered.

After going over the plan to disguise our flight in the large flow of transports between Phoebos and Terra5, he launched into a description of what would follow once we arrived at our destination.

"We have a number of bases hidden on all the major landmasses on Terra5," he explained, "but on this trip we will be going to a smaller destination: a training station tucked away in the mountains of Argos." I knew from my geography classes that Argos was a relatively small island, located in a temperate zone far from the Council's seat of power in Harran. "We don't need a lot of territory to do what we'll need to do, and the less people who know that you're on T5, the better for all concerned."

"What, exactly, will we be doing?" I asked.

"Well, Tiber and Vera will be contacting base commanders to let them know that their time has nearly come. Put them on alert, you might say. You and I, on the other hand, will be repeating a training regimen that has been followed by nearly every eldest Inodian son since the line began, all those cycles ago. We begin on your sixteenth birth din."

"And we end?"

"Whenever you are ready."

"How long did it take you?"

"That's not really pertinent to your situation," Andres said with a dismissive flick of his hand. "For each of us it is different."

"Why?"

"You like to ask questions, don't you?" my grandfather said with a smile showing equal parts amusement and frustration.

"I like to know all I can about whatever I'm doing. Especially if my life is at risk."

"Not just *your* life," Tiber cut in.

"Oh, nicely done," Vera added sarcastically. "Why don't we all see how much pressure we can pile on him."

"Hey, I was just saying…" Tiber began, but Andres cut him off.

"We know what you were saying, Tiber. And you have a point. But it's a point that could have waited for a more suitable time."

For just an instant a flash of anger showed in the young man's eyes. But almost as soon as it appeared, it was replaced by a nod of contrite acceptance.

"Yeh, you're right. It just slipped out. Sorry."

"Don't worry about it," I said before either of the other two could respond. "I don't like my medicine sugar-coated. I need to hear the truth, no matter how much it hurts."

"And so you will," my grandfather said. "But only when you need to hear it."

"Who decides that? You?" I didn't mean to sound snippy, but I guess it came out that way.

"Until I am no longer the leader of our people, yes," the old man said with just a hint of wounded pride. "When you occupy that position, then you can decide. But you are not ready for such decisions quite yet."

I knew he was right. Worse yet, I felt like a fool for challenging his authority. "Hey, you can keep making decisions for us as long as you want," I said, trying to lighten the tension I could see in everyone's face. "I'm not campaigning for that job."

"It will come to you nonetheless," Andres continued, his voice notably more sympathetic. "We can only pray that you will be ready when the time comes."

"I'm sure you'll get me ready…" I began, when suddenly a flashing red light and loud warning announcement interrupted my words.

"Security Force cruisers!" the Commander warned through the ship's sound diffusers. "Looks like they're boarding every transport."

"The Light save us," Andres muttered. Then he turned to me and my two young companions. "Come! We don't have much time!"

I felt my heart leap into my throat. Or at least something big enough to almost make me gag. If they were to find us… I didn't even want to think about it.

Instead, I followed my grandfather and Vera, with Tiber and my bodyguard bringing up the rear. I had no idea where we were going, but wasn't all that surprised when Andres brought us directly to the cargo bay.

"Here, put these on," he told us, taking four breathing hoods from an unmarked container bolted to the wall and handing one to each of us.

As soon as the masks were in place, he opened a small crew hatch into the bay. Or, more accurately, into an airlock. The moment air pressure reached the one-third atmosphere used in the cargo area, a second door slid open with a familiar hiss.

"Hurry!" Andres shouted.

He broke into a jog, taking us between long rows of massive casks labeled: "CAUTION – SPENT DILITHIUM CRYSTALS. DANGER!"

"I don't think this is very healthy," Tiber said loud enough for me to hear.

"Not as unhealthy as being discovered by the Security Force," Vera chimed in from just ahead.

We were two thirds of the way to the end of the row of casks, when Andres suddenly stopped and began to disable the electronic locking mechanism on one of the large yellow and black containers.

"What are you doing?!" Tiber called out, the tension in his voice sending it a half-octave higher than normal.

"You'll see," the old man said, not stopping for even an instant to explain himself further.

All four of us stepped back instinctively as the door to the cask swung slowly open.

"Inside!" Andres ordered, taking Vera by the arm and half-throwing her into the dark opening.

She had time to say only "But..." before she disappeared inside.

"She'll die in there!" Tiber said, and he jumped to the front of our little line to retrieve his friend. I must admit, I was a little ashamed that I hadn't thought to do the same. I waited for him to re-emerge, dragging Vera to safety, but after a few moments I realized he wasn't coming back.

"Move!" Andres ordered, breaking me from my reverie.

I stumbled into the darkness of the container, expecting to bump into the two rebels who'd gone in before me. I took two steps before Tiber's voice came to me from somewhere below my feet.

"Watch your step! There are stairs just in front of you."

As my eyes adjusted I could barely make out a narrow stairway in the floor of the container, leading to...? A dim red light provided just enough illumination to allow me to get down the stairs without breaking my neck. Andres was right on my heels, and Jans just behind him.

I quickly found myself in a small chamber, perhaps 3 meters square, located beneath the level of the loading bay. Vera and Tiber helped each of us navigate the last step into the room, and soon the five of us were reunited in the dim light of the hiding space. Andres pulled a wall lever and the hatch above us slid silently shut.

"How did you know about this?" I asked innocently of Andres, bringing grins and shakes of the head from my fellow rebels.

"We regularly use this transport to move people and materiel from Phoebos to the home planet," he explained patiently. "I've had to take refuge down here more than a few times over the solar cycles."

"But what if they use detection meters? Won't they notice immediately that this cask is different from all the others?"

My grandfather nodded his head appreciatively. "Very good. Luckily, our engineers came to the same conclusion some cycles ago. The exterior of the container is lined with spent Dilithium, so any counter will register the same readings as all the others. Oh, there's probably a small difference in the level of the readings, but the hand-held meters the Security Forces use will never notice the difference."

"We hope," Tiber added, unnecessarily.

"The very fact that I'm standing here proves that it has worked in the past, and there's no reason to believe it won't work again this din."

My sense of relief was interrupted by the Commander's voice over a small diffuser.

"Security Force coming alongside. Boarding in a few clics."

"Sit!" Andres ordered and each of us did as we were told, finding a place on the metallic floor. "No sounds whatsoever!"

In the silence of a small space, with death just meters away, even our breathing and heartbeats seemed overly loud. A tickle in the back of my throat demanded a cough, but I managed to swallow it away.

After some time we heard the muffled sounds of voices and a repeated banging coming from above us. It was clear that both were moving closer.

"What do we do if they find us?" Tiber whispered.

Andres' response was barely audible. "They must not. Now, quiet – please! I have to focus."

As the voices and banging came closer and closer, I could feel the tension grow in our tiny hiding place. I wondered if this awareness was one of my 'powers', or if it were even real. Maybe I was projecting it, since I was plenty nervous. The others showed no outward signs, though in the dim light I couldn't make out their features too well. But I remember that I couldn't hear even a breath as the banging finally arrived at our 'doorstep'. It seemed as if time stood still as the echoes of the metallic hammering reverberated all around us. I found myself clutching my hands together so tightly that the knuckles showed white, while I silently repeated over and over again: *'Please, don't find us, please don't find us.'*

A clock ticked inexorably in my head, measuring the time we had left before the spent Dilithium would begin to kill us. Finally, the sounds above us moved off.

As the pounding gradually faded, all of us began to breathe again.

Vera made as if to ask a question, but was cut off by Andres raising one finger to his lips. "Not yet," he whispered.

We sat in the dim red light for what seemed like a cycle, but was probably not even a clic. Finally the red light blinked several times and Andres stood up.

"They've left," he announced. "Come, we can go back to our flight couches."

He led the way out of the cask, to where two crewmen waited to be sure all was well. Andres thanked them and assured them that we were fine. As we arrived back on the flight deck, Commander Ota repeated the questioning.

"Thanks to you and your crew, we're all doing well," Andres said. "Any trouble with our friends?"

"Nah. Although it was clear that this was more than just a routine search. They're looking for something – or someone." I thought I caught him glancing in my direction, but I wasn't sure.

"Whatever it was, they won't find it this din," my grandfather continued. "Are we on schedule?"

"Close enough. We should be touching down by 03:51."

"Good. Let me know when we're a stunde out, would you?"

"You got it."

I was fascinated by the mix of awe and disregard with which the rebels seemed to treat my grandfather. On the one hand, there was no doubt he was their leader. On the other, nearly everyone called him by his first name and interacted with him as an equal. Clearly, I had a lot to learn.

*****

Andres returned to his briefing, giving us more details about what we could expect in the immediate future. "For you, Vers, training, training, and more training."

"Sorry I'll miss it," Tiber joked.

"You'll have plenty of your own," Andres corrected, "but Vers needs some specialized preparation."

"And me?" Vera asked. "How can I take care of him if I'm excluded from his training?" She sounded almost hurt.

"Don't worry, you'll have your chance when we're done," my grandfather said.

"In the meantime, you can practice on me," Tiber suggested with a sly smile.

"I was talking about care, not vivisection." It was hard for me to tell if she were joking.

"You forget, I've seen you in action," Tiber continued without missing a beat. "It'd be pretty hard to tell the difference between the two."

Andres stepped between us with hands held high. "All right you two, that's enough of that. This will be hard enough without you two at each other's throats."

Vera and Tiber exchanged angry – or were they mock angry? – glances but held their tongues. Andres went on for a full stunde before finally leaving us to our own devices while he left to speak with the Commander.

By the time he'd finished, the brilliant blue and green ball that was Terra5 more than filled the observation port above my head. We were close, and getting closer quickly. I'd be lying if I didn't admit that my heart was racing and I was more than a little nervous. I'd never stepped foot on T5 and my images of the planet were all virtual. Yet there I was about to return as the soon-to-be leader of a movement to overthrow the religious dictatorship that had ruled the Terra system for hundreds of star cycles. Was I nuts?

"Buckle up!" Andres said as he came back to our passenger area. "We're about to begin entry into the atmosphere. The Commander will be trying to mimic a transport for most of the descent, but then he'll break it off to evade their sensors. It may get bumpy."

Bumpy was an understatement. The first part of the descent was actually a lot of fun. The ionization from friction with the atmosphere produced a spectacular light show that we experienced from the perfect vantage point. But when the Commander took evasive maneuvers to try to escape detection in the final phases of our entry, the ship shook so hard I thought my flight couch might break loose from its moorings. I know my stomach almost did.

"He's trying to present a Rascher cross-section to their scans," Tiber said admiringly. "This guy's good."

'He'd better be,' I thought, my fingers grabbing the armrests with every ounce of strength I possessed.

And then, as quickly as it had begun, it stopped. I looked out my observation port as we banked and saw the bright blue of the Terran sky merge with a brilliant blue-green of the sea just a few meters below us. I didn't need anyone to explain that we were skimming the tops of the waves to avoid detection.

"Wow," Vera muttered aloud. "I'd read about this, but it's even more beautiful in real life."

No one was arguing with her. It was breathtaking. After so many solar cycles in the black and white drabness of the mining moon, it was almost overpowering. Just as we'd grown accustomed to the sea colors below us, we banked sharply again and the bright greens of a tropical jungle filled our field of view. We grazed the tops of towering trees for a couple of stundes before slipping between two nearly vertical mountain slopes and speeding on a zig-zag course that traced a raging river just below us. It seemed like we could almost reach out and touch the rock cliffs on either side of us. I marveled at the Commander's skill.

"One din you'll be able to pilot a craft like this," Andres' voice announced as if he'd been reading my mind, "but you will be guided by the Light, not computers."

I didn't want to dispute his expectations, but he hadn't seen me drive a transport. Two citations in the first six lunar cycles of my learner's permit. My mom said her gray hairs were a direct result from teaching me. *I* wouldn't even feel safe if I were piloting.

The whine of the engines changed pitch and I felt us slow markedly. On the sightscreens directly above me I could see us approaching a sheer rock wall, seemingly hundreds of meters tall. I waited for us to change course, or stop, or something, but we continued…slowly, right at the looming cliff. Just as I was about to scream a warning, the cliff *melted* away right in front of our eyes! A projection! The rebels disguised the entrance to their mountain base by projecting a very believable 3D image of the cliff right over a gaping cavern! I was impressed.

We landed very smoothly and I could hear the servos lowering the large craft door to the exit position. We stowed nonessential gear and prepared to depart. I was feeling a little nervous, or maybe excited; it's hard to tell the difference sometimes.

Looking out through the bay door, I saw a single person walk up to, and then into the transport. Our Commander saluted the man, who looked to be in his mid-fifties, trim, with steel gray hair, blue eyes and the slightest of limps on his right side.

"Giles McAllister," Andres said as he followed my eyes. "Commands this sector. Four bases, over two thousand combatants segregated in small cells, spread out over thousands of square kilometers. Good man."

I saw McAllister turn in our direction and smile as he identified my grandfather.

"Andres!" he called out as he came towards us. The two men hugged warmly.

"Giles, may I introduce you to…"

"Let me guess," the rebel leader interrupted, moving to where I stood, "this one is Vers Leitstell." He raised his hand for a touch. "Welcome to Calib Base."

"Thank you. We're happy to be here," I said, and I realized I *was* happy to be there.

"And these three?" McAllister continued.

"Vera Weis, Jans Biggert, and…"

"Tiber Ebram," Tiber cut-in. "It's a great honor."

"Ah, Winder's son, I take it. Yes, yes, I can see the resemblance. I've known your father for a long time."

"He sends his regards."

I was a bit jealous of Tiber's familiarity with our host, but at the same time was glad to see the good will his relationship created.

"Let's get you out of those suits and cleaned up a bit," the sector commander said. "And then a briefing?" He addressed the last to Andres.

"I think so. It wasn't such a long trip that we need time to recover." He looked over at me. "Do we?"

I had no idea what we needed to recover *for*, but I shook my head dutifully. "No sir. I think we're good to go."

"Excellent. Then let's talk a bit and then we'll get you on your way."

On our way? Where was it that we were going? I'd thought that the base was our destination, but obviously it was only an interim stop.

My eyes were so tired that I could barely keep them open and I was forced to stifle a series of yawns that seemed to originate in my toes. Four stundes of sleep will do that to you. "Uh, where are we going?" I finally got up the nerve to ask. "Isn't this where we'll do our training?"

"Here?" McAllister said, glancing over at my grandfather with a questioning look. "This is just a landing port. You'll be heading into Veejy, a small town twenty or twenty-five kilometers from here. Our friends in the Council have too many eyes in the sky and on the ground to keep you here. Heck, we probably won't be here for more than another few lunar cycles ourselves. We have to keep moving to stay one step ahead of them."

No one else said anything, so I decided to keep my mouth shut as well. The four of us men were led to a small chamber where we were provided some warm water and soap, and a change of clothes. For some reason I had been expecting something in camouflage green, so I was a little surprised when we were given simple everydin clothing just like what the locals might wear. Vera got her own space right next to ours and a dark blue hooded dress that covered much more than it revealed.

"Sexy," Tiber quipped when we met her again in the outer hallway.

"When in Veejy…" she said.

"You mean this is how women dress here?" I asked in dismay.

"I think you need this briefing even more than we do," Andres said without any hint of reproach. "Come on."

We were taken to another room, just slightly larger than the first, where Commander McAllister stood next to a table surrounded by 9 chairs. A young aide stood at his right side.

"Come in, come in," he welcomed us. "Take a seat."

As if it had been prearranged, Vera, Tiber and Jans moved to the far end of the table while the Commander's aide pulled out chairs on either side of his boss for my grandfather and me.

"Sorry to hurry you along, but the Security Forces are out in large numbers trying to find any trace of Vers here," McAllister began. He nodded in my direction and I felt my cheeks flush. Me? *I* was who they were looking for? What about Andres?

"We have reports of house-to-house searches back on Phoebos," he continued, "and secondary searches of all transports as they arrive at their destinations down here. With any luck they weren't able to track your final maneuvers, but we can't be sure. So, let's get to it." He pressed a button on a vid-controller and a large image materialized on a screen just behind his back. "This is Argos," he explained as he pointed to a map of the region. "It's a small island, just 42 kilometers by 22, but the rugged mountains and high grade deposits of several key minerals make standard tracking techniques almost useless. It's been home to hijackers and smugglers for generations. And now to us. We're located here, in the Lafros Mountains. You five are headed for Veejy, a town of around 27,000, locate right here." He indicated a point on the edge of a large sea, just at the base of the mountain range. "We have a safe-house all prepared for you. Your cover story is a grandfather and his grandkids coming for a long vacation."

"And me?" Jans spoke out.

McAllister smiled. "You're their bodyguard. Pretty clever, huh?"

Even I knew that many wealthy people on T5 traveled with bodyguards, especially since the 'insurrection' (as the Council called it) had become more public and widespread. Since most of those wealthy enough to afford bodyguards were usually connected in some way to the Council, they were usually given a wide berth by the locals. Sounded like an ideal masquerade.

"And how do we get there?" I asked, eager to show my interest. "Levitors?" The small single-person anti-grav units seemed like an ideal way to get around in the rugged mountain landscape.

"Not on Argos," McAllister answered. "You'd stand out like a sore thumb. The only ones allowed to use that kind of technology here are the SF (Security Forces.)"

"Levitors? Back on Phoebos even teenagers goof around on them."

"That's Phoebos. This is T5. As you'll soon learn, life here is not what it is elsewhere – thanks to the Council."

I was shocked. No one had ever told me of such limitations on T5. In fact, I'd grown up thinking that we'd been somewhat deprived on the mining moon. To hear that we had access to technology – even relatively simple technology – that was better than what the Terrans had was a real eye opener.

"Then how *will* we get there?" Vera chimed in. It made me feel a little better that I wasn't the only one in our little group who didn't know everything about T5.

McAllister's eyes narrowed. "Have you been briefed at *all?*" the Commander asked gruffly, turning directly to Andres. His tone was definitely not as friendly as it had been moments earlier.

"We've been a bit…busy," my grandfather replied, not giving an inch.

"Yes, well, to get from here into town we ride Terran mules," the Commander answered me, his irritation still showing. "Descendants of a pair brought here on the initial migration. It's not fast, and not particularly comfortable if you're not accustomed to riding them, but they're dependable and don't draw attention."

"Mules?" Tiber said.

"Yes, *mules*," McAllister repeated, this time with even more attitude. Apparently we weren't the first visitors to question the locals' mode of transportation. "The Council has decreed mechanical transportation illegal. In this sector, it's mules or horses, and the horses can't handle this terrain." He paused briefly. "Or you can walk, I suppose. But it's a long way on these mountain trails."

He stared at Tiber as if daring him to say another word. The dare was not taken.

"We'll be very happy with mules," Andres said, obviously trying to soothe tender feelings. "When do we go?"

"Not until dark. There's plenty of reflected light from Phoebos, so that shouldn't be a problem. But it makes it a little harder for random satellite sweeps to pick you out. We'll send a good guide with you – he's made the trip a dozen times, at least." He motioned to a young man standing by the door.

"This is Aden," he announced. "McAllister. He'll lead you to town"

One look and we all could see the family resemblance. He bowed his head to Andres (and me?) and then nodded to the others. "Pleasure. Any of you ridden mules before?"

I glanced around. No one was signaling that they had. Except Andres. "I've been down there a couple of times," he said. "But that was long before your time. Haven't been in this sector in many cycles."

"Doubt it's changed much. The one thing I can tell you is to dress in layers. It'll be quite cool in these mountains tonight, but by the time we get down to Veejy, the prime star will be up and you'll be sweating. Other than that, just hang on tight to the reins, keep your animal's head straight, and keep the chatter to a minimum. Sounds are amplified in all the tight passes and ravines, and you never know when an SF patrol might be passing by."

He seemed pretty relaxed and confident, but his words did nothing but raise my anxiety level. Riding some strange Terran animal was one thing, but in the dark on mountain paths with SF patrols buzzing about? Didn't sound like a picnic to me. Of course, I kept my worries to myself. As I glanced around, it didn't look like any of the others was terribly worried, so maybe I was over-reacting. The realization didn't stop my hands from sweating.

McAllister got a quick rundown of the situation on Phoebos from Andres, including details he hadn't yet received about the bombing and our escape.

"Sorry to hear about your Mom," he said to me when he heard. "I knew your folks a little bit some solar cycles back, and they were both good people."

I thought that I'd adjusted to her death pretty well by that time, but just the mention of the attack brought a lump to my throat. I did my best to be sure no one else noticed.

When the Commander'd heard all he thought relevant, he briefed us on the local situation: "There's the standard SF barracks in Veejy, housing 72 of their people. They have a couple of others who work with the local Guard, so don't think of them as your friends. On the other hand, we've got over 100 of our folks scattered all over town. They're broken down into typical six-person cells so that if the SF gets lucky and catches one of them, they can't learn about more than five others no matter what they do to him." No one asked what the SF did to rebels they captured. I knew I didn't really want to know. "I've told Andres about your contact in town – he's the only one who knows you're coming. Try to keep it that way as long as possible. Our people are good, but we don't want to push your luck. Questions?"

Vera raised her hand. "What about us – Tiber and me? What will we be doing?"

"You two will be assigned to a training cell. You'll get hands on training in everything from bomb-making and placement to rumor management."

"Who's going to look after Vers?" Vera asked.

The Commander made a face. "Does he *need* looking after?"

"She's his aide," Andres explained.

"Ah. Well, until your training is completed, I think his grandfather will have to fill that role. Is that right, Andres?"

"I'll do what I can." He didn't try to hide his grin.

"And when we've completed our training?" Vera pressed.

"A dedicated one, eh? Well, if Andres agrees, we'll let you take over the din-to-din assistance. When does he turn 16 again?" It didn't escape my notice that he asked Andres, not me.

"Less than two septs," he said. "The 14th."

"Good, good," the Commander said, nodding thoughtfully. "We are ready."

They were ready? What about *me*?

CHAPTER 11

Terra 5

The High Priest paced anxiously.

"A bomb! You tried to kill him with a bomb!? I told you to keep this quiet so the rebels wouldn't have a martyr to rally around. And you try a bomb!?"

The Fist fought down the urge to lash back, knowing he could not win. "It worked with his father," he said softly instead.

"That was fifteen cycles ago, and it was in a backwater on T3! Not in the middle of the Phoebos mining community! I've spent thirty cycles trying to keep a lid on this rebellion and you try this?"

"We thought it was the best approach..."

"Was it successful?"

Belinger knew that the High Priest already knew the answer to his question.

"We...aren't sure. We haven't been able to find any trace of the boy."

"He can't just disappear!" Rogen spit at no one in particular. Nonetheless, all six of his fellow Council members flinched at his words.

Ofran Belinger, his Fist, spoke cautiously but with the authority that came with his position. "We have found no DNA to confirm his death. However, we've reviewed the output of every DigiCam in the area and interviewed everyone within a kilometer of the event, and we haven't found any indication that he escaped, either."

"So you're telling me he *did* just disappear?" Despite the controlled tone, Antavar was clearly furious. None of the other Council members missed the implied threat.

Only Belinger dared say a word. "We are searching every vessel that leaves the moon. We have our people watching all his associates. We monitor all communications in the sector. We will find him."

"You had better," the High Priest warned coldly. "Now get out of my sight!"

For just an instant the others hesitated, caught off-guard by the sudden dismissal. Did he mean Belinger, or all of us? But one glare from Antavar and they were all soon scrambling to get out of the meeting room.

Left alone, the High Priest reviewed the situation that faced him: the teen, Leitstell, would have his sixteenth birth celebration in less than two septs; at that point, it was only a matter of time before he came into his full powers. If that old fool Andres were already involved – and he had to assume he was – it might be very soon indeed. If they didn't find the kid and eliminate him – or perhaps hold him captive as a bargaining chip? – he would soon take command of the rebel forces opposed to the Council – and to him.

He sighed and walked heavily to the small altar in the center of the room. He entered a sequence of digits into a pad that only became visible with his touch, and a small panel slid open in the latinum and conundrum-encrusted platform. He glanced around to be sure no one was left in the room, and then reached into a recess and pulled out a heavy, ancient paper and ink document encased in a richly decorated binding. He carried the document, *The Rahn* as it had been called in the inner circles of the Council for hundreds of cycles, to a nearby table and took a seat at one end.

He flipped the book open and quickly turned pages until he arrived at the section he sought. He'd visited that section so many times in recent lunar cycles that he knew its location by heart. His eyes slid across the small, neatly penned words. He barely focused on what they said; he'd memorized them long ago.

It was a prediction, a *prophecy* as they'd called them back then. Titled *The Rebirth*, it was written in the last dins of Earth, the home planet of all the Terran colonies. The identity of the scribe had been lost to antiquity, but it was clearly someone of great power and knowledge. Written many cycles before the wars took place, the volume spoke of a diaspora, the establishment of new colonies, and the bloody fight to establish one regime to rule them all. But it also spoke of something much more ominous: *The One*, it was called. It was a small section of the document. Just a few paragraphs, really. And the language, like so much of the document, was cryptic to the point of obscurity. But his heightened awareness told him as much as the words.

He traced a single sentence with one finger as he read, for the thousandth time: *"When the sky is filled by light, The One shall take His rightful place and the peoples of Terran shall rejoice."*

Part of him wanted to sneer in contempt. Typical ancient mumbo-jumbo. Specific enough to warrant concern, but vague enough to fit nearly any situation. He stared out the window at the city below. All those people, all at his beck and call, all of them cowed by the Council and the SF. Almost all. It was those few, a tiny minority really, that kept him awake at night. Not that he ever told anyone about his sleepless nights. They'd see it as a sign of weakness. The High Priest was supposed to be blessed by the Great Creator. How could such a holy man be frightened by a rag-tag gang of would-be usurpers?

He closed the book and sighed. If Belinger couldn't handle the situation, he'd have to get rid of him and find someone who could.

CHAPTER 12

I slept, dreaming of a time when my parents were still on Terra3. I hadn't actually been there, of course but from all my Mom's stories I felt as if I remembered a towering waterfall they'd visited for a picnic just a few cycles before they came to Phoebos. In real life the visit had apparently been benign enough, a few stundes enjoying the sun, the roaring water and each other. But in this dream I found myself wandering alone, entranced by the sound of the waterfall. Nearer and nearer I came, my feet unsteady but the attraction of the water inescapable. Suddenly a brilliant double-rainbow appeared in the cloud of mist that surrounded the falls, and in my overpowering urge to see the colors more clearly, I made my way to the very edge of the sheer rock cliff that overlooked the falling water.

The colors were so beautiful! They changed and pulsed, almost as if they were alive. I knew it was dangerous, but the colors seemed to reach out to me, beckoning, enticing. I took a step to come just a little closer, my eyes glued to the rainbow. Suddenly the ground beneath my feet began to crumble, as first small stones and then the entire cliffside began to slide into the abyss below. I teetered on the edge, fighting to regain my balance, and for a long moment it seemed as if I were suspended in mid-air, neither rising nor falling. But just as a wave of relief began to sweep over me, the pull of gravity won the tug-of-war and I fell head-first over the edge of the cliff, plummeting at impossible speeds toward the rock-strewn river below.

I tried to call out, tried to stop my fall, but it was useless. I saw the roiling water and massive boulders rushing up to meet me and braced for the collision. But just as I was about to smash into the partially submerged rocks, a strong, reassuring hand grabbed me by the shoulder.

"Vers, time to get up," Andres' voice called out to me. The falls disappeared in a twinkling. I opened my eyes tentatively, unsure of what I'd find.

"Come on now," my grandfather continued, "we need to get moving."

The sense of falling still lingered, but I felt my heart slow considerably as I saw a familiar face just inches from my own.

"I was dreaming," I mumbled through heavy lips.

"Sorry about that. But our guide is expecting us in a little over a stunde."

"Okay. Just give me a clic."

"I'll be having dinner with Commander McAllister. Join us when you're ready."

It took me a few moments to realize that I had fallen asleep waiting for nightfall and the trip to Veejy. I shook the cobwebs from my brain while I watched my grandfather leave the sleeping chamber. I washed and dressed quickly, but even the icy mountain water couldn't dislodge the disturbing sense of foreboding that lingered from my dream.

*****

By the time our traveling group had all eaten and packed, Phoebos was just climbing over the mountaintops, a silver-grey beacon to remind me of where I'd come from, and why. McAllister walked us to our departure point, a small clearing some two hundred meters from the rear entrance to the base. There was little chatter in the cool stillness of twilight as each of us pondered the difficult and dangerous journey awaiting us. Even if a rockslide or misplaced hoof didn't get us, the Security Force was an ever-present threat. Lightly armed and mounted on mules, we posed no danger to the professional thugs hired by the Council to keep the masses in place. One false step and we'd be just a footnote in some hidden Council archive.

"Well, at least you look the part," the base Commander said as he surveyed the group. We wore layers of the simple, lightweight clothing typical of the region. On the ornery but sturdy mules we looked every bit the local residents returning from a trip to the mountains or the city beyond.

"I feel naked in this get-up," Tiber complained under his breath, worrying that his sidearm would be hidden deep in a saddlebag.

"That's a nasty image to conjure," Vera joked.

"You wish," was the best he could come up with.

"As long as it keeps the SF from taking a second look, it will have served its purpose," McAllister explained. "If a patrol happens upon you on the way down, it's critical that they have no inkling that you're anyone out of the ordinary. Not only your lives, but the entire struggle may depend on that."

I felt the Commander's words settle heavily upon my shoulders.

"Don't worry. We'll get through. We always do, don't we?" Andres said lightly, belying the tension we all knew he felt.

"Most of the time," McAllister muttered just loud enough for Vers to hear.

With a few last words, the six members of our travel party mounted our mules.

"Stay close behind me, and try to look relaxed," Aden instructed. "The SF – and these mules – can feel nerves."

"Great," Tiber said, more to himself than the others.

I couldn't help but smile. I knew just how the young rebel felt.

Just as I'd suspected, the first stunde or so of the ride was pure hell. I'd never ridden an animal of any kind, and my mule had a very distinct mind of its own. Even my best efforts didn't keep the surprisingly powerful animal from stopping, turning, and even galloping as he saw fit. It wasn't until Aden rearranged the animals so that my mule was located directly behind his own – from where he could grab its bridle and impose his will – that the group moved ahead in a semblance of normalcy.

Even so, it was slow going down the narrow stone pathways. Small rocks and even good-sized boulders toppled down from the steep gorge walls every now and then as we traveled, and in places the path was nearly blocked by small rockslides. On two occasions Aden asked us all to dismount and then half-cajoled and half-pulled the six mules over piles of dirt and stone. At one point we all gasped aloud as one of the mules teetered on two hooves, just inches from the edge of a cliff that dropped off hundreds of feet.

"No problem," Aden assured us when the animal had landed safely on the other side of the blockage. "They know the routine."

"I wonder if he'd still be saying that if it were *his* mule that almost took a nose-dive," Tiber whispered to me. He wasn't smiling.

Still, despite the drama and the danger, our group made steady if slow progress down off the mountain. The constant clip-clop of the mules' hooves became a virtual mantra in my mind, a reassuring if slightly irritating distraction from the ride itself and the challenges that faced me. I had finally settled into the rhythm of the ride, allowing my body to relax slightly instead of constantly fighting the mule and gravity, and was actually beginning to enjoy the rugged scenery and the rocking cadence of my mount, when suddenly I was startled from my lethargic reverie by the sound of a fast-approaching transport.

"Hold it up!" Aden shouted, signaling the same with his hand. "Looks like we have company."

In the pre-dawn darkness I could just make out the outlines of a small C-class transport. Given what we'd been told about the use of higher technology in the area, I assumed it was the Security Force. A jolt of adrenaline shot through my body.

"Let me do all the talking," Aden said. "If they ask you anything, just remember your briefing – we're coming over the mountains from Galena to visit friends and relatives in Veejy."

We all knew the cover story, but I had my doubts whether it would convince a skeptical SF interrogator. My hand unconsciously reached for the phaser hidden in my saddlebag.

A powerful light from the hovering transport swept across the six travelers.

"Remain where you are!" an amplified voice ordered. "Keep your hands where they can be seen. Do not move!"

A hatch on the vehicle opened and two levitors emerged. In the dim light, I could barely make out the distinctive body armor worn only by the SF. I could feel my heart race as the two security officers quickly descended to the path just in front of us. All six of us watched anxiously but said nothing. As soon as the dust had settled, the two Security personnel dismounted and walked slowly toward us, their hands resting on their phasers.

"Officers, what can we do for you?" Aden asked casually as the men neared.

"IDs," the lead officer demanded coolly.

McAllister had provided all of us with appropriate false docs, and each of us dug into our pockets to produce them. One officer held a small light while the other examined the identification. I tried to relax, but when one of the SF officers noticed something and pointed it out to his partner, I couldn't stop my mind from whirling.

'Don't let them find anything, don't let them find anything,' I repeated to myself, my lips moving unknowingly.

I started when Andres hand landed gently on my arm. "It's okay, no problem," my grandfather whispered. I nodded, more out of respect than conviction.

Suddenly, as if they'd heard my thoughts, the two men nodded in agreement and continued to survey the rest of the documents. In just a few clics they were finished – with the docs, but not with us.

"What are you doing out here so late at night?" the first officer asked as the light shifted to Aden's face.

"We're on our way from Galena to visit friends and family in Veejy," Aden said. "The mid-din UVs are brutal, so we travel at night."

The argument made some sense to me – the dinlight stundes were scorchingly hot at this latitude, even at altitude. But would the SF officers believe it?

They stared at Aden for a long moment, briefly shone the light on the rest of us, and then conferred quietly.

"What do you have in those saddlebags?" the other officer asked after a pause.

"Change of clothes, a bit to eat, and some water."

"Let me see," he said, stepping forward to get a better view.

Aden untied the bag and tipped it forward so the SF man could get a better look. He ran his hand through the contents perfunctorily, and grunted his approval.

"How about you?" he asked Vera, who had sat silently – 'as a good Terran woman should'. At that moment she was very happy she'd allowed McAllister to persuade her to wear the gray, loose-fitting outfit and hood preferred by the Council.

She reached down and opened her saddlebag for inspection. The officer was either too lazy or too bored to take a closer look, and so did not notice the bag's false bottom or the weapon and documents inside. He nodded to his partner.

The lead officer communicated with the transport hovering above and apparently received some response via the transponders in his helmet. I closed my eyes and tried to focus as we waited.

"You folks see anyone else out here?" the officer finally asked us.

"Nope. Pretty quiet."

"You have communicators with you?

"Nope. Can't afford 'em."

The officer smiled for the first time. "I know that one. Ok, continue on to Veejy, but be careful. This trail is dangerous enough during the dinlight. At night it can be even worse."

"Thanks, officer. We'll do that."

"May the Great Creator bless your travels," the officer said unconvincingly, striking his chest with a loud *thump* before straight-arming the Council salute.

"You too!" Aden replied, almost too enthusiastically.

The two Security personnel remounted their levitors and flew up to the waiting transport. None of the rebels moved until the bright light on the side of the ship was extinguished and the transport itself began to move away.

"Well done," Aden turned to us and said. "We may get to Veejy after all."

"Then it's okay to start breathing again?" Vera asked. I didn't think she was joking.

"And riding," the young guide answered. "Let's get out of these mountains before any other patrols – or worse – stumble upon us."

"Aden, I think a short break might be in order," Andres suggested, his tone respectful but insistent. The guide got the message.

"Yeh, okay. But let's keep it short. Ten clics?"

"Sounds good to me. Just stretch our legs and have a sip of water."

"And maybe get rid of a bit of water too," Tiber added.

"I thought I was the only one dying out here," Vera said, scrambling down off her mule and tying the reigns to a nearby bush. "Glad to hear the rest of you have bladders too."

As the two young rebels found nearby spots with a bit of privacy to relieve themselves, Andres casually walked over to me as he hefted his canteen and took a long sip of cool water.

"You okay?" he asked.

"Yeh, I'm good. That was a little close for comfort, but close only counts in horseshoes…"

"…And hand grenades," his grandfather finished the sentence for him. "I used to tell that one to your Dad when he was little."

"Had to be. Who else would even know what a hand grenade was?" I glanced up at the older man, his smile only partly hidden.

"Not everyone was born in the last fifteen cycles," Andres countered, his smile broader.

"More like the last 150 cycles."

Andres grabbed me playfully in a gentle headlock.

"I'm still young enough to show you a thing or two!"

I threw up my hands in mock surrender. "You got me. I give!" My grandfather turned me loose with a tap on my shoulder. I saw Aden and Jans staring at us. "Just playing!" I explained, and they went back to their business.

"You felt it, didn't you?" his grandfather suddenly asked, his demeanor becoming unexpectedly serious.

"What? What did I feel?"

"The impact your thoughts had on those two Security officers."

I hesitated. I *had* felt something… "I don't know if that's what it was…"

"That *is* what it was. Your thoughts influenced them. With a little help from me."

"That's crazy!" I sounded defensive even to myself. "Are you saying we made them let us go?"

"I mean, you're coming into your full abilities. It's good that we've got you here so that you can learn how to develop them more fully."

I had heard casual mention of my coming 'abilities' several times by then, and was pretty certain that my confrontations with Nobus had shown at least a hint of the power I possessed. But I had no idea the extent or degree of my 'gifts'. Maybe now I'd finally learn the whole story.

"Time to get moving!" Aden announced, just as Andres seemed about to launch into a further explanation.

"What? No!" I complained, a little too forcefully.

"Don't worry," my grandfather said as he patted me on the back. "You'll hear all about it once we reach Veejy."

A bit reluctantly, I joined the others as we remounted the mules. Aside from my aching thighs and backside, now there was another reason I wanted to get to Veejy as quickly as possible. If I was going to be their big guru, I needed to know what cards I was bringing to the table. I just hoped there were no jokers in the deck.

*****

It was mid-morning by the time we rounded a bend in the rock path and caught our first view of Veejy in the distance. It wasn't much of a town, clearly less than 30,000 people, but even from a distance the bright colors of the buildings shone against the brilliant blue-green of the ocean behind it. Compared to the back of a willful mule it looked like heaven.

"Not far now!" Aden called back cheerily, probably knowing how tired the group was of the endless ride.

"Thank The Creator," I heard Tiber mumble, vocalizing what all 6 of us were thinking.

Somehow the proximity of the town made the last stunde or so pass much more quickly than the preceding 13. Almost before we knew it, we left the dry plains that skirted the foothills to the Lafros Mountains and entered the town that would be our home for the time being. As we rode slowly down the dirt streets at the perimeter of the town, we were surprised and a bit unnerved to not see a single person either in their home, or tending their yards, or even walking the streets. It was as if we were passing through a ghost town.

"Not the liveliest place I've ever seen," Tiber finally suggested.

"That's how the Council likes it," Andres said, his voice just loud enough for our group to hear. "All the men are working. The women and younger children keep pretty much to their homes. If they go out, the women are covered from head to toe. The older children are in school for half the din, and studying the Laws of Light the rest of the time. Usually you don't see much of anybody during dinlight stundes."

"At least we won't stand out like a sore thumb," Tiber added sarcastically. I cringed.

Less than a kilometer from the outskirts of the town, we came to a more densely-populated area where we saw the first townspeople going about their daily chores, a few of them riding mules as well. After what Andres had told us, I wasn't surprised to see only men on the street. Although I knew from news reports that many devoted followers of The Light emulated the High Priest by wearing white flowing robes and shaving their heads completely bald except for a tiny wisp of hair at the very base of their necks, I was unprepared to see so many of the town's men sporting the ultra-religious look. On Phoebos, only priests and high government officials ever adopted the customs of the High Priest. Here, it seemed like more than half the population did so.

"This must be the most religious city on all of Terran," I commented aloud to no one in particular.

"Actually, it's not," Andres answered, his voice pitched even lower than before. "But only the ultra-orthodox qualify for the best government jobs, as well as tax breaks and subsidized housing."

"So why isn't everyone shaving their heads?" Tiber asked.

"Some hate the Council so much they won't do it, benefits be damned. Others have been 'punished' for some offense – real or imagined – by having to wear their hair long. It's considered a disgrace by the true-believers to have a full head of hair."

"Do we have to shave ours?" I asked.

"Or keep them completely covered," my grandfather said. "Otherwise we'll attract more attention than would be healthy."

I contemplated which course I'd take as the group continued on its way. Several times we slowed unexpectedly and the young guide and Andres exchanged hushed words. But I was not at all disappointed when we kept riding for another twenty clics. We'd attracted enough unfriendly stares to put me off introductions to Veejy society for at least one more din.

"We split up here," Aden announced when he'd brought us all to a halt. "Andres will take two of you on one route, and I'll take the rest."

"Split up!" Vera said anxiously. "Why?"

"Because two small groups won't draw as many prying eyes as one large one," I suggested.

"Exactly right," Andres agreed. "Vers, you and Vera come with me."

Jans objected immediately. "I'm sorry, Andres, but I've got to stay with Vers. Orders."

It was immediately clear to all of us that he wasn't asking, he was telling. I was afraid for a second that my grandfather would create a scene, but he just nodded understandingly. "Of course. We all have our orders. Vera, would you go with Aden then? Jans can come with us."

My eyes widened as realization struck me. Jans wasn't there to protect *us*, he was there to protect me!

For the first time I truly understood the full significance of my position; soon I would become the leader of not only the rebel movement, but the entire Terran system. I swallowed involuntarily. The very air around me seemed to buzz in my ears and I found it difficult to take a full breath. I wanted to say something, to let my grandfather know that I really grasped the responsibility that I had accepted, but no words came to my lips. Before I could recover, we were moving again.

As Aden led Tiber and Vera down a narrow roadway to the right, Andres urged his mule down another path to the left. Although my grandfather had reminded us to draw no attention to ourselves, it was hard for me to look natural and relaxed; my immediate instinct was to scan all around me for any sign of SF agents. But I controlled the urge and let the gentle rocking motion of the animal lull me into some semblance of relaxation. In my mind the three of us looked no more like traveling Veejians than a pack of Phoebian mine rats, but I calmed myself by repeating over and over again, "they can't see us for who we are, they can't see us…"

A short while later we turned into a wooded roadway dotted here and there by very basic wooden shacks topped by corrugated metal roofs. Jans shrugged at my inquisitive look, as if to say, "Don't ask me." About halfway down the dirt road, Andres guided my mule off to the left and behind one of the larger, more isolated shacks.

"Welcome to your new home," he announced as I pulled up behind the hut and dismounted. "It's not much, but it'll keep the rain off our heads."

As I surveyed the rusted and dented metal roof, I wasn't sure if it would even do that. But I held my tongue. I'd just gotten down from my saddle, gingerly, when the sound of approaching hooves stopped all three of us travelers in our tracks. We issued a collective sigh of relief when Aden and his two companions came slowly around the building.

"Nice digs," Tiber said sarcastically, "couldn't you find anything smaller?"

"Don't judge by appearances," Andres said softly.

"Or smells," Vera added, scrunching up her nose at the odor of burning trash emanating from somewhere nearby.

"Or smells," Andres agreed. "Come, let's get inside. Bring your things with you. Aden will take care of the mules."

We all followed Andres through the back door into what could only be described as a pleasant surprise. Instead of the old, dilapidated interior we all expected, we were greeted by a modern, simple but eminently functional set of three small rooms. The larger room encompassed a small sitting area, complete with DigiScreen, a kitchen that would have looked right at home in a Phoebos apartment, and a tiny eating area that was little more than a collapsible table that rose out of the floor on hydraulics, and six chairs. Two smaller bedrooms each featured bunk beds and a tiny bathroom with shower.

"It'll be a bit tight," Andres told us, "but I think you'll survive."

"Wow, talk about a pleasant surprise," Tiber said as he threw his saddlebag down on the floor and collapsed into a massage recliner. "It's good to be king."

"We have no king!" Andres barked a bit more harshly than he'd intended. "And never will."

"I was only kidding," the young rebel replied meekly.

"Choose your words carefully," Andres continued more calmly, "especially outside of here. One wrong word, one ill-chosen joke, could result in disaster."

"He knows," I stood-up for my companion. "We all do."

My grandfather looked as if he was going to say something further, but then changed his mind. "Good," he said instead. "Then we don't need to address that issue again. But before we all get too comfortable," he added, glancing down at Tiber, "there's something else you need to see."

As we all watched, the older man went into one of the small bedrooms. "Come, come!" he called back.

We crowded into the room to watch as Andres stepped into the shower stall, pulled the valve mechanism toward him, and rotated it in a counterclockwise direction. There was an audible gasp as the rear wall of the stall, shower head included, rotated backwards to reveal stairs that headed down into pitch blackness.

"I hope none of you have claustrophobia," he said as he started down the stairs.

One by one we followed, cautiously at first but somewhat faster once a dim blue light illuminated the stairway. At the bottom of the stairs Andres stopped, pushed a cleverly hidden button of some kind, and then peered into the small rectangular recess in the wall that suddenly appeared.

"Retina scan," he murmured, holding his head perfectly still.

Moments later a servo motor whirred and a previously unseen panel slid open to reveal a room larger than the footprint of the entire shack. High-tech electronic equipment and multiple SightScreens lined the walls.

"Welcome to our Veejy Control Center," he announced with obvious pride. "It took a lot of time and effort to get this all built and installed."

"Amazing," Vera said as she looked around room.

"Oh, and by the way, no mention of this anywhere in the building aside from down here. We don't think they know we're here, but we take no chances that they can pick up our conversations on a random sweep. Understood?"

We all nodded.

"Good. You'll all be getting training on this equipment, as well as on basic strategy and defense. Vers, you'll get a bit extra. For now, take a shower, relax, get something to eat. If you're as tired as you look, take a short nap. This is your one and only rest din. Starting tomorrow, it's full speed ahead."

"First in this shower!" Vera called happily.

"Speaking of naps," Tiber cut in, "what are the sleeping arrangements?"

"As you can see, we don't have a lot of space," Andres explained. "The bunk beds are pretty comfortable. And there's a pull-out in the main room. I was thinking Vers and I would room together…"

"I'll be fine with a mat on the floor," Jans said, once again more of a statement than a request.

"So I guess it's you and me," Tiber said to Vera with a leering smile.

She wasn't having any part of it. "I'm Vers' aide. I should be with him," she said resolutely to Andres.

"And so you will be," he answered gently, reiterating what she already knew, "once he comes of age. For now, Ver's in training, and I'm the only one who can provide the preparation he'll need. Once he grows into his new role, he's all yours."

I blushed in spite of myself.

"When will that be?" she pushed.

"Yet to be determined. His name-din is in less than two lunar cycles, so it may be then. Or it may be a little earlier or later. It's different for each of us."

"How will we know?"

"We'll know, but more importantly, he'll know."

Everyone turned to stare at me. "If you say so," I said with a shrug. "The only thing I know right now is that I'm tired, hungry and in need of a hot shower. Anyone mind if I take the first shower in the other bathroom?"

"Maybe Vera would like to hand you the soap," Tiber teased, but a testy scowl from Andres quickly sent him back-pedaling. "Just kidding, just kidding," he said. "It's okay with me."

"All yours, then," Andres said to me. "Just don't use all the hot water."

I turned to climb back up the stairs shaking my head. This One thing wasn't going to be quite what I'd imagined.

*****

After a great shower, (well, not great; the water pressure was a bit low and the hot water cut in and out unexpectedly anytime anyone in the house ran a faucet or flushed a toilet), and a decent meal (turned out Jans was also a pretty good cook), I stretched lazily on the sitting room sofa, trying to get the kinks in my back to loosen up. It was clear from our escape to Terra5 and now from the Control Center that the rebel movement was well-coordinated and managed. My only question: how would I fit it? After so many solar cycles working with (for?) my grandfather, how would the various Commanders and other leaders react to a new kid in town? Especially one who didn't know his left foot from his right. I'd just have to wait and see. Despite all the uncertainty, I never really doubted that I could do whatever they'd ask of me. There was something about my grandfather's confidence that was infectious. *'Probably manipulating my thoughts like I did with those Security Force officers,'* I suddenly realized. But even that realization didn't diminish my optimism. *'He should know,'* I decided. *'If **he** thinks I'll be able to do it, then who am I to have doubts?'*

My reverie was interrupted when Vera emerged from her bedroom, her hair wrapped in a twisted towel.

"I don't know about you, but I'm feeling a million per cent better already," she said as she poured herself a cup of the powerful herbal tea that Jans had brewed.

I watched her from the corner of my eye. For some reason, it didn't feel right to stare, but in the skin-tight body stocking she was wearing the sensuous curves of her fit body seemed to call out for closer inspection. I put my hands in my lap to hide any inappropriate reactions.

"Yeh, I'm feeling better too," I managed to sputter.

"Can I get you anything?"

"No thanks, I'm okay." I tried to look away, but my eyes seemed to wander back of their own accord.

"Pretty nice place, huh?" she asked as she came my way carrying her cup of tea.

"Better than I would've thought. I was expecting another cave, or something like that."

"Me too. And that would've been okay. But this is a whole lot better. You sore at all from the ride?"

"A little. You?"

"My thighs are killing me," she said, holding up one leg to reveal the offending limb.

Just then, a clearly refreshed Tiber strolled into the room.

"Wow!" he called out, stopping dead in his tracks. "Am I interrupting something?"

Vera dropped her leg, her cheeks turning nearly as red as mine.

"Of course not!" she answered angrily. "I was just telling Vers that my legs hurt from all that riding."

"My ass is killing me," Tiber answered. "Want to see it?" he turned as if to demonstrate.

"Disgusting!" the young woman groaned as she covered her eyes and turned away. "Is everything a joke to you?"

"Not everything. But most things, yes. Life's too short to take everything too seriously."

"Including the rebellion?" Vera stared at him now, her eyes narrowed.

Tiber shook his head in disgust. "Man, you really are a piece of work, aren't you?" He flopped down into a recliner.

"You didn't answer my question," she pressed.

"I take the rebellion as seriously as any one of you," he answered, his tone matching hers. "I just don't think I have to walk around looking like my mother just died every single cycle of the din."

He only realized what he'd said when he saw Vera look quickly over at me for my reaction. "Sorry," he added. "Just a figure of speech."

"Let's change the subject," I said without any hint of recrimination. "Has Andres told either of you what we're going to be doing tomorrow?"

"No. You?"

"Not really. Think he'd get upset if we asked him?"

"Asked me what?" my grandfather interjected as he came into the room from the subterranean Control Center.

All three of us straightened up involuntarily.

"We were just wondering what you have planned for us tomorrow," I ventured.

"Why, do you have your own plans?"

"No, no of course not," I fumbled. "It's just..."

"You just want to know what kind of strange, bizarre activities we have scheduled for you. Is that about right?"

"Something like that."

Andres smiled. "Just get a good night's sleep. You'll need it." With that he went into our bedroom and closed the door.

"That sounds ominous," Vera said as soon as the door closed.

Tiber glanced over at me. "I hope he meant you, and not all of us."

"Always the team player," Vera jibed. "Maybe Andres will let you stay in bed all din if you complain long enough."

"I didn't mean anything..."

"You two can continue your discussion all night if you want to," I said, getting up from the sofa, "but I'm taking my grandfather's advice. Good night."

Looking appropriately chastised, Tiber and Vera returned my good wishes and watched as I started for the bedroom I shared with Andres and Jans, who appeared from nowhere and followed me toward the room.

"This should prove interesting," Tiber said, half to himself.

"That's one way of looking at it." Vera said as she grabbed her tea and headed for her bedroom. "Don't stay up all night," she called back over her shoulder.

"Yes, Mom," her roommate answered, but his eyes followed her tight butt and aching thighs with nothing like a son's devotion.

CHAPTER 13

The Council Fist was obviously nervous. The more he tried to control his breathing and calm his nerves, the more intimidated he appeared. Of course, he had every right to be intimidated. The High Priest looked down at him from his ceremonial throne with an expression of utter displeasure.

"So? Have you found him?" Rogen Antavar asked. He knew he hadn't, as did all the other Council members staring resolutely at their folded hands.

At this point, some of the Council members expected Belinger to fall to his knees and beg forgiveness. That's what they would have done under the same circumstances. So they were more than a little surprised when the Fist held up a small electronic tablet and stood his ground.

"Not yet, but we're closing in on him," he said with what seemed like complete conviction. "We've found an anomaly in the ion exhaust traces."

"Drop the jargon," Antavar snapped. He wasn't an engineer and hated it when someone used terminology he didn't fully understand. Not that he'd ever admit that, of course.

"We have computers that have been scanning all ion engine traces from every transport and passenger ship flying between Phoebos and Terra5. Each of them is matched with scans submitted with the ships' flight plans. We've found a trace that doesn't match a flight plan."

"How do you know this 'anomaly' is The One?" The High Priest did not sound convinced.

"We don't. But when 236 traces match, and one doesn't, less than 48 stundes after the explosion on Phoebos, it seems like much more than a coincidence." He stared into the High Priest's eyes, almost daring him to argue with his conclusion.

Instead, Antavar nodded thoughtfully. "Yes, maybe so. What's your next move?"

"We've sent a large number of small transports to the general area indicated by the anomalous trace. They're all looking for more information."

"But ion traces dissipate in less than a stunde, don't they?" one of the other Council members suddenly asked, all innocence and light. In truth there was nothing that most of the Council members would like more than to discredit the Fist in the eyes of the High Priest.

Belinger stared at him with undisguised hatred. "Dissipate, yes. But there are lingering traces for up to a full cycle. Those are what we're looking for."

"And if you don't find these *lingering traces*?" Antavar asked.

Belinger cocked his head in a half-shrug. "We've dispatched some of our best operatives to see what we can find using old-fashioned person-to-person techniques. I can assure you, they can be very *persuasive*." Even the High Priest found his Fist's sneering smile a bit much to take.

"I hope they are, persuasive I mean," he said, determined to put the man in his place. "Because if not, *you* might just become their next subject for *interrogation*."

The Fist tried to maintain his façade of confidence, but Antavar could sense his uncertainty, his fear. The High Priest smiled. "But we're getting ahead of ourselves. I have every confidence that you will find this young pup. And when you do… Well, young pups can be taught new tricks, or so they say. And if not? Who'd miss some pimply-faced teenager from a mining moon?"

At that the High Priest laughed, a grating, unhappy sound that put every member of the Council on edge. As it was meant to.

CHAPTER 14

"All right, time to get up!" Andres' voice boomed in my ear.

"Already?" My sleepy voice was muffled by the pile of bedding I had stacked over my head.

"The principal star rose nearly a stunde ago. I've been too lax letting you sleep-in."

"Lax. Right. That's probably your middle name," I muttered.

I was just settling in for another moment of blessed rest, when suddenly my covers flew off in one fell swoop.

"My middle name is Jorus," Andres said with no pity whatsoever. "Come on. Get dressed. We're going for a run."

"Run?"

It was no more than thirty clics later when I found myself jogging in the warm Argos starshine. Improbably, my grandfather led the way, followed by Vera, me, and Tiber, with Jans bringing up the rear. It had been a long time since I'd last jogged further than a few meters to board a transport or catch up to a friend, and after just a short while I could feel my legs rebelling. My outer shirt was already drenched with sweat, and I was breathing as if we'd been running for a full stunde, instead of only a few clics. Vera kept pace with seeming ease, although her top showed the sweaty stains of her effort. I couldn't turn and maintain my pace, so I just assumed that Tiber was keeping up behind me. Despite the hassle, I didn't really mind running, even in the warm, humid air of the coast. Andres had brought us to a deserted path that ran along the sea, and the spectacular views of the steep red rock cliffs as the breaking turquoise waves sprayed us with a cooling mist were almost enough to make me forget the stitch in my side and the burn at the bottom of my lungs.

Still, I was more than a little relieved when Andres finally signaled us to stop a short while later. I stood with the others as I struggled to catch my breath without appearing too winded, eying my run-mates surreptitiously to see how they'd fared with their first taste of training. To my great delight, Tiber was panting and heaving even worse than I, while Vera and Jans seemed a bit less overcome. But it was my grandfather who put us all to shame. Andres stood looking out over the blue-green waters as if he'd just stepped from his front door – calm, collected, with barely a bead of sweat to suggest he'd just run several kilometers.

"How do you do that?" I asked between gulps of air.

"Do what?" Andres answered, but from the gleam in his eyes I was pretty certain he knew perfectly well what I was asking.

"Run all that way without even breaking a sweat."

"And at your age!" Tiber interjected.

The last crack seemed to tickle the older man, as his smile widened. "Your body responds as it's been trained," he said easily. "And as your mind instructs it."

"You're telling us you *thought* your way through that run?" Tiber asked incredulously.

"Something like that. I keep my body prepared so that my mind can ask it to do things that many my age would find difficult."

"*Your* age," Vera muttered, "how about us?" Her cheeks were so red they looked dyed.

"Actually, you've done pretty well for a first run. Better than I'd feared."

"Pretty low expectations," Tiber mumbled.

"Oh? Should they be higher? Then let's take it out another few kilometers. Come!"

Without waiting for a reply, Andres turned and jogged off down the coastal path.

"Oh, wonderful. Can't keep your opinions to yourself, can you Tiber?" Vera pouted.

"I was just saying…"

"Come on!" I urged, setting off even as I spoke. "I am not going to let that old man make me look bad!"

Vera looked to Tiber and shook her head disparagingly. "Men," she muttered, and with that she took off after me and my grandfather.

"Making all sorts of points this din, are we?" Jans asked the stunned rebel. He began to jog before Tiber could answer. Finding himself all alone on the cliffside, the younger man took a deep breath and hurried to catch up.

*****

By the time the five of us got back to our ramshackle hut, everyone but Andres was gasping for breath.

"Was *that* far enough?" the older man asked the group, glancing pointedly at Tiber.

"Great! Great run," Vera answered before her male counterpart could stop his panting.

"Yeh, really good," Tiber finally managed to wheeze.

"Vers?" Andres asked.

"It was plenty far enough for me. I'm wiped out, but I feel good."

Tiber looked to the younger rebel with utter distaste.

"Good! Then you won't mind joining me for a little…extra-curricular training?"

I hesitated, but my curiosity got the better of me. "Sure. Where to?"

Andres signaled the Control Center below us. "The rest of you can shower and relax a bit. You earned it!"

The smile on Tiber's face was genuine. Suddenly, all was forgiven.

"Hey, you have a good time," he said to me with a wave as he disappeared into his bedroom.

I was just about to do just that, when Vera raised her hand to stop me.

"You should have something to drink first," she advised me. "You'll get dehydrated if you don't keep up your fluids."

"And what about Jans and me?" Andres said, only half-joking.

"And Tiber, for that matter," the bodyguard added.

"I suppose I can find four glasses," the lone female rebel answered sourly. "But for future reference, I'm Vers' aide. Exclusively." Her stern look convinced Jans.

"Yes ma'am," he said with a mock salute. "Next time the water's on me."

Even Vera managed a wry smile at that. No sooner had we finished our drink, however, than Andres was herding me down the stairway to the hidden bunker below. Once inside the control room, Andres carefully secured the heavy door to the stairway.

"Is this training some kind of a secret?" I asked.

"Something like that," Andres said distractedly. "Now, come here."

He cleared a spot at one of the work desks and told me to sit. Then he placed a small metal object with four spokes emerging from a ball-like core on the desk.

"Ever see one of these?" he asked me.

I shook my head.

"A little before your time. Even a little before mine. It's called a 'jack', and it was a toy that children played with back on the Home Planet many cycles ago."

The confusion I felt must've played around my eyes.

"You wonder what a children's toy has to do with your training, right?" my grandfather asked.

"It did cross my mind."

"Watch."

Andres took a deep breath and then closed his eyes. My attention was riveted on my grandfather's utterly relaxed face when suddenly a slight sound captured my attention. I glanced down at the desk, and the jack was suddenly spinning – by itself!

"Wha...?" I began, but Andres held up a finger for patience.

As I watched, spellbound, the jack jumped from one spoke, to another, to another, the jack never once wobbling or slowing down. Finally, Andres opened his eyes and the toy clattered across the desktop to a bouncing stop.

"How did you *do* that?!" I asked, excitement in my eyes.

"Practice. And you will too, with time."

"Show me!"

"You think you're ready?"

I wasn't sure whether my grandfather was just teasing me or really had doubts. "Only one way to find out," I answered, watching the older man for a hint.

Andres smiled. "Okay. Examine the jack closely. Go ahead, pick it up."

I did as I was told.

"Now sit back in your chair, close your eyes and picture the jack. Not any jack, this specific one, and I don't want you to just think about the jack, I want you to try to recreate every millimeter of the jack in exquisite detail." Andres' voice was calm, soothing. "Okay, can you see it?"

"Yeh, I think so."

"Good. Now, turn it over in your mind so that you can see every angle, every dimension."

"Okay."

"Now, pick one arm of the jack, one of the spokes, and – in your mind – balance the jack on that one point. Can you do that?"

I struggled to maintain my concentration. Every time I thought I had it balanced, a stray idea or sound would break into my thought stream and the jack would either topple or disappear entirely.

"It's not so easy."

"Not the first time, no. But it will get easier, I promise you. Let me stop talking, and you try to get that point balanced."

I took a deep breath and focused all my energy on that one point of the jack. Time after time my concentration failed. I was getting frustrated, about to give up, when suddenly it was as if a light literally went off in my brain and the jack stood upright on the one point.

"Good!" Andres said.

I opened my eyes and stared at my grandfather. "How did you know?"

Andres smiled. "I gave you a little help – just as my father helped me the first time," he added quickly.

"Was that the light I saw?"

"Everyone experiences it differently, but yes, that was probably it. Want to try again?"

"No help this time." I sounded more petulant than I intended, but I wanted to do this thing myself.

Andres raised his arms above his head. "No help."

I closed my eyes and concentrated. Somehow, it didn't seem as difficult the second time, now that I knew the feeling I was seeking. Within moments I had the jack up on point.

"Got it," I said, and even then the jack didn't wobble.

"Very good," Andres said. "You have a real talent for this. But now comes the hard part. You still see the jack?"

"Yes."

"Okay. Now imagine a wind coming from one side of the jack, as if it were a weather vane. Do you understand?"

"Yes."

"Okay, now, picture the jack spinning in the wind. Slowly, then faster, and faster…"

At first the imagined toy just sat there, unwilling to budge. But then, ever so slowly, I felt rather than saw the light again and the jack began to move! I was doing it!

"It's moving!" I yelled despite myself.

"Now open your eyes," my grandfather said softly.

What I saw nearly made me shout with excitement. The real jack, the one sitting on the desk, was spinning freely – exactly as in my thoughts!

"No way!" I whispered, and in that moment my concentration did waver and the jack toppled over, skidding across the desktop. I was about to try again, but it disappeared! Just like that, right in front of my nose!

"Wha..? How…?" I was speechless.

"Look again," Andres said with a hint of a smile.

As I did, the jack rematerialized, seemingly out of thin air!

"How did you do that?"

"A little sleight of hand, or more accurately, sleight of mind. You'll learn, soon enough."

"How about right now?"

But my grandfather was having none of it. "You've done quite enough for one din." He held out his hand for a touch. "Congratulations. You're on your way."

"Did I do it, or did you help me?"

"Not at all. That was all you. And that's just the camel's nose. Pretty soon, if you work hard, you'll be able to do things beyond your imagination."

"Like you."

The older man smiled wistfully. "Maybe even more. We'll see. For now, let's get you upstairs for a shower and some sleep."

"Just one more time?" I pleaded.

Andres patted me on the shoulder. "Always quit on a success," he advised. "It will help build your confidence and prepare you for the next level. Besides, you must be tired. A rested mind is a strong mind. You'll have plenty of time to practice tomorrow, and the next din. Agreed?"

My shoulders slumped. "Oh, all right. But it's so…amazing!"

"That it is, my boy, that it is. But, for now at least, let's just keep this a little secret between the two of us. Okay?"

I wasn't certain why my grandfather wouldn't want the other members of our little group to know about my progress, but I wasn't about to doubt the old man.

"No problem."

"And no practicing anywhere but down here – for now."

"Okay."

"Good. Come on. You've had a big din."

As we walked up the darkened stairs, I couldn't help wonder what other talents came with being The One. For the first time in dins I thought more about the advantages of my birthright than the dangers. I had a feeling I'd sleep well that night.

*****

The next few dins were a mixture of non-stop exercise, glimpses of my potential, and frustration that it was all so darn difficult and slow. The very next morning Andres took us out for another run, but this time the pace was significantly faster and we ran for several kilometers further, again along the coastline but in a completely different direction. We rode the blasted mules for over a stunde just to reach the new location, which featured tall palm-like trees fringing a flat, irregular coastline. The scenery was not so striking as the din before, but the same incredibly clear blue-green water beckoned just a few meters away.

When the run was completed, Andres waded out into that same warm water towing a large palm frond behind him. "Wait here," he told the others.

"What is that crazy old man up to now?" Tiber muttered as we stood watching our leader walk out further and further into the near-waveless sea.

When the water reached chest-deep, Andres dog-paddled perhaps an additional hundred meters from shore, where he turned the frond loose and quickly swam back to where the four of us awaited him.

"That crazy old man sure can swim," Vera said softly, looking over at Tiber.

"All right!" Andres yelled to us as he walked slowly through the gentle surf. "Strip down to your skivvies!"

The four of us looked to one other as if we thought Andres had lost my mind.

"What the...?" Tiber began, but before he could finish Vera already had pulled her sweat-drenched t-shirt off over her head and was busy stripping off her running shorts as well. Underneath she wore a frilly black bra and panties, a fact that didn't seem to intimidate her in the least.

"Come on you cowards!" she yelled to the three of us men staring helplessly.

Sparked into action, we followed suit immediately, stripping down to our underwear without further comment. Standing there in our skivvies, Jans looked completely at ease, while Tiber and I looked utterly embarrassed.

"Good. Now, first one out to that frond and back gets to sit and watch for half of tomorrow's activities. Your choice," the old man called out. "Now go!"

At first the four of us stood staring like earth deer caught in a transport headlight. It was Jans who finally broke free and ran into the placid salt water. At that, the other three of us shrieked with competitive instinct and galloped into the lapping surf just meters behind. It was a tense competition from the very first, but the lead Jans had grabbed never wavered. He led all the way, followed by Tiber and Vera, with me – who had never swam in open water before in my life – bringing up the rear. In the last forty meters, Vera overtook Tiber and I nearly caught up with him as well as he faded badly in the last few meters. But when all was said and done, it was Jans who stood on the sandy beach, his chest heaving from the effort, smiling broadly as the rest of us struggled to shore.

"Well done!" Andres cheered when all four of us stood panting on the soft white beach. "And don't worry - you'll get better with practice," he said, repeating a mantra that we'd all get sick of in the coming cycles.

My grandfather tried to suppress a smile as he watched Tiber and I try to act casual and relaxed as our eyes swung unerringly toward Vera as she wrung water from her long brown hair, the tight curves of her body accentuated by the tiny black outfit she wore. Jans seemed oblivious, and Vera showed no signs of shyness. But Tiber and I?

"So Jans, that was quite a performance," Andres began, probably to distract attention from a potentially uncomfortable situation. "Looks like you'll be sitting out part of tomorrow's activities."

The big bodyguard nodded his acceptance of the praise, but was quick to reject the offer. "Where Vers goes, I go," he said simply.

"Does that mean I get to sit out?" Vera chimed in immediately.

"Sorry. In these exercises, you get what you earn," Andres said. "There's no award for second place."

The young woman smiled as she shrugged. "Can't say I didn't try."

"No, we can't. Can we gentlemen?" he turned his gaze to me and Tiber.

"No, no, you were great!" "I had no idea you could swim that well!" the two of us tripped over each other trying to praise the lovely young rebel.

"Good. Then we're all in agreement. Take a few clics to dry off and catch your breath, and then we'll be off to our next activity."

Vera, Tiber and I didn't know whether to cheer or complain, but when Jans sat in the warm sand and turned his face to the golden rays of the primary star above, we quickly moved to join him.

"Want something dry to sit on?" Tiber offered as he held out his sweaty t-shirt for Vera to inspect. She wrinkled her nose in displeasure.

"Thanks, but I'm okay," she said as diplomatically as she could. "How about you, Vers? Can I dry you off a bit so the sand won't stick to you?"

I turned as red as if I'd been out in the UV all afternoon. "I...I...uh, I'm fine, thank you though," I finally managed.

Tiber rolled his eyes. Vera, on the other hand, smiled at me as if I'd just said the most clever thing ever.

"You're very welcome," she said. "You know, we'll have to be careful not to get too much UV – we're not used to this climate and could get a nasty burn."

"Yes, Mom," Tiber quipped. Vera shot him an irritated look. I ignored both of them and settled down into the warm sand, my eyes focused on the vast expanse of sea that stretched out in front of me.

As I stared my thoughts drifted, turning eventually to Phoebos, and my mother. She always used to tell stories about the ocean back on T3. She painted such a visual image of the shore that I'd almost been able to see it myself. I thought about how much I missed her, how I'd never see her again, and that familiar lump crept into my throat. I felt a tear forming in my eye and might have embarrassed myself even further if I hadn't been distracted by Vera smoothing out her own t-shirt on the sand nearby. As she bent over to adjust the shirt, I couldn't help but stare, her tiny panties leaving little to the imagination.

"How'd you like a taste of that?" Tiber whispered.

I glared at him. How could he say such a thing?! Although, as I thought about it, I had to wonder what it would be like...

"Okay, time to get moving," Andres suddenly announced.

"Already?" Vera asked, having just moments earlier stretched out in the sand.

"This isn't a vacation," the older man said. "We have a lot more on the agenda for this afternoon."

"I'd like to burn that agenda," Tiber muttered.

"You have something to say?" Andres asked pointedly.

"Who? Me? No, no, nothing," Tiber squirmed.

Vera raised her eyebrows and grinned at him. She seemed to enjoy the older boy's discomfort. So it was even more surprising when Tiber sidled over to her as she brushed the sand from her backside to get ready to leave.

"Can I help you with that?" he asked with the lascivious grin than seemed a constant when it came to Vera.

"I think I can handle it myself," she replied, her voice as icy as the surface of Phoebos after star-set.

Her dismissal didn't seem to faze him in the least. The smile still plastered to his face, he went about his business as if nothing had happened. I found myself wondering why I couldn't be more like him. Maybe not so self-absorbed, but a little more relaxed around Vera, at least. I decided maybe it was an age thing and I'd grow into it.

When all four of us were ready, Andres led us on a fast run back in the direction from which we'd come. However, less than half-way to where the mules were tied he turned away from the shoreline and followed a barely visible path inland toward some foothills in the near distance. We passed through chest-high beach grass, then an area dotted with stunted bushes, until finally we passed into a greener zone where ten meter tall trees provided much needed shade. We ran beside a small stream until we reached the end of the trail, at which time Andres signaled for us to stop. He placed two fingers between his lips and a piercing whistle cut through the humid afternoon air.

As if out of nowhere, a thin dark-haired man suddenly appeared and walked slowly toward the resting group. It was difficult to judge his age, which I thought could be anything from a bit older than Jans to as old or even older than my grandfather, for the stranger had the dark skin and narrowed eyes of a Latasian. As he came toward us with relaxed grace, I had a sudden mental image of a Terran jungle cat. I wondered if the newcomer would prove to be as dangerous.

"Everyone, this is Xerish," Andres introduced the new arrival. "He will provide you with some basic training in the martial arts."

The man nodded to each of us as Andres called out our names.

"Basic martial arts?" Tiber said when his turn came. "Some of us have already had more advanced training." He was obviously proud of his abilities.

"Oh?" Andres said with one raised eyebrow. "Perhaps you'd like to demonstrate to the others?"

"With who? This little guy?" he asked, pointing his chin at Xerish. "I'd be afraid of breaking him in two."

"Oh, I wouldn't be too fearful," Xerish said, his voice clearly mocking, "I'm a little tougher than I appear."

"It's your funeral," the young rebel said with a shrug.

"Good! Watch closely," my grandfather said to the rest of us. "Xerish, Tiber, over here." He led them to a level grassy area. "A pin to the count of three or a simple surrender ends it. Agreed?"

Both men nodded.

"Then go to it!" He dropped his hand and the two of them circled warily, each looking to exploit a weakness or moment of inattention.

"Go get him, Tiber!" I shouted enthusiastically.

"Don't hurt him too badly, Xerish," Vera added. Tiber glanced over at her with a look of utter disdain.

In that one brief moment, Xerish struck. Like a coiled viper he dove for Tiber's arm, yanked it forward, planted his right leg behind Tiber's left, and flipped the larger man onto his back with a dull thud that made me wince. In the blink of an eye he was on top of the red faced rebel, and at the count of three Andres held his hand high overhead.

"We have a winner!" he announced.

I hurried over to the prostrate Tiber, who seemed to be in some pain.

"Are you okay?" I asked the wheezing loser, grabbing his elbow to help him get back to his feet.

"Yeh, yeh, I'm fine," he said, jerking his arm away from me. "Just caught me napping."

"So, that was your first lesson," Andres pronounced as Tiber struggled back to a vertical position. "What did you learn?"

"Speed can overcome power," I offered.

"Good. Anything else?"

"Overconfidence can get you hurt," Vera said plainly. She didn't even bother to look at Tiber, but he could feel her gaze nonetheless.

"Right. And?"

"Never fight with someone you don't know unless you have to. Looks can be deceiving," Jans said with such finality that no one, not even Tiber, thought to contradict him. Xerish bowed ever so slightly in his direction and the big bodyguard nodded back.

"Not bad for a ten second lesson," Andres said. Then, scanning their impressed faces added, "I trust Xerish has established his credentials. Now, let's get to work."

The next three stundes were a blur of activity, as first Xerish put our little group through an assortment of stretches and exercises, and then demonstrated three takedown moves including the one he'd used on Tiber. We rotated pairings so that everyone had a turn with the Master – as Andres called him – and with each other. I had no problem sparring with Tiber or Jans, though both held a distinct age and experience advantage over me, but when it came to Vera... I was so tentative, so ill at ease, that she threw me down on the ground like a sack of potatoes and pinned me in less time than it took Xerish to finish Tiber. Thankfully, she didn't gloat. By the end of the three stundes, all of us were bruised, battered and begging for a break.

"I think that's enough for Din One," Andres finally announced, much to everyone's relief. "You will meet with Xerish twice a sept, sometimes here, sometimes at another location. Each time you will learn three moves. You will practice them among yourselves, and at the next meeting you will be tested. I expect you to know each of the three moves completely. Understood?"

All of us muttered our agreement.

"Good! Master, thank you for your guidance. Now, let's see who can be the first back to the mules. First back gets an extra dessert!"

Even before he'd finished his sentence, Tiber took off running, followed closely by me, Jans and Vera.

"So, what do you think?" the rebel leader asked Xerish as they watched the four rebels disappear down the trail.

"The boy is strong, even without his full powers," the martial arts trainer said.

"Will he surpass me?" The question was matter-of-fact, revealing neither jealousy nor remorse.

"If he learns to master his powers as quickly as he learned those three moves, he will certainly surpass any Terran I have ever known — in time."

"Time is a commodity in short supply," the rebel leader said softly.

"Then he must learn quickly."

Andres nodded thoughtfully. He only hoped Vers would learn quickly enough.

CHAPTER 15

Even before the Fist said a word, the High Priest knew that he brought good news.

"You've found him?"

Rogen Antavar didn't need to explain who he meant. His security chief knew full well.

"We've pinned it down to the east coast of Argos, probably somewhere in the vicinity of Veejy."

The High Priest's expectant look turned to a scowl. "Then he is still out there, preparing for who knows what?!"

"Not for much longer. Our agents are combing the entire area — from the mountains to the sea, and everywhere in between. He can't escape us now."

"Famous last words. How long?"

Belinger fidgeted. There was no way of knowing how long it would take to find the boy, and the High Priest knew it.

"Not long," was the best he could manage.

Antavar leaned forward from his throne chair and stared into the Fist's eyes. He showed no sign of anger, only a cold, resolute glare. From previous experience, Belinger knew he was in real trouble. Even as the thought passed through his mind, a searing stab of pain convulsed his body and sent him crashing to his knees.

"Two septs," the Priest hissed. "That's all the time you have left on this planet if the boy is not found. Is that clear?"

The Fist struggled to formulate words through the agonizing pain. "Y...yes!" he finally gasped. As if the strings to a puppet had suddenly been cut, he fell to the floor in a heap.

"Now go, before I regret my leniency."

Belinger crawled to his feet and limped from the Council chamber. If he was going to suffer for his employees' ineptitude, he fumed, he wasn't going to be the only one. He decided then and there to commandeer a transport and head to Argos. He would either find Vers Leitstell or die trying. Make that find him or *kill* trying.

He smiled at his little joke as he hurried to find an available ship.

*****

As the Security Force transport began its descent into the agency spaceport on Argos, Ofran Belinger looked out the polarized windows at the tangled green vegetation and striking blue-green sea below. *'Not the worst place to die,'* he found himself musing. But as soon as the thought made itself known, he swept it from his consciousness. *'Nobody's dying here,'* he corrected, *'except perhaps the Leitstell kid. If he's lucky.'*

The spacecraft's hatch swung slowly open and Belinger emerged into the steamy hot hanger bay. A small greeting committee stood at attention, led by the regional Commander. The Fist surveyed the group with disdain. *'Incompetent fools!'* he fumed, but he said or did nothing to reveal his inner mood. *'Secrecy is strength,'* he repeated to himself. Only by knowing more than your subordinates, and even your superiors if you could, did you stand a chance of surviving the vicissitudes of the Council.

"Commandant Belinger," the regional Commander said after returning Belinger's straight-armed salute. "What a pleasant surprise!"

''What a supreme pain in the ass' is what you really mean,' Belinger thought. But he kept his thoughts to himself. "Latson," he said with a curt nod. "I've come to see what progress you've made in our investigation into this… Leitstone… Leitstin…"

"Leitstell?" the Commander offered eagerly.

"Ah yes, Leitstell," he said. "How is it going?" No one on Argos other than himself knew that Leitstell was soon to be The One. He couldn't trust any of his underlings to keep the information secret, and once it spread, chaos might result. *'But they haven't managed to bring us down, have they?'* he thought with some pleasure. When he looked up, he realized the Commander had answered him.

"Could you be more specific?" he asked to cover his inattention.

"We have a full complement of agents in the field," the Commander began again. "We're talking to anyone who might have seen the boy, reviewing all the SecureScreen archives, double-checking any departing transports or boats, even posting digital images in markets and bars."

Belinger winced. Such public attention might tip the boy that they were close on his trail. But, then again, with only two septs left before he had to report back to the High Priest, he couldn't afford to overlook any avenue. They *had* to find the young brat!

"Good. When can I review the information you've uncovered so far?"

The Commander blinked, nonplussed. "Well, I mean, immediately if you wish. But I thought, I mean, we thought you might like to freshen up…"

"I didn't come all the way down here to freshen up!" Belinger barked. "I'll review your findings right now!"

The Commander snapped to attention. "Of course, Commandant! We will take you to headquarters at once!"

"Let's go then," the Fist grumbled, sweeping past the startled Commander and his aides, who scrambled to catch up.

It took the locals less than a stunde to find an available transport. The trip began routinely enough, but they had only been traveling for moments, the Commander regaling Belinger with a travel guide's view of the island, when the Fist exploded.

"I don't give a fig about beaches or restaurants!" he yelled red-faced at the terrified Commander as his crew cowered behind him. "I'm here to find Leitstell – can you get that through your valluvium skull!?"

"Yes, of course, Commandant," Latson said dispassionately. It was clear to his staff that he was angry. He was not accustomed to anyone speaking to him in that tone. But Belinger was not just anyone.

The remainder of the trip to headquarters passed in complete silence. Latson didn't offer any further commentary, and Belinger didn't request any. Nerves were on edge when the transport landed behind the massive Security Force Regional Headquarters building. It had been a long time since the Fist had visited Argos, and this was his first time since the new building had been completed just a few cycles earlier. As he stepped out onto the landing pad even he had to admit that the massive stone structure stood out from its relatively low-key, subdued surroundings like a thoroughbred among mules. Twelve stories tall, sheathed in locally quarried black stone, the building itself would have been intimidating even without the massive shield of the SF affixed to the wall above the front entrance.

'Good,' he thought as he strolled into the secure rear entrance, the Commander and his staff trailing sheepishly behind. *'Perhaps a building like this will remind these peons what will happen to them if they should support the rebellion.'*

Belinger barely noticed the SF officers who snapped to attention and saluted as he walked by. They were just interchangeable pieces in his mind, cogs that could be replaced at a moment's notice. And if they didn't locate that infernal boy soon, many of them *would* be transferred to a much less enticing locale for their next assignment – perhaps to the mining moon, or worse. The thought brought him some satisfaction. But when he remembered that his fate would likely be infinitely worse if they failed, his mocking smile quickly faded.

The Commandant and his local staff spent more than a stunde reviewing DigiStills, VidCam recordings, and official logs, before moving on to first person interviews. Belinger hadn't realized that Veejy was such a crossroads for travelers in the region, but after the review he most certainly did. Literally thousands of unidentified persons had passed through the town and its surrounds during the preceding lunar cycle, people the SF could not identify even with the use of its latest facial recognition software that linked their computers to a massive central database back in Harran.

'This would be the perfect place for him to run,' Belinger thought as he shuttled through stundes of footage. *'Out of the mainstream, yet crowded with traders, adventurers, and just plain wanderers.'*

One additional piece of information supported his thinking: Latson casually mentioned that his people had identified suspicious activity in the mountains to the north of the city, leading them to believe that there might be a small landing site (for smugglers? rebels?) hidden in the rugged topography. The ion trail from the unidentified transport that had deviated from its flight plan on the din after the Phoebos bombing had led directly to those mountains. Coincidence? Belinger hoped not.

"I want all this VidCam footage reviewed by hand," he ordered Latson when they'd finished a quick perusal of the mountains of information they'd accumulated. "Start by eliminating anyone under 12 or over 25. This Leitstell *has* to be here somewhere!"

Out of the corner of his eye the Fist could see some of the Commander's underlings roll their eyes when they heard his command. He understood; there were dozens of VidCams located throughout the town and on all the major routes in and out. It would take real effort by a large force to review it all. But he didn't have time to explain. They had less than two septs to find this kid.

Or else.

CHAPTER 16

My fists were beginning to go numb. I'd been pounding a solid wall of wet clay for what seemed like an eternity. I glanced over at Jans, who continued to slam his bare fists into the clay as if it were a feather pillow.

"How can you do that?" I finally asked the older man. "My hands are killing me."

The bodyguard smiled back without missing a punch. "You get used to it," he said, and as if to emphasize his point, he leaned into his next two punches with all his weight.

"Do you think this actually helps?" I whispered.

"Don't you?" the unexpected reply came from several meters away where my grandfather had looked to be resting comfortably while his four trainees went through their paces.

I cringed. I should have known Andres would hear me, or read my mind, I wasn't sure which any more.

"I don't know," I answered truthfully. "It seems kind of pointless. I mean, after all, how often are we going to be going hand to hand with the Council?"

"If this lesson helps you even one time, it might be a time that saves the entire rebellion. Do you think *that* is worthwhile?"

I could see Vera and Tiber off to my left pretending to continue their workout. I could hear the diminished slap of their punches as they eavesdropped.

"Well, of course," I admitted. "But…"

"Keep punching," Xerish ordered. "Your grandfather is right. You need to be ready for any eventuality. You will soon be the leader of the rebellion. Thousands, even millions of your fellow Terrans will be counting on you. Do not forget that."

'*As if I could,*' I thought, casting a glance over to my grandfather to see if the old man had picked up on my complaint. Andres showed no sign of having 'heard'.

The dins of training had slipped by in a rush, even though each clic of the intense physical activity had seemed to last forever. Running, stretching, weights, martial arts, small arms practice – we'd done it all, over and over again. I had to admit that I felt better than I had in my life, and when I caught a glimpse of myself in a still pool of water I barely recognized the buff young man who stared back. But pounding clay?

Truth was, I had already decided that the mental activities that my grandfather practiced alone with just me were infinitely more important than these jock exercises. Sure, they'd gotten me in shape and given me some degree of confidence, but with one well-channeled thought I could do as much as with a dozen chops, kicks and punches. And all these workouts were taking valuable time from the mental preparation. How would I ever be ready to assume a leadership position if I spent so much time pounding a wall of clay?

I'd been debating for dins whether to ask my grandfather if I could forego some of the physical training for more of the one-on-one, but I hadn't mustered the nerve. Now, with my sixteenth name-din celebration just dins away, I'd decided that I'd pose the question then. After all, wasn't I supposed to come into my full powers when I turned 16? Surely Andres would see the logic in my argument.

I went back to pounding my bare fist into the clay hillside, perhaps with just a little more motivation than before. Three more din. Just three more din.

*****

I knew the routine by heart: first I relaxed and found my focus by playing around with the metal jack, spinning it, making it jump, and then stopping it as if frozen in time. Then I moved on to a series of electrical circuits that I opened and closed with just my thoughts. Finally, I moved to a small cage in the back of the underground bunker. There sat two small Terran primates, Shingdu, eating their foul-smelling fruit and looking less than thrilled. I still hadn't mastered this element of my training yet, but I was getting better.

"Do not try to make them do it; convince them that they *want* to do it," Andres counseled as I sat in a wooden chair just centimeters from the cage and stared with undisguised determination at the two Shingdu.

I'd heard it all before, but I'd learned that it was easier said than done. To make the jack move, or open and close circuits, was child's play compared with convincing living, breathing creatures with their own set of priorities.

"Open your mind to theirs. Invite them in," I heard my grandfather say softly. "You are a friend, you are a brother."

'That's me, another caged animal,' I thought, quickly blanking my thoughts to try to block my grandfather from eavesdropping. But despite my momentary irritation, I did as Andres instructed. I pictured a door opening in my mind, an entrance to a place of light, a jungle place strewn with the tropical fruit the Shingdu craved. I could sense their curiosity, 'hear' the unintelligible chatter of their thoughts as they tried to decipher the virtual world that awaited them. But, as usual, that was as far as it went. They were right there, they saw, or felt the opening, but I could not persuade them to step through. Just as I was about to give up in frustration, I 'heard' the voice of my grandfather from inside my head, a calming, reassuring sound that made me feel more confident, more relaxed.

'You are picturing the door in **your** *mind,'* the voice said. *'Picture it in* **theirs.***'*

Picture it in their mind? How could I do that? I'd have to imagine I was one of them, see the world through their eyes.

The thought was so impossible that I was momentarily baffled, my head spinning as if caught in some kind of psychic whirlpool.

'*Don't try so hard!*' the insistent voice of my grandfather intruded into my brain, bringing the whirling mindscape to a gentle halt. '*Relax. Open yourself to their energy. Let it wash over you.*'

I had no idea how to do what Andres requested, but unthinkingly I reached out to the breathing exercises Xerish had taught us to find inner tranquility, and found myself repeating the rhythmic breathing and thought escape that I'd learned just a few cycles ago. As I repeated my lesson over and over again, my conscious thought began drifting away, becoming as indistinct as a distant landscape in the morning mists. And then it happened.

As if a switch had been thrown, I suddenly heard a simple but crystal clear discussion. '*Is it real food?*' '*It looks real.*' '*I cannot smell it, can you?*' '*I cannot.*' '*I am hungry.*' '*As am I.*'

It was the two Shingdu! I didn't know how I knew it was them, but I knew. It was more than just the dialogue. I could *feel* the racing of their hearts, I could smell all sorts of powerful scents I had never really noticed before. I could hear a fan whirl in a computer all the way across the room!

Before I could pose my next question, Andres' voice was in my mind once more. '*Join the conversation. Tell them to push the red button in their cage for some of that food.*'

Join the conversation! How was I supposed to do *that*?!

'*Think the words. Go on now!*'

I didn't have time to question, so I did as I was told.

'*Push the red button to get the food,*' I thought, feeling like a fool. '*Push the button!*'

I watched as the larger of the two Shingdu stared at me with an attentive look that – maybe, possibly – suggested some sort of consciousness, or understanding, a look that sent tinglings of expectation through my body. Tinglings that exploded to lightning bolts when the animal suddenly scampered across the cage and did exactly what he'd been told! A red light illuminated as the animal pushed the button with his paw.

"Now give them some fruit," the older man said, this time aloud. "Positive reinforcement will make it easier next time."

I was so elated I couldn't remember where the fruit was located until my grandfather pulled open the door to the cabinet and reminded me. As I opened the cage to hand the two Shingdu their reward, I 'heard' them once again: *'Food!' 'The red light makes food!' 'Push the button again!'*

And they did. Again. And again. Laughing so hard I thought I might be losing my mind, I handed them piece after piece of the sweet red melon and watched with delight as they feasted on their prize.

"They did it!" I called out to Andres. "They pushed the button!"

"*You* did it," my grandfather said with a proud smile. "They had no reason on Terra to push that button until you told them to."

"They didn't, did they?" I said with wonder in my voice.

Andres put his arm around my shoulders. "You're making excellent progress. Let's call it a din for now."

"Now? When I'm just starting to get the hang of it?!"

"In three Terran din, on your name-din, we will try the next step in your training. Until then, you will practice what you have learned up til now."

"But…"

Andres held up his hand. "We must build a strong foundation if we expect to go ever higher. Practice if you want. Rest if you're able."

Rest! My heart was beating almost as quickly as the Shingdu! How did my grandfather think I could possibly rest? Or did he?

"Show me," Andres said, his voice suddenly low and firm. "Show me you can calm yourself. Show me that you control your emotions."

I shook my head. Another test. Would he never stop?

Despite my disappointment, I responded immediately. I went into the trance state as I'd been taught and sought out a visualization of my beating heart muscle. In moments I had it in my mind's eye, and then, slowly, beat by beat, I 'saw' the muscles slow until they were beating even slower than normal.

"Don't play with such things," my concentration was interrupted by my grandfather's stern words. "If you accidently stop it one din, I may not be around to restart it."

I sighed. In an instant I released the muscle from my control, allowing it to return to its autonomous state. I could feel my pulse return to normal.

"I know this is repetitive," Andres explained, having sensed my frustration. "But it is necessary. Believe me. When you come up against the High Priest, you will need every bit of this training."

'*And maybe even more,*' the old man thought, but he kept his thoughts to himself.

The very idea of meeting the Council's High Priest in one-on-one combat sent a chill through my body. How could I ever hope to match Antavar's power? The High Priest was a direct descendent of Rathma, after all, and had grown up flexing his inherited talent. I'd only just discovered my abilities in the past few cycles. It seemed hopeless.

Andres felt my despair and wasted no time diverting my thoughts elsewhere.

"But you are coming along extremely well!" he said. "With your coming name-din your abilities will multiply geometrically. There will be no one in the Terran Federation whose talents will even come close to yours!"

I knew my grandfather was subtly working to lift my spirits. In a way, it made me feel better, knowing that not even he could hide his true intentions from me. Maybe I would grow into my role, after all.

*****

The first time I noticed it was during a run the morning before my name-din. As always, the five of us were out early, running along the seaside, enjoying the cool morning breeze and the stirring ocean views. But this time was not like all the others.

Andres always led our training group, always pushed us to get as much from the run as humanly possible. But on this din we had barely run four kilometers when he turned back to us, his face a bright red we'd never seen before, and gestured to me.

"Your turn. This old man needs a blow. You take the lead."

I saw the others look to each other, doubt and concern clearly visible in their eyes. But I had learned to do as my grandfather asked, without hesitation or second-guessing, and this din would be no different.

"You okay?" I whispered as I jogged past him.

"I'm old," Andres joked with a broad grin. "I'm as okay as I can be."

I nodded at the explanation, even as I sensed something wasn't quite right. I tried to pick up more from the connection I felt, but it was useless. If it was anyone but Andres, I'd swear the old man had thrown up barriers to stop me from sensing his true feelings. Barriers or not, I did as I was told and continued on, glancing back once to see Andres slow his pace to little more than a fast walk.

By the time the group got back to where the mules had been tied, Andres was nowhere to be seen.

"Should I go back to see if he's okay?" a visibly upset Vera asked before she'd even caught her breath.

"Give him a moment," I said as I looked back down the beach path.

"He didn't look so good," Tiber added after a while.

"The old man's tough," Jans cut in. "Probably just something he ate."

"I don't know," Vera countered. "Maybe, but he looked...tired, to me."

As I stared back along the path, I unconsciously reached out toward my grandfather, searching for an energy signature that I had come to know better and better with each passing din. Driven by my growing concern, I focused intently using the same techniques I'd been practicing with the Shingdu. After a few moments I thought I might have identified the signature, but I wasn't certain. My concern grew as the clics slipped by.

'Do you need help?' I finally asked aloud in my thoughts when Andres still didn't appear.

'You don't need to yell!' a strident response exploded in my mind.

I cringed from the intensity of the message bouncing around my brain. Then a look of utter disbelief came over my face. It took a few moments to realize what I'd just experienced: I'd communicated with my grandfather telepathically!

"Are you okay?" Vera asked, having seen my change of expression.

"I am!" I answered. "And so is my grandfather." To her unspoken question, I added, "I can sense it."

"You can sense what?" Tiber asked.

"He can sense when a tired old man is about to finally show up so you can get back to the hut!" Andres called out as he finally came into view around a curve in the path.

'Better not explain just yet,' his voice appeared in my mind. *'Some things are best kept to ourselves – at least for now.'*

But Vera wasn't going to let it go quite so easily. "How did you know he was coming?" she asked me, her eyes narrowed from confusion – or was it suspicion? Her voice pulled me back from a sort of daze I'd felt since Andres had communicated with me.

"I don't know," I answered truthfully. "I just had a feeling."

"Cool," Tiber said.

I didn't want to answer any more questions and so led the way as all of us hurried back down the path to welcome Andres and to check to make sure that my 'sense' was correct. To all outward indications, it was.

I stood off to one side as the others fussed over my grandfather. I caught Andres' eye as the old man tried to calm all the commotion.

'I'll explain when we get back,' the now-familiar telepathic voice instructed. *'Just be patient.'*

Patient. That was a word I was getting pretty darn sick of.

*****

Once Vera and the others had been convinced that Andres' troubles were not serious and just temporary, we'd made the ride back to the hut in silence. I kept waiting for more unspoken messages from my grandfather, but for the moment he kept to himself. I couldn't be sure, but I had a feeling that Vera was still trying to figure out how I'd known Andres wasn't in any sort of trouble. Tiber was probably thinking about what we'd have for dinner. Jans was scanning the landscape for any sign of trouble.

I'd gotten to know each of them quite well over the past cycles, though I suspected that they hadn't revealed all of their inner secrets, any more than I had. Still, it was really nice having some folks around to share that strange life with, but even with their constant companionship I had to admit I was feeling a bit lonely and missed Amanda, and Jafar, and especially my Mom. Sometimes when I slept I'd dream about one, or all of them, and in those moments I felt a warm sensation of *family* that made me want to just keep sleeping. When I'd eventually wake up I couldn't avoid feeling a letdown, an emptiness that even all the training, and all the interaction, and even having Andres there with me, couldn't completely overcome.

Lulled by the gentle rocking motion of the mule, I found myself dindreaming about Amanda, and what she might be doing right at that moment. I glanced up into the blue Terran sky to try to catch a glimpse of the distant moon, but Phoebos hadn't risen above the horizon.

'Not for another stunde,' Andres suddenly reappeared in my mind. 'We've still got some light left before you'll be able to see it.'

I blushed to realize that my grandfather must have sensed my loneliness and my longing.

'It's natural to miss your friends and Morgan. I miss her too.'

For the first time, I could not only *hear* my grandfather's words, but *feel* his pain! It was a strange, intimate sensation that caused me a bit of initial discomfort, as if I were intruding on a private moment. But then I realized that Andres could have almost certainly blocked me from sensing those feelings if he'd wanted to, and the awareness turned to a warm feeling of trust and sharing.

'How do you manage?' I thought. 'How do you stop missing them?'

'You don't,' came the gentle reply. 'You learn how to go on with your life, to do what you have to do. But you never forget.'

I was about to ask more when suddenly I felt rather than saw my grandfather react to something up ahead. Before I could ask the cause of his concern, two levitors appeared from beyond a small grass-covered dune just meters in front of us! It didn't take more than an instant to realize that they were Security Force personnel and we were in big trouble.

'Let me do the talking!' Andres directed even as he raised his hand to signal all of us to stop.

"Stay right where you are!" one of the cops ordered over a hand diffuser. "Keep your hands where we can see them!"

"Just coming back from a din at the beach!" Andres shouted back to them.

I watched as the lead officer said something to his partner. The partner nodded and my hand drifted to the phaser hidden in my belt as the first officer got down off his levitor and walked slowly toward us.

"Let me see some ID!" he ordered while still several meters away from the five of us.

"I've got your back," Jans whispered. "Just relax and do what they say."

My hands trembled as I struggled to pull my identification from my saddlebag. The officer moved straight down the line of mules, looking first at the ID and then at the person holding it. He seemed to give only passing notice to Andres and Vera, before stopping for a longer inspection of Tiber and his PI card. By the time he got to me, I was struggling to control my breathing.

The SF patrolman looked at my card and then up at my face. I tried to act as if I had no problems in the world, but the officer's stare seemed to burn straight into my psyche. At first I thought I was just being overly anxious, but then something seemed to click inside my mind, as if a hatch door slid open. As I looked into the officer's eyes I saw the man's pupils contract, at the same time I felt a jolt of…something rush through my body.

'He knows!'

'He does NOT know!' my grandfather's voice echoed powerfully inside my head. *'Stay calm. Tell him: It's not the guy you're looking for. He looks a little like him, but it's not him. It's not him.'*

I struggled to clear my mind of the fear that the officer's look had provoked, and gradually I brought my thoughts back under control.

'That's it,' my grandfather coached soothingly. *'Now tell him!'*

I focused all my mental energy on one thought, and one thought alone: *'It isn't him. It isn't the guy you're looking for. He looks a little like him, but it's not him. IT'S NOT HIM!'*

The breath caught in my throat as the Security guard flinched from the impact of my thought barrage.

'Don't try to overpower him!' Andres hissed. *'Softly. Subtly. It's not* **your** *idea, it's* **his**.*'

I forced myself to smile as I looked into the officer's eyes. But it wasn't until I saw the pupils relax that I could take a full breath.

The man shook his head, as if convincing himself that he'd been wrong, and went on down the line to check Jans. It was less than a clic later when he returned to the front of the group and spoke to Andres.

"Have you seen anyone else out here? Young people? Maybe about the same age as your three?"

Andres looked back over his shoulder with a look of utter naivety. "I don't think so. Have any of you seen anyone else this din?" he called back to the others.

"Nope!"

"No one."

"Not me."

The answers came so fast and so unconvincingly that I was certain the SF guards would know we were lying. But they didn't.

"If you do – see anyone, you'll contact your local SF headquarters – right?" the lead patrolman said.

It was an order, not a question. All five heads bobbed in agreement.

"You'll be the first to know," Andres finally said aloud.

"Good."

He went back to his levitor, spoke briefly with his partner, and the two of them were off and away without another word. As the two personal transports rose into the air and disappeared behind the dunes, I felt as if I might vomit.

"Well done," my grandfather said quietly.

"They were looking for us, weren't they?" Tiber asked, his voice tense.

"You don't know that," Andres said, but it was clear to me that he didn't believe what he was saying.

"They were looking for me," I said in a resigned whisper. This time Andres did not challenge the statement.

"But he looked right at you," Vera began, "and I think he had your ID image on his DigiScreen."

I shrugged, but before I could speak my grandfather cut me off.

"Whatever the reason, we were lucky. Very lucky."

'Keep the rest between us,' he said telepathically to me.

"I don't like it," Jans spoke up, sounding just like the experienced bodyguard he was. "This wasn't just a random search. They know we're in the area. And they know him. We've got to make some changes."

"This isn't the time to discuss that!" Andres barked, and all four of us stiffened to hear his hard, commanding tone. "We'll talk it over back at the hut." The last he spoke in a decidedly less aggressive voice.

Jans recognized the request with a curt nod.

"Come on. Let's get back home before those guys change their minds," Andres continued, kneeing his mule into a trot.

'Change their minds?' I thought as I goaded my animal to follow.

What would we do then?

*****

Even when we'd unsaddled the mules and collapsed on the familiar overstuffed chairs and sofa in the hut, I realized that my life had changed irrevocably. In that one moment back on the trail, what had seemed like a great adventure had suddenly been transformed into a deadly threat – to me and my friends. As Tiber and Vera chatted about our close call, I found myself thinking seriously about leaving the hut and my companions, to keep them safe while I traveled the path to my birthright. I debated whether I should tell my grandfather, knowing that I might never reach my full potential without his guidance, yet at the same time feeling tremendous guilt that I had brought the full attention of the Council and the High Priest upon them. I was so deeply occupied with my thoughts that I didn't realize that Andres was watching me intently until I happened to glance up.

"Let's go downstairs," the older man said quietly when he'd caught my eye. "We've got some things to discuss."

I nodded and slipped away while my two young companions continued their discussion and Jans disappeared into a bathroom to rinse the sweat and sand from his tired body. I'd only been down in the hidden control center for a few brief moments before my grandfather appeared, closing the heavy security door behind him.

"You did very well this afternoon," the older man said as he stood in front of the chair where I sat, "but it's clear that the Council has made it a priority to locate you, and they're getting too close for comfort."

I tried to look into my grandfather's eyes, trying to get a feel whether he'd read my thoughts or whether he'd merely come to the same conclusion as I. Not surprisingly, I could get no sense of the man whatsoever.

"I was thinking the same thing," I admitted. "But it's me they're after, so I don't know that it's a good idea for any of you to continue risking your lives unnecessarily."

Andres smiled. "Spoken like a true leader," he said, "but one without the experience to understand all the variables. True, on your own you could discover many if not most of your inherited talents, but it might take you many times longer to master them and during that time you'd be extremely vulnerable. I've spent a lifetime hiding from these people. I could help."

I felt torn: on the one hand, my grandfather's bravado gave me badly needed confidence; on the other, I knew the threat my very presence created for all around me. I didn't know which way to turn.

"Are you familiar with the ancient writing titled *The Rebirth*?" Andres suddenly asked out of the blue. I blinked and shook my head.

"No, I don't think so."

Andres pulled up a chair and sat next to me, leaning forward until our faces nearly touched. "It's a prophesy, written before the exodus from Earth. It predicts the colonization of the Terran outposts, and the wars that would sweep across our system. But it also speaks of The One."

My eyes widened. "How could it?"

"We don't know. We don't even know who wrote it. But it has been extremely accurate in all its predictions, and I think it's the reason the Council is expending so much energy to find you."

"What do you mean?" my voice shook slightly.

"It tells of a time when the sky will be filled with light and The One will claim his rightful position as leader of the Terran system."

"What's that have to do with me?"

Andres took a deep breath and sighed. "Our scientists tell us that we can expect a super-nova in a nearby system sometime within the next few solar cycles – maybe even within this cycle. When the system's principal star explodes, for a brief moment our entire sector will be flooded with light."

"And you think that's what this prophesy if talking about?"

"I don't know. No one does. But I'm very sure that the High Priest and his Council have access to the same archives as we do, and their scientists certainly have warned about the nova. Rogen knows that you are on the verge of coming of age, and I'm guessing that he has decided that it's not worth taking a chance. They will spare no effort to find you and eliminate the threat to their dominance."

"Then I must go," I said, jumping up from my chair. "My presence here puts all of you in danger."

"Whoa, let's not get hasty," Andres said, putting a restraining hand on my shoulder. "Remember: only a calm mind makes a thoughtful decision. Let's think this through. We can be reasonably sure that they don't know you're here, though they think you're somewhere in the area. My principal concern is that their computers will match the digi-vid from the officers' levitors with the digi-stills they have of you. That entire confrontation back on the trail is already in their databanks somewhere. It's just a question of if, or when, a review program matches your facial profile with their video. That could happen tomorrow or never. But we have to assume it will happen sooner rather than later. We can't take the chance on remaining here."

"So you agree I need to leave?" I tried to keep my voice steady, but my apprehension leaked through.

"*We* need to leave. All of us. Once they identify you, it's only a matter of time before they match the rest of us as well."

"Won't they be looking for the five of us traveling together?"

Andres nodded thoughtfully. "They will, yes. And that is why we'll be leaving separately. You and I will go off together, while the other three will have to find their own way."

I frowned. "How exactly do you intend to get Jans and Vera to let me out of their sight? They're like guard dogs."

That brought a smile to my grandfather's face. "Well put. And because of that, there's only one way for us to go – in secret."

"You're not going to tell them? They'll be fuming."

"I'm sure they will. But we all must make sacrifices for the good of the movement. That includes them. In this case, by drawing some of the SF resources in their direction, they'll actually be making you and me a little safer. I'll tell them that in the message I'll leave."

"When? I mean, when do we go?"

"Tonight. As soon as everyone is asleep, we will set out."

"Do you know where? Is there anywhere that's safe?"

Andres looked at me closely, and for the first time in cycles saw the frightened kid that hid behind the bravado and bluster. "I wish I could tell you that such a place exists, but I very much doubt it does. I do have a place in mind, however. We'll be as safe there as anywhere."

I waited for further elaboration, but when I realized none was coming, I spoke up.

"Are you going to tell me, where we're headed?"

"Better than that," Andres said, leaning forward until his forehead touched mine. "Relax. Clear your mind. Think of nothing but your existence."

I wanted to ask a thousand questions, but I felt the urgency in my grandfather's voice and so went along with the request without hesitation. As Xerish and Andres had taught me, I cleared my mind of all thoughts, sounds and images of the here and now, replacing them with a steely focus on a single sound and a single brilliant spot of light deep within my mind. I silently repeated the sound over and over again, trying to bring my mind's eye closer and closer to the brilliant light...

Suddenly I was jolted by a flash of light even brighter than my focal point, and a fleeting whisper as if a sea breeze had swept past me on a deserted beach.

"Okay, you can open your eyes now," I heard my grandfather say.

When I did I was shocked to see my grandfather standing half-way across the room.

"Now you know – where we are going and who we will meet. You may not think you know, but you do. If for any reason I'm unable to accompany you, all you have to do is bring yourself back to this place and this moment, and the route will reveal itself to you."

I felt slightly dazed, confused. "But, how...what...?"

"If I told you the information, an experienced SF interrogator could pry it from your consciousness, with or without your cooperation. This way, you might say the message is encrypted. No one, not even you, can access it without the key to the memory. It's hidden from your conscious mind, you might say."

I shook my head. What other fantastic knowledge would I learn in the coming cycles?

"Come. Let's go upstairs and go about our business as if nothing out of the ordinary was happening," Andres said as he went toward the door.

"But, what about the others?" I called after him. "They're in nearly as much danger as we are! We can't just leave them."

I sensed as well as saw Andres experience a surge of pride. "No, of course we can't. I'll send them to another safe house, and put them in contact with some people there who can help keep them safe. They may be even safer there than they were here with us."

It wasn't much satisfaction, but it was better than nothing. I nodded solemnly and followed my grandfather up the stairs.

*****

I thought I'd never be able to get to sleep, but when a hand shook my shoulder in the pitch blackness of the room I shared with Jans and my grandfather, I started awake with a gasp.

"It's okay," Andres' calm voice reassured. "It's time to go. Put this on."

I tried to shake the cobwebs from my head as Andres handed me a hooded cloak before he turned to throw his few belongings into a knapsack.

It took me a few moments before I finally focused on the cloak. It wasn't mine, but it seemed familiar…Was it Tiber's? I rolled over and threw off my covers, expecting to find Jans sitting up on his floor mat, watching my every move. So I was more than a little surprised when I instead heard his heavy breathing and watched his shoulders rise and fall in sleep.

"You didn't wake Jans?" I whispered.

'Practice communicating without talking,' my grandfather's reply sounded in my head. 'As for Jans, I decided that Vera and Tiber need him more than we do.' He went back to packing as if he'd just told me about the weather outside.

'He'll never forgive you!' I told him telepathically.

'Never is a long time. Now hurry, I can't keep him oblivious to all our banging around forever.'

Another trick of my ancestry. I wondered how many more I'd learn before all this was over. If it was ever over.

I packed my few things as quickly and quietly as I could, and in just a short while we stood at the back door to the hut, ready to start the next chapter in this incredible journey.

"Goodbye, friends," I said softly as I surveyed the simple interior one last time.

Andres patted me on the shoulder. *'The Great Creator willing, we will meet again,'* he *minded* me.

I certainly hoped so.

As we stepped outside I saw at once that the Great Creator had blessed our escape with a moonless night sky peppered with enough stars to help us see, but not so many as to make us easily visible by either SF patrols or their innumerable VidCams. *'Pull up your hood,'* Andres instructed me without a word. *'Any doubt works in our favor.'*

So that was why he'd given me Tiber's cloak. Any DigiStills or video would reveal the old man and a young friend traveling through the Argos night, a young man whose cloak would match with other, earlier shots taken of our older rebel companion. If the ruse only bought us a few stundes head start, it was better than nothing.

The saddling of the mules seemed both interminable and noisy, but finally we had the two animals outfitted and ready to go.

'No more conversation until we're well away from this sector,' Andres minded me. *'And if we run into anyone, let me do the talking.'*

I certainly had no argument with that, and so we set off that star-lit night on the next leg of a journey that would take me many kilometers from my only friends on Terra5, and ever deeper into a rebellion that could cost me, and countless others, their lives. It was a solemn moment, but if I were honest I'd have to admit a thrilling one as well. Perhaps it was my naïve youth; perhaps it was a natural protection mechanism. Whatever the reason, I breathed in the cool night air with a feeling of renewed hope and a determination to see the people of the Terran Federation safe, free and prosperous under a government that *they* chose, a government that cared about them as people, not just lost souls.

A meteorite streaked across the night sky – a sign, I thought, of better times to come.

CHAPTER 17

At almost that same moment a computer system somewhere inside the massive Security Forces building in Harran signaled its bleary-eyed operator that a facial match had been found to the unknown young man who everyone in the building, including even The Fist himself, wanted to lay their hands on. The operator sighed. This wasn't the first such match. In fact, over the past sept the computers had spit out six such 'matches', but each one had turned out to be a false alarm. "Pludy machines," he mumbled as he manipulated the data. Most of the populace thought the SF could perform magic tricks with all their DigiStills, VidCams and computers. He knew better. They were pretty good, he admitted, but nowhere near as good as the people had been led to believe.

He looked at the readout accompanying the piece of video that had been sent in from a routine patrol earlier that night. Of the nineteen facial characteristics the computer analyzed, this face had fourteen confirmed matches, five probables, and NO disqualifying hits! He enlarged the digitized still on his vidscreen and placed it side by side with the ID shot they were using as the control. It *did* look like the same person!

Normally he would have immediately contacted a superior to take a second look. But he'd heard The Fist let loose with a string of oaths when the last 'hit' had proven false. He did *not* want to be on the receiving end of anything like that dressing-down!

Instead, he called over another young analyst to take a look.

"What do you think?" he asked the woman, who'd worked there a full cycle longer than he had.

She eyed the video still closely and then reviewed the facial analysis. "Looks good to me," she finally said.

"Good enough that you want to call it in?"

Her eyes widened. "I'll leave that honor to you. You'll probably get a promotion."

"I'll probably get fired," he mumbled to her back as she quickly returned to her work station, but he did as she suggested. He had barely hung up his communicator when three supervisors arrived at his vidscreen, literally pushing him out of his chair to get a better look. As they debated whether the slightly blurred video image was indeed the kid that they'd been told to find, the buzz in the large room grew louder by the clic. The excited chatter was nearing a crescendo when suddenly it stopped – dead. The smile on the young operator's face disappeared in a heartbeat as he looked up and saw Ofran Belinger – The Fist himself – striding toward his workspace with the regional Commander scurrying along in his wake. Other operators who'd been crowding around his terminal fell back out of Belinger's path like stalks of grain before a combine.

"This had better be good," Belinger muttered as he flopped down into the chair that had been emptied for him. He glanced at the kid's ID shot, then at the video still, and then at the facial analysis.

"Where and when was this video taken?" he asked gruffly. The three supervisors turned immediately to the young operator.

"Last night, on a trail between Ayton Beach and the city," the operator squeaked, adding as an afterthought, "Sir."

"We don't have VidCams out there, do we?" The Fist asked, directing his question again toward the anxious supervisors. Once again they stared at the operator.

"No Sir, we don't," the young man answered.

"Then how did we get this video?" His patience was obviously running thin.

"Two SF officers intercepted the group and this is from their levitor cams."

"Group? Nobody mentioned a group," Belinger said, his attention piqued. "How many?" This time he asked the quaking operator directly.

"Five."

"Where are those two officers?!" Belinger suddenly shouted, jumping up from the chair. "Get them here – NOW!"

Orders were delivered, messengers sent running, and within just a few clics the two SF officers found themselves face to face with an angry Ofran Belinger.

"Did you screen a group of travelers coming back to the city from Ayton Beach last night?" he asked the two of them, his voice barely controlled.

"Yes, Sir," the more senior officer answered, his tone cautious.

"And did you follow standard procedures? Did you check their IDs and put eyes-on from close up?"

"Yes, sir!"

Belinger's eyes narrowed dangerously. "Then how in the Creator's good name could you fail to recognize this young man, who I'd given specific orders to apprehend and hold?!" The Fists' face was turning purple; veins bulged in his neck.

"I, uh…we, uh…" The lead officer turned to his junior partner. "How did you fail to recognize him?!"

The junior officer flinched noticeably. "It wasn't him, Sir. I mean, it looked a little like him, but it wasn't him."

The Fist's eyes narrowed further. 'Come over here," he directed the man. "Take a look at this image from your levitor, and this ID image that we circulated. Are you telling me these aren't the same man?"

The officer stared at first one, and then the other image. Then he blinked as if hit between the eyes with a brick.

"Well, now that you mention it, they do look very similar," he said softly.

"Similar!?" Belinger roared. "Are you an idiot, or are you blind!?"

"I have perfect vision!" the officer answered.

"Then how...?" The Fist stopped in mid-sentence. "Was there an older man, maybe 60 cycles or more, in the same group?"

"There was."

"Vrash!" he said, turning at once to the regional Commander, who'd been hovering by the door to the small office. "I want every person you've got available to review output from every VidCam on that side of the city. You're looking not only for the kid, but any of the five in this group. Go back two or three septs. Understand?!"

"Perfectly," Latson said as he snapped to attention. He passed the order to an aide, who passed the order to the base commander, who passed the order to the three supervisors, who in turn told their staff to "Find those five people!" Workers who were on leave or home asleep were called in. No one would sleep or rest easy until the five were found.

*****

It took them nearly a full stunde but they found the digi-vid they were looking for. A half dozen underlings surrounded the screen as Belinger reviewed the new material.

"It's them all right," The Fist finally announced as he switched from one VidCam view to another. "Looks like they're in the northern sector. Get every available officer out there, now! Have them go door to door if necessary. I want them found, THIS DIN!"

Latson virtually emptied the entire city of officers, sending all of them to the area where their VidCams had spotted the five rebels. Of course, only Belinger and Latson knew why they wanted the five so badly. All the rest only knew that they had to find them before Phoebos disappeared from the night sky, or else...

Everyone kept their distance from The Fist while he waited to hear from the officers in the field, even Latson. He invented some pressing responsibilities that required his attention outside the building in order to get as far away from Belinger as possible. The Fist, meanwhile, paced inside his office like a caged tiger just before meal time.

It was only three stundes later when the report came in to headquarters. They'd found a hut on the outskirts of the city where they believed the five were staying.

"Do NOT try to seize them," Belinger ordered Latson's Deputy, the highest ranking official still in the headquarters building. "Tell your people to watch them closely, especially the boy. Do NOT let him out of your sight once you get positive identification. But keep your distance. I don't want them to know we've found them – not just yet."

The orders were passed to the field officers, who had already closed off all streets leading to the neighborhood in which the hut was located. They set up listening, infrared, and close-up viewing devices, and waited.

Belinger commandeered the first transport he could find and rushed to the scene, where he immediately took control of the entire operation. He was taken directly to the ground commander.

"What do you have?" he asked eagerly before the SF officer even had time to salute.

"Multiple sightings over the past two to three septs. It seems nobody has actually met or spoken with them, but there's general agreement that there are five of them in there, including one woman and one older man."

"And the boy?"

"Our interviews suggest that there are *two* young men."

Belinger nodded. "Who does the hut belong to?"

The officer frowned. "It appears that the owner may have died some cycles ago."

Unexpectedly, The Fist took the news calmly. "No surprise there. How many heat signatures inside?"

"Our techs aren't entirely sure, but they think three."

Belinger actually smiled. Maybe the kid was one of them.

"Anyone go in or out since you got eyes-on?"

"No one."

"Any communication – in or out?"

"None."

Belinger kept his expression completely neutral, but inside he was elated. Finally he'd get the High Priest off his back! He could almost see the other Council members' faces when he dragged this rebel teen in front of them. Maybe now he'd get the praise he deserved. Or, more importantly, a salary increase or at least a new home.

Part of him wanted to wait, to see if they could uncover any links between these five and the rebel organization they knew existed in the area. But the rebels were weak, scarcely worth worrying about. And he knew full well that if he let the kid slip through his hands, Rogen would *not* be happy.

"Tell your people to move in," he ordered the local commander. "Quietly. We don't want them to know we're here until it's too late. And I want them alive! No one uses a weapon or they will answer to *me*!"

Belinger knew he was taking a risk. He knew all too well that if the older man in the group was Andres Leitstell, as he believed, the officers would be exposed to his dangerous mind games. But he was willing to bet that the old man wouldn't be able to manipulate all of them, especially since *he*'d be on his guard. Let the old fool try!

Communicators crackled as the SF force began to tighten its noose around the ramshackle hut. Belinger considered taking the point, but then thought better of it. Better to let someone else share the glory if they succeeded, and take the full blame if they failed. That strategy had gotten him where he was this din. No sense changing it.

In the dim early morning light he could barely make out the dozen or so heavily armored S&D robots that moved silently toward the hut, let alone the small army of SF officers that waited in the shadows for the robots to enter and secure the building. But he followed every move on the communicators and the computer screens in front of him. When the hut was completely encircled, Belinger grabbed the diffuser input and called out to the five rebels trapped in the rundown building:

"By order of the Holy Council of Harran, I order you to come out with your hands clearly visible! If not, we will be forced to come in after you."

The amplified words echoed in the stillness of the sparsely populated area. Several white seabirds flushed from the trees surrounding the hut, the sound of their flapping wings the only sounds to break the sudden stillness. The Fist waited several clics, until it was clear that the rebels were not going to respond.

"This is your last warning!" he announced once again over the diffusers.

This time he waited scarcely long enough for the reverberations of his words to disappear before signaling the local commander to send the robots in.

"Go get them," he said. "But NO WEAPON FIRE!"

A battering-bot moved into position at the faded and warped front door. The operator looked to his commander for final approval. He nodded. One plunge of the bot's hydraulic ram and the door splintered into a dozen pieces with a loud crash.

The commander was just about to send survey-bots into the building, when suddenly a small herd of goats – three, exactly – came running from the house, their eyes wide in sheer terror.

Belinger realized the significance of the animals before any of the others.

"VRASH IT ALL!" he shouted as he jumped up from his secure position. "Send those pludy survey-bots in there – NOW!"

The local commander nodded as if struck, and the operator responded instantaneously. Four of the small flying video platforms swept into the hut with barely a sound. Belinger's eyes stared ferociously at the computer screens in front of him as he watched the video from the flying bots in real time. As he'd suspected when he'd seen the goats, the hut was empty. He waited a few moments until the operator gave the "All Clear!" call, and then walked resolutely toward the hut.

"Commandant!" the local commander called after him in horror. "We still haven't swept the place for IEDs!"

Belinger heard the man, but he didn't stop. He'd been doing this for a long time now, and he had a gut feeling that the hut was as empty as it looked on the monitor. Besides, if he was right he was as good as dead anyway. The rebels had penned the goats inside the house to give the IR readings that they'd misinterpreted as human. '*By now, they might be half way to Terra 3,*' he thought with a clenched jaw.

Sure enough, a thorough search revealed recently-abandoned living quarters, and a subterranean control center with every piece of remaining equipment smashed beyond repair.

"Looks like they were here until quite recently," the local commander suggested as if to prove to The Fist that he was not as incompetent as the rest of his force.

The Fist was not impressed. "I can see that," he hissed. "What I want to know is where they are *now*!?"

"We will find them!" the commander said, saluting before he literally ran from the hut.

Belinger sighed. Hearing it from that fool probably sounded a lot to his ears like his guarantees sounded to the High Priest. He could feel the clics and stundes passing as the rebels moved further and further away from where he now stood, while he moved closer and closer to his fate at the hands of Rogen, a fate he did not want to contemplate.

CHAPTER 18

The dense green foliage that surrounded us seemed at times a single sentient being, determined to slow our progress and drain every bit of strength from our dripping wet bodies. I'd grown up on Phoebos and so was accustomed to climate-controlled environments, not the mind-numbing temperature and 90 per cent humidity found in the jungles of Argos. The air was so thick I could hardly breathe.

"How much further?" I asked my grandfather, unable to ignore my discomfort a moment longer.

"Not much," he said tersely.

I watched him rock side to side in rhythm with his mule, and wondered how someone of his age could tolerate such an inhuman climate. It was several clics, however, before I realized that the back of his shirt was dry, with no sweat stain like the one that extended along my spine from my neck to my hips.

"I thought you were going to explain how you do that," I said aloud, my mind so muddled from the heat that I could no longer censor my thoughts.

"Do what?" he asked. I was about to explain when I saw his knowing smile. "Oh, do you mean the heat?" he continued, the smile firmly set. "How do I seem to ignore the heat?"

I nodded weakly. "Yeh, the pludy heat."

He pulled up his mule and motioned for me to come up next to him.

"It's a question of control," he explained softly. "I know that it's hot, but I refuse to let it affect me."

"How?"

"It's easier for me to demonstrate. Close your eyes. Go ahead, close them," he insisted when I hesitated. "Now, think of a clear spring din. Warm, but not hot."

I did as he said, the sweat dripping down my nose as well as my back.

"Now, let yourself feel the din, feel the warm light on your skin. A gentle breeze ruffles your hair."

At first I could only feel the heat and humidity that engulfed us as I listened to the shrill cries of strange animals and insects in the green canopy above. But then I slowly began to actualize my vision, to make it my reality. It's hard to explain, but I just ignored the heat and instead concentrated on the imagined starlight and gentle breeze as Andres had suggested. Slowly, ever so gradually, I began to cool down.

"Better?" he asked moments later.

"Yeh. A little."

"Keep at it. When you've mastered the technique you'll be able to keep the thought of your alternate reality in place even as you go about your normal din. For now, just recreate it every time you feel the heat and moisture overpowering you."

"Why don't I just think of a colder scene? Wouldn't it be faster?"

"Actually, no. Our minds can bridge the gulf between reality and a similar imagined alternative better and faster than if the two images are too disparate. *Cognitive dissonance* is what they used to call it long ago on Earth."

"Cool."

"Literally. Are you ready to continue?"

I quickly took stock. To my amazement, I felt impossibly revived. "Yeh, sure. Thanks."

"My pleasure. By the way, there will be more, much more, if we get the time."

As he turned and urged his mule forward, his words echoed in my mind: *'If we get the time.'*

*****

By the time we reached our final destination, the principal star was high overhead and I should have been drenched with sweat, but I wasn't. Even in the relatively brief time between Andres' lesson and our arrival, I'd managed to refine my control over my body temperature considerably. I still couldn't hold the cooling mental image indefinitely, but far longer than the first time. Somehow that neat little trick gave me immense pleasure and a sense of optimism for our future far beyond its actual difficulty or utility. If I could do *that*, why couldn't I do much more?

My optimism was sorely tested, however, when we came upon a clearing in the dense jungle occupied by a thatched roof hut that made our previous shelter look like a mansion.

"Well, here we are," Andres said as he stopped his mule at a tie-post by the front steps – or what was left of them.

No sooner did the words leave his mouth than an old dark-skinned local woman stepped out of the front door carrying what appeared to be an antique gunpowder-propelled projectile weapon! She wore a colorful local skirt with a matching bandana tied around her graying hair. It was clear from her expansive girth that food was not a problem, even at such a remote, isolated location.

"This ain't no hotel!" she yelled sourly, the weapon held loosely at hip level but pointed in our general direction.

"And you aren't much of a hostess!" Andres shouted back. I cringed and braced for a quick escape if the old lady took offense at his brash words.

"Andres? Is that you?" she said after an interminable moment of indecision. She squinted mightily to see through ancient eye glasses.

"Who else would come all the way out here to see you?" he answered, climbing down off his mule.

To my surprise, and relief, the woman put the weapon down on the rickety porch and hurried with more speed than I would've thought possible down the crumbling stairs, to be met halfway by my grandfather. I watched in stunned silence as they embraced and held each other tightly.

"Andres, my sweet little boy," the woman said through tears of joy.

"Mama Jaydu, it's so good to see you again."

I felt uncomfortable, almost like an uninvited guest, as I sat atop my fidgeting mule and watched the whole scene unfold. What in the world was going on?!

Finally, Andres stepped away from the woman and turned back to me.

"Vers, come over here and meet Mama Jaydu."

I did as I was told, tying my mule to the same post he had.

"Mama Jaydu," he introduced, "this is Vers Leitsell – my grandson." He said the last with such emphasis that I understood immediately that this woman didn't know of my existence, or at least hadn't heard much about me for a very long time.

"My word," she said softly, and peering through the thick old glasses she walked to where I stood open-mouthed and pinched my cheeks with her fingers!

"You sure he's yours?" she asked my grandfather lightly. "Too good-lookin' to be related to an ugly ol' cuss like you!"

I blushed, but my grandfather burst into loud, unrestrained laughter. It was the most utterly uncontrolled reaction I'd ever heard from him and I think my face must've shown my surprise.

"Don't worry, Vers, she won't bite," he said after catching his breath. "At least I hope not."

The woman took her cue. "Not unless you're as stubborn and ornery as your grandpa was!" she said with glowing pride in her eyes.

By this time my head was swimming. Obviously this Mama Jaydu had known my grandfather when he was young, but how? Why? Andres smiled and answered as if he'd heard my questions, as well he might have.

"Mama Jaydu was my mother's housekeeper," he said proudly. "'Nanny' they used to call the position. She helped raise your father as well."

My father?! I'd never met anyone who'd known my father when he was young. Suddenly our escape into the jungle took on a whole new dimension.

"You knew my father?" I asked in awe.

"Knew him? I jus' about raised him!" the woman said with a laugh. "Andres and Lenore were always running off here and there, so your father spent a lot of time here with me."

I glanced over at my grandfather, who nodded – a bit sadly I thought.

"Wish we could've spent more time here on Argos, but it wasn't to be."

"And now a third generation of Leitsells. My, my – how quickly time passes," Jaydu said wistfully.

"Speaking of which, we've got some things we've got to get done, right away," Andres said. "Everything still operational?"

Jaydu frowned. "I don't mess with all your equipment. You know that." She sounded defensive, almost hurt.

He ignored her. "We'll see. For now, though, any chance you can whip us up something to eat? We've been traveling all night."

Her smile returned. "I think I *might* be able to find something. You two just keep out of my way and I'll see what I can come up with."

At that, Andres and I went into the hut and through the small but tidy sitting room into one of two rear bedrooms. "I imagine we'll be staying in here," he announced as he dropped a knapsack on one of two small beds. "But we can work that out later. Now, I need to get the word out that the Council is searching for us and we're on the move."

He moved to a beat-up bureau, pulled out a middle drawer and reached inside to push or pull an unseen switch. I heard a clunk come from inside a small closet to my left.

"Come on. You need to get familiar with this," Andres said as he led the way toward the closet.

I followed, not knowing exactly what to expect. But I was hardly surprised when he opened the closet door to reveal a stairway leading down to a room hidden beneath the hut. I could see the floor of the closet hanging on hinges as a hatch to the stairway, a square of floorboards festooned with shoes and slippers nailed to the wood.

"It's not as elaborate as the other place, but it serves the purpose," my grandfather explained as he flipped a light switch and headed down.

That was an understatement. The tiny control room wasn't much larger than the bathroom in the other shack. It was packed full with a small desk, two chairs, and a bench overloaded with electronic equipment.

As soon as he reached the bench he threw a switch and an assortment of colorful LEDs sprang to life.

"Thank goodness," he mumbled as he sat in front of a VidCam and focused a small key light on his face.

In few words he described what had happened in the past 24 stundes, reassured everyone that we were safe (without giving any hint as to where we might be), and then repeated three or four sentences that seemed utterly incongruous to me at the time.

"Code," he explained as soon as the VidCam and light were turned off. "Although the messaging is already encrypted and sent in micro-bursts on frequencies that vary according to a predetermined pattern, we take no chances with strategic information."

"When will *I* learn those codes?" I asked, half-hoping I wouldn't need to.

"As soon as your birth-din has passed and you master a few more control techniques, you will be *entrusted* with these codes, and others. Many people's lives depend on maintaining the integrity of this information. Not just here on Terra5, but throughout the system."

His voice was so solemn, so serious, I felt my gut turn flip flops.

"You know I'll do the best I can," I said, the only thing I could think of in response to his declaration.

He took a deep breath. "I know you will, Vers. I know you will. It's hard sometimes for an old man like me to remember what it was like to be your age. So if I come on a little strong every now and then, just remind me you're not even 16 yet."

"You're not so old."

He smiled kind of sadly and messed my hair. "Thanks for that, but I'm getting older by the clic. Come on. Let's see what Jaydu's whipped up for us."

As he walked past where I was sitting to head up the stairs, I looked closely at his worn and care-lined face. You know, he *did* look older than I'd remembered! His hair even seemed a little grayer. I wondered if it were just the power of persuasion or if I hadn't been paying attention. In any case, I decided right then and there that I'd redouble my efforts and take as much responsibility off his shoulders as I could. He deserved better than a life running from dilapidated old hut to even more dilapidated old hut, babysitting his grandson while the whole system waited for us to lead them to independence from the Council. The sooner I could assume some of his leadership responsibilities, the better.

*****

Of course, saying that I'd take over some of his duties was a lot easier than doing it. After two cycles during which we never even left the hut, I was more than ready to resume my outdoors training. I would have been ready to get started again even sooner, but he reminded me that half the Council's agents were probably still looking for us and so discretion was the better part of valor. Cool saying. I decided to steal it for use when I'm The One. If that time ever comes.

Finally, on the third din, I awoke ready to get to work. To my surprise, Andres hadn't awakened me at star-rise, instead allowing me to loll around in bed until the principal star was half way through its morning arc.

"What's going on?" I said, probably sounding as offended as I felt. I thought he was taking it easy on me because of our troubles with the SF. I was wrong.

"Your time has come," he said softly, and for a moment I had no idea what he was talking about. But then he smiled and added, "You only turn sixteen once."

I had completely forgotten that it was my birth-din. I assumed that I'd feel something special as I assumed the *talents* that came with my bloodlines, or that there'd be some kind of big ceremony, like I'd witnessed at the rebel base. But there was nothing special and I felt just the same as I had the din before. I was confused.

"I thought…" I began to explain, but Andres cut me off.

"That you'd suddenly feel like some demi-god with the world at your feet?" he said, only half in jest.

I laughed in spite of myself. "Something like that."

"Sorry to disappoint. Your abilities are still just potential, until we make them something more."

"When do we start?"

Now it was his turn to laugh. "Let's get some food in your stomach before we do anything else. Then, we'll see just how enthusiastic you are when you don't have your buddies around to absorb half of my irrational demands."

Just the mention of our three companions made me wish that they were still with us, and reminded me that I hadn't heard a word about them since the din of our escape.

"They're fine," Andres said, not even waiting for me to vocalize my concern. "Got a message this morning that they're all moved-in at the new place and continuing with their training. They asked about you."

"Tell them I miss them and look forward to the time we can all be together once again."

He nodded. "I already did. Of course, the sooner you learn everything I can teach you about your powers and how you can use them, the sooner that reunion will take place."

"I don't need any additional motivation," I said. "I'm all ready to go right now."

"You two aren't going anywhere until you've had breakfast," Mama Jaydu said as she carried a steaming plate of scrambled chicken eggs, pig bacon and fruit to the kitchen table.

"I think I can be persuaded to wait a little longer," I said, pulling out a chair.

"I bet you can," she teased.

I had no inkling how much I'd dindream about that breakfast over the next few septs. It was to be my last *normal* meal for quite a while. If my training back in Veejy was intense, this was triple-intense – both physically and mentally. Looking back, I suppose Andres was getting anxious to transfer as much of his knowledge and know-how as possible as quickly as he could. I assumed at the time that he was nervous about the SF forces looking for us. Now I realize that that was only part of the reason.

Whatever the cause, we upped our daily training regimen to six stundes per din physical activity – including much more concentrated personal defense training, and 4 stundes per din mental exercises. Except for one meal each din, my nourishment (I can't bring myself to call it food) consisted of a disgusting combination of dried sea plants, ground seeds and nuts, and a health drink that tasted like old socks smell. The only positive thing I can say from those septs is that my body rapidly transformed from a thin, modestly athletic frame to solid, rangy, and surprisingly muscular. As grandfather often said, 'there's nothing free in this life.'

At first I was so excited and determined to achieve every goal Andres set that the workouts actually energized me. I couldn't wait to get up each morning while Phoebos still lit up the night sky, and begin exercising: running, cutting trees, moving boulders, you name it – if it built strength or endurance, I did it. I say *I* because Andres became more and more of a spectator as the septs rolled by. He still ran beside me on our increasingly long and challenging morning jogs, but more often than not he'd drop off after just a kilometer or two and rejoin me on the return leg. He demonstrated many of the self-defense moves, but I was left to practice on a mountain of a local man that Andres had brought in for just that purpose. It would have been difficult enough if the guy were just a dozen centimeters taller and ten kilos heavier than me. But no, he'd also been the Argos heavyweight mixed martial arts champion for several cycles running – until he'd landed on the wrong side of the Council on a fight-fixing scandal (he'd refused to take a dive). Now he worked as a laborer at night and helped train me during the din.

Every night, immediately after what I sarcastically referred to as ART (appetite reduction training), otherwise known as dinner, my grandfather would take me down into the claustrophobic confines of the underground control room to practice the mental aspects of my 'gifts.' On the plus side, as soon as I turned 16 I suddenly found a whole new level of power and diversity in the skills at my disposal. Each and every din Andres demonstrated some new technique or talent, and every din I found that I not only grasped the new information, but often exceeded Andres' expectations within just a few stundes.

Maybe it was the incessant workload, maybe the lack of contact with anybody even close to my own age, but as the septs crawled by I began to lose some of my earlier fervor. Don't get me wrong, I'd come to love and respect my grandfather, and Mama Jaydu was the grandmother I'd never had. But there were things, many things, that I just didn't feel comfortable sharing with either of them. They tried, but the age gap was just too great. As time went on I caught little knowing looks pass between the two of them whenever I answered glumly or dragged my feet coming or going to another session. I knew my attitude stank, but what could I do about it?

I debated every alternative I could think of and had rejected every possibility except one. I'd just about screwed up enough courage to ask Andres if we could visit with Tiber and Vera, or have them come visit us, when my whole world turned upside down.

It was just another din, another in the seemingly endless progression of workouts and training. Nomar, my sparring partner, was busy tossing me around like a ragdoll as he usually did. (Perhaps I'm being a little too humble. Actually, by that time I'd learned to put up a pretty good defense, at least for a short while.) Of course, I didn't use any of my 'talents' on him – at least none that he could recognize as such. But, in any case, on that morning I was certainly getting a workout at his hands. If I remember correctly he had me in a reverse shoulder lock and I was trying – without much luck – to break free, when suddenly I heard a voice I'd thought I'd never hear again!

"Man, if that's the best you can do I can see why they brought me in to help out with your training."

Jafar! For just an instant I thought I was dreaming, so often had I thought about seeing my old friend once again. But when I saw that smile and the teasing twinkle in his eye, I knew he was really standing right there in front of me. I don't know exactly what happened, or what I did, but the next thing I knew Nomar was lying on his back on the ground and I was crushing Jafar in a bear hug.

"Take it easy, take it easy!" he gasped as I accidentally hugged the breath right out of him. "Man, what have you been eating? You're like, Ultra-Man!"

"How did you get here? How long can you stay?" I was throwing questions at him so fast he didn't even have time to answer.

"Woa, slow down!" he said, his breathing nearly returned to normal. "We can talk about all that later. I thought you might want to say hi to another old friend first."

My look must have matched my confused mind, for he smiled and cocked his head toward the path behind him. I glanced back just as a familiar form stepped shyly from behind my grandfather a few meters down the pathway, a faint dirt scar carved out of the thick Argos jungle. Amanda!

I don't know if she ran to me or I ran to her, but the next thing I knew she was in my arms and we were kissing as if we might never kiss again.

"Hey, let her up for air!" Jafar yelled after several long moments.

I stepped back just far enough to look into her eyes.

"I can't believe you're here!" I said, shaking my head. I held her by her shoulders as if afraid she'd disappear. Perhaps I *was* afraid.

"It wasn't the same back there without you," she said softly.

I felt light-headed, like I was falling into those limpid pools of violet. My knees felt so weak I almost stumbled.

"I'm…I'm training…" I mumbled like a drunken fool.

"I think we can curtail your work-out – for the rest of the din," Andres announced loudly. "What do you think Nomar?"

"I think he's much stronger than he knows," the martial arts champion answered, rubbing his right arm. "No man has ever thrown me down like that."

It wasn't until that moment that I really realized what I'd done. I felt both elated and embarrassed in equal parts. "I'm sorry, Nomar! I don't know what happened."

"I know what happened: you saw your friends standing there and I was in your way. I wouldn't want to be the next person who stands in your way."

"Are you okay?"

"He's fine!" my grandfather intervened. "Although we may need to get you some extra padding from now on." He glanced over at Nomar and winked.

"I wouldn't say no to that offer. I want to still be in one piece when we throw Antavar and his gang of thugs out into the street."

"We'll do the best we can to keep you that way until then," Andres said. "But for now, what do you say we all go back to the hut and get some lunch. I'm starving!"

We all agreed, and as soon as we'd picked up Nomar's equipment we were on our way back through the jungle, Andres and Nomar leading the way with the three of us *kids* bringing up the rear.

"I can't believe we're actually here!" Amanda said as we walked hand in hand. "It's like a dream."

"If it is, then don't wake me up," I said, eliciting a groan from Jafar. I felt my face turn red.

"Don't listen to him," she said, coming to my rescue. "He's jealous."

"Of this big glook?" Jafar shot back. "You've got to be kidding me."

Amanda took a playful swipe at him, which he ducked easily. "He does look bigger, doesn't he?" she asked rhetorically. "What have you been doing – aside from fighting huge Argonians that look like they could break valluvium bars with their bare hands?"

"Just some exercises my grandfather came up with," I said, hoping to sound humble when I really didn't want to get into it too deeply.

"Maybe he should be doing them too," Jafar answered, his voice dropped low so that Andres couldn't hear.

"What do you mean?"

"Well, I mean he looks like crap. He looks *a lot* older than however old he was in that photo you used to show us."

"That photo was five solar cycles old."

"He still looks bad."

I tried to rationalize his observation, but I had to admit that I didn't think Andres was looking too great either. I turned to Amanda, hoping she'd set us both right.

"What do you think?"

She glanced up at me out of the corners of her eyes, and before she even spoke I knew what she was going to say.

"He doesn't look real healthy."

I didn't know what to say. So I didn't say anything. Amanda and Jafar picked up the conversational slack, and I mainly just acted as if I were listening as we made our way back to the hut. But my mind wasn't in it. All I could think of was, what if he is sick? What could we do? We couldn't take him to any public hospital in the system. The Council would be all over him in a stunde or less. Even if the medical personnel at one of the bases could help him, I doubted that their best would be state of the art. Could I just keep making believe that nothing was wrong, until…?

CHAPTER 19

The Fist felt his heart pounding as he walked into the Council chamber, his eyes kept respectfully lowered. He could almost feel the waves of anger roiling off the High Priest.

"So, you have returned from Argos. Did you bring me the boy?" Antavar's voice was unnaturally calm. Belinger knew he was in big trouble.

"We traced him and the others to a shack on the outskirts of Veejy…"

"Did you bring me the boy?" Now the voice was cold, steely cold.

"I…I brought one of his key contacts."

Belinger saw one of the High Priest's eyebrows arch ever so slightly. He'd surprised him. He didn't know about the guide.

"Oh? And what did this conctact tell us?"

The Fist took a deep breath. "We used all the usual methods on him, but he refuses to tell us anything more than that he led them from the other side of the mountains to Veejy."

"That's all?"

Belinger felt his chest tighten. "I was hoping…I mean, I thought you might…"

"Help him remember? Where is he?"

Belinger took out a communicator and spoke briefly to someone outside the room. In just a few clics two SF thugs dragged a bruised and bloodied Aden into the room, his limp body sagging between them.

"Is he still alive?" the High Priest asked skeptically.

"Of course, the Light willing," Belinger answered quickly. He saw a slight sneer cross the Priest's lips and he wondered if he'd gone too far.

"He'd better be. Bring him over here." The two guards did as they were told and dropped the battered rebel onto the floor at the foot of Rogen's throne.

"Step away," Antavar growled. The guards jumped back as if burned.

"What is his name?" the High Priest asked.

"Aden. Aden Laskus. We think he joined the rebels…"

"I didn't ask for his life history!" Antavar screamed, and Belinger flinched.

Then he and his two guards watched, spellbound, as the High Priest closed his eyes and lifted one hand to point at the motionless body lying on the floor. Suddenly, as if high voltage electricity were running through his body, Aden began to twitch, his arms and legs moving spasmodically of their own accord. Then, to the horror of all three spectators, the body rose to its feet, a jerky, fitful move that spoke of overwhelming power. The rebel guide hung in mid-air, his arms and legs splayed outward as if he were a dangling from a string.

Suddenly, the man's eyes flew open.

"What is your name?" the High Priest asked in a calm, even voice.

The rebel's mouth moved awkwardly, no words coming forth. Then, as if requiring an enormous effort, a raspy pained whisper answered, "Aden…Laskus."

"Aden, did you lead a group of rebels through the mountains to Veejy about 3 or 4 septs ago? About five of them, one an old man and another a teenage boy."

The man's body shook, whether from an effort to resist answering or from the pain of the interrogation, Belinger didn't know.

"Yes," the answer finally came.

"Good. That's good, Aden. When you answer correctly, I can make the pain go away. Would you like that, Aden?"

The puppet rebel nodded eagerly. Immediately the jerking movement of his muscles stopped and he hung motionless in the air before the Priest's throne chair. A relieved groan issued from deep inside his chest.

"Is that better? Good. Now, where did you take the five rebels?" Antavar's voice was smooth as silk, consoling, even friendly.

But the rebel was not yet broken. Belinger watched with grudging admiration as the guide tried once more to resist. Small tremors swelled to waves of muscle contractions.

"I need an answer!" Antavar bellowed, and a violent spasm shook Aden's body.

"A shack," the answer came, weak and hesitant.

"On the outskirts of Veejy, isn't that right, Aden?"

The rebel's head nodded feebly.

"Where are they now, Aden? Where are the five people you took to that shack now?" The High Priest was not able to hide the urgency and desire from his voice. Anyone who looked could see the intensity of Antavar's need in his eyes.

"I…don't know…" Aden barely managed to answer.

"You *do* know!" the High priest roared. "And you will tell me – NOW!"

The rebel's body snapped to rigid attention, the muscles in his neck straining against the forces that were ripping him apart from within.

"TELL ME!"

Belinger saw the man's mouth working soundlessly, spittle dribbling down his chin. His eyes seemed to bulge from his head. Blue-green veins pulsed in his temples.

Suddenly, as if a proton beam had struck a watermelon, the man's head exploded in a shower of blood and bone. His body slumped to the floor, all strings cut.

Even Belinger glanced away for a moment, acid rising into his throat.

"This is all you have to offer to me?" the High Priest asked, his tone once again low and threatening. "He was useless!"

"He might have been able to tell us something, if you'd let him talk a while longer!" the Fist answered reflexively, and at once he knew he'd overstepped his boundaries.

The High Priest didn't shout or rage against his security chief. Instead, a small, almost imperceptible smile crept over his lips. A smile that made Belinger quake in his place.

"I wouldn't have needed to have him talk if I had the boy, would I?" he asked placidly. "If you'd done your job."

"We're getting closer, Your Grace. It's just a matter of stundes now." He tried to keep the fear from his voice, but he knew he'd been only partly successful. Rogen knew. He always knew.

Antavar seemed to consider his Fist's words, nodding thoughtfully. But then he looked down at Belinger, and the security chief knew his time had come.

"Unfortunately, those are stundes that you no longer have available," he said, and then closed his eyes as if resting.

For just a clic The Fist thought he might get another chance, might live to see another din. But then a pain like a thousand lightning bolts swept through his body from head to toe and the very breath in his lungs seemed to roar into flame.

The two guards standing just meters away saw their Commandant stiffen, cry out in an inhuman, nerve-flaying cry, and fly backwards across the room as if shot by a mass accelerator. By the time they turned to see what had become of him, all that remained was a pile of smoldering ash, wisps of smoke rising languidly into the tense chamber atmosphere.

"Get that cleaned up," the High Priest ordered abruptly.

When they hesitated, to see if he'd ask for anything else, he stared at them with a black fury that turned their guts to jelly. "Go!" he yelled, and they literally ran from the room.

The High Priest took a deep breath and stood up from his throne chair. He would have to do this thing himself, he realized. The boy must die. Now.

CHAPTER 20

The next din dawned with a morning light that seemed brighter and more hopeful to me than it had for septs. Maybe longer. Just seeing my old friends had lifted my spirits more than I can say. When we'd arrived back at the hut we'd spent literally stundes talking about Phoebos, and our mutual friends, and how Jafar and Amanda ended up there on Argos in our little hut in the middle of the jungle. Turns out their world had been shaken nearly as badly as mine by the explosion all those many cycles ago back home. With my disappearance, SF forces had swarmed all over the area, picking up even the smallest bits and pieces of wreckage from the blast site and interviewing everyone who ever knew me.

They made it clear from the very first that their investigation had the blessing of the High Priest himself, and made it equally clear that any perceived lack of cooperation would be seen as treason – and punished accordingly. Initial interviews had been more or less friendly, or at least not overtly hostile. Well-dressed young SF reps had come to our school and interviewed both Jafar and Amanda (and more than two dozen other kids as well) in an empty classroom. The questions had been general at first, becoming increasingly pointed and more focused as time went on. All my friends were eager to help the SF find the people who'd killed my mother and her new husband, and – they assumed – me as well, but as the interviews continued and the kind face of the Council evolved into the hostile, paranoid sneer they had all heard whispered about but never witnessed in person, they came to realize that they would never be free of suspicion and would never get their old lives back. Amanda's father was sacked from his prestigious position at the Mines. Jafar's dad was passed over for a promotion that had been promised him, and let know that his early retirement would be accepted readily. It took less than a cycle before they knew they had to leave Phoebos. But to where?

Jafar's family had relatives on Terra3, and so they decided to pack up and move there. They didn't know if their reputation would follow them, but T3 had a reputation of its own as the kind of place that Terrans from other parts of the system who'd had problems could find a new start. 'A bit of the old Wild West of Earth' was how they described it. Amanda's folks decided to stick it out on Phoebos. Somar Velding was convinced that all the fuss over Amanda's *friendship* with Leitstell would soon blow over, at which time he'd rely on the vast network of friends and associates he'd developed over the many cycles he'd spent in the mining biz to get him back to the level of management he knew he deserved. His wife was less than sanguine about his plans, but as a good Terran wife she went along with them without public disagreement (after several intense nights of private discussion.)

Since both Jafar and Amanda had celebrated their sixteenth birth-dins, each of them was – in theory, at least – an adult, capable of making their own decisions. Not that their families saw it that way, of course. But the two of them spent a lot of time together in the wake of the bombing, both to commiserate and to discuss alternatives to the dismal futures they both saw facing them if they stayed on Phoebos. Jafar had no interest in moving to Terra3. He didn't like his cousins who lived there, and he was utterly convinced that even the Wild West wouldn't be big enough for him to escape his ties to me. Amanda was a mess. As she described it, "With you gone, I didn't really have a reason to get up in the morning."

And so, when Winder Ebram showed up one din, both Jafar and Amanda were open to hearing his tale of what had befallen my mom, me, and the broad brushstrokes of what we hoped to accomplish under the guidance of my grandfather.

"I thought the guy was off his rocker," Jafar explained, "but I hoped he wasn't."

Amanda had smiled shyly when retelling her part of the tale. "I wasn't surprised. I always knew you were special."

The hardest part had been leaving without saying goodbye to their parents. They each left a note saying they'd decided to try their luck on Terra2, the Terran planet most like 5 in nearly every respect but with less strict Council oversight. They doubted that the SF would believe the explanation, but it might set them off looking in that direction and so buy some time. Amanda still worried that her disappearance so soon after Vers' death would make the SF even more suspicious of her link to him than they already were, but she had every confidence that her dad could take care of himself and her mom. Or at least she told herself he could. Jafar was equally sure that his family would make a go of it on T3 no matter what the SF thought of him.

"I was already public enemy number one in their eyes," he embellished without a smile, "or maybe number two. In either case, I doubted they'd think more or less of me for taking off."

And so they left. Ebram managed to sneak them aboard a freighter transport headed for Terra2, with a quick, unscheduled stop-off on 5, where they were met by some of McAllister's people. The rebels took them by mule to Argos, and then local members of the rebellion took them to a meeting place where Andres had personally met them and led them to the hut. As I watched them tell their tale, I thought I saw a dazed, dislocated look in their eyes. Or was I just imaging it? I needed to know.

"So, are you glad you came?" I asked when they'd finished. I'm not sure, but I think I was holding my breath.

"*I* certainly am," Jafar blurted without hesitation. "I couldn't take much more harassment from those SF glooks, and I sure as heck wasn't going to 3 to live with my crazy relatives."

I looked over to Amanda. She looked me straight in the eye, no wavering. "I would've come sooner, if I'd know where you'd gone."

I exhaled. "You have no idea how glad I am to hear that," I admitted. "5 isn't such a bad place, and I really like being able to spend so much time with my grandfather, but…" I hesitated, unsure of my own feelings.

"But he's an old guy and you need some young blood to keep you goin'!" Jafar completed my sentence, his cock-sure smile bringing an even bigger smile to my face.

"Yeh, something like that. Only thing is, you've gotta understand that the Council is out to get me. They've got SF all over the place trying to find us."

"We know," Amanda said. "Andres already told us all about it."

"We're in it for the duration," Jafar added.

For the first time in ages I felt almost normal. Maybe this whole crazy rebellion thing would work out after all. If they didn't find us first.

*****

Septs passed in the depths of the jungle and my lessons continued and increased both in number and intensity. The physical tests weren't so bad. But the Kin-zah mind control was something else completely.

At first it was just more telekinesis – lifting things, moving them, basic techniques that were little more than refinements of that very first spinning jack trick. Then it got much more complicated. Andres spent nearly two complete septs teaching me the Kin-zah methods he'd used on the SF patrol out in the mountains when we first came to Veejy. As it turned out, I had a talent for that facet of the gift, but even so it turned out to be extremely complex. Each person has his or her own thought patterns, preconceived notions, a unique way of looking at the world. To influence that perception, I needed to find a way into the inner core of their beliefs, past all the external stimuli and rote training that were like the outer layers of an onion. Perhaps a maze is a better example. Every mind has a way into the innermost reaches of the inner self, but every mind is different. I needed to find how to get through each maze and make the changes I wanted, all without being detected. Just when I got that skill more or less under control, Andres took me to a whole new level: he showed me a brute force method that was more or less an overpowering of one – or more – minds at the same time. It took tremendous concentration and was utterly exhausting. But after dins of frustration, splitting headaches and a whole host of near-misses, I finally mastered it. Of course, I only had a handful of people to practice on: my grandfather, Jafar, Amanda, Nomar and Mama Jaydu. So my final exam, if that's what you call it, required me to use the brute force technique on them. Of course, only Andres knew exactly what I was up to. Otherwise, it wouldn't be a real test.

So when both he and I were somewhat confident that I could pull it off (he more than me, I must admit), Andres gave me an envelope with instructions inside. I had no idea what he was going to ask me to do – I'd been forbidden to tap into his thoughts without his expressed permission, so I was a bit nervous as I tore open the sealed document and read the terse directive: 'I want you to make Amanda, Jafar, Nomar and Mama Jaydu dance the Kritska of their own volition. They MUST decide to do this themselves, with no compulsion by you or anyone else. Good luck.'

The Kritska is a Terran traditional dance that celebrates the landing of the first Earth party on Terra 5 all those many cycles ago. It is normally danced by school children, and involves holding hands and dancing in a circle while singing an inane tune about the Great Creator and His Blessed Argia. I took one look at the instructions and nearly burst out laughing. Amanda *might* be amenable to performing the dance, just for the fun of it, but Nomar and Mama Jaydu? Let alone Jafar! No, this was not going to be easy. Not easy at all. I glanced up at my grandfather, who watched my reactions with a small satisfied smile of his own.

"Questions?" he asked.

I shook my head. "You never make it easy, do you?" His smile widened.

To give me *some* chance of success Andres had gathered all four of my test subjects in the hut. Mama Jaydu was in the kitchen, while Amanda and Jafar were practicing defensive moves under the watchful eye of Nomar out in the main room. So that they couldn't see me, I took a position just outside the rear hut door.

As I had been instructed, I took a deep breath and repeated my sita-ra until I could feel my heartbeat slow and my mind focus on the task at hand. I pictured each of the four dancing the Kritska in the main room, *heard* the music that moved them, and tried to imagine every detail possible about each of them: from the clothes they wore, to the expressions on their faces, to the very thoughts that ran through their minds. And then, when all of that was flooding through my psyche in a controlled torrent, I *channeled* all that mental energy from my mind to theirs. I can't really explain how I do it. I didn't really *force* them to dance; I just let them *feel* like it was something they wanted to do. I'd learned the basic techniques by repeating my grandfather's lessons over and over. A sixth sense, I think it was once called. Then, as if watching through *their* eyes – each in turn – I *saw* them come together in the main room, take each other's hands, and begin to dance as if listening to some hidden diffuser. Faster and faster they twirled round and round, laughing and singing as if they were having the best time ever. To be real honest, I was a bit jealous of all the fun they were having.

I could hear their singing and dancing through the thin walls of the hut, but sitting there completely alone I felt anything but happy and satisfied. Truth is, I found myself feeling depressed by everything that separated me from them, and always would. Suddenly, as if he'd heard my thoughts, Andres appeared by my side.

"Well done! Why don't you go inside and join them?" he asked.

"But if I stop projecting their reality…" I began, but he held up one hand to cut me off.

"I'll keep them going. At least long enough for you to take a spin. Go!"

I did as he suggested, and the dancers allowed me to join them without a word of protest or question. I felt the least bit guilty knowing that I had manipulated them, but only a bit. I could see the joy on their faces and hear the delight in their song. I joined my voice to theirs and the five of us danced with wild abandon for another few clics, until gradually, as if air were leaking from a balloon, we slowed, and slowed, and then stopped.

"That was a blast!" Jafar shouted as the Kritska finished, leaving only sweating, panting dancers in its wake.

"I haven't done that in…forever!" Mama Jaydu added.

"I've *never* done it," Nomar said, and from the look on his face, he – and gradually the others – realized that what they'd just experienced was anything but normal.

"Strange," Amanda said. "I can't explain for the life of me why I wanted to do that."

"Neither can I," Jafar agreed. With just a moment of hesitation, he turned towards me. "Is this *your* doing?" he asked, his eyes pinched in confusion.

"Guilty as charged," I said, unable to hide the pride I felt.

"*We* were your exam?" Amanda asked.

"Wouldn't have been fair to let you know ahead of time."

"Not fair, or not as much fun?" Jafar pressed.

"Both. It *was* fun, wasn't it?"

"Next time you need to take a final exam, count me in," Mama Jaydu said before disappearing back into her kitchen.

"Very impressive," Nomar said, and I could tell from the way he looked at me that our relationship had changed, probably forever.

Amanda looked as if she were going to grill me further, so I did the prudent thing and started for the door. "Let me go see how Andres is doing," I excused myself. I didn't want to answer any more questions, and I had a few of my own that only my grandfather could answer.

Beside I wanted to hear my grandfather's evaluation of my *performance*. I thought I'd done pretty well, but I knew how tough he could be and was ready for some constructive criticism. What I wasn't ready for was to find Andres lying on the ground, his face pale, his eyes barely open.

"Grandfather, what it is?!" I called out as I ran to his side.

He tried to smile, but his lips fell back in a lopsided impersonation of a grin.

"Guess I overdid it a bit," he whispered.

"Can you get up?"

"I think so – with a little help."

I took his arm and gently helped pull him to his feet. He leaned against my arm, unsteady and tentative. His breathing was ragged as he struggled to fill his lungs.

"Let's just keep this between the two of us, okay?" he said as soon as he recovered enough to speak.

"We need to get you some help – there must be one of our doctors nearby…"

He cut me off. "I'll be all right. There's nothing a doctor can do except tell me to take it easier. And we can't risk the SF following him here. You're not ready to face them yet."

I didn't doubt for a moment that he was right, but that wasn't my principal concern. If he were really sick, our entire movement might be at risk. Besides, he was my *grandfather*.

"I'm feeling better now," he said, pulling away from my support. "Just stay close by in case I need a little help navigating those stairs."

What could I say? I walked close behind him as he made his way ever so slowly to the rickety hut steps and then, one-by-one, up to the peeling blue door. At the top of the stairs he rested, his eyes shut as he labored to catch his breath.

"See? Not a big deal. No mention of this, right?"

I nodded, even as every instinct told me that it *was* a big deal. However, I'd given my word, and so as we stepped into our ramshackle home I did my best to clear the concern from my face as I followed him inside.

CHAPTER 21

The High Priest was in one of his moods; his wife could see that at a glance. Octana had lived with the man for over 20 cycles — there was nothing about him she didn't know. He was more than angry, perhaps even a tiny bit unnerved. She didn't need all her experience to grasp the reason, either.

"So you removed Belinger?" she asked, her voice revealing nothing of her inner thoughts.

"He failed the Council. He failed me. He failed the Great Creator." She heard the defensiveness in his voice. He tried to disguise his feelings, but she could always see through every attempt to mask his true self.

"You know this will create problems on T2," she said, knowing full-well that he already knew the likely reaction on Terra2 to the death of the planet's most renowned citizen and its sole representative on the Seven. She did it to gauge the extent of his lingering anger. If he were still incensed by the killing, she'd need to take the appropriate steps to keep him from any interaction with the rest of the Six Sisters, as she sarcastically called his fellow Council members. Or Five, with Belinger now just a pile of disassembled molecules.

"I am well aware of the reaction we can expect on T2," he answered, his voice now calmer, in control. "I've already sent instructions to our people to spread the rumor that Belinger was killed while coming to the aid of good Terrans under attack from rebel scum. We might as well get some benefit from the useless glook's death."

Octana smiled. Good. That was more like the Rogen she'd come to know over all those cycles. Maybe he wasn't the easiest person to live with. Maybe his temper got the better of him on too many occasions. But he was good-looking enough, and not bad in bed. Besides, the perks that came with being the wife of the High Priest were substantial. Of course, it wasn't as if all the benefits of their union fell on her side of the ledger. Not at all. In fact, both of them knew that their marriage had been more a negotiated merger of two powerful families than a love match: his roots were there on T5, and hers on T3, the next-largest and most prosperous planet in the Terran system. Her family was one of the Five – the wealthy, powerful clique that ran the everydin workings of the planet – under the watchful eye of the Council, of course. They brought money, prestige and military might to the relationship, and received prerogatives, trade preferences, and the occasional blind eye from the powers-that-be on T3 in return. The Moral Code was perhaps the regulation most honored in the breach, as Five members regularly drank fermented beverages, engaged in public demonstrations of affection, and generally ignored many of the most restrictive of the Code's demands.

With so many half-brothers and cousins scattered all over the system, the High Priest needed a strong support mechanism on each of the Terran planets to vouchsafe his legitimacy. Too many descendants of Arod could make a claim to his throne if he wavered. With the fool they call The One once again coming forth from the shadows – where he'd apparently spent the many cycles since the rebels last made a big public splash – Octana knew all too well that her husband would be looking for ever more public and grandiose gestures of fealty. Without the support of the equivalent of the Five on each of the planets, the Council would be little more than a religious dictatorship, a small group of unelected officials kept in power by brute force alone. In the short term that might suffice. But over many cycles, it took financial and interpersonal relationships at the top to grant legitimacy.

Rogen knew that. As did the families. They played a delicate little game of charades in which no one publicly admitted their mutual need, but every one of them knew its import full well. Octana was the link between the Council and the Families, not only on T3, but on all the six other planets as well. She and Rogen had done quite well for themselves with that arrangement, both politically and financially. They had more money than she could count in hidden off-planet bank accounts, and luxurious homes purchased in the names of family members throughout the galaxy. Octana wasn't sure Rogen could even conceive of a time when they would not wield the power that came with the Crown of Arod. She, on the other hand, had been taught from her youngest dins how to protect her family – personal and extended. No matter what the political climate, no matter what unexpected event might shake their society to its foundations, they would survive. And prosper.

CHAPTER 22

Despite my worries about Andres, my training continued without so much as a pause; I could feel my heritage growing stronger inside me with every passing din. Andres, on the other hand, seemed to grow weaker with each passing din, despite his best efforts to disguise the fact. My attempts at broaching the subject were always met with a quick dismissal. After a while I began to think maybe I *was* worrying too much, so I let the matter lie for a while.

Even more amazing than the power of my new talents was their diversity. Telepathy, telekinetics, shielding – physical and mental, force projection: after a while I began to wonder if there was any limit to the abilities my ancestors had passed down to me.

"Don't get too cocky," my grandfather would warn me. "You're still a human being. Still vulnerable. You can be injured, even killed. Don't let your powers become a weakness by relying on them too much. Your greatest asset is still that grayish lump of gelatinous cells between your ears. Use that, and you won't need the others so much."

I took his advice to heart, and practiced my tactics and various methodologies twice as hard as my inherited talents, which didn't leave much time for anything else. I could sense a growing feeling of disquiet, or maybe it was frustration, coming from both Amanda and Jafar. Both had given up there previous din-to-din lives in order to support me and the cause, but they got precious little in return. I tried to spend as much time as I could with either or both of them, but there simply weren't enough stundes in the din. They volunteered to learn some defensive skills from Nomar, but for the most part we studied, and practiced, separately. When I complained to Andres that I was feeling a bit isolated, he replied, "It's necessary. It's better for you, and the rebellion, if the Council and their minions think of you as a superman. The more they know about your strengths, and weaknesses, the worse it will be for us."

I tried to explain that to Amanda, and she acted as though she understood, but I couldn't help but feel that she was disappointed by how little time we spent alone, just the two of us. So I was startled – and more than a little pleased – when one din about three septs after they'd arrived, Andres suggested that Amanda and I take a din off and go to the shore to 'relax.' He didn't have to ask twice.

Nomar was tasked by Andres with keeping Jafar occupied and content, which he achieved by offering to teach him several new defensive moves. I did feel a little guilty. Normally I would have asked him to come along too, but somehow the friendship I shared with him was becoming increasingly overshadowed by what I felt for Amanda. There's that old earth saying about separation making emotions grow stronger; with Amanda and I, being so close and yet so far apart made the two of us eager for time separate from the others – and the rebellion.

It was a warm sunny morning, just after breakfast, when we set out on our mules. We'd packed a lunch, more a mini-feast prepared by a chuckling, winking Mama Jaydu, and in just a few clics the hut disappeared in the thick foliage behind us and we were on our own. Or as on our own as I was likely to get. Although no one specifically told me that I was prohibited from going off without a body guard, my newfound talents allowed me to sense the presence of someone close by keeping an eye on us. In fact, I could tell at once that it was Jans, returned from who-knew-where to resume his old post. I suppose I could have protested, or even used my talent to confuse or disorient him, but I didn't. He stayed out of sight and I made believe he wasn't there.

We didn't talk much as we rode, but instead soaked in the greenery and the sounds of the jungle that surrounded us. By the time we got to the shore, the morning haze had burned off completely and we were greeted by clear blue skies and sparkling turquoise water. We found a small patch of shade beneath one of the palm-like trees that lined the shoreline, and spread a blanket for an old-fashioned beach picnic.

"So, what do you think?" I asked as we lay there under the swaying fronds, a gentle breeze keeping the jungle heat under control. "Better than back on old Phoebos?"

I saw a look of concealment, or perhaps it was pain, pass over her eyes for just a second.

"It's...beautiful," she said, but the hesitation in her voice confirmed my suspicion.

"But?"

"Well, I know it's silly, but I kind of miss that old space rock. The way we had to go everywhere by transport, the small communities... It wasn't so bad."

"I dream about it sometimes," I said before I even realized I was speaking. "Usually my Mom is there. Sometimes even my Dad."

Amanda reached over and touched my arm. "It's hard, isn't it?"

I swallowed. For just an instant I thought about lying. Thought about assuming the *persona of the leader* as my grandfather called it. But one look into her worried eyes changed my mind. "Sometimes, yeh. I try to keep as busy as possible so I don't have time to think about it," I said. "But late at night, when I'm lying there trying to fall asleep, that's when I think about them. Remember trips we took. Vacations. Sometimes even just din-to-din life."

"Do you think you'll ever go back there?"

I had to think for a moment. I hadn't really looked that far into the future for a long time. I suppose because I was afraid to jinx myself. But now that I did, I knew the answer almost immediately. "If I can, I will," I said. "I'd like to see some of the old places, and visit with old friends. And maybe stop by my parent's burial crypt." On Phoebos, because of all the rock, people who died weren't buried underground like on the Terran planets. They were 'laid to rest' in tiny drawer-like crypts, each with a 3-d hologram of how they looked in life mounted on the front of the drawer. It was kind of creepy, actually, but I suppose it was the best they could do given the circumstances.

I don't know if it was the food or the sun, but I must have dazed-off for a moment, because I was startled to hear Amanda's voice so near.

"I can only imagine," she said, "how it must be for you. It's not fair."

I smiled. "If the universe were fair, I don't think Rogen Antavar would be High Priest, and the Council would definitely not rule the system."

"It'll be a whole lot better when you're the leader, won't it?" Her voice straddled the gap between hopefulness and doubt.

"I hope so," I said as honestly as I could. Truth be told, I wasn't sure myself how much better things would be if our revolt were successful. Andres had made me read a ton of histories about people who thought they were going to make the world a better place and ended up just substituting one terrible regime for another. 'The best plans oft-times go awry' some philosopher or writer said back on Earth a long time ago. There's no doubt he – or she – was right.

Amanda didn't seem to have any such qualms. "I know it will," she whispered, leaning in so close to me that I could feel the warmth of her breath on my cheek. "I have no doubt."

I turned to answer, to say something befitting such faith, but when I saw the look in her eyes I forgot everything I'd thought to say. My breath caught in my throat. As her eyes closed I felt my heart pound in my chest.

I leaned forward, hoping against hope that I hadn't misread the signs. I paused for just a moment, whether to gather my own courage or give her a chance to back out, I'm not sure which. But when she didn't move, didn't open her eyes, I knew it was now or never. I was just about to close the gap between us when she tired of waiting and kissed me gently, her lips soft and warm. We had kissed before, of course, back on Phoebos, but somehow that moment was different. That kiss spoke of much more than just youthful play.

When we finally parted I felt as if I were floating.

At first neither of us spoke a word. Then, she smiled.

"It's been too long."

"I hope it'll never be that long again," I said, and I meant it.

Her smile changed. How, I can't describe, but the word enigmatic seems to fit. She suddenly grabbed my hand and jumped up.

"Come on. Let's find a more private place." She jerked her head in the direction I knew Jans stood guard. Until that moment I had no idea that Amanda even knew he was there.

"You knew?"

"I may not have special powers, but I know when someone is riding a mule just a few hundred meters behind me. I take it he's one of *your* people."

No one had ever referred to any of the rebels in that way, and I felt a rush of exhilaration as I realized that some of them, at least, already saw me as their leader. Or one of their leaders. I couldn't imagine doing what needed to be done without my grandfather.

"He is," I answered.

"Well friend or not, there's only so much I'm willing to share." She began to pull me toward the denser undergrowth.

I don't know what came over me, but I stopped dead in my tracks. "Are you sure?" I asked. I think my voice may have quaked.

Her smile was so bright I could almost feel the heat. "I've had a long time to decide," she said. "Now, are you coming, or not?"

I surrendered peacefully.

CHAPTER 23

Sometime later, I'm not really sure how long, we were laying there wrapped in each other's arms, the sounds of the waves in the distance and animals and insects chirping all around us, when from not far off we both heard footsteps, approaching quickly. By the time I broke out of my enamored daze, the steps were a scant few dozen meters away. I chastised myself for not having kept my mental guard at full alert, until moments later I became aware that it was only Jans and relaxed a bit. Amanda, on the other hand, sat bolt upright holding her clothes to her chest.

"It's only Jans," I said.

"Why is he running?"

Good question. I tried to probe his mind, but his thoughts were so scrambled that I wasn't able to sift through them for an answer before he was already nearly on top of us.

"Vers!" he called out from a respectful distance. "May I approach?"

I could tell from his voice that there was an urgency to his request. "Sure. Come."

Amanda looked at me with questioning eyes.

"Sorry to interrupt," he said when he finally appeared through the dense green undergrowth, addressing his apology more to Amanda than me. "It's Andres. They need you back at the hut. Now."

I felt a stab of fear rush through my guts. "We'll be right with you," I said jumping up at once, utterly mindless of the fact that I wasn't wearing a stitch of clothes. Jans turned away without comment and waited with his back turned while Amanda and I got dressed.

As we hurried back to the mules, Jans explained that he'd received a communication from Mama Jaydu that Andres had collapsed. He was still alive, but not doing well. Not well at all.

We drove those mules as fast as we dared, bouncing on their backs like sacks of potatoes. By the time the shack came into view, all three of us were shaken to our cores and exhausted from trying to keep our balance on the constantly shifting animals. That didn't stop me from jumping down almost before my animal came to a complete stop and running into the shack.

As soon as I stepped through the door I saw the fear and desperation on Jaydu's face.

"He's in there," she said, pointing to the room we shared. "Please, help him!"

I took a deep breath to steady myself and opened the door to our room. The image I saw is still engrained in my mind: my grandfather, paler than I'd ever seen him, stretched out on his tiny cot, his eyes closed, his breathing shallow and labored.

"Andres…Grandfather," I whispered from his bedside, "it's me, Vers."

His eyes fluttered open. "Vers. Sorry to interrupt your picnic…" He began to cough and I saw for the first time how utterly frail and feeble he'd become. Even though I'd noticed for some time that he hadn't been his normal self, why hadn't I seen this deterioration?

"Grandfather, what is it? What's happening?" I could only imagine that the High Priest or one of his flunkies had somehow gotten to him and caused this sudden collapse.

"It's nothing," Andres said softly, waving his hand as if to swat a buzzing fly. "Just the natural order of things."

"What do you mean, nothing?!" I said, my voice louder and more strident than I'd intended. "What can I do for you?"

He smiled. Despite his weakness and pain, he smiled at me. "You're a good boy," he said, "but not even you can stop the ravages of Time. This is one battle none of us can win."

I didn't want to hear that. In fact, I refused. I didn't know what was wrong with him, and had no idea what I should do, but I was determined to do something. So I did as I'd learned: I put myself into a Kin-zah trance, and probed his mind.

"No, no use," he mumbled weakly, but he had neither the strength nor the resolve to stop me. In an instant I was pulled into the maelstrom of thoughts, demands and unseen communications that filled his mind. I was stunned. Until that moment I'd had no idea that a human being could possibly handle such a storm of mental activity. I gasped and took a step back, the impact as if someone had punched me in the middle of my chest.

But I didn't give up.

Much like the old Digi-Vids of Earth cowboys riding wild horses, I held on for dear life. For a few moments I felt as if I might be thrown aside, or even worse, sucked into the whirlpool of images and sensations. But although I wobbled, I held firm. Slowly, precisely, I re-found my center and then worked my way toward my grandfather's. To me it seemed just like the images I'd seen of Earth hurricanes; eventually I found a stillness in the heart of all the madness.

With my confidence renewed, I took my time sorting through all the conflicting impulses. It was obvious at once that Andres had been hiding his illness, if that's what you'd call it, from all of us. He was weaker than I could ever imagine. In fact, I was stunned that he'd been able to maintain a façade of relative health despite having lost so much of his strength. I also realized that the reason he'd lost so much so quickly was that he'd been channeling a great deal of his energy to me, in order to help me learn what I needed to know faster than it should have been possible.

I did what I could to bolster his system, to ease his mind by blocking some of the dozens of inputs that streamed through his synapses, rechanneling others to my own. Despite my best efforts, however, I could only stop the progression of his deterioration, not roll it back. I knew, somehow, that his illness was terminal. I only hoped that he would be with us long enough to see the Council fall.

By the time I slowly eased myself out of his mind, I was sweating from the exertion. I sat, or more accurately fell back into a chair by his side.

I stared down at him, my expression a mixture of pain and fear.

After several moments, his eyes opened and he looked up at me, his face pale but relaxed.

"You are strong," he whispered. "Thank the Great Creator."

"Why?" I answered. "Why didn't you tell us? I might have been able to do something…"

He shook his head. "Don't even think about it; there's nothing anyone can do. I've sustained myself well past my given time, and no one but Him can stave off the passage of cycles forever."

"We *need* you, grandfather. How can we hope to defeat them without you?"

His eyes narrowed and for just an instant he seemed to regain much of his old fire. "Don't even think such a thing!" he snapped. "You are already stronger than I ever was. You will lead our people to a new life. It is your destiny."

I know it sounds crazy, but I believed him. It *was* my destiny. But I still wasn't ready to go it alone. I wasn't ready for my grandfather's death. I could sense how he had shielded me from the fact of his weakness, how he had used my self-absorption to keep me from seeing the obvious. I felt embarrassed, hoodwinked. But I also felt terribly sad. I will use that as the excuse why I took liberties that I would not have normally even considered. I wandered through every corner of Andres' mind, looking for what, I didn't know. I only knew that I wanted him to live a while longer, and I wasn't going to give up just because he said to.

"There's no way," he said after a time. "I've tried everything I could think of."

"If I really am stronger than you, maybe I'm smarter too," I replied. He smiled and closed his eyes.

"I won't argue the possibility," he said softly.

I roamed at will, hoping against hope that I'd stumble on something, *anything* that would help me help him. It was hard work, harder than anything I'd practiced up till that time, and after just a few clics I grew tired. I was about to give up, 'surrender to the inevitable' as Andres would've said, when I felt rather than consciously perceived an unexpected weakness in an electrical impulse from his heart. How I knew what it was, or what it indicated, I have no idea. Even now I'm constantly amazed by the insights that just pop into my head. On that afternoon, I simply *knew* that I'd stumbled on something important.

"Relax," I told him, trying to do the same myself. "Think of some other place, some other time."

I could sense his reaction to my words almost immediately. The tension that had reflected his resistance to my intrusion melted away. With the doors to his psyche now wide open, I entered like an electronics tech working on a complex circuit problem, tracing the electrical impulses that formed a closed loop between his brain and his heart. Everything seemed okay, everything as it should be... Then, I noticed it! There was a disturbance, a short-circuit if you will, that was drawing off much-needed energy and forcing his heart to work much too hard just to keep him going. *'What now?'* I remember thinking, and for just an instant I panicked. I had no answer. I didn't have any idea what to do next. And so, as Andres had taught me, I opened myself to the universe, dropped all barriers. To this din I don't know what I did. I felt rather than heard Amanda and Jans enter the bedroom and pause just inside the door. They told me later I looked so intense, so focused, they were almost afraid to breathe.

I ignored them. All that mattered at that moment was Andres and the frail spot in his autonomous nervous system that needed to be repaired. Somehow I channeled energy, the likes of which I'd never experienced before, from a source so powerful, so dynamic, that I was awestruck to be in contact with it. The Great Creator? I had no idea. But I felt it, felt the warmth of it pass through my body and into his. He drew in a quick breath, more like a gasp, and sat up with a start. He stared at me as if I were an alien from another world.

"How did you do that?" he asked.

"I don't know," I admitted. "I just wanted it to happen, and it did."

He touched his chest as if it were a new-found body part and glanced over at Amanda and Jans, who now stared in disbelief. Andres looked several cycles younger, his eyes beaming with a life-force beyond anything that any of us had seen in our brief association with him.

"What have you done?!" Amanda asked, her voice a mix of awe and fear.

"I...fixed what was broken," I stumbled. I didn't realize until much later that I was as awestruck as they were.

As we soon learned, Andres felt better than he had in quite some time — stronger, more alive. The three of them, and then Mama Jaydu too, peppered me with questions. I side-stepped most of them, not because I was being coy, but because I had no idea what to say.

That was the beginning of a new life for me, a life unlike anything I could have imagined. A life that would change the course of history.

CHAPTER 24

Rogen hated the warm, tropical climate of Argos, always had. It was too hot, too sticky, too… unlike his home. He preferred the cool, sophisticated environment of Harran and its surrounding sub-states. But the one preference that took priority over all others was the necessity of finding – and destroying – the young successor to Inod: The One, as they so arrogantly called him. To accomplish that end, Rogen would have travelled to the ends of the universe and through the fiery gates of Rim.

As he stepped from his modified warship, the hot humid breeze brought immediate discomfort to the High Priest. *'Maybe the gates of Rim would be preferable,'* he thought as the local SF Commander scurried over to greet him with head appropriately bowed.

"Your Worship," the security man said, dropping to one knee. "Welcome to Argos."

"Is that building air-conditioned?" Antavar asked, his face flushing a most un-regal shade of red.

Latson glanced over at the SF Headquarters building. "Some of the sections, yes, Your Grace."

"Then let's get over there before I melt right here and now." He strode away without waiting for the Commander, who scrambled to catch up to Antavar along with a sizeable retinue of bodyguards, advisors and various other hangers-on. *'It's almost enough to make one solar cyclen for a simpler life,'* Rogen mused. *'Almost.'*

Not until he was ensconced in the relative coolness of the Commander's personal office did he address the mass of associates who traveled with him.

"Gillan!" he called out to his personal secretary, "check to be sure my quarters are prepared – and that the air-conditioning is working!" The attractive young woman, who moments earlier had been standing a short ways away from the mass of retainers with a look of deep disdain on her face, ran from the room as if pursued by Artegan Death Sworls. "Antos!" the High Priest continued, this time directing his attention to his military aide, "get me the latest intel reports and satellite readouts – visible and infrared." The heavily-medaled young man saluted and turned crisply. "Hermis – get all these loafers out of here and into offices where they can get started tracking down any lead to where this young Mr. Leitstell might be hiding. I don't want to stay in this place a clic longer than is necessary!" he yelled after the quickly receding form of his administrative assistant.

Then he turned to Regional Commander Latson, who stood behind the High Priest as if hoping to both bask in his reflected power and hide from his sharply-delivered demands.

"Latson…It is Latson, isn't it?" he asked.

The Commander jumped to attention and gave the familiar straight-armed salute. "General Ramsey Latson, at your service!" the Security Chief barked.

"Put your arm down," Rogen said tiredly, "you look like an idiot." Latson did as he was told, glancing around surreptitiously to make sure no one else had heard the High Priest's comment. To his relief, the two of them were alone.

"So, Latson, I understand you were some assistance to Commandant Belinger when he was here, is that right?"

Latson swallowed heavily. Did he admit that he'd helped The Fist fail, or deny the obvious? He felt the High Priest's eyes penetrate into the innermost recesses of his mind. "The Commandant was very much his own man," he said cautiously. "I tried to help him as best I could, but he was determined to handle the investigation himself."

The High Priest nodded thoughtfully as he walked over to a large window that overlooked the town of Veejy. "How sure are you that Leitstell is still out there somewhere?" Antavar asked, his voice low and distracted.

"I...*we* are reasonably confident that the subject has not left the area." He winced, his words sounding feeble even to his own ears.

"*Reasonably confident,*" the High Priest repeated as if weighing the value of the words given their source and lack of assurance. "Are you confident enough to wager your career, your *life* on it?"

The room seemed suddenly smaller, warmer, and Latson struggled to take a breath. "I...I..."

"The question is rhetorical," Antavar said with a dismissive wave of his hand. "You've already made your wager. Now, I hope – for both our sakes – that you can deliver. Am I clear?"

The cold, cutting edge to his voice sent a chill down the Commandant's spine.

"Y-yes sir," he managed to mutter.

"Good. Then we understand each other. Now go find me this rebel, and make it quick. My patience is not inexhaustible."

Latson saluted quickly and scurried from the room. It was perfectly clear to him that the High Priest's patience was a good deal less than inexhaustible.

*****

Rogen glanced at the raw information flashing past his eyes on the VidScreen monitor. It was a very good thing that he was able to absorb such information nearly as quickly as it could be provided, he thought for the umpteenth time that afternoon. With all the VidCams at their disposal, all the first-person investigation results, and all the hearsay and worse that flooded the SF offices once they'd announced a reward for information leading to the arrest of Leitstell, he'd need to spend stundes if not dins in order to wade through it all. As it was, he was growing tired of looking at all the garbage that flashed before his eyes. Couldn't they at least edit it down to probable leads? He'd have to discuss procedures with Commander Latson. The man was either lazy, incompetent, or too secure in his position. None of the possibilities sat well with Antavar.

After nearly a half din of review, he'd had enough. He ordered the computer to turn itself off and then just sat there for a while, trying to get a handle on his next move. He'd hoped to avoid taking a personal role in the investigation; it made him look weak, Octana argued, and made the boy look much too strong. Perhaps she was right. But he could feel the boy's strength growing, growing much too rapidly. From this distance he couldn't pinpoint the source, but he knew he was out there. Soon he would be a formidable opponent, much too soon.

Finally, after an unseemly amount of vacillation, he made his choice: better to look a bit weak than to risk the boy gaining so much power that he posed a serious threat. He'd take charge of the search himself, perceptions be damned.

"Gillan!" he yelled toward the outer office. "Get Latson in here, and Hermis and Antos as well. We've got some work to do."

CHAPTER 25

After just one din of rest, Andres was back up and pushing me harder than ever. Yet despite his ardor, or perhaps because of it, I felt strangely calm, strangely self-confident. When I'd mentioned my changed perception to my grandfather, he'd looked at me with narrowed eyes and a small nod.

"I didn't think it was possible," he said, as much to himself as to me.

"What? What isn't possible?"

"You. Unless I'm mistaken, you've already reached Ton Yap, or *critical mass* as they used to call it back on Earth."

I'd never heard of either term. "Is that good or bad?"

He smiled. "It means that my efforts are now just icing on the cake. You've reached a point in the development of your heritage powers at which you will 'learn that which cannot be taught, know that which cannot be known, and do what cannot be done.' That's how it's worded in *The Rahn* – or so I've been told."

He'd stumped me again. "*The Rahn?*"

"Remember I told you about *The Rebirth*, and how it tells the story of our ancestors' flight from Earth and the spread of The Light throughout the system?"

I nodded.

"Well, *The Rebirth* is just one section of *The Rahn*, which is a collection of all the holiest writings of Rogen's cult. He keeps it locked up in that obscene castle of his in Harran. He thinks it's his big secret, but we've uncovered many original documents over the cycles, and a few members of previous Councils have told us of some of the prophecies and portents it records. It's a very powerful work, not least of which because it describes you and what you can accomplish."

"Me?" I was dumbfounded. Why hadn't he ever mentioned this to me?

"Well, not by name, of course" he corrected, "but it tells of the coming of The One who will remake the Terran system in the image of the original Swords of the Light."

"And you think that's me?"

"I know it is. All the portents fit. The timing is right. You are *The* One."

"But..."

He held up his hand. "No use arguing. You will soon know yourself whether I'm right or whether I'm wrong. Nothing either of us can say will change that. What we can do, however, is make sure you're every bit as prepared as possible. So, let's get back to your lessons."

As he turned and walked back toward our training space, my thoughts flew in every direction imaginable. *Remake the system in the image of the original Swords of the Light?* I didn't even know what the original Swords believed, let alone whether I agreed with them. What if my beliefs didn't match-up with theirs? For that matter, what exactly were my beliefs? I felt suddenly light-headed as I realized that I'd gotten myself into a situation I didn't really understand. I had thought to free our people from the tyranny of the Council, not to replace them with a new religious dictatorship. What was I doing?

*****

I guess my confusion must have been pretty obvious; Amanda confronted me the very next din to ask whether there was a problem.

"How do you mean?" I asked, knowing I was being only half-truthful.

"You haven't been your usual self these last couple of dins. Moody. Closed-mouth. Not at all like the Vers Leitstell we all know and love."

Her smile couldn't disguise her concern. "Just some stuff about my training," I lied. I don't know why I didn't just tell her the truth, except I felt like it'd be unfaithful to my grandfather and the whole rebellion if I admitted my doubts. So, I kept them to myself.

She accepted my explanation, or so I thought at the time. However, just a few stundes later Jafar tracked me down and continued the interrogation. I'm pretty sure Amanda had put him up to it.

"Hey man, how's it going?" he asked, his smile a little too broad, his look a little too concerned.

"Okay," I said. "Just working through a few rough spots."

"Anything I can help with?"

If anyone could understand my dilemma, it'd be Jafar. Heck, I'd known him since we moved to Phoebos. Still, I hesitated.

"Nah, not really."

He nodded understandingly. "Sometimes it's hard to talk about it."

"I…it's nothing."

But I could tell he'd picked up the scent of a problem, and I knew Jafar well enough that he'd never turn it loose until he got to the bottom of it. Besides, I have to admit that I really wanted to talk it through with someone, and who better than him?

The conversation began slowly, as I danced all around the real predicament, but Jafar kept at it and at it until he wore me down.

"You see," I finally admitted, "I don't know if I'm the right person for this rebellion thing." It felt really good to finally get it out of my head and into the outside world.

"Wow. That's one big rough spot. What changed? You never said anything about doubts before now."

I sighed. "Andres mentioned yesterdin that he expects me to lead the system back to the ways of the original Swords of Light. I don't know that I can do that."

I don't know what I expected my old friend to do. Probably jump all over me for letting down the rebellion and my grandfather and all the other Leitstell ancestors. I know what I didn't expect was a story from our shared childhood.

"Remember the time when we were in Third Form and our class was doing that play about Linth Vaden for the celebration of his, what was it – 400th birthdin or something? Mr. Weetu wanted you to play Vaden, but you were against it – to put it mildly."

"I think I threw a fit."

"That's how I'd describe it. You were adamant that you'd screw it up, that your fear of public speaking would ruin any chance of you, or the class, pulling it off. But Weetu talked to your parents, and I guess he really leaned on them, because I remember us going to class one din and you telling me you 'had to do it.' Remember what I told you?"

I vaguely recalled some advice, but he was on a roll so I let him finish. "Not exactly."

"I said, 'you have to look like you're doing it. Whether you actually do it or not, well, it's not unheard of for an actor to get sick the night of his big performance.'"

As he said the words I could remember his smiling face and devilish eyes as if it had happened only the din before.

"Your point?" I wanted something more than innuendo and good memories. I was about to make a decision that would probably change my life and many, many others.

"You are The One. I believe that. Both because I've seen what you can do, and because I know you. Whatever you decide, I trust. Whatever you need to do to make that happen, other than dead-out lie to people – which you'd never do, I support. You *are* The One. You will lead the Terran system into a new time of freedom and prosperity. The Great Creator will make it happen. Through *you*. So, whatever you decide, even to let people think that your goals are theirs, the Great Creator is behind you. I'm behind you. All of us are behind you."

I'd never seen Jafar so serious, never heard him speak so convincingly. It actually sent chills up my back.

"Is it really that simple?" was the only thing I could think to say.

"Look, I'm no expert. But I think I've heard Andres telling you that what someone believes, he can make real. Believe in yourself. Believe in all of us who believe in you. You can do this — with our help."

I felt a large lump in my throat and on the spur of the moment threw out my arms and embraced my friend in a bear hug.

"Hey, hey!" Jafar grumbled as he squirmed to get out of my grasp. "Don't want Amanda getting jealous or anything." His face was red, but his eyes were calm. I could feel the power of his friendship, and it made me stronger.

*****

The long, exhausting dins of physical and mental exercises gradually dissipated, replaced by equally long and even more exhausting dins of strategy, and public messaging, and every possible element of getting and keeping the Terran system free and secure. Not that we stopped my sessions of Kin-zah telekinetics and telepathy entirely; Andres challenged me every din to do more and do better. Both Nomar and Jans made occasional appearances to test my physical capabilities in unannounced 'ambushes', leaving all three of us with the bumps, bruises and superficial cuts that come from all-too-realistic hand-to-hand combat. No quarter asked, and none given – until a final surrender.

But the physical and mental weaponry of my preparation gave way to more abstract battle planning, practice at delivering public speeches (I was still less than stellar, though I learned how to talk to a crowd of strangers without barfing), persuasion (both with and without the aid of my Gift), and so much more. It became a blur. What was perfectly clear, however, was that our time was running short. I don't think any of us knew quite how short, however, until a rebel messenger appeared at Mama Jaydu's hut very late one night.

We had finished our training for the din and all of us were sitting in the main room talking about what the future might hold, when the future arrived all too unexpectedly.

"The Security Forces have seized Tiber and Vera, among others," Andres explained after a quick private briefing by the messenger. "They've been taken to SF Headquarters in Harran."

The uproar was predictable. "How did they find them?" "What are we going to do?" "Are we in danger?" The questions flew unedited. It was clear that everyone, and particularly Amanda and Jafar, were badly shaken.

Andres held up his hand for quiet. "I don't know how they found them, but it's clear that they're now the bait to draw us out into the open. We have to think our next steps through very carefully."

"Should we move to another safe house?" Jafar asked, his anxiety now more under control.

"I'm guessing that's what they expect us to do," Andres said. "They probably have all their satellites and drones scanning this general area, looking for movement. If they knew where we were, they'd already be here. So I think we stay put, for now."

"What about Tiber and Vera? We can't leave them to the SF, bait or no bait," I said. My grandfather breathed deeply and nodded.

"No, we can't. But we can't go off half-cocked either. That's what they want."

"What's your thinking?"

"If you mean, do I have a plan, the answer is no. We need to contact some of our other cells and get their input. That'll be a start. But the main thing we need to do is keep calm. Don't let them spook us."

"Easier said than done," Amanda said softly. I went over to where she stood and took her hand. I knew how hard it must be for her, and Jafar. Mama Jaydu and Andres had lived with the threat of the SF for decades. I'd had many septs to adjust. They'd only just recently been thrown into the storm. "It'll be fine," I said softly. "We'll be fine."

I don't know if my words helped, or if she found some hidden reserve of resolve, but I remember very clearly that she looked up at me and smiled.

"That's good enough for me," she said.

"Me too," Jafar chimed in.

"Good," Andres said, "then why don't the two of you get with Mama Jaydu and put together some travel packs – just the minimum we'd need to camp out in the jungle for a few dins, while I steal Vers away for some discussions."

"One to One?" Jafar said with a grin. There was no better sign that he was holding up well under the stress than his sarcasm.

"Exactly," my grandfather fired back. Then, turning to me he added, "Let's go downstairs."

We left our three housemates to fend for themselves and went down to the subterranean control center. No sooner had he closed the heavy security door than he turned to me, his expression stern.

"I don't want to mislead you; this is bad, very bad."

"I know," I said, and I did, both because of the circumstances and because I could by that time read my grandfather's thoughts almost without trying. He was worried, more worried than I'd ever seen. I could feel that he needed reassurance just like the rest of us. "We'll get them back," I said, with no real idea of how we'd do that, just the sense that it would happen.

He patted me on the shoulder. "You *are* a Leitstell. Come. Let's talk."

I didn't fully realize it then, but for me the rebellion had just begun.

CHAPTER 26

The cell was damp, with the moldy smell that all underground spaces seemed to develop after a time. The only light in the room came in through small slits in the metal door. A bucket in the corner had been provided for their *comfort*.

The High Priest didn't say a word as he walked slowly toward the two bound and kneeling prisoners. None of the seven rebels they'd captured had shared anything more than routine, unimportant information, but he sensed that these two knew more than they let on. He could try to force his way into their consciousness and simply take what he wanted, but if they'd been trained in even basic Kin-zah techniques – and he was betting they had, that would take more time and energy than he was willing to expend and might even destroy their usefulness as pawns in the little game of move and countermove that was about to play out with his distant cousin and the boy. Musn't forget or underestimate the boy.

He saw the young man glance up quickly and then lower his eyes, his chest rising and falling noticeably as he struggled to regularize his breathing. The woman seemed calmer, but he knew from experience that outward impressions were often misleading. He reached out to her mind, gently, imperceptibly, and felt the chaos of fear and confusion flooding the overwhelmed synapses. Good. Excellent. Both were feigning greater control than they possessed. Those sorts were often the easiest to break.

He didn't say a word as he circled them, watching closely for any reaction that might increase his advantage. Not that he needed any. But he'd learned from past…experiences, that overconfidence could be problematic, even deadly. So he waited.

When he was confident that their heart rates had peaked and the adrenaline in their bloodstreams was playing games with their concentration, he spoke.

"Did you really think you could hide from us?"

The question was more statement than threat. He wanted them to know how little they meant in the overall picture. Of course, neither of them said a thing. He could feel them bracing against a frontal mind attack. They were modestly strong, but inexperienced. Amateurs. He could rip their psyches from their moorings with a blink of his eye. But that wasn't what he was looking for. He wanted information, yes, but more than anything he wanted pawns. Yes, that was the word they used back on Earth for the little chess pieces that could prove critically important in any attack. *Pawns.*

"Tiber Ebram." At the mention of his name the young man looked up for just an instant. An automatic reaction. He immediately returned his gaze to the floor. "That is your name, isn't it?" Rogen continued. He wanted them to know how much he knew about them. The more they thought he knew, the easier it would be to get them to tell him more. "Well?"

"Yes, sir." The young rebel peeked over at the woman beside him, who returned his look with wide-eyed disapproval.

"You don't think Tiber should've answered me, Miss Weiss?" Her eyes widened just a millimeter further.

"Yes, I know who you are, and why you're here in Veejy. In fact, I know a great deal about the two of you. I know you think you're fighting for a noble cause in support of The One, as you call him. But I also know something you don't know." He paused to watch their reactions. "I know that he's *using* you. Both of them, actually: the old man *and* his grandson." He let his energy move into their bodies and raised their heart rate and breathing a notch. They didn't even notice. "You think they want a free, non-sectarian

Terran system – am I right?" He knew he was. They'd captured and interrogated enough of the rebels to have a pretty good idea of what they'd been told about the rebellion. "And you think your *One* will lead you there?" He continued to pace, circling, always circling. It kept them just a bit off guard. Didn't let them focus. "Well, they won't. Neither of them. What they won't tell you is that their real goal is a new religious order, based on their own beliefs. Their own Council. Their own Security Force. Their own Shining Light commandments to rule our worlds. Have they ever shared that little secret with you? Did either of you know?"

In fact, Antavar didn't know either, not really. His people had pieced together enough bits and pieces from enough informants and prisoners to have a pretty good idea of the rebels' philosophy and plans, but nothing definitive. Could one of these two have heard the words from the old man's lips? Or maybe from the teen? That would be worth the time he was spending with them. But no, he could immediately sense that neither had heard any such thing.

"Do you actually expect us to *believe* that?" the woman snapped, her cheeks dotted with bright red blotches of hormonal overreaction. He wanted to laugh, but didn't allow himself the pleasure. One goal; no deviation.

"Ah, so you *can* talk. Good. I was getting tired of hearing nothing but my own words. Why don't you tell me what *you* think the rebellion is all about?"

"Don't do it!" the young man hissed. "He's just playing with us."

The High Priest smiled, a lopsided sneer the best he could muster. "Am I? To what end? If I wanted to break you, I could – you must know that. No, my young rebel friend, all I'm trying to do is tell you the truth about your misplaced loyalty. I appreciate your steadfastness. The Security Forces could use good, smart young officers like the two of you in positions of leadership."

"Your Security Forces are nothing but thugs who force Terrans to follow a philosophy most of them don't believe in!" The young woman stared at him with fury in her eyes. "They should be disbanded!"

"To be replaced by what? You and your friends? And then what? We saw what happened back on Earth when there was no centralized governing body to hold people together: chaos. Every little group that shared a religion, or language, or just a geographic space, wanted to dominate their neighbors. As some writer once said, 'the Center could not hold.' What would you prefer: a world at peace, with some disagreement over minor philosophical differences, or a world engulfed in near-constant war? I think if you asked your fellow Terrans, they'd opt for peace."

"That's pluda, and you know it!" This time it was Ebram. Rogen was impressed: even faced with a hopeless predicament, the two young rebels remained defiant and focused. Of course, he wasn't about to show *them* that he was impressed. With just a casual thought he sent a carefully calibrated bolt of mental energy surging through the young man's body. He watched as muscles spasmed and a weak cry escaped from the rebel's clenched jaws.

"You forget yourself!" Antavar thundered with long-practiced indignation. "I am the High Priest of Terra, Guardian of The Light, right hand to The Great Creator! You will not use that sort of language in my presence!" He saw a flicker of fear pass across the woman's eyes. Good. Very good.

"I think you need some more time to think about your commitment to those false prophets," he said, softly this time. "I will come back when you are ready to hold a civil conversation."

Actually, he wanted to give them time to digest the information about the old fool and his grandson, give some time for qualms to take root. He doubted that they knew anything about their leaders' whereabouts. At least he could sense no such knowledge. No, his goal was to slowly break their resolve, and if possible bring them over to his side. And if they wouldn't cooperate, if they insisted on remaining loyal to their pathetic conspiracy? Well, as soon as their value as bait was determined, one way or the other, they would either swear allegiance to the Council and join the SF or... not.

He glanced down one last time at the two of them lying in the near-darkness on the cool stone floor; she cradled her companion's head in her arms as he lay curled in a tight fetal position, panting from the pain.

"A pity," he mumbled, as if to himself. "What a waste."

He turned and walked quickly from the cell, the heavy metal door clanging shut immediately behind him. The solemn sound echoed down the stone-lined corridor, and then all was quiet once more.

*****

"Are all the men in position?" The High Priest barely glanced at Argos Commander Latson, who stood at attention directly in front of him.

"Yes, sir!"

"Deployed as I suggested?"

"All of them, sir."

"Good. Now we wait."

Antavar could see that Latson was chomping at the bit to ask him something. He let him chomp for a bit, until it was clear who was in control.

"So? Did you have a question, Commander?"

Latson pulled himself even further to attention, if that was possible. He looked stretched to the breaking point.

"Yes, sir. You said we would wait – for the rebels to come and try to free our prisoners, I assume."

Rogen bit back a snide reply. "Yes, Commander, go on."

He saw the senior SF man take a deep breath as if to steel himself. *'I've got to replace this fool once this is all done,'* the High Priest thought as he waited. *'I need someone with titanium in his spine, not silicone.'*

"What I wondered," the SF Commander finally continued, "is how long you suggest we wait – for the rebels to come, I mean. It's not just curiosity," he went on nervously. "We'll need to make up rotational schedules to be sure we're always fully manned, and bring in enough consumables – food, drink, even ammunition, so that we're prepared at all times."

Rogen pursed his lips. Maybe he'd been too quick to judgment. Even if the man wasn't entirely courageous, maybe he had a good mind for this sort of thing. He'd have the new Fist review Latson's personnel records. Maybe they could find a use for him after all.

"Good point, Commander," he said, and he noticed Latson's spine disengage a notch. "I don't know these people – I've never even met them. But I'd be very surprised if they let their friends spend more than... two din here at Headquarters. Think we can stay on full alert for that long?"

"Yes sir!" he barked with a bit too much enthusiasm. "I'll make certain of it!"

"You do that," the High Priest said. "Let me know when everything's in place."

"The men are in position now."

"I said *everything*," Rogen snarled. "Is *everything* ready? Supplies, schedules..."

"You'll have it right away!" the senior SF commander answered, clicking his heels together as if to emphasize the point.

"Good." He looked up to see Latson standing rigidly at attention, waiting to be dismissed. *'More a lapdog than commander,'* Antavar thought. "You're dismissed!' he ordered. "Go get this done!" As soon as the Commander turned to leave, he stopped him in his tracks. "And Latson?"

"Yes sir?"

He lowered his voice to little more than a whisper. "You screw this up and there won't be enough of you left to bury. Is that clear?"

Latson swallowed heavily. "Yes, sir. Completely."

"Good. That'll be all."

As soon as the door to the office closed, Rogen walked slowly to a large window that overlooked Veejy and the jungle beyond. He stood staring out across the dozens of buildings that comprised the small city, a hodgepodge of styles and materials that might have been called ugly, if anyone had had the courage to say such a thing aloud. At the far eastern edge of the city, far enough that he couldn't make out detail, the ugly wound of a city stopped abruptly and the green savagery of the jungle began.

'That's what we've done for these people,' he mused. *'That's just how close they are to reverting back to the primitive creatures they truly are. We're all that stands between them and the wild.'*

Feeling more in control, he took a deep breath and cleared his mind. The Kin-zah preparation was second nature to him by now. He projected his life energy out toward the dense palms and undergrowth, searching, scanning for a kindred energy, a ping that would tell him that the old man, or the kid, or both were out there somewhere. He projected out in a complete circle, slowly, carefully, allowing nothing to escape his attention. But there was no response. No ping, no reflection of the Light force. If they were out there, they were too far away to detect.

But they were coming. He was certain of it.

CHAPTER 27

I knew we couldn't abandon our people to the torment of SF interrogation. Even if they weren't friends. They were part of the movement, and no rebel could ever be left behind.

But that didn't relieve the waves of doubt that roiled my gut as I thought of walking into an SF trap. Oh, it was a trap, all right. We all knew it. Even Mama Jaydu had become unnaturally soft-spoken and deferential since the decision had become common knowledge. I'd only slept a couple of stundes the previous night, my mind constantly turning trying to find a way to save our friends without risking the entire mission.

No matter what scenario I came up with, however, I didn't see any way to avoid risking the lives of Andres, Jafar, Amanda and many, many others.

Unless, that is, I went alone.

I knew Andres would go ballistic if I even broached the subject. And with good reason. I was the future. I was The One. I was their leader.

But what kind of leader hides behind his people? That's what I'd be doing, I decided, since when it came right down to it, success or failure would depend on me — and perhaps to a lesser extent on Andres — to set Vera and the others free. We didn't have the manpower to overwhelm the SF Headquarters, especially since they were almost certainly expecting us. No one else had the Gift to help them get past the intricate security systems that no doubt encircled the building.

Andres was old, I could see that. And ill. He'd already given a lifetime to the cause. It wasn't fair to ask him to do this, especially given the state of his health. No, this was something *I* needed to do. Myself. Why had I spent all that time preparing if not to use my talents when they were most needed? Besides, how better to show my leadership, to rally the far-flung rebel units, than to steal into an SF Headquarters building and walk out with high profile prisoners?

Was I naïve? Perhaps. Was I cocky? Most likely. But there was also something else: I don't know how to describe it, but I had a feeling, a *sense*, that this was my time. After all the training I'd endured, one thing I'd absorbed was the need to believe. To reach beyond logic and calculation to a higher power. That's what it was: I *believed*.

That din crawled past as slowly as any in my life. I didn't see much of Andres, who was in near-constant contact with units on the other planets, trying to come up with a plan that would free the prisoners without endangering me or the rebellion. He kept me out of the discussions, for the most part, because he didn't want me to feel that my well-being was the sticking point. Although I'm pretty sure it was. When it came right down to it, I think most of our commanders were willing to sacrifice Vera, Tiber and the others in order to keep me safe. That was a trade-off I couldn't countenance. It was clear to me that I had to make my move, and it had to be that night.

Probably the hardest part of getting through that din was trying to hide my plans from Jafar and Amanda. I don't know if Andres told them to stay close to me, or whether it was their own doing, but every time I turned around one of them – or both – were right there trying to raise my spirits, or was it their own?

"It'll all work out," Amanda told me, all the while looking more serious than I'd ever seen her. "Andres and the other commanders will come up with a way. We just have to stay patient."

Part of me wanted to yell at her: "Patient?! Our friends are probably being tortured even as we sit here, and you want me to be patient?!" But I knew she was only trying to ease my guilt at having led them into that mess in the first place, and her concern for me was obvious. So I held my tongue. I played along, feigning patience I didn't feel.

When she went off to help Mama Jaydu prepare lunch, Jafar appeared miraculously as if summoned – which he probably was. He was equally upbeat, and his words so clearly echoed Amanda's that I felt certain they'd both been briefed. I suppose I could've just reached into his mind and learned the truth that way. But I'd made myself a promise cycles earlier that I wouldn't use my Gift with friends or family unless it were absolutely necessary. There was something of the voyeur, or worse yet, the sneak thief in using my powers to *eavesdrop* on friends' thoughts. I knew that I'd feel violated if someone intruded in my mind. So I kept my thoughts to myself and allowed those around me to do the same.

To accomplish that goal with all the pressure building up around me, I perfected a way to divide my conscious mind into two distinct segments: one, in which I kept mulling my plans for the night's rescue mission, the other in which I answered questions and engaged in casual conversation as if I had no other concerns in the world. It was a strange balancing act: engaging in back and forth dialogue with people who knew me well, all the while keeping the majority of my mind locked into the difficult task that awaited me at SF Headquarters.

Somehow, I managed it well enough to survive the din without tipping my plans to anyone at the hut. As the principal star began its slow descent into the jungle canopy that surrounded us, I actually felt a sense of relief. As difficult as it would be to go into the enemy camp alone, I would be *doing* something, not just talking. I would have a chance to use my Gift, a chance to save my friends. Of course, as a nagging doubt whispered far in the back of my brain, I'd also be risking everything that Andres and all our predecessors had built up over hundreds of cycles.

No pressure there.

CHAPTER 28

Rogen Antavar left the security systems room after just a brief visit. More than a dozen young men and women pored over a flood of data that came to them from sensors throughout the Headquarters building and all along the two meter wall that surrounded it, from pressure sensors and infrared cams outside the wall, to satellite images and humint from SF forces hidden throughout the jungle at the outskirts of town. From the outside, nothing looked out of the ordinary. Inside, the place was abuzz with energy.

Not that he expected all the SF precautions to stop a rebel attack. He knew that the heretics had to try to free the prisoners, to maintain morale if nothing else. But he very much doubted that even the young pretender would be so foolish as to attempt a frontal attack. It would be suicide. So what then?

He felt a sense of relief as the hubbub of the systems control room disappeared behind the heavy blast-resistant door. It was hard to think with all that noise, with all those people giving off their nervous, even frightened energy. Better to be off on his own where he could focus. True, he'd humored them by listening to all their plans, all their preparations. But that didn't mean that he thought for an instant that they'd be successful in stopping the non-believers. He pretty much knew it would all come down to him. It almost always did.

He slipped into the situation room he'd prepared for just this eventuality and ordered his ever-trailing security team out in the hallway to only allow Latson or his top lieutenant access to the room. Nothing worse than being besieged by a panicky crowd of fools when the going got tough. Even Latson was questionable. Most of the others: chaff.

The High Priest settled down in a high-backed chair in front of the only vidscreen in the room. On it he could access all the key security scanners and sensors individually or collectively. He had no way of knowing how long he'd have to wait, but his instincts told him it wouldn't be long.

And his instincts were nearly always right.

CHAPTER 29

I waited until quiet finally came to our tiny hut. Andres was the last to allow himself to fall asleep, finally surrendering to the reality that he might not have another such opportunity for many dins. I lay still in my small bed, feigning sleep even as I projected a delicate barrier to my conscious mind – a barrier to prevent Andres from accidentally discovering my plans and trying to stop me before I could carry them out. I listened until his breathing assumed the rough, regular cadence I had grown accustomed to over the many cycles we had roomed together. It was a soothing sound, one constant in our otherwise ever-shifting world.

When I was certain he slept, I used a simple sound muffling cast to ensure that he stayed asleep through my brief preparations. I wasn't bringing much with me; my greatest chance of success lay in the skills I'd developed. Still, I brought some rope, a tempered valluvium blade, a pocket torch and a flare, just in case. Lastly, I slipped into a black shirt and pants that would give me some degree of invisibility in the shadows of the night. I ran through my mental exercises to try to keep myself calm as I packed for the mission. I was only partly successful.

I assumed that my greatest advantage would come from surprise, that the SF forces would expect a much bigger attack. That, and of course the powers I'd been granted through the Gift. But I was neither so young nor naïve that I didn't realize that the Headquarters building would be bristling with men, weaponry and sensors – all of which I hoped to bypass rather than engage. My plan called on stealth and deception, not brute force. I wasn't afraid to use force if necessary; I only hoped it wouldn't come to that.

When I felt as ready as I'd ever be, I took one last look down at my sleeping grandfather.

"Sorry, Andres," I whispered. "Wish me luck."

With that I slipped quietly out the door to our room and, without pausing, out the back of the hut. I must've been totally focused on the mission at hand, because I'd only taken a few steps when a completely unexpected voice shocked me to my very core.

"And where do you think you're going?"

I spun around as quickly as I could, blood pounding in my temples, my awareness suddenly on full alert, only to find myself facing Jafar and a *very* angry Amanda.

"Did you really think we were going to let you do this on your own!?" Amanda's voice increased in volume and pitch with each spoken word.

"Keep it down!" I whispered as loudly as I dared. "This isn't a game!"

"We know what this is, Vers," Jafar took up the argument. "What we don't know is why you're trying to run off on your own, with no backup. Are you crazy?"

As my heartbeat slowly returned to something approaching normal, I was able to focus on my two friends and see through the anger on their faces to the concern and determination in their hearts. At that moment I didn't know whether to laugh or cry. The one thing I did know is that I didn't want them to risk their lives to help me.

"I'm the only one who can possibly pull this off without leaving piles of dead bodies in my wake," I explained. "Both ours, and theirs. I think I can do this without major bloodshed. I *know* I can. You just have to trust me."

"Oh, we trust you all right," Jafar said. "But you don't seem to trust *us* very much. We can help."

"We've been training for septs now. We're not just a couple of goofy twelfth formers!" Amanda fumed.

My immediate inclination was to use the Gift to send them back into the hut with no memory of my leaving whatsoever. I almost did exactly that. But then, as I heard their words echoing in my mind, I reconsidered. Maybe they *could* be helpful. Maybe I *was* thinking of them as I'd known them back on Phoebos. That wasn't any more realistic than thinking of myself as I'd been way back then. I knew I was a different person. And I knew having them with me would give me the extra bit of confidence I needed to pull this off. I'd just have to have some faith.

"We're not letting you go without us!" Jafar said as if he could see my indecision.

"And don't try any of that telepathy stuff on us either." I looked over at Amanda, her eyes flashing, her lips thrust forward in a defiant pout, and it was all I could do to stop myself from kissing her. Instead, I smiled.

"All right. You can go – on one condition."

"What?!" they asked simultaneously.

"You do what I say, when I say it. No arguing, no disagreements. Understood?"

Instead of a reply, the two of them spontaneously threw their arms around me, and each other, in a giant bear hug.

"Don't worry – we'll get them out of there," Jafar said with an assuredness I envied. "No problem."

I only wished I fully believed him.

*****

The jungle at night is an alien world of moonlit swatches of brilliant green edged with inky pools of utter blackness. The familiar sounds of the din are replaced by freakish howls, high-pitched screams and the occasional guttural roar of large carnivores. And on Argos, the night hunters were large indeed.

The responsibility for keeping my two friends safe weighed heavily on me as we made our way toward Veejy and the SF Headquarters building. Although they'd both volunteered to come

– insisted, really – I knew they wouldn't be there if it weren't for me. We maintained complete silence along the convoluted route that I'd chosen, taking us well north of the town, and then west until we approached from a very different direction than I hoped the SF expected.

As much as it felt a little like a betrayal, I secretly probed both Amanda and Jafar as we hiked, to get some sense of whether they could be counted on in a moment of high stress. To my great surprise and relief, both of them seemed preternaturally calm. If anything, Amanda was even more in control of her emotions than Jafar, whose normal effervescent excitement was now bubbling off the charts. But neither seemed overly frightened. I took some comfort from that, and tried my best to match their tranquility even as I ran through myriad possibilities for the attack and reached out to try to identify any SF ambush that might block our way.

Time passed all too quickly as we picked our way through overhanging branches and dense undergrowth, all the while harassed by the ever-present whine of blood-sucking insects of every stripe. Although it wasn't hot compared to normal din temps, all of us were sweating profusely in the heavy humid air of the jungle. Twice we stopped to swig some cool water and take stock. After just a few moments, we pushed on.

We'd come nearly halfway to our final target with no contact of any kind, when I suddenly pulled up short and signaled my two friends to hold perfectly still. Somewhere not too distant, maybe four to five hundred meters, I sensed a small group of people hidden on either side of the trail we followed – SF, if my intuition was right.

"What is it?" Amanda whispered, her voice a half-tone higher than usual.

"SF, I think."

"Can we get around them?" Jafar asked.

I shook my head. "This is the only trail that goes in the direction we're headed. Or at least the only one I know. If we try to outflank them we'll lose too much time, and probably get lost in the bargain."

"What then?"

A fair question. I took great pains to slow my breathing and focus my thoughts. But it didn't help. I was about to admit that we might need to blast our way through the ambush, when a completely different approach came to me.

"Follow me," I instructed. "And whatever you do, don't speak or look at anything except the person in front of you. Understand?"

I saw doubt in their eyes, but to their credit Amanda and Jafar never argued. I didn't explain what I intended, both because I didn't want to start a debate and because I'd never attempted what I was about to do. Or at least, try to do. If I were wrong, we'd find ourselves in a very difficult predicament. To say the least.

I pulled a flare from my small backpack and started back down the path, my two friends following close behind. As we walked, I put myself into a deep Kin-zah trance, keeping just enough of my conscious mind alert to keep us on our path. When we'd come as close as I dared to the SF personnel guarding the path, I waved Amanda and Jafar down.

When I move, you stay with me. Understood?' I projected into both their minds. They looked startled, but nodded their agreement.

I took a deep breath, hoping desperately that my confidence in my abilities had not been misplaced. There was no time to dwell on doubts. I focused all my energy on creating a reflective ion cloak all around the three of us, an energy field that reflected the surrounding jungle as precisely as a mirror. Or nearly. Small fluctuations caused the occasional ripple in the field, but given the faint light and the chaos I expected to break loose in the next few moments, I hoped it would be good enough. From within the shield the world around us looked a shade dimmer than normal, but in the gloom of the jungle I doubted my friends would even notice the difference.

As soon as I had the shield stabilized, I aimed the flare up through a narrow slit in the thick foliage above us and pulled the igniter. As the bright red ball reached the zenith of its flight well above the treetops, I heard pandemonium break out from just ahead. At that moment I turned back to Amanda and Jafar.

'Now – walk directly behind me. Don't stop, don't fall behind, and don't say a word!' I knew I sounded harsh, but at the moment that was the least of my worries.

I saw Amanda's eyes widen, but the two of them did as they were told. Slowly, calmly, the three of us walked straight down the pathway, directly into the impending ambush! I could feel their level of discomfort soar as heavily armored SF agents crisscrossed our path, shouting orders, weapons ready to fire. The jungle sprang to life as floodlights blossomed and the screams of wildlife echoed the yells of the ambush party. I tried not to let my concentration waver, but I prayed for a bit of luck, for I was using all my energy to maintain the shield. I had nothing left to try to redirect the agents around us. They couldn't see us, but if one of them happened to stumble into us in the darkness…

We were almost through the ambush zone, almost past the insanity, when my worst fears were realized. From out of nowhere a young SF agent came crashing through the brush and slammed headfirst into Jafar, knocking him from the protective cocoon of the ion field! The two men were momentarily stunned, both from the violent impact and from the shock of suddenly finding themselves lying face to face on the jungle floor.

As if in slow-motion I saw the SF agent recognize his peril and reach for his weapon. Jafar froze, his body taut with adrenaline. I didn't have time to think, only react. If the agent fired his weapon, or managed to communicate with the rest of his unit, we were done! I merely glanced at him and wished him silenced. Just the briefest of thoughts.

I saw his eyes fly open, spittle foam at the corners of his mouth. Then, with a violent spasm, he fell back onto the ground, lifeless. I looked down at him, saw the youthful features and staring brown eyes, and felt a wave of sickened regret surge through my body. I'd killed him! With just a thought! What kind of person could do such a thing?!

Suddenly I realized that Amanda was gripping my arm tightly, pulling me forward.

"No time!" she whispered. "We've got to go!"

For the first I noticed that the ion screen was down and the three of us were standing in the middle of the path, fully visible to anyone who might look in our direction. I suppose I should've reformed the shield immediately, moved beyond the body at my feet. All for the greater good. But I couldn't. I could no more organize my thoughts than forget the tranquil face staring up at me.

"Vera and Tiber need you!" Jafar said much too loudly. He grabbed me by the shoulders and shook me until my teeth rattled. "Let's go!"

I saw the frenzied look on his face and, somewhere deep within me, knew that he was right. With bile rising into my throat, I stumbled down the pathway toward Veejy, Amanda and Jafar pushing and pulling me as best they could. I felt numb. Cold. As if something had died within me. But they would not let me stop, and I had no fight left in me.

*****

Andres awoke with a start. Flashes of light, screams, proton explosions! He'd seen it in his sleep, but he knew it wasn't a dream.

He pulled himself from his bed and dressed quickly. Vers was in trouble, and unless he moved quickly the entire revolt was in jeopardy. He contacted his Commanders on the other planets and with only token questioning, they all agreed: it was time. The prophecies had spoken of just such a moment, or at least that's what he told them. And they allowed themselves to be convinced. They would launch simultaneous attacks against the Council on all seven Terran colonies. At the same time, Andres would lead a small contingent in support of Vers. For if he failed, no matter how successful the other units were, the rebels would ultimately lose.

It took him nearly a full stunde to awaken and organize the fourteen members of the Argos underground into something resembling an attack unit. They were all experienced fighters, but they'd never worked as a coordinated group. Nothing he could do about that now. Vers and his two young friends were already pretty far ahead of them, and as weak as he'd been feeling he only hoped he wouldn't slow his men too much. With a hug to Mama Jaydu, he set off into the pitch-dark jungle, the future of the revolt and of the entire Terran system resting in the balance.

*****

It took me a while to clear my head, and even then I still felt sick to my stomach by what I'd just done. But Jafar's words rang loud and clear – I had to help Tiber and Vera, and time was running short. Any reflection would have to wait.

By the time I fully recovered my senses we were already three-quarters of the way to the Headquarters building. I assumed that the patrol had communicated with their command center, and although the element of surprise was lost I still hoped that the audacity of our attack would give us a better than even chance of getting out of there alive. As the brightly-lit building appeared through the thick foliage in the distance, I stopped our little group for a last-clic attack review.

"So, any questions?" I asked after running through the sketchy details one last time.

"Not here," Amanda said.

"I'm good," Jafar added.

I had to smile. How lucky was I to have two such friends, who would follow me into a certain ambush with confidence and pluck?

I gave each of them a quick hug, and received a passionate kiss from Amanda in return.

"It will work," she said calmly, staring into my eyes. I looked over to Jafar who nodded in agreement.

"Then let's do it," I said, and the three of us moved toward the heavily fortified building.

In the stillness of the night our every step seemed to reverberate much too loudly, but by weaving our way between sensors and outposts we got within just a few dozen meters of the outer wall without being discovered. Of course it helped that I could *listen* to the thoughts of both the patrols in the jungle and their superiors inside the building, allowing us to counter every move they made even before they made them. Once I got a little too confident and almost marched us right into an outlook that had been sitting quietly, hidden in the shadows of the undergrowth, but my Gift managed to alert me just moments before we showed ourselves.

We bypassed the outlook and took up a position just meters from where the jungle ended and the well-trimmed landscaping of the SF Headquarters began. As we surveyed the scene, I knew it was time to share one last element of my plan with my two companions, to give them an opportunity to back out. For what I hadn't revealed to Amanda and Jafar was that I'd only been able to identify one glaring weak point in the Headquarter's defenses, and that was the dilithium loading bay for the power reactor. No one in their right mind would enter that room without bulky radiation suits, which we didn't possess.

"That's suicide!" Jafar responded concisely.

"Let him explain!" Amanda ordered defensively, with a bit more passion than I would have expected.

"Normally, you'd be right," I began, "but I think I can use the same ionization field that I used back there on the trail to hide us from the patrols, to protect us from the radiation."

"You *think*?" I wouldn't say Jafar was skeptical, exactly, but he definitely wanted some reassurance.

"It should work. But, I've never tried it before."

"Never?" Amanda asked, and then looked chagrinned that it had slipped from her lips.

"If you don't want to come with me, I'll understand…" I began, but before I could finish I was cut off by their protests.

"Don't even think about it," Jafar barked.

"If you go, we go," Amanda added. They both stared at me with such determination that I didn't even consider trying to talk them out of it.

"Okay. Then it'll be the same drill as before. Stay close behind me, in line, so I can maintain the ion barrier and still scan ahead and around us for any SF response. Ok?"

They both nodded.

"Then let's do it!"

I focused on the ion barrier and in just moments the wavy distortion that told me that the barrier was in place filled my field of vision. It was a little like looking through the old glass that some of the early colonists brought from Earth. The stuff you only found in museums now. You could see pretty much everything, but not clearly. I only hoped I wouldn't miss anything important.

As we stepped out from the shadowed protection of the jungle undergrowth, I glanced back at my two friends and saw that fear now shared their expressions with the earlier determination. I didn't blame them; I was feeling more than a little shaky myself. But there was no time for second-guessing. From that moment on it was 100 per cent commitment. Or else.

We walked across the open green space surrounding the walls of the SF Headquarters, feeling as exposed as if we were stark naked. I was having some trouble filtering out key information from among the many competing thoughts, verbal communications and casual conversations among the SF forces both inside and outside the building, while at the same time maintaining the barrier and picking our way past pressure and motion sensors.

We were half-way across the yard, when suddenly I felt rather than heard a sudden awareness that hadn't been there before. Something – or someone – inside the building was projecting Kin-zah barriers! I focused on what I took to be control room chatter but picked up nothing that suggested a wider alarm. Confused, and perhaps a bit rattled, I reached out to try to identify the source and severity of the threat. At first it was like trying to see through smoke. I knew something was there, but it was vague, indistinct. And then I knew.

It was the High Priest: Rogen Antavar! From what I could tell he wasn't aware of our presence. He seemed relaxed, almost cavalier in his lack of concern. But he was inside the Headquarters building!

I was so surprised I let myself linger within his consciousness a bit too long. I felt a change in the Kin-zah link between us and realized that he'd begun to become aware of my intrusion! As if slapped, I pulled back and threw up a mental barricade that I hoped would stop return probes. It was just a moment before I grasped that a barrier would be as much of an announcement of our presence as actual contact, and I struggled to transform the barrier into something that would absorb rather than deflect any energy sent in our direction. The revised concealment was barely in place when I felt his *gaze* slide over us. I stopped dead in my tracks, so quickly that Amanda walked right into my back.

"What is it?!" she whispered, a note of terror creeping into her voice.

'Don't move. Don't speak. Just wait,' I spoke directly to her mind.

Antavar's probe probably only lasted a few tenths of a clic, but it felt like an eternity. Finally, I sensed his return to his previous state of mind, and I chanced another short mindwave communication to my friends.

'Ok, let's go. Quickly!'

I didn't wait for any questions or reaction, but broke into an immediate jog. I felt a short hesitation behind me, then both of them followed at a brisk clip. Jafar and Amanda were clearly nervous, but their determination continued strong as ever. I took strength from their belief in me. I had to. Knowing that Antavar was just meters away, I struggled to keep my focus. I'd never juggled so many inputs and so many simultaneous adjustments, and certainly never in such a difficult environment. But to my relief – and yes, my pride – my concentration never wavered as we fled across the open grass between the edge of the jungle and the loading bay door.

As we approached the massive auto-door, I surveyed the area to try to detect where the human SF assets might be. I immediately saw the infrared and motion detectors mounted high up on the building wall, but they didn't concern me. The first would be virtually blind in the sweltering early morning heat, and the second couldn't see past the ion field encompassing us. But real live SF agents could be another story entirely. To my surprise, and consternation, I saw no one. Not a single agent. I used my Gift to sweep the area for any stray thought patterns, but there were none. How could they leave such an obvious entry point unguarded? What was going on?

I didn't have time to stop and ponder the situation, so I pushed on with fingers crossed. We stopped in front of a small personnel port right next to the massive loading door, and I thanked my lucky stars that I wouldn't have to tackle the huge electro-mechanical system that lifted the larger door. Instead I focused all my energy on the interior bolts that held the smaller door shut. As I identified each of the three reinforced locking rods, I willed them to slide back, one after the other. With three soft clicks the door opened.

As soon as we stepped inside I projected my sensory outreach throughout the loading bay: nothing. I was beginning to get a very bad feeling about that place. It was too easy. There should've been people running all over the place. They *had* to know we were coming, or at least be pretty sure. What was their plan?

I dropped the ion barrier and my two friends materialized as if from thin air.

"That was cool!" Jafar said, his eyes aglow.

"Where are all the SF glooks?" Amanda asked, looking around skeptically. "How come there weren't any alarms, or anything?"

With that, Jafar's eager enthusiasm dropped down a notch.

"Yeh, now that you mention it, where is everybody?"

"They're exactly where I told them to be," a voice announced from the shadows at the rear of the bay. "And so are you."

All of us froze. Suddenly a figure materialized out of the darkness.

"Nice trick, the ion barrier. Did your grandfather teach you that one?"

I'd never seen him before in person, but we'd all seen that face a thousand times on the DigiScreen – Rogen Antavar, the High Priest!

I wanted to say something snide, to show him that he didn't scare me. But my mouth was so dry and my heart was beating so hard that I couldn't form the words.

Antavar walked slowly toward us, seemingly unconcerned by our presence.

"It's a waste, you know. You, following that old man and his crazy dreams. You must know it's hopeless."

I don't know if it was his Gift or my own insecurities, but what he said reverberated deep inside of me. I felt a wave of fear slide through me, doubts that I'd never shared with anyone suddenly surfacing. I swallowed and was struggling to answer, when Amanda stepped forward and let him have it.

"It's you that's the waste!" she shouted, so loudly that I flinched. "You've ruined our system and distorted the Great Creator's teachings!"

"Keep your mouth shut!" the High Priest roared, and with a single flick of his finger sent her tumbling head over heels across the floor.

I shook my head numbly. It was as if I'd just awakened from a bad dream. He'd hurt her! He'd hurt Amanda!

I didn't really think, just reacted. I reached out to him with a fury that was unlike anything I'd ever conjured before. With a concussive crash, the High Priest of the Council of Seven flew back against the rear wall of the loading bay, smashing into the concrete blacks with a sickening thud!

For a moment there was complete silence in the bay, as all of us froze in disbelief. Then Amanda groaned involuntarily and Antavar pulled himself back to full height.

"Bad mistake, kid," he said dismissively. But I sensed something else, something not so completely self-assured. He was *shaken*! As incredible as it seemed, he felt doubt! But in the moment I made the realization he was already fighting back.

I barely raised my defenses before a blast of energy exploded all around me, knocking the unprepared Jafar all the way back to the bay door. I chanced a quick look to make sure he was all right, but even that nearly cost me dearly. A second wave of energy swept over me, and in the blink of an eye Antavar disappeared back into the shadows from which he'd come. I scanned for him furiously, certain he couldn't have escaped, but there was nothing. No energy sign whatsoever. It was as if he'd never been there at all!

"Where is he, Vers?!" Amanda called out, her voice a half-pitch too high.

Jafar raised himself up on one elbow. "Did you get him?"

I exhaled deeply. I hadn't even realized I'd been holding my breath. "I don't think so," I admitted, trying to keep my tone neutral. "He just…disappeared."

"Then we'd better get moving!" Amanda said as she struggled to her feet.

I could see she was in pain, and out of the corner of my eye saw Jafar even worse off. I made a split-second command decision. "I think it'd be best if the two of you stay here," I said.

They both started to object. I raised my hand. "I know you want to help. But at this point we've got to assume the High Priest will sound the alarm and this whole building will soon be crawling with SF. You two are hurt – you'll only slow me down. I think I can create an ion barrier that will hide you from prying eyes until I get back. Sorry, but that's how it has to be."

Amanda nodded numbly. Jafar took a heartbeat longer, but finally acquiesced as well.

"Make it fast," he said.

"I will." I could see Amanda wanted to say something too, but she reconsidered and just mouthed the words: *'I love you.'*

I only had time to smile before I became aware of a large group of SF fighters making their way quickly to where we stood. "Gotta go," I managed to say before I threw out a mental command that swept the two of them together off to one side of the bay and hid them from view. I scrambled up to the entry port at the back of the bay, which exploded open just moments after I got in place and threw up a second ion barrier.

Twenty heavily-armed SF forces poured into the bay and took up fighting positions all across the back wall.

"Surrender or we will fire!" their leader called out into the emptiness of the huge chamber. His words echoed harmlessly. With their attention entirely directed into the bay, I slipped out through the port into a hallway lined with empty offices. I'd studied a schematic of the building made available to my grandfather by one of our people inside the SF, and so knew that the detention cells were located one floor below and on the far side of the structure. What I didn't know was whether Antavar was holding Tiber and Vera there, or whether they were elsewhere. I reached out to try to identify their thought patterns, but found something else instead.

"I am waiting for you, Leitstell," the High Priest's voice spoke clearly in my mind. "We're *all* waiting for you." For just an instant I saw an image in my head of Tiber writhing in pain, suspended from manacles chained to a wall. "Hurry. I don't know how long they can last."

He didn't sound worried in the least. I shivered in spite of myself.

I struggled to create a mental blockade to Antavar's intrusions, rotating the frequency of my interference on a random basis as my grandfather had shown me. But I had more to deal with than just the High Priest's taunts and threats: there were probably three hundred meters of hallways to navigate without getting myself killed. I knew that the ion barrier might not fool Antavar any longer, but the security vidcams and sensors were another matter entirely. At least I could keep myself invisible to the SF forces within the building – or so I hoped. If the High Priest tried to contact them with my whereabouts, I'd know. So unless they got lucky – or I got unlucky – I had a fighting chance.

I made my way as quickly as possible through the hallway leading to the lifts and stairs down to the detention cells. With every step, every turn in the route, I fully expected to find myself facing a phalanx of heavily armed SF agents. And yet, as meter after meter disappeared behind me, I met no one. Not a single person. The hallways were unnaturally silent and empty, as if Antavar had ordered all his people to move back and let me pass through. Could it be?

I suddenly realized that I was being passively herded along the exact route that they – He – wanted me to travel. I wasn't overpowering or deceiving their defenses: they wanted me to do what I was doing!

As soon as that realization dawned, I knew that I had to do something to put me back in control of the situation. I scanned the building's schematics in my mind and identified an access panel not thirty meters ahead that led into the maze of plumbing, environmental and electrical conduits that crisscrossed the Headquarters building. Under normal conditions it would be nearly impossible for someone to find their way through that jumble, but I had the drawings etched in my mind's eye and I quickly determined a route that would lead me to an equipment room just down the hallway from the detention cells. I extended the ion curtain around the site and managed to quickly open the panel and crawl into one of the larger conduits, an enviro tunnel that was just large enough for me to crawl through toward the far side of the building.

Going was slow, as various other pipes and conduits intruded into the tunnel, but I knew that I needed to get to Antavar quickly enough to throw him off-stride and so I pushed on despite banged knees and a bloodied head. I was sweating profusely by the time I came to the ladder that led down to the center level.

Even though I was fairly confident that the High Priest had no intention of confronting me until I stepped into his trap, I crept to the edge of the tunnel and peeked down just to make sure his SF goons weren't waiting there for me. They weren't. It took just a few clics to descend the ladder and just a couple more to open the panel in the equipment room and escape out into the pitch blackness of the musty storage space. I used the torch on my communicator to get my bearings, to pick my way through office supplies and unlabeled boxes stacked from floor to ceiling.

As I cracked open the door leading out to the corridor, I forced myself to breathe even as I expected to find an empty hallway. I felt the drain on my energies as I struggled to maintain my Kin-zah control, both to keep the sensors and digicams ignorant of my movements and to hide my very thoughts from the High Priest. I had never attempted anything so difficult in a real world setting, where even the slightest mistake could result in not only my own death, but that of my friends and possibly of our entire movement. I felt sweat drip down my temples and my head throb. I suddenly realized that the weight of that responsibility threatened to overwhelm me, but then – as if in a dream – I heard my grandfather's voice speaking to me: 'You are The One. You are strong, you are prepared, you *will* triumph.' I honestly didn't know if

I was hallucinating or whether Andres had found some way to communicate with me. It didn't matter.

Whatever the truth, his words came at just the right moment. I felt my life force swell and my confidence return to the levels I needed to take on the High Priest in that precarious setting. I took a deep breath, and opened the door to the detention cells.

CHAPTER 30

Andres looked at the 14 men and women who surrounded him. They were young, so young! But they were all members of the underground rebellion, and he knew they would do their best to help distract Antavar and the entire SF from his grandson's rash rescue mission. He was so worried he didn't know whether to be angry at Vers or proud of him for taking such a terrible risk in order to save his friends. What he did know was that even with the coordinated attacks on the other Terran planets to distract his old enemy, Vers was greatly overmatched in a contest with the High Priest. Not that he didn't have the potential, but potential did not always translate into success, especially when confronted with an older, more experienced, equally powerful adversary. He needed to make Antavar's life a little less predictable, a little more difficult, and he needed to do it immediately.

"You know what we must do," he concluded his talk to the rebel fighters. "Vers must survive at all costs. You – and I – are expendable." He glanced around to see how they were taking it. To their credit, not one of them looked away from his stare or showed any sign of backing out. He felt a surge of pride. They were going to win this thing; they were going to rid the system of Antavar and all his deluded followers.

The Great Creator wouldn't let them fail.

*****

The 14 moved through the dense jungle without making contact with any SF forces, due primarily to Andres' ability to sense their hidden locations before they could ambush his small party, but also because the SF forces didn't seem to expect a second rebel patrol to be moving toward the Headquarters building as din dawned. The two SF units they'd bypassed both seemed overly relaxed, almost cocky. Some of his younger team members had wanted to engage the enemy units – remove them from any future battlefield then and there. But Andres had explained – telepathically – that their job wasn't to fight the outlying SF patrols that din, their job was to make sure that Vers – and his friends, if at all possible – escaped from the SF Headquarters building in one piece. He felt their reluctance, their urge to fight and kill their hated enemies. But they followed his orders like the well-trained and motivated fighters they were, and slipped through the humid green twilight like a gentle breeze, leaving the SF patrols lolling in self-congratulatory ignorance as they moved closer and closer to where Andres felt his grandson to be.

He sensed Vers' struggle to balance the needs of his cloaking field with the equally demanding mental block to hide from Antavar's incessant searching. He felt the drain on his physical and mental powers, felt the strain to keep both at optimum intensity. So he did the one thing that might give his grandson a tiny edge he'd need to succeed – he let Antavar feel their presence. All fourteen of them.

The reaction was instantaneous and predictable: alarms sounded throughout the Headquarters building and searchlights swept the awakening jungle that surrounded it.

"What the…?" one of the rebels said aloud as the protective silence of thick vegetation exploded into chaos.

'It's all part of the plan,' Andres projected telepathically. *'Keep strong.'*

He could see the doubt reflected in their expressions, could sense the confusion in their thoughts. But they obeyed. When he signaled for the patrol to move out at double-time, not a single one of them hesitated.

CHAPTER 31

I jerked my hand back from the sensor that opened the door to the detention cells the moment the alarms began to wail. For just an instant I thought that I'd been discovered. My heart pounded in my chest and for an instant my concentration wavered. But then, like the faintest hint of a cry soaring above the howl of an ocean gale, I 'heard' my grandfather speak to me: *We are coming! You are not alone!'*

The message revived my dwindling stores of energy and lifted my spirits. I was not alone!

I took a deep breath and touched my hand to the sensor beside the detention area entrance. I focused the little mental acuity I'd held back from the two cloaking projections to add a third: a constantly morphing fingerprint pattern that would eventually trigger the opening mechanism. A nagging headache began to throb in my temples. I ignored it. Finally, after what seemed like several long clics but was probably much less, the servos whirled and the door slid open.

I don't remember now what I expected to see, but a long, narrow, dimly lit corridor with Tiber chained to the far wall was probably not it. As red lights flashed behind me and the wavering alarm sirens blared incessantly, I hesitated, scanning the shadows for any hint of Antavar or his people. There was none. Could I have fooled him? Could my grandfather's attack have drawn him away from the cells? Part of me wanted to run the length of the corridor right then and there and free Tiber from his chains. But the part of me that my grandfather had so carefully cultivated knew better.

I crept cautiously from one deep shadow to the next, expecting at any moment to be confronted by SF agents or the High Priest himself. And so I was more than surprised, shocked really, when I got to the far end of the corridor unimpeded. Tiber looked bad, his near-naked body bruised, his face distorted in pain.

"Tiber! Tiber, can you hear me?" I whispered, the pain in my head preventing me from projecting the thoughts directly into his battered brain.

My friend didn't move, but just hung there, his arms straining against the shackles that pinned him to the wall. Fearing the worst, I grabbed his face and turned it up to mine. I felt the nearly indiscernible touch of his meager breaths against the back of my hand. He was still alive! Supporting his weight as best I could with my left arm hooked beneath his right, I touched the shackle on his left arm with my free hand. It exploded from the energy I over-eagerly poured into it, the metal shards cutting Tiber on his face and chest! I felt his body weight sag onto me, and I moved to better support it. But even as I did, a thought suddenly occurred to me: something wasn't right – how could I maintain both projections and still generate such power?

I had no time to worry about it. I knew that it was only a matter of time before Antavar or some of his minions discovered my presence. But even as I moved to free Tiber's other hand, the manacle flew off and clanged against the stone wall behind it. What was happening? I hadn't done this!

My instincts told me to run, but Tiber would have collapsed to the floor without my help. Fighting the urge to flee with every ounce of courage I still possessed, I lowered him carefully to the cold concrete floor. I had just begun to gently slap his cheeks to try to revive him, when an all-too-familiar voice echoed through the corridor as a door to my left slowly swung open.

"Well, well, well – young Mr. Leitstell, is it? So we meet again. Come in, come in…" Despite all my preparations, a sense of physical dread ran through me.

It took me a moment to collect myself and remember something Andres had taught me: 'In a high-pressure situation, the person who keeps his cool and doesn't panic will always have the edge.' I took a deep breath and stepped through the open door.

I found myself in a largish room, perhaps eight or nine meters on a side, with high ceilings but no windows. Along the outer edge of the room sat a variety of electro-mechanical devices, many of which looked to be from solar cycles long past. Red stains splattered the walls and traced rivulets on the floor. Although I couldn't identify most of the machines, their purpose was instantly clear: *enhanced* interrogation. Torture. And at the far end of the room sat the High Priest himself, ensconced in an elaborate throne chair that seemed utterly out of place in that room of horrors.

"I'm impressed," he began as I walked slowly in his direction. I had dropped all of my cloaking projections and was busy trying to ready both offensive and defensive energy fields. I could feel him teasing at the edge of my consciousness. "I didn't think you'd get this far. Congratulations."

I wanted to say something snide, to show him I wasn't intimidated by his position and trappings of power. But I needed to concentrate and so I kept silent, scanning the room to be sure no surprises awaited me.

"What's the problem – cat got your tongue?" he asked pointedly, his eyes never leaving mine. "Don't have anything you'd like to say to me?" I kept moving, slowly but without hesitation, sensing somehow that my silence was beginning to bother him.

"We're very much alike, you and me," he said after a long pause. "The blood of Arod Tolanfar runs in our veins. We have his Gift, and the responsibility that comes with it."

I held my tongue. If I could keep him talking perhaps he'd reveal something that I could use, something to give me the edge I so badly wanted. And needed.

"You think I'm a tyrant, and you and your grandfather's supporters could do better for our people?" He laughed, a shallow, humorless sound that sent a chill along my skin. "Is that what he's been telling you? I know it is – I can read it in your thoughts."

For just an instant I could feel him pushing to get inside my mind, but with an effort I slammed the door shut. His eyes widened slightly.

"Impressive. You're stronger than I'd imagined." His tone was cautious, and I suddenly realized that he was evaluating me, keeping me off-balance so he could determine my strengths and weaknesses while he finalized his plans. I needed to turn the tables.

"Where is she?" I asked, my voice weaker than I'd planned. "Where's Vera?"

He leaned forward in his throne chair. "Ah yes, the lovely Miss Weis. Is she your girlfriend?" His eyes narrowed as he increased his efforts to get inside my head. But I was ready this time, and his probe was blunted before he learned a thing.

"Where is she?" I repeated, circling his chair slowly, like a big cat stalking its game. I could sense just the faintest hint of confusion coming from the High Priest – or was it fear?

"All in good time," he said, smiling as if we were the best of friends. "But first, you and I need to talk."

"Do we? About what?" I'd decided to engage him to keep him from concentrating on me, and Andres. Where *was* he?

"About your foolish little rebellion, and all those little black lies your grandfather has been telling you."

I felt a tiny stab of doubt but kept my voice as calm as I could. "How do you know what he's told me?"

He smiled. "I know a great deal – more than you think." He suddenly frowned and motioned to me brusquely. "Do you think you could stop that? You're making me dizzy circling like some hungry animal."

I stopped. "My apologies."

"Accepted." He leaned back in his chair, apparently feeling pretty good about the situation. "So, you think you can help the people of the Terran System by doing away with me and taking my place. Is that about right?"

"Something like that."

"And just why do you think you're qualified to lead the Terran people? Or do you think just anyone can do this?" He motioned expansively with his hand.

"As you just said," I answered, "I'm a Tolanfar."

"You're a child!" Antavar snapped with more vehemence than I suspected he meant to reveal. "A child whose head has been filled with nonsense by that crazy old grandfather of yours." For nearly a clic neither of us spoke. Finally he stood and walked slowly down the steps leading to his throne. I backed involuntarily. "Did you ever ask yourself why *he* didn't lead the rebellion himself, but kept a low profile, stayed out of sight?" His words were soft but carried a sting.

I tried not to show it, but I *had* wondered, actually. "The Prophesy says I'm The One who will lead us to freedom," I said with more conviction than I felt.

"The Prophesy? You mean that old, worm-eaten book I keep locked up in a case in my office back in Harran? That's what he bases your success on?" Sarcasm dripped from his words. I knew he was trying to manipulate me, but I felt compelled to listen. "He's never even seen the book, has he?"

I had no intention of giving him any more information than he already possessed. "I don't know. I only know that he can quote the Prophesy word for word, and it says that your time is coming to an end."

"He's afraid. You know that, don't you?"

He didn't have to tell me who he was talking about. I knew he meant Andres.

"Of you?" It was my turn to use sarcasm.

"Of me, my Security Forces, and more than anyone – of the people of Terra." His voice dropped to little more than a whisper. "He fears that they will reject him. And you."

He tried to move closer, but as he moved to my left I circled slowly to my right.

"The people have *already* rejected *you*," I managed to spit out through suddenly wooden lips.

"Heretics," he fumed, flicking his wrist as if tossing them in the refuse bin. "Not worthy of my attention. There will always be those who do not believe. Always those who listen to apostates, madmen who want to believe that they are true guardians of the Light. But you know that *we* are the true representatives of the Great Creator here on Terra, and throughout the system! It is *our* responsibility to keep His laws and educate His people. Our birthright is to lead not only the Terrans, but one din much, much more."

In the dim light of the chamber I could almost see his eyes glow with fervor, or was it madness?

"It is insanity for the two of us to fight; it can bring nothing but death and destruction. How much better if we joined forces, worked together for the good of all the Terran people!"

I was awestruck. Work *together*? Was this…dictator suggesting that we forget the generations of evil perpetrated by him and his predecessors in the name of The Great Creator? He *was* mad!

I struggled to keep the revulsion from my face. "Tell me more," I said instead, hoping to lull him into carelessness, looking for a chink it what I knew to be a most formidable armor.

"I am not an unreasonable man," he continued, his voice perfectly modulated to give the impression of an equitable mediator. "I am more than willing to share. We already have seven planets, and thousands more just waiting for the blessings of the Light! I will continue to govern four, and to compensate you for your smaller realm you'll choose which three of the seven will be yours – with the one proviso that I maintain Terra5."

"Of course," I said, my mind whirling.

"As we reach out into the galaxy, our two branches of the family will share the spoils evenly. Together no one and nothing can stop us. We will be *invincible*!"

Maybe I should've reacted differently. Maybe I should've played his game a little longer, pretending to accept his crazy ramblings as a real possibility. But all I could think of were my two friends.

"You've obviously been thinking about this for quite some time," I began, hoping to win a respite with faint praise. "It's a big step - I'd like to take some time to think it over." I paused and took a deep breath. "Until then, as a show of good faith, why don't you release Vera and Tiber? You don't need them any longer."

I could see from the hardening of his eyes that I'd said the wrong thing. I scrambled to correct my mistake.

"Of course, I'll stay here so we can talk further. Perhaps you can tell me more about your plans…"

I don't know how I knew, what sixth sense or offering of the Gift made it possible, but in that instant I knew that he was about to betray me. As if in slow motion I watched him raise his hands, felt the surge of power that signaled an imminent attack. Without a thought I threw up a protective barrier.

Suddenly the air sizzled like raw meat on a red-hot grille as the very molecules between us exploded from the intensity of the blast he leveled at me. I barely had time to stabilize my field when the wave of energy struck. I was knocked back by its power and blinded by the discharge as his Kin-zah projection struck mine with a detonation that rocked the very foundations of the Security Force building! Un-neutralized fragments of the blast ricocheted off the walls and ceiling, tearing huge chunks of metal and stone from both that landed all around us with a deafening crash.

For just an instant I stood stunned, shaking my head to clear the echoes from the blasts. In that instant, he prepared to strike again. But I was not as dazed as he supposed. Before he could launch another assault I hit back, firing wave after wave of focused energy at the High Priest with no regard for myself or anything around me. As the first wave hit I saw him smile, a cocky, self-assured grin that told me he wasn't impressed by my efforts. But as the waves continued and increased in intensity and impact, I saw his expression change: first to surprise, then to grudging acceptance, and finally to something very close to fear.

But the effort was weakening me. I felt it, knew that I couldn't keep it up much longer. I had never expended that kind of energy before, and I wasn't experienced enough to know how to vary the wave to keep him on his back foot while I caught my breath. Even as the last of my attack sequence broke against the barrier he'd surrounded himself with, I braced for the return attack I knew would come.

And come it did.

The first blast nearly swept me from my feet, a blue wave of pure energy so intense it nearly blinded me. I felt my protective barrier weaken as the tell-tale headache returned with a vengeance. I was focusing every bit of my mental energy on repelling his assault; I had none left to counter-attack. A second blast, and then a third! I grit my teeth and hung on for dear life as the building shook around us.

And then, just as I felt my force field waver, just as doubt began to worm its way into my consciousness, I saw a massive green beam of energy crash into Antavar from his left side, catching him completely unawares! He was pushed back, grudgingly, his concentration suddenly turned toward the unexpected attack. I reached out to try to learn what was happening, and immediately my grandfather's voice sounded loud and clear in my head:

"We are here, Vers – hang on!"

I saw the High Priest's eyes widen, whether from the strain of his efforts or because he too realized that Andres was nearby, I didn't know. But it was clear he was struggling to maintain any semblance of an attack while warding off my grandfather's blows. His narrowed eyes and pained expression revealed the terrible effort required, but he held firm and continued to rain down bolts of energy on me. I fought back with renewed hope, sensing the overwhelming power of Andres' assault and the corresponding deterioration of Antavar's offensive with each new wave that broke over my shields.

I stared spellbound as the air around the High Priest's shield began to glow from the energy expended on both sides. I gasped as he staggered backwards, sweat dripping from his stringy black hair. We were winning! We were beating him!

And then, in a moment I will never forget, I saw his face distort into a mask of pure hatred as he drew himself to his full height and closed his eyes tight.

"NOOOO!!!" he screamed in a voice that exploded all around me like a thunderclap, a sound both wounded and determined.

In that moment I felt a surge of energy unlike any I had ever experienced before and the rock and metal surrounding us groaned in agony. At first I was confused. What was he doing?! Was he mad? And then, as the pained sound coming from the walls and ceiling heightened in both pitch and intensity, I suddenly realized: he was bringing the building down on top of us!

At that moment Andres knew as well.

Fight back – don't let him focus!' his voice directed.

I drew on reserves of strength I didn't know I possessed and released a wave of energy that exploded against his shield with such power that I was knocked to the ground. The concussion was deafening as pieces of stone began to fall all around me and thick dust filled the air. I struggled to draw another breath, choking in the cloud of debris that engulfed everything in the room. For several long moments visibility was nil, but finally, ever so slowly, it began to clear. I strained to see what our blow had accomplished, but when I turned back – Antavar was gone!

Find your friends!' Andres directed telepathically. *'You've got to get out of there – now!'*

My head was pounding and I felt barely strong enough to stand, but I reached out with my Gift and located Vera's energy signature not far away. It was weak – so very weak!

Stumbling like a drunk, I made my way back down the corridor to a reinforced metal door on my left. I tried the opening mechanism, but as I expected it was locked. I had neither the time nor the patience to finesse the situation, so I placed my hands against the door and channeled all the energy I had left into the metal. It exploded back into the room beyond with a loud *crack* and I hurried inside.

What I saw almost made me gasp. Vera was strapped to a crude wooden cross attached to the back wall of the chamber, naked and bleeding from head to toe!

"Vera! It's me – Vers!" I called out as I tore at her bindings with my bare hands. "Hang on – we'll get you out of here."

She fell from the bindings lifeless, collapsing into my arms. I carried her from the room and back to where Tiber sat half-dazed but conscious.

"Can you stand?!" I screamed to him as he looked at us with glazed eyes.

"I...I think so," he said with an effort. I helped him to his feet, my Gift so expended I didn't dare even try to carry him as well. Leaning heavily on my shoulder, he managed to stagger out of that terrible place and back to a stairway that led up and out of the Headquarters Building. But that was as far as we got. There was no way I could carry the two of them further – I was barely functioning myself.

I stopped to collect my thoughts and was just about to explain that I needed to go see if a nearby service lift was still operating, when the sound of running feet coming down the stairs froze me in mid-sentence. It was too late to hide, so I put my two friends behind me and braced for a fight, at least the best I could manage. I only hoped I looked more threatening than I felt.

"Stop right where you are or I will destroy you all!" I called up to them in a voice that quavered despite my best efforts.

The footsteps stopped briefly, but then continued even faster than before.

"I'm sorry," I whispered to my friends. "I did the best I could…"

Just then a figure dashed around the last bend in the stairs and virtually leapt down to where I stood. I raised my hands to try to defend myself, but then dropped them in utter disbelief as Jafar's smiling face slid into my field of vision.

"Destroy us, will you?" he mocked gently. "You look barely able to stand." He turned back up the stairs. "He's here! Hurry!"

In just a moment a half-dozen rebel volunteers surrounded us. Jafar barked a few orders and the men and women responded immediately, carrying Vera and Tiber and shepherding all of us up the stairs as quickly as they could move. As soon as we reached the next floor up, I heard the explosions and screams of a pitched battle in the main area of the Headquarters' building, just a short distance from where we stood.

"Your grandfather and the rest of our people are giving them something to remember us by," Jafar explained when he saw my inquiring look. "But they can't hold them off forever. Let's get out of here!"

We left through the same loading area we had come in through, though now the large open space was dotted with fallen, bloodied bodies, both ours and theirs. As soon as we emerged into the morning sunlight a barrage of proton beams from somewhere off to our left locked in on our position and tracked our every movement. We couldn't negotiate the narrow strip of open ground between the building and the surrounding jungle without leaving ourselves open to blanket fire that would quickly decimate us. We were trapped.

"They've got us pinned down!" one of the rebel lieutenants explained to Jafar. "Can *he* do something?" Through a haze of exhaustion I realized the rebel was referring to *me*. Jafar looked my way with expectant eyes.

"I can try," I said, but it was soon obvious that I could not even muster the energy to hide us from the SF guns, let alone counter-attack. I was drained. Desperate, I reached out to my grandfather.

'We're under attack!' I mentally communicated. *'I'm too spent to get us out of here.'*

'Hold tight,' his answer came immediately. I could sense he was being assailed from all sides, but somehow he held his attackers at bay for just an instant as he projected a deadly wave of energy in the general direction of our tormenters. A huge blast rocked the jungle beside the far end of the building, followed by fallings trees and the screams of SF agents caught unaware.

"Now – let's go!" I shouted, and the entire group of us ran for the relative safety of the nearby jungle. I could hear the telltale discharge of energy weapons all around us, the thud and searing detonations that tore up pieces of earth and set tree branches ablaze above and beyond us. I don't know if Andres managed to somehow shield our small unit from the withering firepower that sought to obliterate us, or whether the Great Creator Himself took us under his care, but somehow we made it across the 10 meters of open space and dove into the undergrowth on the other side.

I struggled to stand, my legs rubbery beneath me, when a firm hand took me by the shoulder and helped me to my feet.

"Let's get out of…" I began, before I saw the shock of red hair out of the corner of my eye. Amanda!

I grabbed ahold of her like a drowning man and held on for dear life. I could feel her sobs through my chest, sensed the relief she experienced seeing me alive. I was so tired, so spent, that all I could do was mumble her name, over and over again. "Amanda…"

The next thing I knew we were stumbling through the thick vegetation, explosions and fire erupting all around us. I don't think I could've stayed on my feet without the support I got from

Amanda and Jafar, but somehow we managed to plow through the huge leafy ferns and low-hanging branches until the battle behind us began to fade.

And then, suddenly, it stopped. It all stopped.

"What happened?" I managed to whisper while sinking to one knee.

"I don't know. It sounds like somebody's won," Jafar answered, his stare riveted on the jungle behind us. "But who?"

I could not even focus my thoughts well enough to try to contact my grandfather, and for several long moments all I could sense was silence – an utter stillness that made my skin crawl.

"Can you communicate with them?" Jafar finally asked. "Do you know what happened?"

I was about to admit that I couldn't and didn't, when I heard Andres' voice, weak but sustained, reaching out to me.

'Our forces surprised them – we've taken the capital,' he said. *'The enemy is on the run!'*

"We've won!" I muttered deliriously, not completely sure I hadn't hallucinated Andres' voice. I remember seeing Jafar's eyes open wide, heard Amanda cry out with joy, and then I fell face first into the thick decomposing mulch of the jungle floor.

CHAPTER 32

When I next opened my eyes, the first thing I saw was Amanda's worried face staring down at me. I attempted to sit up, but her hand in the middle of my chest gently pushed me back down.

"Take it easy – you've been out for a long time," she said softly.

Out? "How long?" I whispered, my lips thick and swollen.

"More than a din. Your grandfather was getting worried."

"Just my grandfather?" I forced a feeble smile.

"We've all been worried," she corrected herself with a shake of her head. "Though why, I'm not sure."

"Probably because he's such an obedient, thoughtful young man," Andres answered sarcastically as he strode into my field of vision, looking tired, bruised, but surprisingly strong. "What in the Creator's good name did you think you were doing over there?" He sounded genuinely ticked.

I had neither the inclination nor strength to go into detail. "Saving my friends," I said simply.

"And you couldn't tell us – your other friends and *family* – so that we could help?"

I felt a momentary flash of guilt. It passed. "I didn't want to put you all in any more danger than I already have."

"But you didn't mind putting our entire movement – the well-being of the entire Terran system – in danger? *That* didn't cross your mind?"

"They were *my* friends, *my* responsibility."

"Your responsibility?! What do you know about…?"

He would've continued but for Amanda's intervention.

"Andres, he's half-dead. Can't this wait?" Her tone was part entreaty, part demand.

I saw a rainbow of emotions pass across my grandfather's face. Finally he shook his head and sighed. "Yes, I suppose it can. But just understand, this discussion is *not* over." The last bit was directed straight at me.

"I'm not going anywhere. At least not soon," I managed to joke.

"Don't even think about it!" both Amanda and my grandfather said in unison. They smiled at each other.

"Great. Now there's two of you watching my every move."

"Make that at least five," a familiar voice chimed in from the door to the recovery room. I looked back past my grandfather to see Jafar just entering, followed close behind by Tiber pushing Vera in a wheelchair.

"You look like I feel," I said as they rounded into view. Tiber and Vera, in particular, clearly showed the effects of the High Priest's attention.

"Not so bad, really," Vera said. "I'm sure Antavar got worse than he gave."

Suddenly it all came back to me. Antavar! The battle!

"Where is he?! Is he dead?!" Without even thinking I pushed myself up on one elbow. I knew the news wasn't as good as I hoped when all the younger folks turned to my grandfather.

He shook his head. "Not dead, but not in power in Harran, either," he said solemnly, waiting a moment before continuing. "We think he escaped."

"Escaped?! From the island?"

"From the planet." He held up a hand to stop the flood of questions he could sense coming his way. "I've done everything I can do to try to locate him, but he's gone. Disappeared into thin air."

It took me a short while to digest the news. "And the Security Forces? Have they been neutralized?"

"Here on T5, yes. And on 2 & 3. The rest…not yet."

Suddenly I felt weak. I lowered myself slowly back to the cot. "They still control four of the planets?"

"For now," Jafar said defiantly.

"Don't you worry, we'll get them all before long," Tiber chimed in.

Andres was more forthcoming. "On T1 our forces were overmatched. We hadn't intended on making a move there for at least a cycle. Shouldn't have done it this time around. I tried to talk them out of it, but they weren't listening. The SF cut us up pretty bad, but I'm told we've regrouped in the mountains east of the capital. On Four it's still uncertain – the fighting goes back and forth. Six and Seven were never in play. We just weren't ready there to take on Antavar's people at this stage of the game, and *they* listened when I told them to wait this one out."

"But we've freed three of our planets, Vers!" Amanda interrupted. "Over 12 billion people no longer living under the High Priest and his Guardians of the Light!"

I nodded, my feelings mixed. I had always expected the entire empire to fall when we made our move. Had I jeopardized everything by putting the lives of my two friends before the success of our mission? Or had Andres gone too far by giving the go-ahead to our forces on so many of the outlying planets? In either case, I had to squint a bit to see the basket as half-full.

"I guess we should be thankful for the success we've had," I managed to say. "We'll get the rest in due time."

I saw Andres' face relax as he exhaled. "That's right. Let's take this moment to give thanks to the Great Creator for giving us this din." He knelt and we all bowed our heads. I, for one, was curious to hear what he would say. "Creator, we give you thanks for our victories and ask that you continue to guide our way with your Holy Light," he began. "Everything we do, we do for you. Please protect us and lead us to ultimate victory over those who have enslaved your servants. For yours is the Light that reveals the Truth and chases away the shadows."

This was the first time I'd participated in a blessing such as this, outside the framework of the High Priest and his people, and I felt awkward to say the least. Until that moment we had scrupulously avoided any show of overt religious fervor that would echo the regime we hoped to replace. And now, with our first real victory, *this*.

Perhaps my discomfort showed on my face, for Amanda quickly spoke up.

"All right – let's give Vers a chance to recuperate, all right? Come on now, everyone out."

She shooed them all out the door, even Andres, then turned back to tuck me in before she left.

"You're worried," she said simply as she sat next to me on the cot.

"Not exactly," I lied. "It's just that everything is moving so quickly now."

She smiled, a rueful grin that barely reached her eyes. "I guess everything will change now, huh?" She was the one who sounded worried.

"Not everything," I said, and I pushed myself up until my lips touched hers. "Some things are too good to change."

Her smile broadened, and the twinkle in her eyes shone brightly. "I guess I'd better let you rest, huh?"

Part of me wanted to object, but I knew only too well how weak I still felt and how much help my grandfather would need to hold Antavar at bay while our forces consolidated their gains, and so I sent her away. She blew me a kiss from the doorway as she left.

As I lay there in the dim light of late afternoon, despite the tremendous strides of the last din I couldn't help but feel that we'd only taken one step in a very long journey. True, Antavar was on the run, but he still had four planets to sustain him and his forces. We had won a battle, but now had to prove to the people of the three planets we'd liberated that we could win the peace. Could we govern well enough to win their faith and confidence? Or would the War drag on interminably, preventing any semblance of real life for the people of the Terran system?

With such thoughts running feverishly in my head, I closed my eyes and prayed for sleep.

CHAPTER 33

Rogen Antavar stared out the large panoramic window that formed one wall of his quarters on the camouflaged shuttle that hurried at top speed to carry him to safety on Terra1. A soft buzzing brought his thoughts back to the sparsely outfitted cabin.

"Enter."

He didn't even bother to turn, but reached out mentally to the new arrival: it was the Captain of the modified military shuttle, Shars Hanover. The tall, thin Security Forces airman had served as his personal pilot for many cycles.

"Captain?"

Hanover bowed his head respectfully. For the first time the High Priest noticed just a hint of gray hair at the Captain's temples. "Your Grace, we should arrive on Terra1 in a little over two din. So far, all aspects of our flight are within expected parameters."

"Very good, Captain." Rogen smiled. He enjoyed the unemotional tech talk of his military personnel. It reassured him that there were still Terrans under his control who could be counted on, despite the apparent disaster of the previous din. Three planets lost! And a fourth teetering on the verge. It was almost unbelievable.

Antavar suddenly realized that Hanover was still standing there, awaiting his response.

"If there's nothing else," he continued. "let me know when we're one stunde out. Until then, instruct the crew to give this cabin a wide berth. I've got a number of…situations to address, and I don't want to be disturbed while I do so. Understood?"

"Yes sir!" The pilot hesitated just an instant to make sure Antavar didn't want to explain further, and then bowed once more and did an about-face. He was almost out the door when the High Priest stopped him.

"Oh, and Captain," Antavar said as if it were an afterthought, which it most assuredly was not, "let the crew know that this little *disturbance* by my cousins is nowhere near finished. Believe me, they have no idea what they've gotten themselves into. But they will soon enough."

Hanover seemed to straighten perceptibly and a broad smile swept across his face.

"Yes sir! I will do that!"

As the hatch door slid shut behind him, Rogen Antavar returned his gaze to the countless stars that seemed just beyond his grasp on the other side of the massive window.

'*I underestimated your Gift once, Vers Leitstell,*' he thought, focusing on the distant light that he knew to be Terra5. '*It won't happen again.*'

He nodded to himself, and then turned to the Replicator to program some food. Suddenly he felt ravenously hungry.

www.ingramcontent.com/pod-product-compliance
Lightning Source LLC
Chambersburg PA
CBHW050555260626
47157CB00002B/571